ALICE LECCESE POWERS

TUSCANY IN MIND

Alice Leccese Powers is the editor of the
anthologies *Italy in Mind*, *Ireland in Mind*, and
France in Mind, and coeditor of *The Brooklyn
Reader: Thirty Writers Celebrate America's Favorite
Borough*. A freelance writer and editor, she has
been published in *The Washington Post*, *The Bal-
timore Sun*, *Newsday*, and many other newspapers and magazines. Ms. Powers also teaches
writing at the Corcoran College of Art and
Design. She lives in Washington, D.C., with
her husband.

France in Mind, edited by Alice Leccese Powers

Ireland in Mind, edited by Alice Leccese Powers

Italy in Mind, edited by Alice Leccese Powers

Paris in Mind, edited by Jennifer Lee

Cuba in Mind, edited by Maria Finn Dominguez

India in Mind, edited by Pankaj Mishra

TUSCANY IN MIND

TUSCANY IN MIND

AN ANTHOLOGY

Edited and with an Introduction by

Alice Leccese Powers

Vintage Departures

VINTAGE BOOKS

A DIVISION OF RANDOM HOUSE, INC.

NEW YORK

A VINTAGE DEPARTURES ORIGINAL, MAY 2005

Permissions acknowledgments can be found
at the end of the book.

Library of Congress Cataloging-in-Publication Data
Tuscany in mind : an anthology / edited and with an
introduction by Alice Leccese Powers.
p. cm.—(Vintage departures)
ISBN 1-4000-7675-7 (pbk.)
1. English literature. 2. Tuscany (Italy)—Literary collections. 3. Tuscany (Italy)—
Description and travel. 4. Americans—Italy—Tuscany. 5. British—
Italy—Tuscany. 6. American literature. I. Powers, Alice Leccese.
PR1111.T87T87 2005
820.8'032455—dc22   2004061155

Book design by Jo Anne Metsch

www.vintagebooks.com

Printed in the United States of America
10 9 8 7 6 5 4 3 2 1

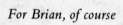

For Brian, of course

ACKNOWLEDGMENTS

With grateful acknowledgment to my editor Diana Secker Larson and my agent Jane Dystel; to my friends and fellow writers Erich Parker, Kem and Jon Sawyer, Jane Vandenburgh, and Jack Shoemaker, to Deborah Warin and Frank D'Ambrosio and everyone at Villa Le Balze for their hospitality during our stay in Fiesole; to Antonio Alcalá, Johan Severtsen, and Pat Taylor, my colleagues at the Corcoran College of Art and Design; to my extended Italian family, especially Gaetana Leccese, Maria Leccese Kotch, Michael Leccese, and my godparents Dan and Lil DiSanto; to Dave Gregal for his wise counsel; and to my dear daughters Alison, Christina, and Brenna and my new son, Steve.

Ghosh shook his head. "You are still young. Free," he said, spreading his hands apart for emphasis. "Do yourself a favor. Before it's too late, without thinking too much about it first, pack a pillow and a blanket and see as much of the world as you can. You will not regret it. One day it will be too late."

"My grandfather always says that's what books are for," Ashoke said, using the opportunity to open the volume in his hands. "To travel without moving an inch."

From *The Namesake: A Novel*
by Jhumpa Lahiri

CONTENTS

INTRODUCTION

Writers drew me to Tuscany. This, my fourth volume in the "In Mind" series, is a collection of fiction and nonfiction, poetry and prose, the best writing by English and American authors on Tuscany. Like its predecessor, *Italy in Mind, Tuscany in Mind* reveals the Anglo-Saxon attempt to solve the puzzle that is Italy.

My job as an anthologist is to render a portrait of a place, balancing authors, genres, and subjects. Starting with the literary heroes of my college days, Byron, Shelley, the Brownings, Twain, and Dickens, I culled thousands of pages by almost a hundred authors. I pored over the work of travel writers like Kate Simon, Eric Newby, and H. V. Morton, discovered twentieth-century authors like Kinta Beevor and Iris Origo, and added recent émigrés like Paul Gervais, David Leavitt, Frances Mayes, and Ann Cornelisen. I noted the entwined friendships of many in this book: Byron and the Shelleys, Robert Lowell and Mary McCarthy, Edith Wharton and Henry James, and Frances Mayes and Ann Cornelisen. Finally, the preliminary manuscript—rational and well considered—was completed.

Then I went to Tuscany.

"There are places one comes home to that one has never been to," wrote Barbara Grizzuti Harrison. I had been to Tuscany twice, briefly. Years of travel writing should have armed me against insensate infatuation. But like many of the writers in this book, I fell hopelessly for this place.

My emotions were magnified by circumstance because my research trip doubled as a long-delayed honeymoon. More than thirty years after our wedding, my husband and I traveled unencumbered by children and untethered to babysitters. I was surprised to find I was able to write away from my Washington desk. In coffee-houses, piazzas, and pensiones, I filled spiral notebooks with over-heard conversations and observations. Bruce Chatwin wrote, "Those of us who presume to write books would appear to fall into two cat-egories: the ones who 'dig in' and the ones who move." I have always belonged to the former group, comforted by my books, my com-puter, and my quiet routine. In Tuscany I found myself in the latter category, having passed into the august society (junior member) of expatriate writers liberated by Italy.

This collection is different from the one I initially compiled—it is more personal and more emotional. In a small way, I proved the con-ceit of this book, *Tuscany in Mind*: the Anglo-Saxon sensibility is fun-damentally altered by the northern Italian landscape. It is not only geography and the region's history, art, and architecture that leaves their mark, but the sound of cicadas in the countryside or an alfresco rendition of a Puccini aria at midnight in a medieval walled town, the feel of cobblestones through the soles of shoes bought in a tiny Flo-rentine shop or the smell of pork basting on a spit in a butcher's stall in the Cortona market. Falling in love with Tuscany means embrac-ing a different life and implicitly rejecting traces of the old one.

Many writers did this gratefully. The Shelleys, the Brownings, and Byron escaped censure in England. (In a letter Shelley called Tuscany a "paradise of exiles.") Both Byron and Shelley fled unhappy mar-riages; the Brownings' marriage made everyone in Elizabeth's family unhappy. But not all of the early travelers fell under Tuscany's spell. The dyspeptic Tobias Smollett did not like anyplace but England. Ironically, he died in Livorno. Dickens and Twain liked Tuscany, but disliked Italians.

The twentieth century brought a new round of immigrants. Kinta Beevor's bohemian family bought a castle overlooking the Gulf of Spezia. She and her lifelong friend Iris Origo were part of Bernard Berenson's Florentine intellectual circle until Origo married an Ital-ian and moved to a *fattoria*, or farm, in the country. Edith Wharton met Berenson and they became friends and traveling companions. After World War II the grand lifestyle of the wealthy expatriates faded, replaced by the more modest one of less affluent settlers. Ann

Cornelisen, Paul Gervais, Matthew Spender (visited by his father, the poet Stephen Spender), David Leavitt, and Mark Mitchell bought villas and farmhouses and made Tuscany home. Frances Mayes wrote, "The house is a metaphor for the self, of course, but it is also totally real. And a foreign house exaggerates all the associations houses carry."

Luigi Barzini theorized that people are drawn to Italy by dead Italians and find themselves entertained by the live ones. But to some writers, their hosts were nearly invisible, at best supernumeraries to the house tenor. Some writers were simply confounded by Tuscans or regarded them merely as necessary intermediaries in the "Italian experience." David Leavitt could not get a driver's license without an *agente* to smooth the way. Frances Mayes needed a bevy of real estate brokers and lawyers to purchase Bramasole. Kinta Beevor's family was tended by Italian servants who were "disarmingly straightforward . . . friendly without being familiar."

The Tuscan is an enigma. (In the interest of full disclosure, I am a hybrid Italian American, half Sicilian, half Barese. None of my ancestors traveled north of Rome.) To an outsider he appears a natural actor, an uninhibited thespian. In a deli in Siena, my husband and I witnessed a bravura performance by the proprietor Michele and his silent assistant ("the new guy") who made us two sandwiches. Michele appeared to have missed his calling in the theater, and we were his captive audience. ("Come in! We love you here!") Without interrupting his stand-up routine ("Take my picture. Now let the new guy take your picture with me!"), he and his assistant fashioned our ham-and-cheese sandwiches. ("Look at the amount of cheese in that sandwich! The new guy loves you!") Michele convinced us to buy a *panforte*, the Sienese dessert that is the Italian equivalent of our Christmas fruitcake ("It keeps for two years. Some say three, but we like ours fresh.") We left with a hefty bill and the memory of an impromptu star turn.

These superficial extroverts can deceive. The Tuscan world is divided into family and strangers, *paesani* and foreigners. The suspicion of *stranieri* is well-founded as Tuscany has been invaded again and again, most recently by a wave of foreign homesteaders. The walled city is an architectural embodiment of insularity. "To leave a

walled city is to feel evicted, cast out—cast out of paradise," wrote
Barbara Grizzuti Harrison, "no matter that the countryside outside
the walls is paradisical."

If the signature element in American vernacular architecture is the
front porch (according to my friend Michael Dolan's book *The American Porch*), the Italians favor the piazza and the courtyard. Their living space is either very private (note the heavily barred windows and
shutters) or very public. Communal life flourishes in the nightly
after-dinner *passeggiata*, or traditional evening promenade. Kate
Simon wrote, "The boys stroll together, as do the girls, except for an
engaged or extremely enlightened pair. Fluffy baby carriages act as a
prow for a family cutting its way through the crowd. A girl in a
smock, carrying a pile of shoe boxes, a boy with a tray of cakes, still
in his white work coat, press purposefully through this leisured world
of which they are not yet part . . ."

Tuscany combines the untamed and the controlled, decay and
regeneration. It always seems to verge on disappearing, hit by legions
of invaders, visited by floods, catastrophe, and benign neglect. In the
late nineteenth century Henry James wrote, "Everything is cracking,
peeling, fading, crumbling and rotting." In his novel *The Sixteen Pleasures* Robert Hellenga described the devastation of priceless Florentine art after the flood in 1966: frescoes vanished from wet walls, art
conservators attempted to save endangered work by Botticelli,
Titian, Rubens, and Rembrandt, and irreplaceable documents simply
washed down the Arno. Tuscan gardens exemplify the twin forces of
construction and destruction with flower-filled terra-cotta pots, man-
icured topiaries, frayed lawns, and crumbling statuary. Paul Gervais
wrote, "A formal garden's abandon is most evident at its edges: where
gravel meets grass, grass meets soil, soil meets plantings."

English and American writers often chide Italians for their stew-
ardship of their history. Even while sympathizing with them, Henry
James sounds like an authoritarian, scolding father when he writes,
"We may plead moreover for these impecunious heirs of the past
that even if it were easy to be clean in the midst of their mouldering
heritage if would be difficult to appear so." I could not help but note
in one particularly quarrelsome entry in my journal, "If Florence

were America, this would be [like Colonial] Williamsburg with actors walking the streets dressed as the Duke of Urbino or Michelangelo. But it is Italy, so there is graffiti on fifteenth-century walls."

Anglo-Saxons worship order; Tuscans, like all Italians, thrive in anarchy. Stores and museums seem to open and close at will. In Florence's Church of the Santo Spirito my husband and I were ushered out at noon by a monk who extinguished our just-lit holy candles with a flick of his bamboo fan, despite a posted closing time of one o'clock. In Siena we witnessed a general strike announced casually by a notice in the lobby of our hotel. "Gentle Patrons: Tomorrow will be a general strike. Thank you." No trains? We asked the concierge. No. Buses? No. Post? No. What of people who have schedules, and planes and trains to catch? She shrugged. In Tuscany, time is expansive and deadlines are merely suggestions.

The Italian chaos theory extends to the roads. Except on the modern autostrada, roads are a warren of hairpin turns, punctuated by roundabouts and an abundance of often contradictory signs. Unable to discriminate between a circle with a horizontal line and a circle with a slanted line, we drove our car to a precipice in the upper city of Colle di Val d'Elsa. A finger-wagging policeman on motorcycle helped us back off the cliff and escorted us out of town. We were resigned to getting lost. The ubiquitous but mysterious sign "*tutti direzione*" comforted us when we went astray; it seemed impossible to be going in the wrong direction following a marker that read "all directions."

In Tuscany the counterweight to anarchy is formality. From the Vatican down, Italians love uniforms. The carabinieri and the clergy are handsomely attired, but so are many other workers. In an ornate *pasticceria*, in the lower city of Colle di Val d'Elsa, two waitresses stood at attention behind the counter, dressed in prim navy blue dresses and little boat-shaped hats, like Pan Am stewardesses from the 1950s. Ordinary commerce often assumes unexpected ceremony. Bureaucrats stamp official documents—and then stamp them again for good measure. Jewelers reveal their wares and then wrap a purchase lovingly—in a box secured by an extravagant bow with another box inside an embossed bag—as if they cannot bear to part with it. We went into a stationery shop in Lucca that was more museum than store. The proprietor stocked only one of every item—to buy the bottle of handmade *inchiostro turchese* was to exhaust his supply. In a hotel in Cortona the manager totaled our bill. "Of course, minus the discount," he said, "and a gift," handing me an elegantly wrapped piece of pottery. I protested gently that I did not expect a discount or a gift. "And that is when it is the best," he assured me, "when you expect it the least."

If there is an organizing principle to Tuscan life it is food. The two most important places may be the kitchen and the market. Kinta Beevor wrote that Tuscan cooking is based on "*la cucina povera*, peasant cooking, which made the best use of home-grown raw materials—maize flour for polenta, semolina for gnocchi, onions and beans for soups, fresh vegetables from the *orto* for stuffing and tomatoes for sauces, while the wild mushrooms, herbs, nettles and particular grasses gathered from hillsides went into *torte* (flans) and even *tortelloni*. But almost every meal depended upon that ancient trinity of bread, olive oil and wine." Every region has its own version of the soul-warming bean soup *ribollita* plus signature specialties. In a restaurant in Monteriggioni I tried to order sweet-and-sour wild boar prepared with a combination of chocolate and balsamic vinegar. "It is too dangerous," cautioned the waiter. "This dish is very particular." He let me order roast boar instead, but gave me a sample of the sweet-and-sour boar. It was exquisite, like a chocolate sundae of pork with a sour aftertaste. Very good, very particular.

A Tuscan meal would not be complete without wine. Production is tightly controlled by the government, mandating that real Chianti can only be made in seven defined zones. In Penelope Fitzgerald's novel *Innocence*, Cesare, the patriarch of the Valsassina estate mourns the "tragedy of 1932 . . . [when] authorities had declared Valsassina to be just outside the boundary line of the Chianti area. This meant that none of the Ridolfi wines could be labelled or sold as classic, and their market value was reduced by a quarter." In Italy even the tomato-cheese ratio on pizza is prescribed and only certain recipes are given the official stamp of the Associazione Verace Pizza Napoletana (AVPN).

Romance can be neither quantified nor controlled, and it abounds in *Tuscany in Mind*. James Boswell reveled in the licentiousness of eighteenth-century Siena. "It was the custom of the society," he wrote. "I yielded to custom." Lord Byron also yielded to "custom" before settling down with his married mistress and her much older husband. Shelley wrote, "La Guiccioli his cara sposa who attends him impatiently, is a very pretty sentimental, [stupid *deleted*] innocent, superficial Italian, who has sacrificed an immense fortune to live [with *deleted*] for Lord Byron; and who, if I know any thing of my friend or her, or of human nature will hereafter have plenty of leisure & opportunity to repent of her rashness." Erica Jong satirized Italian gigolos in her poem "Ritratto," but in Laura Fraser's *An Italian Affair* the author's Florentine friend says that the only remedy for a broken heart is an Italian man. "You need an Italian lover. That's the only solution. . . . To everything." In E. M. Forster's *Where Angels Fear to Tread*, British Philip Herriton goes to Tuscany to rescue his widowed sister-in-law Lilia from a young Italian suitor, Signor Carella. Philip demands that Lilia break off her relationship. "I am not blaming you now. But I blame the glamour of Italy—I have felt it myself, you know." Philip adds that Carella is "probably a ruffian and certainly a cad." "There are no cads in Italy," replies Lilia.

The twentieth century challenged the conventions of love, even in Tuscany. Italian television (with game shows in which, for no apparent reason, contestants disrobe) is even more inane than American programming. I was mesmerized by a program aptly called *Amori e Tormenti de Due Pandolini*. Interviewed in their apartment, the Pandolinis fought in front of the camera (*amori* may have been off the mark, but *tormenti* was spot on). Finally, Signor Pandolini left in a huff and stormed out to the street. The camera followed Lucia Pandolini as she ran to the window and yelled to her husband. "Don't leave me. Don't go out. And take an umbrella—it's raining."

Above the infernal buzz of the Vespas, the ring of cell phones, and the clamor of tourists, romance endures. Tuscany could have been scored by native composer Giacomo Puccini. Its beauty inspired Michelangelo, who said, "If there is anything good in me it comes from the pure air of your Arezzo hills where I was born." I found that Tuscany's overpowering spell could even transform long-marrieds into newlyweds.

Bruce Chatwin wrote, "The places you work well in are the places you love the most." And I worked well in Tuscany. My final selections for *Tuscany in Mind* were based on my own beloved places. Everyone has different favorites and Tuscany evokes strong opinions. A good friend dismissed my adored Lucca with "It's just a city." Our Florentine desk clerk disliked Monteriggioni ("A square and about four houses"), but recommended Viareggio on the coast ("Where the life is!"). Its cheek-by-jowl beach clubs with names like Miami, Texas, and Florida reminded me of Long Island. The concierge in Lucca warned us off Pisa ("It's full of thieves!"), echoing Dickens's sentiments one hundred years earlier. An artist friend recommended Pietra Santa and its Carrara marble sculpture studios. There I was transfixed by plaster molds of the Pietà, Jesus, David, and Robert Kennedy, a pantheon of the afterlife waiting to be completed in stone.

To come home from Tuscany is to long to return. Next time we'll travel north to Carrara, spend more time in Florence, make another visit to Cortona, enjoy two days in Piensa, overnight in Arezzo. Next time we'll take the train to Lucca, drive the shore road to Spezia. Next time . . . next time. "Nothing is new in Tuscany," wrote H. V. Morton, "we were merely the latest of those who had laughed and joked upon that hilltop under the same blue sky."

TUSCANY IN MIND

Kinta Beevor

(1911–1995)

In 1916 when British-born Kinta Beevor was five, her father, the painter Aubrey Waterfield, bought a sixteenth-century castle, La Fortezza della Brunella, near the village of Aulla. Waterfield, his wife, the writer Lina Duff Gordon, and their three children moved into the imposing fortress with its improbable rooftop garden that looked like "it had been abandoned under an enchanter's spell." For the next twenty-five years they lived a bohemian life, punctuated by visits from friends like Aldous Huxley, Bernard Berenson, D. H. Lawrence, and Iris Origo. Kinta and her brothers were often left to the care of Aullan servants while her parents devoted themselves to their work and the rehabilitation of Fortezza della Brunella. Beevor wrote, "It was often said of my parents that they had all of the luxuries of life, but none of the necessities . . . they seldom had money for those things that their relations considered the basis of civilized life."

Their lives in Tuscany ended with World War II. Beevor's parents had a harrowing escape from Italy and relocated, unhappily, in England. Her two brothers and her husband served with the British military; her brother John was killed in combat. Aubrey Waterfield died in 1944. But the indomitable Lina Duff Gordon returned to the heavily damaged Fortezza after the war. The destruction of her husband's frescoes and the memories evoked by his rooftop garden proved too much for her and, after several years, she returned to England. Kinta Beevor's only book, *A Tuscan Childhood*, from which this is excerpted, was published in 1993, two years before her death. She concluded that La Fortezza was "the most beautiful and magical place in the world. But when I look back, I can easily see why friends and relatives . . . considered my parents wildly imprudent, if not mad, to settle in such a place. Thank God for imprudence."

from A TUSCAN CHILDHOOD

In those days, just after the First World War, the kitchen was the best place in which to get to know the region. And the herbs and vegetables, still smelling of the warm volcanic earth, could start a love of Tuscan cooking that would last a lifetime. For the servants, as well as their friends and relations who dropped in on visits, the kitchen was not simply a place of work but the centre for their favourite subject of conversation. Everyone, men and women alike, compared recipes. When somebody talked of a particular dish, another might say that a cousin of theirs who had married a Piedmontese prepared it a slightly different way. They would argue the relative merits, go away and experiment, and discuss it again the next time.

The cooking of the Lunigiana, while essentially Tuscan, reflects its geographical reality as a border region and its history of "armies, pilgrims and merchants" passing through. Surrounded by Genoese Liguria, Parma and Reggio nell'Emilia, it has borrowed what it likes: *pesto* with pine nuts in the Genoese style; the curing of hams and the preparation of sausage and *coppa* from Parma (the *pecorino* cheeses from up the valleys also bore a strong affinity to Parmesan); and the local favourite of *panigacci*—a form of unleavened maize bread cooked between iron dishes and eaten with *pesto*—from Emilia.

The basis of life sixty years ago was *la cucina povera*, peasant cooking, which made the best use of home-grown raw materials—maize flour for polenta, semolina for gnocchi, onions and beans for soups, fresh vegetables from the *orto* for stuffing and tomatoes for sauces, while the wild mushrooms, herbs, nettles and particular grasses gathered from hillsides went into *torte* (flans) and even *tortelloni*. But almost every meal depended upon that ancient trinity of bread, olive oil and wine.

Polenta, a pale golden colour from the flour of Indian corn, formed the solid staple of winter months when no fresh vegetables were available. Cut into strips, it was eaten fried in olive oil, baked with Parmesan or served with a sauce and a little meat if available, such as goat, garlic salami or *zampone*—a pig's trotter made into sausage. So central was polenta to the diet of the northern Italian that southerners used to call them *polentoni*. Tuscans were also called the bean-eaters, because the *fagioli* gathered in the summer, then dried, shelled and sacked up for the winter, provided the bulk of their protein, usually in the form of minestrone.

Beef was almost unheard of, unless an old animal had been killed, and veal was a rare luxury. Often the tougher bits were boiled, making a consommé, then the meat was served with *salsa verde*, a green sauce made from very finely chopped parsley, onion and capers with oil and sometimes an anchovy. Any pieces of meat left over were minced, then augmented with egg, breadcrumbs, parsley and basil or other herbs in season, and used to make *ripieni*—stuffed vegetables, such as tomatoes, onion, aubergines, zucchini, or lightly boiled cabbage leaves made into a parcel.

Most fresh meat came from chickens, pigeons and rabbits, which were cheap to raise. One of my favourite dishes, which both Mariannina and Adelina cooked superbly, was a *bomba di riso* of squabs or fledgling pigeons. For this you line a bowl with partly cooked rice mixed with egg, then fill the remaining cavity with young pigeon breasts in a mushroom sauce with chicken livers. It is a dish you do not often find today, but as soon as you mention it, people suddenly remember the taste from their youth with a reawakened longing.

I never really liked eating rabbit, not because I thought of the animal as a cuddly pet, but because I was exasperated by Adelina—whose lack of scientific reliability was all too apparent even to us children—insisting that it contained lots of iron and so was especially good for *padroncini*, or little masters and mistresses.

Tuscans have deeply held beliefs about the effects of food, some of which are no doubt true, while others are fanciful. Figs, they say, are bad for you at night. You will avoid illnesses of the liver if you use only the very purest olive oil. Red chilli is good for stomach trouble. A tea made from fennel seeds helps soothe a baby's colic. Eating raw garlic keeps mosquitoes away, and also, one might add, other species from vampires to Lotharios.

Another range of sayings I remember concerned the preparation of food. Basil should be torn, not cut with metal, otherwise it loses its taste as well as its goodness. Parmesan should never be grated because the friction cooks it. And each cooking utensil—knife, cutting board or pan—should be used for one purpose only so that flavours do not mix.

Variations in the cooking of the Lunigiana are, like in other areas, dictated by the seasons, but certain foods are clearly associated with specific feast days. For the Aullesi, one of the most important annual events, the Feast of San Severo on the first Saturday of September, is even known by the name of the dish—the *Festa della Capra*. For this celebration of that local favourite, kid and polenta, the meat is slowly brought to the boil. The water that is produced, known as the *selvatico*—the wild element—is thrown away. The purified *capra*, a very lean meat, is then cooked in oil with *soffritto*—lightly fried onions, celery and dry sausage with herbs—capers and *mortadella di Maiale*. Meanwhile, a sauce for the kid and the polenta is prepared consisting of tomatoes, onions, carrots, celery and white wine.

The calendar ran roughly as follows. In Carnival, exotically stuffed *tortelloni* were popular; and a surprisingly unfestive choice at this time was boiled chickpeas. The onset of Lent was a penance that sat easier on the poor who could seldom afford to eat meat. And since fresh fish was also too expensive, the diet of peasant families changed little, except for the addition of *zuppa di magro*—or Lenten soup. It was also a time when people remembered the story of the "*zuppa dei poveri*." A poor man arrives at the door of a house and asks the wife if he could have some water for his soup. She peers into the saucepan he is holding and sees only a stone.

"What?" she exclaims. "Soup made with just a stone and some water?"

"Well, signora," says the man, "it is true that it would taste better with a carrot as well."

"But soup made with just a stone and a carrot . . ."

"Well, it would be better with a potato if you happen to have one to spare." And so on.

Easter was a time for peasant families to kill a chicken, either to prepare *pollo in umido* or *pollo al cacciatore* served with carrots and shallots cooked whole. Chicken in those days, thoroughly free-range and fed on maize, had a deliciously gamy taste. But the paramount importance of the chicken for producing eggs was borne out of the year-round popularity of *frittate*—cold omelettes—and quiche-like *torte*. We were always given onion *frittate* in a picnic basket. And fairly often appearing on the table would be an onion tart, known as *la barbuta*, or "the bearded woman," because the fine slices of vegetables were supposed to look like hair; or a *torta* of spinach cooked in the bread oven, or even, in the spring, a *torta* made with nettles when they were still young and fresh.

The centre-piece of Aullese Christmas fare was usually a capon, but most of the other dishes were very different to British tradition. The first course was often *tortelli* stuffed with ricotta and wild herbs or mushrooms, followed by a *torta di verdura*—a rich quiche with pumpkin, leeks, spinach, beet, onion, nettles and borage.

The seriousness of the whole enterprise, above all when preparing for a feast day, was not to be underestimated. Tasting was not just a formality; Mariannina's expression was genuinely preoccupied until reassured both by the taste and, after a loaded silence, by the after-taste. Only then would she pronounce her work satisfactory.

Much later, when all was eaten and the copper saucepans cleaned, polished and hung up, Mariannina would sit down in the large kitchen chair and take out her embroidery. This was the best time to beg her to tell us fairy tales. In a typically Tuscan way, most of them involved delicious food produced by magic as well as the more con-ventional rewards of great riches, or marriage to a prince or princess.

MARKET THEATRE IN AULLA

For Mariannina, as for any Tuscan, the first step in the preparation of the day's meals was seeing which vegetables were ready in the *orto*. Only then would she consider what produce was fresh and reason-ably priced—either in the market, or available from travelling ven-dors. Anything not grown at home was automatically regarded with suspicion, so selection was as important as the cooking itself.

Vendors used to turn up unannounced with frequent irregularity. Coming down to breakfast, we would often find a peasant woman seated upon the hall steps, surrounded by scrawny chickens with their legs tied together. She would pinch the poor fowls to show how fat they were while Mariannina or my mother bargained. Others arrived with sacks of chestnuts or baskets of apples, eggs or home-made cheeses.

On one occasion, Mariannina opened the door of the *salone* and shepherded in a live turkey as if announcing a rather shy guest. The turkey stalked haughtily around the room and eventually came to a halt, contemplating the fire in fascination. Mariannina wanted my mother's agreement on the price before concluding such a major purchase. They decided to buy him. He would be quartered outside by the magazine and fed on maize and acorns in preparation for Christmas.

Our turkey, an apparently tame and complacent creature, took on the habits of a domestic pet, wandering in through the *portone*, up the steps to the hall and even to the kitchen. His imprisonment was incomparably more civilized than that of most large birds destined for the pot. In many farmhouses the capon or cock being fattened up for Christmas was kept in a wicker cage near the kitchen fire. Yet perhaps our turkey suddenly perceived his fate on one of his perambulations, for one day this hitherto willing prisoner jumped from the outer wall into the ilex wood below, softening his fall with an energetic flapping of stubby wings.

Ramponi, who had spotted the escape, was certain that such a slow bird could not elude him. He delayed his pursuit until he had finished what he was doing. But this proved a severe miscalculation for which Mariannina never forgave him—or indeed herself, since she had been the one who had persuaded my mother to buy the bird in the first place. She and Adelina had long discussions afterwards about whose pot the turkey had disappeared into, but their speculation on his fate only increased their frustration.

The temptation for both travelling vendors and stallholders in the town to get the better of the English—to be *furbo*, or cunning—with stones in the bottom of the sack or other such devices, was often too great for them to resist. In those days, when the *lira sterlina* was still on the gold standard, English travellers and residents were automatically assumed to be milords and charged acordingly, which meant at least double the price demanded from Italians.

Local friends would laugh at my mother's disappointment after a particularly nice vendor turned out to have been dishonest in a transaction. "Never trust your neighbour," they would tell her. "Your neighbour does not expect it." Life was a process of cheat and be cheated, a circle of rough justice. Peasant women who could neither read nor write were constantly tricked by shopkeepers in the town, and they in turn would get their own back from anyone they thought could afford it.

The only weighing machine anyone trusted was the one at the railway station, and many people used to rush there to check their purchases. It was Signora Fortunata, the wife of a local merchant, who eventually mustered the courage to turn the butcher's scales upside down. She tore off the weights that were concealed on the underside and lectured him so loudly that a crowd gathered, peering in at doors and windows to watch him quiver under her magisterial tongue-lashing.

In a small town like Aulla, shopping and social life were closely linked. The local inhabitants were of course keenly interested in the price as well as the quality of the food on offer, yet the market itself provided the main source of excitement. This meeting-place, inevitably the main centre for gossip, was above all a stage for declamatory theatre and dialogue—a public contest in which the bargaining reputation of both stallholder and housewife was at stake.

Bargaining was an immensely serious business, a matter of state; yet for many it was also the most exciting part of the day, and a subject for endless discussion afterwards. But once the duel, however acrimonious, had run its course, it was suddenly resolved. The purchaser, extracting the money from a purse hung round the neck, maintained a watchful eye in case a different article to the one she had chosen was placed in her basket or bag, then the whole encounter was concluded with nods and smiles and mutual compliments. My mother, although a writer with no natural interest in housekeeping, was fascinated by the game that was played out there each day, but she found it very hard to follow Mariannina's advice to be constantly on guard.

Aulla market started early, usually around five in the morning. The noises of assembly—the creak and rattle of handcarts, the cries of greeting and raillery between peasant women coming in from the two valleys—mingled and, if the river mist was not heavy, drifted up to the castle. The little town's more prosperous matrons, each one closely followed by a maid bearing large baskets, would make their appearance later, but not too late. As if to emphasize the dignity of their position, they would not show any sign of pleasure at the colourful and lively scene but would circle the stalls with pronounced disdain as they eyed them for bargains.

Alongside the proper stalls with tables and awnings, peasant women squatted in the shade of huge umbrellas with hefty baskets in front of them filled with eggs, or vegetables from their own *orto* or, if they were shepherds' wives, heavy, round *pecorino* cheeses.

I loved to accompany Adelina when she went down to the market, if only because of the variety of produce and its colours. In summer it was like looking through a kaleidoscope—the red, yellow and green of peppers, the glossy purple of aubergines, and the orange of persimmons. Even the less garish produce—cardoons, cabbages, spinach, strings of onion and plaits of garlic—were all displayed to attract the eye. And the whole time one would hear the singsong cries of the vendors—"*O signori, la mia bella verdura*"—chanted in what sounded like the proud lament of an opera without music.

The fish stall fascinated me most, with its red and grey mullet, crayfish, prawns, cuttlefish and whiting laid out on glistening marble slabs. Every so often, when no customers were in the way, a young lad threw a bucket of water over them to keep them cool and fresh-looking in the heat. Inland, fish was expensive—except in the unap-petizing form of *baccalà*, or dry salt cod—so any member of the household returning from La Spezia would bring some fresh fish back from the large market there. On days when Mariannina had asked somebody to do this, she would go out on to the dining-room balcony to watch for the train from La Spezia. If a handkerchief was waved energetically from a carriage window as the train drew into the station, she knew that all was well and that she would not have to pre-pare an alternative meal at the last moment.

When there was a feast day Adelina used to take us down to the town. She took great care with her appearance—she was a clever dressmaker, whether refashioning an old dress of my mother's or making her own. I was fascinated by what she could achieve with a length of material from one of the bolts of cotton print that came from Genoa. Dresses were generously cut, full-skirted and down to the ankle, and a shawl or scarf was worn round the neck, ready to be draped over the head when entering church.

Once mass was over in the church of San Caprasio, the day was for seeing—the crowds, the stalls, the sideshows and the spectacles—and for being seen—either in the general *passeggiata*, or showing off a new dress by dancing in the Piazza Fontana to the music of a concertina. In the background, as if to confuse the dancers, the town's brass band, in which Ulisse played a trumpet until his death, could be heard going through its repertoire—mainly excerpts from Verdi and Rossini.

In a way, a feast day was rather like market day, but the stalls were designed, as was the occasion itself, for pleasure, not daily needs. They sold ribbons and materials for dressmaking, cheap gewgaws or delicacies to be consumed on the spot such as chestnut cake, sticky as marrons glacés and cut into segments with a wire.

Vendors walked around offering unusual wares, from large grasshoppers in crudely fashioned little cages to patent medicines. Other men, standing by baskets of pears, figs and other fruit, loudly declaimed their virtue, then, having selected a fine specimen, proceeded to eat it with a conspicuous display of relish.

The local letter-writer did not miss the opportunity to set up his tent: he increased his charge when asked to compose love-letters, and there was a further supplement for verses. Meanwhile, fortune-telling crones spun wildly optimistic predictions for lovesick girls. Small crowds gathered round travelling organ-grinders, jugglers, tightrope walkers and acrobats or *saltimbanchi*. All the sounds competed: the brass band, the hubbub of voices and the hurdy-gurdy of the merry-go-round, on which we had as many rides as possible.

The feast day of San Caprasio, the patron saint of Aulla, on 1 June was one of the high points of the year. It finished with a religious procession following the statue of the Virgin, borne by relays of perspiring volunteers. At Corpus Christi, also in early summer, flowers were scattered in the road and attached to lampposts. On such occasions the procession round town, with an embroidered canopy held over the priest who carried the chalice and host, ended with a blessing outside the railway station.

Religion, in a small community like Aulla, was down-to-earth and personal. God seemed to be addressed like an understanding yet feared head of the family from whom favours were constantly sought. There was an innate flexibility that Protestants never seemed to understand. Even anticlericals, like the amiable Ulisse, still went to church and accompanied religious processions out of respect for ancient custom. And while devout Catholic wives insisted on remaining chaste during Lent—the birth rate dropped sharply in the month before Christmas—they were more pragmatic on the question of food. One Ash Wednesday, for example, an aunt of Mariannina's, who had made a large quantity of ravioli stuffed with meat for Carnival, found only a small proportion had been consumed. "What am I to do?" she demanded. "Here we are in Lent and we should not be eating meat in any form. But it would be such a *peccato* to throw them away." (The word *peccato* conveniently means a sin as well as a shame.)

"I agree," said Mariannina. "But let's look at it this way. The real sin is what comes out of the mouth, and not so much what goes in."

James Boswell

(1740–1795)

Famed biographer and diarist James Boswell was also one of the first Grand Tourists. His papers, long thought to have been lost or destroyed, were discovered in Ireland in the early twentieth century and then acquired by Yale University. In addition to his London diaries, Boswell wrote accounts of his travels to Holland, Corsica, France, and Italy. Tourism suited Boswell's personality; he was adaptable, cheerful, and loved to meet all kinds of people. Unlike his contemporary, the cranky Tobias Smollett, Boswell enthusiastically embraced Continental society, describing the language, the wine, the food, and his many love affairs.

In this excerpt from *Boswell on the Grand Tour* (1765–1766) he wrote that he was "very attentive to the ladies at Siena. I found that people lived there in a completely natural fashion, making love as their inclinations suggested . . . I allowed myself to become all sensation and immediate feeling . . . To enjoy was the thing. Intoxicated by that sweet delirium, I gave myself up, without self-reproach and in complete serenity, to the charms of irregular love."

Although best known for his diary and its record of the life of Samuel Johnson, Boswell's travel writing stands alone. Like many young travelers released from the restraints of British society, James Boswell was unalterably changed by Italy, its people, and its culture.

The following is from a letter that summarizes his Italian tour written to Jean-Jacques Rousseau. Although three copies of the letter exist, it was apparently never sent.

from BOSWELL ON THE GRAND TOUR

From Parma I went to Florence, where I remained a fortnight, to see the curiosities and a little of the society, which I did not find very agreeable. The Florentines (especially the Florentine women) are very proud and very mercenary. I shall not give you a detailed report on all the cities where I passed some time and in which I saw the nobility. I found in Florence one of the best teachers of the flute in Europe, Dothel, a Lorrainer. He gave me several lessons, and started me on a good plan of study.

From Florence I went to Siena, where I passed a portion of my existence in perfect felicity. The nobility there form a society of the most amiable sort. They have a simplicity, an openness, a gaiety which you cannot imagine without having been there. They have no society manners, none of that affected air which to the philosopher betrays artificial beings. You, Sir, as delicate as you are, could live in the society of Siena. Since there is no Court there and the nobles think only of living within their moderate incomes, you never see in Siena those gentlemen with great interest who spoil every company in a city where it is thought that something may be gained by paying court. The Sienese are independent, equal, and content to be so, and when a great prince comes among them he is politely received, but they do not put themselves out for him. While I was in Siena, the Constable Colonna spent several days there, and I, with my monarchical ideas, was scandalised to see him treated in so easy a fashion. "Come! Il Conestabile Colonna!" They laughingly replied to me, "Ma che fa a noi il Conestabile Colonna?" Never have I seen so much of what I should call true humanity as at Siena. People there do not embarrass a stranger by giving him a studied reception. He comes recommended by some person of distinction, as I was by my Lord Mountstuart. They greet him naturally. An easy conversation immediately ensues. He forgets that he is a stranger, and no longer is one.

I had excellent apartments at Siena. I ate well. The wine of the district was very good, and on holidays I regaled myself with delicious Montepulciano. The air is fresh, and the weather is always fine. My health was very quickly restored. An Abbé of talent and obliging disposition dined with me every day, and accommodated himself perfectly to the little variations of my temperament. He helped me as teacher in Italian. Every morning for two hours I read the divine Ariosto, and you can imagine the effect which that produced on my romantic soul. I also wrote in Italian with equal regularity, and as I used no other language in conversation, I made rapid progress. The Sienese dialect is the most agreeable in all of Italy. For me it was a continual melody. I had lively sensations of pleasure when I heard people merely discussing the good weather. A "professor" of music, who had very fine taste, came to me every afternoon, and we sang and played fine airs on the flute. Little by little I shall come to know something of music. I can already amuse myself with it tolerably. I lack application, but that will come. I have not forgotten you in a land where I have heard six different operas. I am sorry not to have some of your music with me. I remember only "Quand on sait aimer et plaire" and a little air with which you amused a lady of Neuchâtel:

> Nous habitons une maison,
> Où les biens pleuvent à foison. . . .

Ariosto, music, and pleasant company occupied my days at Siena. The circumstances were most precious to my imagination. I was in a provincial city in the heart of beautiful Tuscany; a city completely at peace where not a single soldier was to be seen, not even a pensioner. I was the only foreigner there. I was as though in the most remote of countries, the most hidden of retreats. My mind was healthy, easy, and joyful. Neither past nor future entered my thoughts. I thanked God for my present existence. It is an extraordinary mind which can do so.

But, Sir, I must tell you of more interesting things. Your Scot was very attentive to the ladies at Siena. I found that people lived there in a completely natural fashion, making love as their inclinations suggested. It was the custom of the society in which I lived. I yielded to custom. I allowed myself to become all sensation and immediate feeling. I did not wish to extend my mind to encompass a series of prudent considerations. I did not wish to be more profound than the others. To enjoy was the thing. Intoxicated by that sweet delirium, I gave myself up, without self-reproach and in complete serenity, to the charms of irregular love.

I paid court to a lady who had lived much in Florence, and whose noble manners incited my vanity; and through vanity I so heated my imagination with a desire to obtain that lady that I thought myself madly in love with her. As a matter of fact, I *did* suffer from her severity. She saw me frequently, showed a genteel esteem for me, called me her friend, wrote me tender letters, but assured me that she had really loved my Lord Mountstuart, and that he would be her last lover. I wrote her the most curious of letters on that subject. It was a delicate question whether to try the constancy of a friend's mistress, but as my Lord had given me permission to adore a goddess whom he scarcely gave a thought to any more, and as I was quite sure that Signora _____ had considerable inclination to be persuaded to change her mind, I continued to press her with great eagerness.

I was wicked enough to wait at the same time on a very amiable little woman to whom I made declarations of the most sincere passion, as can be easily done when one feels only a slight inclination. I fancied that she had no heart, and as I believed everything fair in the war of gallantry, I lied to her certainly no fewer than a hundred times a day. Behold me, then, very busy indeed, with two affairs going at the same time. It required an unparalleled dexterity, and I had it. Then nothing was difficult for me. I drifted pleasantly between my two loves, and my *valet de place*, a lout who could neither read nor write, was dispatched with his face turned towards the east to carry a letter for Signora A. in his right-hand pocket and a letter for Signora B. in his left.

In a fortnight Signora B., who was the most trusting of persons, and with whom I had used the full force of my reasoning powers to prove that in me she would have the most faithful of lovers, but that my sufferings were so excruciating that, if she did not soon assure me of her affection, I feared so much the sad effects of a strong passion on a melancholy mind that I was determined to set out at once—and what a pity it would be to miss in this short life so fine an occasion for mutual happiness. This amiable person, whose heart was already touched, listened to me kindly and granted me all, saying, "Ebbene, mi fido a voi com' a un galantuomo." My conscience reproached me. It happened that Signora A. revealed her character to me. I saw that she conducted intrigues strictly according to the rules, without being touched by love. I abandoned my design upon her. I attached myself completely to my dear little mistress, through a principle of true gratitude.

I studied her character. I found many good qualities in her. I even found charms in her which the dissipation of my spirit had caused me to overlook previously; and with extraordinary joy I found myself truly in love with her. I opened my heart to her, made a full confession of the deceit I had practised on her, while assuring her that she had gained my love. I enjoyed with her the exquisite pleasure of Italian gallantry, whose enchantments I had heard so much of; and I swear to you that experiencing them measured up to my ideas. She was struck with what I had told her. She reproached me tenderly for my treachery. But from that time on she had complete confidence in me. I was utterly happy and I risked nothing.

The times, Sir, are much changed in Italy. No longer does one have to fear the stiletto of a jealous husband. But as the dispositions of a people always persist under one form or another, and as the lively wit of the loose-living Romans is displayed in sonnets, in songs, and in ecclesiastical intrigues, so Italian jealousy survives feebly in the hearts of *cavalieri serventi*, of whom every lady has one or two. A *cavaliere servente* is a being whom I regard as illustrating the last stage of human degradation. A lover without love, a soldier without pay, a being who is more a drudge than is a *valet de chambre*, who does continual duty, and enjoys only appearances! Since Signora B. had to keep some of these gentlemen in her train, we had to manage them, and we were sometimes a little embarrassed how to do it.

I loved her more and more. She had a natural *allegria* which never changed and which so alleviated my sombre humour that it buoyed me up until I was quite free of melancholy. I found her a woman made for a life of virtue. When I explained to her the sweet and durable bonds of the conjugal union, she was enchanted and regretted infinitely that she could not experience them, insisting strongly on the advantage which a virtuous mother of a family must enjoy in old age. But said she, "They took me out of the convent and married me at sixteen, when I did not have the slightest idea what marriage meant. Ero totalmente senza malizia. Quando ero messa in letto col mio marito, trovava roba intorno di me, a pensava ch'era una bestia." The naïveté with which she made that remark and the laughable word *roba* diverted me infinitely. "I am married," she continued, "to a man considerably older than myself; a man whom I not only cannot love but whom I cannot even respect, for to tell the truth he has no liveliness of mind at all, and he is very coarse."

Hear me, illustrious philosopher! I dare ask you to tell me honestly without prejudice whether that woman was really married, whether she had made a true contract, whether she was obliged to remain faithful to a man to whom her parents had bound her, whether it was her duty to sacrifice her finest inclinations to the hard circumstances in which she found herself. I could not answer her arguments, but in my moments of virtue and piety I warmly repeated to her the common sentiments against adultery. She was very fond of your works. I read to her with a grave and serious air the beautiful and affecting words of Julie on that terrible vice. I was so moved by them that she could not but feel something. But an onrush of passion overcame me. I embraced her with a kind of frenzy and repeated our criminal ecstasies. She said, "Voi siete precisamente quel Rousseau. Tale quale. Parlate moltissimo della virtù, e però fate il male." I was stirred by a pride of sentiment. She confessed to me all the love affairs in which she had engaged. She told me the names of her lovers, one of whom was always at our *conversazioni*. I wished him dead many and many a time. My extreme jealousy was tormented even by what no longer existed.

My Signora was sorry that I felt so. She assured me that I was the first for whom she had felt a true passion, because it was the first time that love had made her uneasy. The same thing, indeed, has happened to women of intrigue many times. I wished to believe her. But I could not endure the thought that she had been the mistress of others. Ah, I groaned from the heart. Signora B. made a rather subtle observation on that. She told me that a man is wrong to boast that he possesses the affections of a girl, because the poor ignorant being knows no better, never having had opportunity to know the merits of lovers. But when a woman has had a little experience and knows men, then her attachment is truly flattering. I believed that also. But do not call me a dupe. Do not say that I fell into very good hands. Have no suspicions of the sincerity of my charming Signora. No, Sir, although not from the richest of families, she was completely generous, completely disinterested. Although she could not doubt that I would lay everything at her feet that she might demand from me, she never made me play, never told me that she wanted the least thing; and, take my word for it, such a character is very rare among the ladies of Italy, especially those of Tuscany where they make a regular business of English "milords," as they call all us British gentlemen in general. She was a careful manager and advised me how to bargain so as not to be taken in, so as to spend my money wisely. I felt as though I were really married, so well did she play the part of an excellent wife. Never was vice so sanctified by virtue. She made me go to mass with her, and I dare say that while we were there we were as pious as if our conduct had been completely innocent.

Thus my life slipped away in a delicious dream, while my principles of systematic morality were melted down by the fire of a heated imagination. But time was fleeing. My father was in momentary expectation of news of my arrival in France, and before going there I had secretly resolved to make a tour of Corsica. How was I to decide? My inclination, and, according to the principles of true gallantry, my duty—for vice, when it is social, has its principles also—demanded that I remain with a woman who had made me happy and to whom I owed so much. I thought also that a being who has had so sad an existence as mine would do badly not to profit as much as possible from happiness which he had finally found—if he did not drink from the stream of pleasure as long as Heaven caused it to flow. I was utterly happy. Everything seemed agreeable to me. Even God took on for me the most agreeable aspect, as he will appear to us when at the end our souls will be all purified and exalted into the divine perfection. O dear St. Preux! Yes, my soul is bound to yours. I have loved like you, I am pious like you. If we have committed crimes, we have also expiated them.

I resolved to leave Siena, and I told Signora _____ a week beforehand. I was firm though sad. Her good sense was such that she admitted my reasons for leaving were irrefutable. But she could not but complain of her lot, which had made her taste real happiness only to feel its loss. When we enjoyed those delicious murmurs which your divine delicacy prefers to the moment of ecstasy itself, she said, "Ah, io piangerò questi momenti." Her sighs pierced my heart. I was gentle in moments of . . .

O love, passionate fever of the soul, meteor of joy whose essence it is to be brief, how dearly we buy your transports! I tried to console us both for the sadness of parting by depicting the beautiful prospect of an eternal friendship. But the Signora insisted absolutely that she must see me again. . . .

[*c.* 2 SEPTEMBER. SIENESE REFLECTIONS.][1]

It seems to me that men have been much mistaken in their search for happiness, and I believe I see clearly the reason why. They have wished to establish the same general system of living for everyone, without realising that men differ as much in inclination as in appearance. It is not surprising that men who have devoted themselves to thought and who are honoured with the great name of philosopher—it is not surprising, I say, that their pride and ambition should make them wish that they could lay down the law to all their fellows and thus be almost kings of mankind. And it is not even surprising that the majority of men have submitted to this intellectual domination, since a great part of mankind are timid and lazy when it comes to thinking for themselves. As for me, who have found myself in every possible frame of mind and have experienced life in great variety, I think that the general rules are very badly conceived and hold men in a tiresome dependence, with no other advantage than to aggrandise certain famous names which have almost become oracles.

It is true that a society cannot exist without general rules. I agree. Let us therefore have laws, and let those laws be the general rules. But I want no others. The laws which are really necessary for public happiness are beyond all question very few. Men have many unwritten laws, and this is exactly the evil against which I am trying to argue. These are the laws of fashion, of custom, and of so many other particular sorts, that those who live "in the world," as the phrase goes, are little better than slaves. I wish everyone to live naturally, as he himself pleases, and then possibly we might not hear so many people complaining of this evil world. To me those lamentations seem like the cries of animals in chains or in cages.

So I think when I live retired from the world and my spirit has

[1]These Reflections written in Italian are a counterpart of the French themes Boswell composed in Utrecht (see *Boswell in Holland*). They were written rapidly as linguistic exercises on any subject which came into his mind. Since they carry no dates, they have to be ordered on internal evidence and on the type of paper and ink used.

complete liberty. So I think here at Siena, where I find myself in a pleasant Tuscan city in the midst of a simple and gay society; and if the moralist would judge some persons living here to be dissolute, then it must be said that the libertinism of Siena is like St. Paul's charity: it thinketh no evil. Marriage here is tacitly considered a different compact from that of civil law, for the *consortium omnis vitae* between married couples is never presumed. And really gentlemen and ladies here do nothing against their consciences, for their consciences are of quite another sort than those of people who live in a country where rigid morality is observed. So I can say philosophically that I have lived among very good people.

So I wish every man to live precisely according to his own inclination, without minding those of other people. I am living in this fashion now. I have been a week in Siena and have not as yet seen any *maraviglia*, as the Italians say. I should not be able to say why to anyone who demanded a proper reason, but I can explain it very well to myself: it is because I have been so busy with women that I felt no curiosity about inanimate objects. I have resumed the study of Italian; I have read Ariosto with a fire worthy of that sublime author and, as I am making clear perhaps at this moment, I have been trying to write a little in *la bella lingua*. I feel peaceful and happy, and though there may be more estimable people, I am sure there are none happier than I am. My philosophy aims no higher.

Elizabeth Barrett Browning

(1806–1861)

Elizabeth Barrett Browning and Robert Browning are nearly overshadowed by the mythology of their great love affair. She was an acclaimed poet and an invalid; he, a poetic upstart six years her junior. Her family opposed their marriage and the couple eloped to Italy and lived in Florence. Elizabeth's *The Sonnets of the Portuguese* (1850) is addressed to her husband and remains her greatest work.

Elizabeth was ardent about her adopted country and wrote somewhat strident poems about its nationalist cause. One of her early biographers wrote, "A noble devotion to and faith in the regeneration of Italy was a prominent feature in Mrs. Browning's life. To her, Italy was from the first a living fire, not the bed of dead ashes at which the world was wont to sneer."

Elizabeth's passion for Tuscany is evident in the poem "Bianca Among the Nightingales." The narrator, a Tuscan woman who has followed her faithless lover to England, contrasts "gloomy England" with her "Native Florence! dear, forgone!" While parts of the poem seem forced or even gruesome to a modern reader, some of its imagery sparkles, particularly in the descriptions of her beloved Tuscan landscape.

On June 6, 1861, Count Camillo Benso di Cavour, the architect of Italian unity, died. Elizabeth was heartbroken that "the patriot pilot was hurried from the helm." Despite reassurance that Cavour's successor would carry on his fight, Elizabeth's always fragile health failed three months later. Elizabeth Barrett Browning is buried in the Protestant Cemetery in Florence.

BIANCA AMONG THE NIGHTINGALES

I

The cypress stood up like a church
    That night we felt our love would hold,

And saintly moonlight seemed to search
    And wash the whole world clean as gold;
The olives crystallized the vales'
    Broad slopes until the hills grew strong.
The fireflies and the nightingales
    Throbbed each to either, flame and song
The nightingales, the nightingales!

I I

Upon the angle of its shade
    The cypress stood, self-balanced high;
Half up, half down, as double-made,
    Along the ground, against the sky;
And *we*, too! From such soul-height went
    Such leaps of blood, so blindly driven,
We scarce knew if our nature meant
    Most passionate earth or intense heaven
The nightingales, the nightingales!

I I I

We paled with love, we shook with love,
    We kissed so close we could not vow;
Till Giulio whispered "Sweet, above
    God's Ever guaranties this Now."
And through his words the nightingales
    Drove straight and full their long clear call,
Like arrows through heroic mails,
    And love was awful in it all.
The nightingales, the nightingales!

I V

O cold white moonlight of the north,
    Refresh these pulses, quench this hell!
O coverture of death drawn forth
    Across this garden-chamber . . . well!
But what have nightingales to do

In gloomy England, called the free . . .
(Yes, free to die in! . . .) when we two
    Are sundered, singing still to me?
And still they sing, the nightingales!

V

I think I hear him, how he cried
    "My own soul's life!" between their notes.
Each man has but one soul supplied,
    And that's immortal. Though his throat's
On fire with passion now, to *her*
    He can't say what to me he said!
And yet he moves her, they aver.
    The nightingales sing through my head,—
The nightingales, the nightingales!

V I

He says to her what moves her most.
    He would not name his soul within
Her hearing,—rather pays her cost
    With praises to her lips and chin.
Man has but one soul, 'tis ordained,
    And each soul but one love, I add;
Yet souls are damned and love's profaned;
    These nightingales will sing me mad!
The nightingales, the nightingales!

V I I

I marvel how the birds can sing.
    There's little difference, in their view,
Betwixt our Tuscan trees that spring
    As vital flames into the blue,
And dull round blots of foliage meant,
    Like saturated sponges here
To suck the fogs up. As content
    Is he too in this land, 'tis clear.
And still they sing, the nightingales.

VIII

My Native Florence! dear, forgone!
    I see across the Alpine ridge
How the last feast-day of Saint John
    Shot rockets from Carraia bridge.
The luminous city, tall with fire,
    Trod deep down in that river of ours,
While many a boat with lamp and choir
    Skimmed birdlike over glittering towers.
I will not hear these nightingales.

IX

I seem to float, *we* seem to float
    Down Arno's stream in festive guise;
A boat strikes flame into our boat,
    And up that lady seems to rise
As then she rose. The shock had flashed
    A vision on us! What a head,
What leaping eyeballs!—beauty dashed
    To splendor by a sudden dread.
And still they sing, the nightingales.

X

Too bold to sin, too weak to die;
    Such women are so. As for me,
I would we had drowned there, he and I,
    That moment, loving perfectly.
He had not caught her with her loosed
    Gold ringlets ... rarer in the south ...
Nor heard the "Grazie tanto" bruised
    To sweetness by her English mouth.
And still they sing, the nightingales.

XI

She had not reached him at my heart
    With her fine tongue, as snakes indeed
Kill flies; nor had I, for my part,

Yearned after, in my desperate need,
And followed him as he did her
    To coasts left bitter by the tide,
Whose very nightingales, elsewhere
    Delighting, torture and deride!
For still they sing, the nightingales.

XII

A worthless woman; mere cold clay
    As all false things are: but so fair,
She takes the breath of men away
    Who gaze upon her unaware.
I would not play her larcenous tricks
    To have her looks! She lied and stole,
And spat into my love's pure pyx
    The rank saliva of her soul.
And still they sing, the nightingales.

XIII

I would not for her white and pink,
    Though such he likes—her grace of limb,
Though such he has praised—nor yet, I think,
    For life itself, though spent with him,
Commit such sacrilege, affront
    God's nature which is love, intrude
'Twixt two affianced souls, and hunt
    Like spiders, in the altar's wood.
I cannot bear these nightingales.

XIV

If she chose sin, some gentler guise
    She might have sinned in, so it seems:
She might have pricked out both my eyes,
    And I still seen him in my dreams!
—Or drugged me in my soup or wine,
    Nor left me angry afterward:
To die here with his hand in mine,

His breath upon me, were not hard.
(Our Lady hush these nightingales!)

X V

But set a springe for *him*, "mio ben,"
      My only good, my first last love!—
Though Christ knows well what sin is, when
      He sees some things done they must move
Himself to wonder. Let her pass.
      I think of her by night and day.
Must *I* too join her . . . out, alas! . . .
      With Giulio, in each word I say?
And evermore the nightingales!

X V I

Giulio, my Giulio!—sing they so,
      And you be silent? Do I speak,
And you not hear? An arm you throw
      Round some one, and I feel so weak?
—Oh, owl-like birds! They sing for spite,
      They sing for hate, they sing for doom,
They'll sing through death who sing through night,
      They'll sing and stun me in the tomb—
      The nightingales, the nightingales!

Robert Browning

(1812–1889)

During his wife's lifetime Robert Browning was often eclipsed by the more famous Elizabeth. His early work—heavily influenced by Shelley—garnered some recognition, but he was best known as the suitor who rescued Elizabeth from an oppressive family and a life of invalidism. For fourteen years they lived in a flat in the Casa Guidi, across from the Pitti Palace in Florence. The Brownings were not young star-crossed lovers; he was thirty-five, she was forty-one. They eloped with a maidservant and a dog. She was so small and thin that one visitor said that shaking her hand was like holding on to the foot of a bird.

After Elizabeth's death, Robert moved back to London with their son, Pen, and his poetic star rose. He has been lauded as the master of the dramatic monologue; generations of schoolchildren have memorized "My Last Duchess" (1842) in which the Duke of Ferrara, pointing to a portrait of his late wife, lets drop that he had arranged for her murder. In this poem, "Old Pictures in Florence," Browning explores the relationship between his adopted city and her art treasures. He sees the paintings as the embodiment of great masters. "Wherever a fresco peels and drops, / Wherever an outline weakens and wanes / Till the latest life in the painting stops, / Stands One whom each fainter pulse-tick pains . . ."

Browning died in Venice at the home of his son. He is buried in Westminster Abbey.

OLD PICTURES IN FLORENCE

I

The morn when first it thunders in March,
    The eel in the pond gives a leap, they say:
As I leaned and looked over the aloed arch
    Of the villa-gate this warm March day,
No flash snapped, no dumb thunder rolled
    In the valley beneath where, white and wide

And washed by the morning water-gold,
    Florence lay out on the mountain-side.

I I
River and bridge and street and square
    Lay mine, as much at my beck and call,
Through the live translucent bath of air,
    As the sights in a magic crystal ball.
And of all I saw and of all I praised,
    The most to praise and the best to see
Was the startling bell-tower Giotto raised:
    But why did it more than startle me?

I I I
Giotto, how, with that soul of yours,
    Could you play me false who loved you so?
Some slights if a certain heart endures
    Yet it feels, I would have your fellows know!
I' faith, I perceive not why I should care
    To break a silence that suits them best,
But the thing grows somewhat hard to bear
    When I find a Giotto join the rest.

I V
On the arch where olives overhead
    Print the blue sky with twig and leaf,
(That sharp-curled leaf which they never shed)
    'Twixt the aloes, I used to lean in chief,
And mark through the winter afternoons,
    By a gift God grants me now and then,
In the mild decline of those suns like moons,
    Who walked in Florence, besides her men.

V
They might chirp and chaffer, come and go
    For pleasure or profit, her men alive—
My business was hardly with them, I trow,

But with empty cells of the human hive;
—With the chapter-room, the cloister-porch,
    The church's apsis, aisle or nave,
Its crypt, one fingers along with a torch,
    Its face set full for the sun to shave.

VI

Wherever a fresco peels and drops,
    Wherever an outline weakens and wanes
Till the latest life in the painting stops,
    Stands One whom each fainter pulse-tick pains:
One, wishful each scrap should clutch the brick,
    Each tinge not wholly escape the plaster,
—A lion who dies of an ass's kick,
    The wronged great soul of an ancient Master.

VII

For oh, this world and the wrong it does!
    They are safe in heaven with their backs to it,
The Michaels and Rafaels, you hum and buzz
    Round the works of, you of the little wit!
Do their eyes contract to the earth's old scope,
    Now that they see God face to face,
And have all attained to be poets, I hope?
    'Tis their holiday now, in any case.

VIII

Much they reck of your praise and you!
    But the wronged great souls—can they be quit
Of a world where their work is all to do,
    Where you style them, you of the little wit,
Old Master This and Early the Other,
    Not dreaming that Old and New are fellows:
A younger succeeds to an elder brother,
    Da Vincis derive in good time from Dellos.

IX

And here where your praise might yield returns,
    And a handsome word or two give help,
Here, after your kind, the mastiff girns
    And the puppy pack of poodles yelp.
What, not a word for Stefano there,
    Of brow once prominent and starry,
Called Nature's Ape and the world's despair
    For his peerless painting? (See Vasari.)

X

There stands the Master. Study, my friends,
    What a man's work comes to! So he plans it,
Performs it, perfects it, makes amends
    For the toiling and moiling, and then, *sic transit!*
Happier the thrifty blind-folk labor,
    With upturned eye while the hand is busy,
Not sidling a glance at the coin of their neighbor!
    'Tis looking downward that makes one dizzy.

XI

"If you knew their work you would deal your dole."
    May I take upon me to instruct you?
When Greek Art ran and reached the goal,
    Thus much had the world to boast *in fructu*—
The Truth of Man, as by God first spoken,
    Which the actual generations garble,
Was re-uttered, and Soul (which Limbs betoken)
    And Limbs (Soul informs) made new in marble.

XII

So, you saw yourself as you wished you were,
    As you might have been, as you cannot be;
Earth here, rebuked by Olympus there:
    And grew content in your poor degree
With your little power, by those statues' godhead,
    And your little scope, by their eyes' full sway,

And your little grace, by their grace embodied,
    And your little date, by their forms that stay.

XIII

You would fain be kinglier, say, than I am?
    Even so, you will not sit like Theseus.
You would prove a model? The Son of Priam
    Has yet the advantage in arms' and knees' use.
You're wroth—can you slay your snake like Apollo?
    You're grieved—still Niobe's the grander!
You live—there's the Racers' frieze to follow:
    You die—there's the dying Alexander.

XIV

So, testing your weakness by their strength,
    Your meagre charms by their rounded beauty,
Measured by Art in your breadth and length,
    You learned—to submit is a mortal's duty.
—When I say "you" 'tis the common soul,
    The collective, I mean: the race of Man
That receives life in parts to live in a whole,
    And grow here according to God's clear plan.

XV

Growth came when, looking your last on them all,
    You turned your eyes inwardly one fine day
And cried with a start—What if we so small
    Be greater and grander the while than they?
And they perfect of lineament, perfect of stature?
    In both, of such lower types are we
Precisely because of our wider nature;
    For time, theirs—ours, for eternity.

XVI

To-day's brief passion limits their range;
    It seethes with the morrow for us and more.

They are perfect—how else? they shall never change:
    We are faulty—why not? we have time in store.
The Artificer's hand is not arrested
    With us; we are rough-hewn, nowise polished:
They stand for our copy, and, once invested
    With all they can teach, we shall see them abolished.

XVII

'Tis a life-long toil till our lump be leaven—
    The better! What's come to perfection perishes.
Things learned on earth, we shall practise in heaven:
    Works done least rapidly, Art most cherishes.
Thyself shalt afford the example, Giotto!
    Thy one work, not to decrease or diminish,
Done at a stroke, was just (was it not?) "O!"
    Thy great Campanile is still to finish.

XVIII

Is it true that we are now, and shall be hereafter,
    But what and where depend on life's minute?
Hails heavenly cheer or infernal laughter
    Our first step out of the gulf or in it?
Shall Man, such step within his endeavor,
    Man's face, have no more play and action
Than joy which is crystallized forever,
    Or grief, an eternal petrifaction?

XIX

On which I conclude, that the early painters,
    To cries of "Greek Art and what more wish you?"—
Replied, "To become now self-acquainters,
    And paint man man, whatever the issue!
Make new hopes shine through the flesh they fray,
    New fears aggrandize the rags and tatters:
To bring the invisible full into play!
    Let the visible go to the dogs—what matters?"

XX

Give these, I exhort you, their guerdon and glory
    For daring so much, before they well did it.
The first of the new, in our race's story,
    Beats the last of the old; 'tis no idle quiddit.
The worthies began a revolution,
    Which if on earth you intend to acknowledge,
Why, honor them now! (ends my allocution)
    Nor confer your degree when the folk leave college.

XXI

There's a fancy some lean to and others hate—
    That, when this life is ended, begins
New work for the soul in another state,
    Where it strives and gets weary, loses and wins:
Where the strong and the weak, this world's congeries,
    Repeat in large what they practised in small,
Through life after life in unlimited series;
    Only the scale's to be changed, that's all.

XXII

Yet I hardly know. When a soul has seen
    By the means of Evil that Good is best,
And, through earth and its noise, what is heaven's serene,—
    When our faith in the same has stood the test—
Why, the child grown man, you burn the rod,
    The uses of labor are surely done;
There remaineth a rest for the people of God:
    And I have had troubles enough, for one.

XXIII

But at any rate I have loved the season
    Of Art's spring-birth so dim and dewy;
My sculptor is Nicolo the Pisan,
    My painter—who but Cimabue?
Nor ever was man of them all indeed,
    From these to Ghiberti and Ghirlandajo,

Could say that he missed my critic-meed.
    So, now to my special grievance—heigh ho!

XXIV

Their ghosts still stand, as I said before,
    Watching each fresco flaked and rasped,
Blocked up, knocked out, or whitewashed o'er:
    —No getting again what the church has grasped!
The works on the wall must take their chance;
    "Works never conceded to England's thick clime!"
(I hope they prefer their inheritance
    Of a bucketful of Italian quick-lime.)

XXV

When they go at length, with such a shaking
    Of heads o'er the old delusion, sadly
Each master his way through the black streets taking,
    Where many a lost work breathes though badly—
Why don't they bethink them of who has merited?
    Why not reveal, while their pictures dree
Such doom, how a captive might be out-ferreted?
    Why is it they never remember me?

XXVI

Not that I expect the geat Bigordi,
    Nor Sandro to hear me, chivalric, bellicose;
Nor the wronged Lippino; and not a word I
    Say of a scrap of Frà Angelico's:
But are you too fine, Taddeo Gaddi,
    To grant me a taste of our intonaco,
Some Jerome that seeks the heaven with a sad eye?
    Not a churlish saint, Lorenzo Monaco?

XXVII

Could not the ghost with the close red cap,
    My Pollajolo, the twice a craftsman,
Save me a sample, give me the hap

Of a muscular Christ that shows the draughtsman?
No Virgin by him the somewhat petty,
    Of finical touch and tempera crumbly—
Could not Alesso Baldovinetti
    Contribute so much, I ask him humbly?

XXVIII
Margheritone of Arezzo,
    With the grave-clothes garb and swaddling barret
(Why purse up mouth and beak in a pet so,
    You bald old saturnine poll-clawed parrot?)
Not a poor glimmering Crucifixion,
    Where in the foreground kneels the donor?
If such remain, as is my conviction,
    The hoarding it does you but little honor.

XXIX
They pass; for them the panels may thrill,
    The tempera grow alive and tinglish;
Their pictures are left to the mercies still
    Of dealers and stealers, Jews and the English,
Who, seeing mere money's worth in their prize,
    Will sell it to somebody calm as Zeno
At naked High Art, and in ecstasies
    Before some clay-cold vile Carlino!

XXX
No matter for these! But Giotto, you,
    Have you allowed, as the town-tongues babble it,—
Oh, never! it shall not be counted true—
    That a certain precious little tablet
Which Buonarotti eyed like a lover,—
    Was buried so long in oblivion's womb
And, left for another than I to discover,
    Turns up at last! and to whom?—to whom?

XXXI

I, that have haunted the dim San Spirito,
 (Or was it rather the Ognissanti?)
Patient on altar-step planting a weary toe!
  Nay, I shall have it yet! *Detur amanti!*
My Koh-i-noor—or (if that's a platitude)
 Jewel of Giamschid, the Persian Sofi's eye;
So, in anticipative gratitude,
  What if I take up my hope and prophesy?

XXXII

When the hour grows ripe, and a certain dotard
 Is pitched, no parcel that needs invoicing,
To the worse side of the Mont Saint Gothard,
  We shall begin by way of rejoicing;
None of that shooting the sky (blank cartridge),
 Nor a civic guard, all plumes and lacquer,
Hunting Radetzky's soul like a partridge
  Over Morello with squib and cracker.

XXXIII

This time we'll shoot better game and bag 'em hot—
 No mere display at the stone of Dante,
But a kind of sober Witanagemot
  (Ex: "Casa Guidi," *quod videas ante*)
Shall ponder, once Freedom restored to Florence,
 How Art may return that departed with her.
Go, hated house, go each trace of the Loraine's,
  And bring us the days of Orgagna hither!

XXXIV

How we shall prologize, how we shall perorate,
 Utter fit things upon art and history,
Feel truth at blood-heat and falsehood at zero rate,
  Make of the want of the age no mystery;
Contrast the fructuous and sterile eras,
 Show—monarchy ever its uncouth cub licks

Out of the bear's shape into Chimæra's,
     While Pure Art's birth is still the republic's.

XXXV

Then one shall propose in a speech (curt Tuscan,
     Expurgate and sober, with scarcely an "*issimo*,")
To end now our half-told tale of Cambuscan,
     And turn the bell-tower's *alt* to *altissimo*:
And fine as the beak of a young beccaccia
     The Campanile, the Duomo's fit ally,
Shall soar up in gold full fifty braccia,
     Completing Florence, as Florence Italy.

XXXVI

Shall I be alive that morning the scaffold
     Is broken away, and the long-pent fire,
Like the golden hope of the world, unbaffled
     Springs from its sleep, and up goes the spire
While "God and the People" plain for its motto,
     Thence the new tricolor flaps at the sky?
At least to foresee that glory of Giotto
     And Florence together, the first am I!

George Gordon, Lord Byron

(1788–1824)

By the time he was an adolescent, Lord Byron had learned Italian, read parts of the *Inferno*, translated a thirty-volume history of Italy (in "not very choice Italian"), and amassed an impressive library of Italian dictionaries. He had yet to step foot in Italy.

In 1815 Byron married Anne Isabella Milbanke, a serious young woman and a complete mismatch to her hedonistic husband. After the birth of their daughter and an acrimonious separation, Byron fled first to Switzerland and then to Italy. For a time he became part of the fluid Shelley household and had an affair with Mary Shelley's half sister Claire Clairmont that resulted in another daughter. Again, he moved on. In a letter, Shelley wrote to a friend, "I daresay you have heard of the life he lived in Venice, rivaling the wise Solomon in the number of his concubines." Byron finally found stability with Countess Teresa Guiccioli, a married woman with a husband three times her age. Much of Byron's enthusiasm for the Italian nationalist movement is attributed to her influence.

After Shelley's death Byron moved to Greece to participate in the independence movement. He died there of fever and his body was returned to England. He remains one of the best known of the Romantic poets and wrote some of his best work during his six years in Italy.

"Stanzas Written on the Road Between Florence and Pisa" reflects Lord Byron's obsession with youth, beauty, and love.

STANZAS WRITTEN ON THE ROAD
BETWEEN FLORENCE AND PISA

1

Oh, talk not to me of a name great in story—
The days of our Youth are the days of our glory;
And the myrtle and ivy of sweet two-and-twenty
Are worth all your laurels, though ever so plenty.

2

What are garlands and crowns to the brow that is wrinkled?
'Tis but as a dead flower with May-dew besprinkled:
Then away with all such from the head that is hoary,
What care I for the wreaths that can *only* give glory?

3

Oh FAME!——if I e'er took delight in thy praises,
'Twas less for the sake of thy high-sounding phrases,
Than to see the bright eyes of the dear One discover,
She thought that I was not unworthy to love her.

4

There chiefly I sought thee, *there* only I found thee;
Her Glance was the best of the rays that surround thee,
When it sparkled o'er aught that was bright in my story,
I knew it was Love, and I felt it was Glory.

Bruce Chatwin

(1940–1989)

Born in Sheffield, England, Bruce Chatwin went to work as a porter at Sotheby's right after secondary school. He quickly rose from auctioneer to director and acquired his own collection of antiquities. Curious about their origins, Chatwin studied archaeology at the University of Edinburgh and then did fieldwork in Afghanistan and the African Sahara. Although he never finished his degree, he parlayed his experience into a job for the London *Sunday Times* magazine as a travel writer.

Chatwin specialized in exotic places like the southernmost tip of South America, which he described in his travelogue *In Patagonia,* or Dahomey, West Africa, which he described in *The Viceroy of Ouidah*, his fictionalized biography of an eighteenth-century Brazilian slave trader. *The Songlines*, his most famous book, was based on several trips to Australia. This selection, "A Tower in Tuscany," written in 1987, is uncharacteristically contemplative about the process of writing. His biographer, Nicholas Shakespeare, said, "He was a genuine grasshopper and couldn't work in his own space. Maybe that was about some dissatisfaction with himself . . ." A tower in Tuscany was one of the places in which Chatwin felt comfortable.

Chatwin once said, "I quit my job in the 'art world' and went back to the dry places: alone, traveling light. The names of the tribes I traveled among are unimportant: Rguibat, Quashagai, Taimanni, Turkomen, Bororo, Tuareg—people whose journeys, unlike my own, had neither beginning nor end."

from ANATOMY OF RESTLESSNESS

A TOWER IN TUSCANY

Those of us who presume to write books would appear to fall into two categories: the ones who "dig in" and the ones who move. There are writers who can only function "at home," with the right chair, the shelves of dictionaries and encyclopaedias, and now perhaps the word processor. And there are those, like myself, who are paralyzed by "home," for whom home is synonymous with the proverbial writer's block, and who believe naïvely that all would be well if only they were somewhere else. Even among the very great you find the same dichotomy: Flaubert and Tolstoy labouring in their libraries; Zola with a suit of armour alongside his desk; Poe in his cottage; Proust in the cork-lined room. On the other hand, among the "movers" you have Melville, who was "undone" by his gentlemanly establishment in Massachusetts, or Hemingway, Gogol or Dostoevsky whose lives, whether from choice or necessity, were a headlong round of hotels and rented rooms—and, in the case of the last, a Siberian prison.

As for myself (for what that's worth), I have tried to write in such places as an African mud hut (with a wet towel tied around my head), an Athonite monastery, a writers' colony, a moorland cottage, even a tent. But whenever the dust storms come, the rainy season sets in, or a pneumatic drill destroys all hope of concentration, I curse myself and ask, "What am I doing here? Why am I not at the Tower?"

There are, in fact, two towers in my life. Both are mediaeval. Both have thick walls, which make them warm in winter and cool in summer. Both have views of mountains, contained by very small windows that prevent you from getting distracted. One tower is on the Welsh border, in the water meadows of the River Usk. The other is Beatrice von Rezzori's signalling tower—in her idiomatic English she calls it a "signallation tower"—built in the days of Guelph and Ghibelline and standing on a hillside of oak and chestnut woods, about twenty-five kilometres east of Florence.

For years I had to admire Beatrice Monti della Corte (as she then was) from afar. She had been a golden girl of the postwar generation on Capri. When she was twenty-three, long before big money clamped its leaden and rapacious hand on the art market, she had opened a gallery in Milan, the Galleria dell'Ariette, one of the first in Europe to show the new New York School of painting. She had bought a sixteenth-century "captain's house" in Lindos (long before the days of deafening discotheques). Next I heard she had married the Austrian novelist Gregor von Rezzori (or was he Romanian?) and had settled in a Tuscan farmhouse.

One summer evening in England, this couple, whom my imagination had inflated into figures of mythology, were brought to our house. Within minutes we were all old friends: within months I was a regular visitor to Donnini.

The house is a *casa colonica*: the colonists in question being settlers from the Arno Valley who fanned out in waves over the Tuscan countryside from the fourteenth century onwards. Its solid architecture, of stone and tile, is unchanged since that of classical antiquity. Indeed, until about thirty years ago, what Horace had to say of his Tuscan farm could also be said of the life in any *casa colonica*.

At nights the thirty-odd members of an extended family would curl up to sleep under the rafters. By day they would tend their sheep or their beehives, vines and olives. They ploughed the narrow terraced fields with white oxen and lived, austerely, on a diet of bread and beans, cakes of chestnut flour, and meat or pigeon maybe once a month. Then, in the postwar industrial boom, the farmers went to work in the factories, leaving thousands of farms untenanted.

Grisha Rezzori, by temperament and upbringing, is a "mover": it would be impossible for any biographer to trace his zigzagging course through Europe and America. The Rezzoris were Sicilian noblemen who Austrianised themselves and ended up in the Bukovina, the farthest-flung province of the Austro-Hungarian Empire, now swallowed into the Soviet Union.

A marginal man, cast adrift as a civilian in wartime Germany, he fastened his ironic stare on the fall of the Nazis and its aftermath, and with his prodigious gift for storytelling settled down (more or less!) at Donnini and wove these stories into his monumental novel *The Death of My Brother Abel*.

In summer he would work in a converted hay barn; in winter in a cavernous and book-stacked library where, among his rescued souvenirs, there is a faded sepia photo of the rambling manor, now presumably a collective farm, which was once his family house. Yet to watch Il Barone (as his Tuscan neighbours call him) re-emerging from a snowstorm in a greatcoat after a night walk alone in the woods or to see him strolling through the olive groves with his dogs (or the two tame wild boars Inky and Pinkie) was to realise that he had recovered, or reinvented, the "lost domain" of his boyhood.

I associate visits to Donnini with hoots of belly laughter. The Rezzoris have a knack of attracting farcical situations. Their immediate neighbours are a well-known German film director and his wife. This couple had friends among the European Far Left. Their guests included Daniel Cohn-Bendit, better known as Danny le Rouge; and somehow the Italian *carabinieri* got it into its collective head that they might be harbouring *Brigate Rosse*. They also got the wrong house and with helicopters and Jeeps staged an "attack" on the Rezzoris, calling them with loudhailers to come out, unarmed, with their hands up.

The Tower stands a short way from the house on a spur of land overlooking the Arno Valley. When I first went to Donnini, it was lived in by a peasant family and still belonged to the Guicciardini family, whose forebear was the patron of Dante's friend, the poet Guido Cavalcanti. And although Beatrice used to say, with a slightly predatory glint, "I have a fantasy to buy that Tower," I confess to having had designs on it myself. As a boy, on a walking tour of Périgord, I had spent hours in Montaigne's famous tower, with the Greek and Latin inscriptions on the rafters, and now I, too, had a fantasy— the fantasy of a compulsive mover—that I would settle down in the smiling Tuscan landscape and take up scholarly pursuits. Beatrice's fantasy, however, was a lot stronger than mine. Besides, I have noticed in her a flair for putting fantasies into action. The tenants left the Tower. She bought it and began the work of restoration. Her friend the Milanese architect Marco Zanuso designed the outside staircase that leads to the upper room. Inside, it became a "turquerie"; for the Tower of her particular fantasy was another "lost domain," lying somewhere on the shores of the Bosporus. This part of the story goes back to the mid-twenties when Beatrice's father, an aristocrat and expert in heraldry with a great knowledge of history and the fine arts, went to Rome for the winter season and married a fragile Armenian girl who, since the massacres, had been living in Italy.

She died seven years later. Yet the memory of her, of a person unbelievably beautiful and exotic, gave Beatrice an idea to which she has clung all her life: that glamour—real glamour, not the fake Western substitute—is a product of the Ottoman world. Once the rooms of the Tower were plastered, she employed a fresco painter, an old rogue called Barbacci, the last of the locals who could paint a *trompe-l'oeil* cornice or an angel on the ceiling of a church. But when he came to paint the pink "Ottoman" stripes of the room I write in, he was forever peering from the window at the *baronessa* in the swimming pool, and some of the stripes have gone awry.

I have never known Beatrice to buy anything but a bargain, even if she has to travel halfway across the world to get it. She bought dhurrie carpets in the Kabul carpet bazaar. Nearer to home, she bought chairs from the Castello di Sammezzano, a fake Moorish palace on a nearby hill. She had, in addition, an assortment of strange objects, of the kind that refugees pack in their trunks: a gilded incense burner; engravings of odalisques; or a portrait of her grandfather, the pasha, who was once Christian governor of Lebanon—objects which needed a home and which, with a bit of imagination, could conjure echoes of lazy summer afternoons in summerhouses by the water.

Whenever I have been in residence, the place becomes a sea of books and papers and unmade beds and clothes thrown this way and that. But the Tower is a place where I have always worked, clearheadedly and well, in winter and summer, by day or night—and the places you work well in are the places you love the most.

Ann Cornelisen

(1926–2003)

In 1954 Ann Cornelisen arrived in Italy intending to pursue archaeology, but instead worked for the nonprofit Save the Children Fund. In twenty years she helped established three hundred nurseries in Abruzzi. Two books resulted from her work: *Torregreca: Life, Death, Miracles* (1969) and *Women of the Shadows: Wives and Mothers of Southern Italy* (1976). Cornelisen's eye is unsentimental and she lets the women of southern Italy speak for themselves, revealing lives of grueling work in the harsh, bare land of postwar Italy.

Eventually, Cornelisen moved to a thirteenth-century house in Tuscany, the setting for her comic novel *Any Four Women Could Rob the Bank of Italy* (1983) from which this excerpt is taken. Although the book is a caper romp compared to her nonfiction work, it has a serious feminist underpinning. The female perpetrators of a mail train robbery elude Italian police because their gender makes them above reproach. One character says, "I say women are as innately evil and grasping or selfish as men and fully as criminal . . . they have a right to equal suspicion."

While living in Tuscany, Cornelisen befriended recent émigré Frances Mayes, who dedicated *Under the Tuscan Sun* to her. At the end of her life Ann Cornelisen returned to the United States and died in Rome, Georgia.

from ANY FOUR WOMEN COULD ROB THE BANK OF ITALY

Five miles away the town of San Felice Val Gufo, which lends its name, albeit grudgingly, to the station, is invisible from the highway except for the Medici fortress, a church, and a ragged string of houses all clumped together on the top of a high hill. The cathedral, the palaces and squares with their arches and loggias, are saved for a smaller, gentler valley, hidden behind the hill, away from the Val Gufo. There, Renaissance villas and large stone farmhouses sparkle in the morning light and cypress trees sway gently, nodding their allegiance to the town. Exposure, not snobbery, they say, dictates this position, southwest for the greatest amount of sun and the least buffeting from the north wind. The excuse, though always an excuse, allows the San Feliciani to be arrogant and a bit smug. As their ancestors ignored Hannibal's encampments and later those of the condottieri, so today's residents keep their backs to the clusters of concrete boxes in the valley below, the petrol stations and grain silos, the asphalt plants and building-supply yards, which the railway and through roads have attracted. A crass world, appropriate for storage, perhaps. No greater affinity need be acknowledged.

San Felice's claims to superiority are confirmed by serious guidebooks, those with small print and florid prose. They are tempted to lead the visitor from doorway to doorway on a five-hour inspection, but are too wise in the ways of tourists, who take in only what lies between the parking lot and the best restaurant in town, to put much faith in it. Instead they lavish stars and blocks of boldface on those things that must, absolutely, be seen: the Etruscan walls, the medieval battlements and portals, the Hall of the Signoria, and the museums. About two churches, one Romanesque, one Baroque, they are fulsome and at the same time resigned to the reader's inattention. Still, there can be no doubt: San Felice Val Gufo is one of those little-known gems that cognoscenti boast of as their secret discovery. It also has very good wine.

Change is not a mania in such places and too, San Felice has been fortunate. Wars and disasters have not plagued it. Already two hundred years ago there was no land left within the walls for new structures, and no real need for them. The town is much as Napoleon might have seen it. The streets are cobbled. Most are steep and uncomfortably narrow for modern cars. One just allows delivery trucks to reach the Piazza. Another shunts them straight out again. Traffic jams are not tolerated, parking spaces are few. Electrification has left braids of wires along the palace façades, and at vital corners where they must all meet and somehow join, they weave veritable pergolas. Neon has not caught on: the signs are modest and seldom lighted. No one denies the sewers are erratic. They dispose of the materials consigned to them quite efficiently, but on damp, still days they turn sulky and exhale mephitic warnings of displeasure. The mayor and the majority of the town council, all Communists of the Tuscan, bourgeois subspecies, are, as in most nondoctrinal matters, loath to tinker with a system that works. If the weather is slow to change and the miasma too pungent to deny, they mutter darkly about political enemies, subversives all, or the nefarious activities of American nuclear submarines. Only the ingenuous try to fathom the cause-and-effect relationship implied.

The San Feliciani are happy with their inheritance and determined to take care of it. Individually they paint their shutters and repair their roofs and polish the brass mountings on their front doors. Collectively they expect the same attention for their public buildings. Italian politicians, of whatever persuasion, are pragmatic: they satisfy their constituents' more obvious whims, so that peculation may remain a private affair. All that is visible is in exquisite order. The rosy stone of the town hall, the Signoria of old, is well pointed. The clock on its tall tower still pings the quarter hours accurately, though the adjustments required by daylight saving time stimulate attacks of tachycardia. Twice a year for several days time twirls by at a most unsettling pace. Convents, abandoned by their nuns, have been converted to other uses, to schools, even hostels, and the palaces, which now serve as museums and public offices, are maintained with a precision that would startle their former noble owners. No window pediment is allowed to crumble, no column to sag.

The services are impeccable. The sanitation workers, as they choose to be called, never strike. The garbage is *always* collected, the streets *always* swept. The town *Vigili*, in full battle dress, goggles, and helmets, strut importantly about the Piazza, looking for someone to chastise. Squads of men in blue twill trim the hedges of the public gardens, sweep the gravel of leaves, and scrub the fountains. They even sluice down the statues of long-forgotten local dignitaries often enough to keep them white and arresting in their niches. Only the pigeons who roost on the windowsills and in the crannies of the town hall have defied discipline. The slightest noise sends them up on a bombing run of the stairs, and off across to blitz the Piazza.

Not that the town is perfect. It could hardly be that. By the end of a long dry summer the water tastes distinctly peculiar, froggy. The two cinemas, one in the creaky old opera house, can rarely raise a quorum: many films are announced, few are ever shown. In the last twenty years no satisfactory site, visually satisfactory that is, has been found for the hospital the government insists it will build. Not even Michelangelo could design a structure the size of the Ministry of Foreign Affairs that would not be obtrusive on a Tuscan hillside, so the hospital is still in a seventeenth-century palace. The exterior is charming with its narrow arches and graceful columns, its galleries and medallions. The interior, at best, is a *lazzaretto* whitewashed once a year, sloshed with formalin once a week. The equipment is mid-Victorian except for an "intensive-care unit" that was installed several years ago. As yet no technicians who understand it have been assigned to the staff. The San Feliciani admit that it is wiser to be sick in Siena. In most other ways they are satisfied with the town and themselves.

They stay there. They marry each other, gossip about each other, prosper, and die in serenity, a pattern so uncommon today that it is almost suspect. No need to be wary. The circuit is closed, and they like it: they are merely complacent. They are not attracted by life on a large scale. Industry would not have suited them. They judged the dozen or so landowners who still struggle to keep sprawling estates together as idle men with appropriate hobbies. Proper occupation is the gentle commerce of selling each other goods and services, which is much more complex than normal supply and demand. Old feuds must be honored with unflinching devotion; new ones perceived in embryo. An inordinate amount of time is spent watching neighbors through half-closed shutters on the assumption that each splinter of information has or will have its value. Skeletons are everywhere, waiting to be rattled. At least one to a family, which is a powerful incentive to tolerance and neutrality. A murmur, a shrug is warning enough. It is an armed truce and a quiet day, any day, in town can be exhilarating.

The San Feliciani keep themselves armed and potentially ferocious, but are in practice quite kind to each other. They celebrate birth with smiles and delicate gold chains. To the sick they take bowls of fresh chicken broth. They mourn with grave faces. No matter what they may have said about the *caro defunto* in life, they never speak ill of the dead. They condole with the parents of a daughter who marries outside the community, a situation fraught with uncertainties. The tenor of her future life cannot be exactly analyzed, and they still hold the *tenor di vita* to be important: a question of caste. The departure of a son finds them tactfully silent. They suspect instability: ambition, for instance, is an illusional ill.

They do not doubt such judgments. They have inherited a clear code. The generalizations that follow from it assume the power of tenets. Foreign travel is dangerous and uncomfortable: the beds are poor, the food worse, and the natives thieves. All cities are corrupt and corrupting. Politicians are pirates in double-breasted suits. Civil servants are lazy and foreigners—well, foreigners have lately presented a problem for the San Feliciani.

In the summer there had always been a few tourists, German couples doggedly following Baedeker, stray Americans with hired cars and drivers, maybe a busload or two, tours in search of St. Francis or hedge gardens and herbaceous borders. They tramped down the Corso, looked around, bought postcards, and went on to the next place. At least they did until Conte Maffei married his young English wife. It was generally agreed that the change in San Felice began with Caroline's arrival, which, had she known it, would have surprised her. Like most well-bred Englishwomen she considered herself inconspicuous and far too busy keeping up with Giordano Maffei and her kennels to have any influence on town affairs.

Of course she was wrong. She might have melted into a crowd in England. She did not in San Felice where, anyway, the streets were only crowded on market day. She was too tall, too fair with her long streaked blond hair and skin that the palest April sun could turn pink. Even the way she strode along was different, less languid than that of local matrons, less self-conscious. She was obviously pleased with the world, her world at least, which is an infectious pleasure. People who had scowled a moment before suddenly smiled broadly as she passed. Everyone knew her and spoke to her. The women said a few words and then moved quickly away from her: she made them feel dumpy. The men followed her with their eyes and enjoyed the improbable fancies that do flash across the male mind. The grocers, the pharmacists, the town clerks, the people she did business with on her daily round of errands, went out of their way to talk to her. Her pronouns were erratic and her use of the subjunctive was entirely personal, but her Italian was fluent—and they were amused by her. Her opinions were so curious, so original, and she had causes. Who but Caroline would have lectured a peasant, right in the middle of the Piazza, in front of everyone, after he had kicked a dog out of his way? "*Scusi, signora. Mi scusi*, but I didn't know the dog was yours," which enraged her further. The dog was *not* hers. She did not know whose it was, nor care. It was a matter of principle: no dog deserves cruelty. Did he understand? And, of course, he did not.

They learned soon enough that Caroline was tenacious about her causes, and were confused. What she wanted to change had long been established as man's right or man's immemorial vice. All hunting should be banned. Animals protected. Corruption in government ought to be exposed. The illegal flow of Italian capital to safe Swiss bank accounts should be curbed. So original, so very English, they decided.

The Conte had waited a long time, but it was agreed that when he finally chose, he chose the perfect wife. The twenty years' difference in their ages was unimportant. He was still a "fine figure of a man." So tall with a large head, lapping gray curls, and strong, craggy features, which, helped by a constant tan, seemed cast in bronze, he looked as a count should and was satisfactorily eccentric. He had lived in exotic places, Africa and the Far East. He toyed with the idea of sailing the Atlantic alone. Or he might do it in a balloon. Airplanes fascinated him and Chinese dialects. He had managed to learn three of them, though of the languages that might have been more useful to him he spoke only French. He was a frustrated inventor, the owner of one of the district's last large estates, therefore also the resident of its crumbling Renaissance castle, and a *soi-disant* Socialist. He saw no conflict. Certain aspects of life were as they were, inheritance being the most obvious.

Giordano Maffei admired reason and logic in all things and believed that his own decisions were arrived at through their strict application. The results, as everyone agreed, were remarkable. He had come home to manage his land, which was his main source of income. Reasonable. Logical. Now his myriad interests left him no time to do it; he had hired a factor. A liberal, he deplored the effect of prosperity on the peasants. Cars, schooling, store-bought clothes, and television had ruined them. They should have stayed in the condition natural and proper to them, that of a hundred, even two hundred years ago. With the first rumor of the oil crisis, he required Caroline to use her motorbike for all chores in and around San Felice, then bought a tractor, a medium-sized Fiat, and a Mercedes for himself. His friends listened carefully to his explanations, shook their heads, and asked him to repeat that again. Perhaps they had missed a step. Finally they gave up, dazzled by this wizardry that bent logic to prove contradictions.

Caroline, whom Giordano insisted was flighty and emotional, had surprised him by sorting out the confusion of his affairs into something close to order. He was so pleased that, when she wanted to raise Italian shepherd dogs, he encouraged her. Comfort led to benevolence, and he allowed her to invite for weekends the English and American friends he had been sure he would not enjoy. Then he found he liked them. They came back. They delighted in the countryside and their host, whose deep quiet voice seemed to confide and whose brown eyes danced with some ambiguous amusement.

They were artists, writers, journalists who could work almost anywhere, and there were at that time lots of small stone farmhouses, abandoned by the peasants who wanted modern cube houses on a paved road and "regular" jobs, even as unskilled construction workers. These Italianized foreigners bought the abandoned houses for very little and remodeled them a bit at a time or all at once, as their bank accounts allowed. Some used them for weekends. A few, like Hermione Hendricks, the inventor of "The Female Imperative," and Eleanor Kendall, who wrote highly praised, if not highly remunerative, books about Italy, settled down to be permanent residents.

It was this first wave of newcomers that overcame the San Feliciani's misgivings. Foreigners were almost like real people. They would argue and explain and discuss. They *were*, of course, different—they preferred old clothes to fashionable ones, did not go to church, and drank strange fiery liquors—but they could be forgiven because they were semi-famous. They popped up on television screens or were interviewed in newspapers with gratifying regularity. Shopkeepers approved of them wholeheartedly. They were consumers of high-quality goods with high profit margins to match, and they paid their bills. When, finally, they were included in the parties of the local gentry, the matter was settled: the San Feliciani would be cordial to foreigners.

Inexplicably there did seem to be more general tourists, which gave rise to an idea that would not die: obviously all foreigners knew each other and, like migrating birds, called their friends down to share in fertile fields. Each year a few remained behind or came back out of season and more houses were bought and rebuilt and more permanent customers for high-quality goods acquired. But these did not have the other winning habit of paying their bills at once. They paid a bit this month, a bit next—maybe. The gentry did not, would not, know them and, as everyone observed later, Contessa Maffei's friends were courteous, if they met them in the street, but they were never seen together otherwise. When this second wave sold their houses at large profit—never as outlandish as rumored—the situation was reassessed: foreigners should be treated with caution.

The San Feliciani could also speculate and did on a much more daring scale. They put light, water, and roads into several huge abandoned houses and sold them for more money than they were sure the local bank had on deposit. The third wave of foreigners knew no Italian, but that slight impediment did not make them shy. They swarmed over the town, shouting in their own languages for whatever they wanted, or grunting with simian determination. To everyone's relief the novelty of shopping soon wore off, and platoons of servants took over the chore of keeping their new masters and the armies of guests comfortable. Majordomos ordered the provisions required, haggled over the prices, and at the end of each month went around, very conscious of their new importance, paying the bills. Canned and boxed goods were purchased by the case. Mops by the dozen. All most confusing, for what were these things? Cornflakes? Tonic water? Peanut butter? Water biscuits? Mock turtle soup? Why not take a pan and one mock turtle . . . ? Bottles of whiskey and gin appeared on grocers' shelves, the toilet paper available was somewhat softer, and three new butchers sprang into existence. The San Feliciani were presiding, a bit late, over their own "Italian Miracle." Now they greeted strangers with wan, hopeful smiles and spoke only in infinitives.

Some of the more obnoxious foreigners were weeded out by circumstances beyond their control—time, two severe winters, anxiety over the Communist party's intentions, and a fixation about kidnapping, which, since no one had offered, sounded like another way to emphasize their eligibility. They put their houses up for sale, packed, and departed for . . . ? California? The Seychelles? Who knows? Simplicity took its toll with others of more acceptable manner and greater expectations. San Felice failed them. There were no dukes and duchesses, movie stars, or heads of state they could invite for formal dinners. So they too left to follow the seasons elsewhere and talk longingly of their villas in Tuscany.

These rites of settlement puzzled the San Feliciani. Foreigners, they decided once and for all, could not be understood. They were accustomed now to the ones who had stayed. They did not panic at the sight of new arrivals or itinerant tourists. They accepted the unfathomable, but when the day was over and they met for an *aperitivo*, they exchanged funny stories about the foreigners, who were strange, very strange indeed. Society has a certain just symmetry, for when two or three foreigners sat quietly in a garden, surrounded by cypresses and the golden light of a Tuscan sunset, they exchanged funny stories too—about the Italians, who were strange people, very strange indeed, perhaps the strangest of them all.

Charles Dickens

(1812–1870)

In 1844 Charles Dickens and his large family spent a year in a villa in Genoa. While Dickens rationalized the trips as educational for the children, he was also attracted to Italy because it was relatively cheap compared to England. Like Mark Twain, Dickens earned large sums and spent them as quickly. And also like Twain, he supplemented the income from his novels with travel writing and lecturing.

Dickens's first intention was to rent Lord Byron's former home, but he found it neglected and used as a wineshop. The Dickens family was forced to take up residence in "the most perfectly lonely, rusty stagnant old staggerer of a domain that you can possibly imagine." In his letters, Dickens keeps up a running complaint about the weather, the bugs, the architecture, and the Italians ("Two friends of the lower class conversing pleasantly in the street, always seem on the eve of stabbing each other forthwith. And a stranger is immensely astonished at their not doing it"). However, he allows "such green, green, green, as flutters down below the windows, that I never saw; nor yet such lilac and such purple as float between me and the distant hills; nor yet in anything, picture, book or vestal boredom, such awful solemn, impenetrable blue, as in that same sea . . . When the sun sets clearly, by Heaven, it is majestic." As was his habit, Dickens produced sketches for *Pictures from Italy* (1846) in serial form.

In this excerpt Dickens traveled away from his base in Genoa to Rome via the Tuscan coast road. Note Dickens mentioned the gravesite of his fellow Englishman and equally crabby traveler, Tobias Smollett.

from PICTURES FROM ITALY

TO ROME BY PISA AND SIENA

There is nothing in Italy, more beautiful to me, than the coast-road between Genoa and Spezia. On one side: sometimes far below,

sometimes nearly on a level with the road, and often skirted by broken rocks of many shapes: there is the free blue sea, with here and
there a picturesque felucca gliding slowly on; on the other side are
lofty hills, ravines besprinkled with white cottages, patches of dark
olive woods, country churches with their light open towers, and
country houses gaily painted. On every bank and knoll by the wayside, the wild cactus and aloe flourish in exuberant profusion; and the
gardens of the bright villages along the road, are seen, all blushing in
the summer-time with clusters of the Belladonna, and are fragrant in
the autumn and winter with golden oranges and lemons.

Some of the villages are inhabited, almost exclusively, by fishermen; and it is pleasant to see their great boats hauled up on the
beach, making little patches of shade, where they lie asleep, or where
the women and children sit romping and looking out to sea, while
they mend their nets upon the shore. There is one town, Camoglia,
with its little harbour on the sea, hundreds of feet below the road;
where families of mariners live, who, time out of mind, have owned
coasting-vessels in that place, and have traded to Spain and elsewhere. Seen from the road above, it is like a tiny model on the margin of the dimpled water, shining in the sun. Descended into, by the
winding mule-tracks, it is a perfect miniature of a primitive seafaring
town; the saltest, roughest, most piratical little place that ever was
seen. Great rusty-iron rings and mooring-chains, capstans, and fragments of old masts and spars, choke up the way; hardy rough-water
boats, and seamen's clothing, flutter in the little harbour or are drawn
out on the sunny stones to dry; on the parapet of the rude pier, a few
amphibious-looking fellows lie asleep, with their legs dangling over
the wall, as though earth or water were all one to them, and if they
slipped in, they would float away, dozing comfortably among the
fishes; the church is bright with trophies of the sea, and votive offer-
ings, in commemoration of escape from storm and shipwreck. The
dwellings not immediately abutting on the harbour are approached
by blind low archways, and by crooked steps, as if in darkness and in
difficulty of access they should be like holds of ships, or inconven-
ient cabins under water; and everywhere, there is a smell of fish, and
sea-weed, and old rope.

The coast-road whence Camoglia is descried so far below, is

famous, in the warm season, especially in some parts near Genoa, for fire-flies. Walking there on a dark night, I have seen it made one sparkling firmament by these beautiful insects: so that the distant stars were pale against the flash and glitter that spangled every olive wood and hill-side, and pervaded the whole air.

It was not in such a season, however, that we traversed this road on our way to Rome. The middle of January was only just past, and it was very gloomy and dark weather; very wet besides. In crossing the fine pass of Bracco, we encountered such a storm of mist and rain, that we travelled in a cloud the whole way. There might have been no Mediterranean in the world, for anything that we saw of it there, except when a sudden gust of wind, clearing the mist before it, for a moment, showed the agitated sea at a great depth below, lashing the distant rocks, and spouting up its foam furiously. The rain was incessant; every brook and torrent was greatly swollen; and such a deafening leaping, and roaring, and thundering of water, I never heard the like of in my life.

Hence, when we came to Spezia, we found that the Magra, an unbridged river on the high-road to Pisa, was too high to be safely crossed in the Ferry Boat, and were fain to wait until the afternoon of next day, when it had, in some degree, subsided. Spezia, however, is a good place to tarry at; by reason, firstly, of its beautiful bay; secondly, of its ghostly inn; thirdly, of the head-dress of the women, who wear, on one side of their head, a small doll's straw hat, stuck on to the hair; which is certainly the oddest and most roguish head-gear that ever was invented.

The Magra safely crossed in the Ferry Boat—the passage is not by any means agreeable, when the current is swollen and strong—we arrived at Carrara, within a few hours. In good time next morning, we got some ponies, and went out to see the marble quarries.

They are four or five great glens, running up into a range of lofty hills, until they can run no longer, and are stopped by being abruptly strangled by Nature. The quarries, or "caves," as they call them there, are so many openings, high up in the hills, on either side of these passes, where they blast and excavate for marble: which may turn out good or bad: may make a man's fortune very quickly, or ruin him by the great expense of working what is worth nothing. Some of these caves were opened by the ancient Romans, and remain as they left them to this hour. Many others are being worked at this moment; others are to be begun to-morrow, next week, next month; others are unbought, unthought of; and marble enough for more ages than have passed since the place was resorted to, lies hidden everywhere: patiently awaiting its time of discovery.

As you toil and clamber up one of these steep gorges (having left your pony soddening his girths in water, a mile or two lower down) you hear, every now and then, echoing among the hills, in a low tone, more silent than the previous silence, a melancholy warning bugle,— a signal to the miners to withdraw. Then, there is a thundering, and echoing from hill to hill, and perhaps a splashing up of great fragments of rock into the air; and on you toil again until some other bugle sounds, in a new direction, and you stop directly, lest you should come within the range of the new explosion.

There were numbers of men, working high up in these hills—on the sides—clearing away, and sending down the broken masses of stone and earth, to make way for the blocks of marble that had been discovered. As these came rolling down from unseen hands into the narrow valley, I could not help thinking of the deep glen (just the same sort of glen) where the Roc left Sindbad the Sailor; and where the merchants from the heights above, flung down great pieces of meat for the diamonds to stick to. There were no eagles here, to darken the sun in their swoop, and pounce upon them; but it was as wild and fierce as if there had been hundreds.

But the road, the road down which the marble comes, however immense the blocks! The genius of the country, and the spirit of its institutions, pave that road: repair it, watch it, keep it going! Conceive a channel of water running over a rocky bed, beset with great heaps of stone of all shapes and sizes, winding down the middle of this valley; and *that* being the road—because it was the road five hundred years ago! Imagine the clumsy carts of five hundred years ago, being used to this hour, and drawn, as they used to be, five hundred years ago, by oxen, whose ancestors were worn to death five hundred years ago, as their unhappy descendants are now, in twelve months, by the suffering and agony of this cruel work! Two pair, four pair, ten pair, twenty pair, to one block, according to its size; down it must come, this way. In their struggling from stone to stone, with their enormous loads behind them, they die frequently upon the spot; and not they alone; for their passionate drivers, sometimes tumbling down in their energy, are crushed to death beneath the wheels. But it was good five hundred years ago, and it must be good now: and a railroad down one of these steeps (the easiest thing in the world) would be flat blasphemy.

When we stood aside, to see one of these carts drawn by only a pair of oxen (for it had but one small block of marble on it), coming down, I hailed, in my heart, the man who sat upon the heavy yoke, to keep it on the neck of the poor beasts—and who faced backwards: not before him—as the very Devil of true despotism. He had a great rod in his hand, with an iron point; and when they could plough and force their way through the loose bed of the torrent no longer, and came to a stop, he poked it into their bodies, beat it on their heads, screwed it round and round in their nostrils, got them on a yard or two, in the madness of intense pain; repeated all these persuasions, with increased intensity of purpose, when they stopped again; got them on, once more; forced and goaded them to an abrupter point of the descent; and when their writhing and smarting, and the weight behind them, bore them plunging down the precipice in a cloud of scattered water, whirled his rod above his head, and gave a great whoop and hallo, as if he had achieved something, and had no idea that they might shake him off, and blindly mash his brains upon the road, in the noon-tide of his triumph.

Standing in one of the many studii of Carrara, that afternoon—for it is a great workshop, full of beautifully-finished copies in marble, of almost every figure, group, and bust, we know—it seemed, at first, so strange to me that those exquisite shapes, replete with grace, and thought, and delicate repose, should grow out of all this toil, and sweat, and torture! But I soon found a parallel to it, and an explanation of it, in every virtue that springs up in miserable ground, and every good thing that has its birth in sorrow and distress. And, looking out of the sculptor's great window, upon the marble mountains, all red and glowing in the decline of day, but stern and solemn to the last, I thought, my God! how many quarries of human hearts and souls, capable of far more beautiful results, are left shut up and mouldering away: while pleasure-travellers through life, avert their faces, as they pass, and shudder at the gloom and ruggedness that conceal them!

The then reigning Duke of Modena, to whom this territory in part belonged, claimed the proud distinction of being the only sovereign in Europe who had not recognised Louis-Philippe as King of the French! He was not a wag, but quite in earnest. He was also much opposed to railroads; and if certain lines in contemplation by other potentates, on either side of him, had been executed, would have probably enjoyed the satisfaction of having an omnibus plying to and fro across his not very vast dominions, to forward travellers from one terminus to another.

Carrara, shut in by great hills, is very picturesque and bold. Few tourists stay there; and the people are nearly all connected, in one way or other, with the working of marble. There are also villages among the caves, where the workmen live. It contains a beautiful little Theatre, newly built; and it is an interesting custom there, to form the chorus of labourers in the marble quarries, who are self-taught and sing by ear. I heard them in a comic opera, and in an act of "Norma"; and they acquitted themselves very well; unlike the common people of Italy generally, who (with some exceptions among the Neapolitans) sing vilely out of tune, and have very disagreeable singing voices.

From the summit of a lofty hill beyond Carrara, the first view of the fertile plain in which the town of Pisa lies—with Leghorn, a purple spot in the flat distance—is enchanting. Nor is it only distance that lends enchantment to the view; for the fruitful country, and rich woods of olive-trees through which the road subsequently passes, render it delightful.

The moon was shining when we approached Pisa, and for a long time we could see, behind the wall, the leaning Tower, all awry in the uncertain light; the shadowy original of the old pictures in school-books, setting forth "The Wonders of the World." Like most things connected in their first associations with school-books and school-times, it was too small. I felt it keenly. It was nothing like so high above the wall as I had hoped. It was another of the many deceptions practised by Mr. Harris, Bookseller, at the corner of St. Paul's

Churchyard, London. *His* Tower was a fiction, but this was a reality—and, by comparison, a short reality. Still, it looked very well, and very strange, and was quite as much out of the perpendicular as Harris had represented it to be. The quiet air of Pisa too; the big guardhouse at the gate, with only two little soldiers in it; the streets with scarcely any show of people in them; and the Arno, flowing quaintly through the centre of the town; were excellent. So, I bore no malice in my heart against Mr. Harris (remembering his good intentions), but forgave him before dinner, and went out, full of confidence, to see the Tower next morning.

I might have known better; but, somehow, I had expected to see it, casting its long shadow on a public street where people came and went all day. It was a surprise to me to find it in a grave retired place, apart from the general resort, and carpeted with smooth green turf. But, the group of buildings, clustered on and about this verdant carpet: comprising the Tower, the Baptistery, the Cathedral, and the Church of the Campo Santo: is perhaps the most remarkable and beautiful in the whole world; and from being clustered there, together, away from the ordinary transactions and details of the town, they have a singularly venerable and impressive character. It is the architectural essence of a rich old city, with all its common life and common habitations pressed out, and filtered away.

SIMOND compares the Tower to the usual pictorial representations in children's books of the Tower of Babel. It is a happy simile, and conveys a better idea of the building than chapters of laboured description. Nothing can exceed the grace and lightness of the structure; nothing can be more remarkable than its general appearance. In the course of the ascent to the top (which is by an easy staircase), the inclination is not very apparent; but, at the summit, it becomes so, and gives one the sensation of being in a ship that has heeled over, through the action of an ebb-tide. The effect *upon the low side*, so to speak—looking over from the gallery, and seeing the shaft recede to its base—is very startling; and I saw a nervous traveller hold on to the Tower involuntarily, after glancing down, as if he had some idea of propping it up. The view within, from the ground—looking up, as through a slanted tube—is also very curious. It certainly inclines as much as the most sanguine tourist could desire. The natural impulse of ninety-nine people out of a hundred, who were about to recline upon the grass below it, to rest, and contemplate the adjacent buildings, would probably be, not to take up their position under the leaning side; it is so very much aslant.

The manifold beauties of the Cathedral and Baptistery need no recapitulation from me; though in this case, as in a hundred others, I find it difficult to separate my own delight in recalling them, from your weariness in having them recalled. There is a picture of St. Agnes, by Andrea del Sarto, in the former, and there are a variety of rich columns in the latter, that tempt me strongly.

It is, I hope, no breach of my resolution not to be tempted into elaborate descriptions, to remember the Campo Santo; where grass-grown graves are dug in earth brought more than six hundred years ago, from the Holy Land; and where there are, surrounding them, such cloisters, with such playing lights and shadows falling through their delicate tracery on the stone pavement, as surely the dullest memory could never forget. On the walls of this solemn and lovely place, are ancient frescoes, very much obliterated and decayed, but very curious. As usually happens in almost any collection of paintings, of any sort, in Italy, where there are many heads, there is, in one of them, a striking accidental likeness of Napoleon. At one time, I used to please my fancy with the speculation whether these old painters, at their work, had a foreboding knowledge of the man who would one day arise to wreak such destruction upon art: whose soldiers would make targets of great pictures, and stable their horses among triumphs of architecture. But the same Corsican face is so plentiful in some parts of Italy at this day, that a more commonplace solution of the coincidence is unavoidable.

If Pisa be the seventh wonder of the world in right of its Tower, it may claim to be, at least, the second or third in right of its beggars. They waylay the unhappy visitor at every turn, escort him to every door he enters at, and lie in wait for him, with strong reinforcements, at every door by which they know he must come out. The grating of the portal on its hinges is the signal for a general shout, and the moment he appears, he is hemmed in, and fallen on, by heaps of rags and personal distortions. The beggars seem to embody all the trade and enterprise of Pisa. Nothing else is stirring, but warm air. Going through the streets, the fronts of the sleepy houses look like backs. They are all so still and quiet, and unlike houses with people in them, that the greater part of the city has the appearance of a city at daybreak, or during a general siesta of the population. Or it is yet more like those backgrounds of houses in common prints, or old engravings, where windows and doors are squarely indicated, and one figure (a beggar of course) is seen walking off by itself into illimitable perspective.

Not so Leghorn (made illustrious by SMOLLETT's grave), which is a thriving, business-like, matter-of-fact place, where idleness is shouldered out of the way by commerce. The regulations observed there, in reference to trade and merchants, are very liberal and free; and the town, of course, benefits by them. Leghorn had a bad name in connexion with stabbers, and with some justice it must be allowed; for, not many years ago, there was an assassination club there, the members of which bore no ill-will to anybody in particular, but stabbed people (quite strangers to them) in the streets at night, for the pleasure and excitement of the recreation. I think the president of this amiable society was a shoemaker. He was taken, however, and the club was broken up. It would, probably, have disappeared in the natural course of events, before the railroad between Leghorn and Pisa, which is a good one, and has already begun to astonish Italy with a precedent of punctuality, order, plain dealing, and improvement—the most dangerous and heretical astonisher of all. There must have been a slight sensation, as of earthquake, surely, in the Vatican, when the first Italian railroad was thrown open.

Returning to Pisa, and hiring a good-tempered Vetturíno, and his four horses, to take us on to Rome, we travelled through pleasant Tuscan villages and cheerful scenery all day. The roadside crosses in this part of Italy are numerous and curious. There is seldom a figure on the cross, though there is sometimes a face; but they are remarkable for being garnished with little models in wood, of every possible object that can be connected with the Saviour's death. The cock that crowed when Peter had denied his Master thrice, is usually perched on the tip-top, and an ornithological phenomenon he generally is. Under him, is the inscription. Then, hung on to the crossbeam, are the spear, the reed with the sponge of vinegar and water at the end, the coat without seam for which the soldiers cast lots, the dice-box with which they threw for it, the hammer that drove in the nails, the pincers that pulled them out, the ladder which was set against the cross, the crown of thorns, the instrument of flagellation, the lantern with which Mary went to the tomb (I suppose), and the sword with which Peter smote the servant of the high priest,—a perfect toy-shop of little objects, repeated at every four or five miles, all along the highway.

On the evening of the second day from Pisa, we reached the beautiful old city of Siena. There was what they called a Carnival, in progress; but, as its secret lay in a score or two of melancholy people walking up and down the principal street in common toy-shop masks, and being more melancholy, if possible, than the same sort of people in England, I say no more of it. We went off, betimes next morning, to see the Cathedral, which is wonderfully picturesque inside and out, especially the latter—also the market-place, or great Piazza, which is a large square, with a great broken-nosed fountain in it: some quaint Gothic houses: and a high square brick tower; *outside* the top of which—a curious feature in such views in Italy—hangs an enormous bell. It is like a bit of Venice, without the water. There are some curious old Palazzi in the town, which is very ancient; and without having (for me) the interest of Verona, or Genoa, it is very dreamy and fantastic, and most interesting.

We went on again, as soon as we had seen these things, and going over a rather bleak country (there had been nothing but vines until now: mere walking-sticks at that season of the year), stopped, as usual, between one and two hours in the middle of the day, to rest the horses; that being a part of every Vetturino contract. We then went on again, through a region gradually becoming bleaker and wilder, until it became as bare and desolate as any Scottish moors. Soon after dark, we halted for the night, at the osteria of La Scala: a perfectly lone house, where the family were sitting round a great fire in the kitchen, raised on a stone platform three or four feet high, and big enough for the roasting of an ox. On the upper, and only other floor of this hotel, there was a great wild rambling sála, with one very little window in a by-corner, and four black doors opening into four black bedrooms in various directions. To say nothing of another

large black door, opening into another large black sála, with the staircase coming abruptly through a kind of trap-door in the floor, and
the rafters of the roof looming above: a suspicious little press skulk-
ing in one obscure corner: and all the knives in the house lying about
in various directions. The fireplace was of the purest Italian architecture, so that it was perfectly impossible to see it for the smoke. The
waitress was like a dramatic brigand's wife, and wore the same style
of dress upon her head. The dogs barked like mad; the echoes
returned the compliments bestowed upon them; there was not another
house within twelve miles; and things had a dreary, and rather a cut-
throat, appearance.

They were not improved by rumours of robbers having come out,
strong and boldly, within a few nights; and of their having stopped
the mail very near that place. They were known to have waylaid some
travellers not long before, on Mount Vesuvius itself, and were the
talk at all the roadside inns. As they were no business of ours, however (for we had very little with us to lose), we made ourselves merry
on the subject, and were very soon as comfortable as need be. We
had the usual dinner in this solitary house; and a very good dinner it
is, when you are used to it. There is something with a vegetable or
some rice in it, which is a sort of shorthand or arbitrary character for
soup, and which tastes very well, when you have flavoured it with
plenty of grated cheese, lots of salt, and abundance of pepper. There
is the half fowl of which this soup has been made. There is a stewed
pigeon, with the gizzards and livers of himself and other birds stuck
all round him. There is a bit of roast beef, the size of a small French
roll. There are a scrap of Parmesan cheese, and five little withered
apples, all huddled together on a small plate, and crowding one upon
the other, as if each were trying to save itself from the chance of
being eaten. Then there is coffee; and then there is bed. You don't
mind brick floors; you don't mind yawning doors, nor banging windows; you don't mind your own horses being stabled under the bed:
and so close, that every time a horse coughs or sneezes, he wakes
you. If you are good-humoured to the people about you, and speak
pleasantly, and look cheerful, take my word for it you may be well
entertained in the very worst Italian inn, and always in the most
obliging manner, and may go from one end of the country to the

other (despite all stories to the contrary) without any great trial of your patience anywhere. Especially, when you get such wine in flasks, as the Orvieto, and the Monte Pulciano.

It was a bad morning when we left this place; and we went, for twelve miles, over a country as barren, as stony, and as wild, as Cornwall in England, until we came to Radicofani, where there is a ghostly, goblin inn: once a hunting-seat, belonging to the Dukes of Tuscany. It is full of such rambling corridors, and gaunt rooms, that all the murdering and phantom tales that ever were written might have originated in that one house. There are some horrible old Palazzi in Genoa: one in particular, not unlike it, outside: but there is a winding, creaking, wormy, rustling, door-opening, foot-on-staircase-falling character about this Radicofani Hotel, such as I never saw, anywhere else. The town, such as it is, hangs on a hill-side above the house, and in front of it. The inhabitants are all beggars; and as soon as they see a carriage coming, they swoop down upon it, like so many birds of prey.

When we got on the mountain pass, which lies beyond this place, the wind (as they had forewarned us at the inn) was so terrific, that we were obliged to take my other half out of the carriage, lest she should be blown over, carriage and all, and to hang to it, on the windy side (as well as we could for laughing), to prevent its going, Heaven knows where. For mere force of wind, this land-storm might have competed with an Atlantic gale, and had a reasonable chance of coming off victorious. The blast came sweeping down great gullies in a range of mountains on the right: so that we looked with positive awe at a great morass on the left, and saw that there was not a bush or twig to hold by. It seemed as if, once blown from our feet, we must be swept out to sea, or away into space. There was snow, and hail, and rain, and lightning, and thunder; and there were rolling mists, travelling with incredible velocity. It was dark, awful, and solitary to the last degree; there were mountains above mountains, veiled in angry clouds; and there was such a wrathful, rapid, violent, tumultuous hurry, everywhere, as rendered the scene unspeakably exciting and grand.

It was a relief to get out of it, notwithstanding; and to cross even the dismal dirty Papal Frontier. After passing through two little towns; in one of which Acquapendente, there was also a "Carnival" in progress: consisting of one man dressed and masked as a woman, and one woman dressed and masked as a man, walking ankle-deep, through the muddy streets, in a very melancholy manner: we came, at dusk, within sight of the Lake of Bolsena, on whose bank there is a little town of the same name, much celebrated for malaria. With the exception of this poor place, there is not a cottage on the banks of the lake, or near it (for nobody dare sleep there); not a boat upon its waters; not a stick or stake to break the dismal monotony of seven-and-twenty watery miles. We were late in getting in, the roads being very bad from heavy rains; and, after dark, the dulness of the scene was quite intolerable.

We entered on a very different, and a finer scene of desolation, next night, at sunset. We had passed through Montefiaschone (famous for its wine) and Viterbo (for its fountains): and after climbing up a long hill of eight or ten miles' extent, came suddenly upon the margin of a solitary lake: in one part very beauitful, with a luxuriant wood; in another, very barren, and shut in by bleak volcanic hills. Where this lake flows, there stood, of old, a city. It was swallowed up one day; and in its stead, this water rose. There are ancient traditions (common to many parts of the world) of the ruined city having been seen below, when the water was clear; but however that may be, from this spot of earth it vanished. The ground came bubbling up above it; and the water too; and here they stand, like ghosts on whom the other world closed suddenly, and who have no means of getting back again. They seem to be waiting the course of ages, for the next earthquake in that place; when they will plunge below the ground, at its first yawning, and be seen no more. The unhappy city below, is not more lost and dreary, than these fire-charred hills and the stagnant water, above. The red sun looked strangely on them, as with the knowledge that they were made for caverns and darkness; and the melancholy water oozed and sucked the mud, and crept quietly among the marshy grass and reeds, as if the overthrow of all the ancient towers and house-tops, and the death of all the ancient people born and bred there, were yet heavy on its conscience.

A short ride from this lake, brought us to Ronciglione; a little town like a large pig-sty, where we passed the night. Next morning at seven o'clock, we started for Rome.

As soon as we were out of the pig-sty, we entered on the Campagne Romana; an undulating flat (as you know), where few people can live; and where, for miles and miles, there is nothing to relieve the terrible monotony and gloom. Of all kinds of country that could, by possibility, lie outside the gates of Rome, this is the aptest and fittest burial-ground for the Dead City. So sad, so quiet, so sullen; so secret in its covering up of great masses of ruin, and hiding them; so like the waste places into which the men possessed with devils used to go and howl, and rend themselves, in the old days of Jerusalem. We had to traverse thirty miles of this Campagna; and for two-and-twenty we went on and on, seeing nothing but now and then a lonely house, or a villainous-looking shepherd: with matted hair all over his face, and himself wrapped to the chin in a frowzy brown mantle, tending his sheep. At the end of that distance, we stopped to refresh the horses, and to get some lunch, in a common malaria-shaken, despondent little public-house, whose every inch of wall and beam, inside, was (according to custom) painted and decorated in a way so miserable that every room looked like the wrong side of another room, and, with its wretched imitation of drapery, and lop-sided little daubs of lyres, seemed to have been plundered from behind the scenes of some travelling circus.

When we were fairly going off again, we began, in a perfect fever, to strain our eyes for Rome; and when, after another mile or two, the Eternal City appeared, at length, in the distance; it looked like—I am half afraid to write the word—like LONDON!!! There it lay, under a thick cloud, with innumerable towers, and steeples, and roofs of houses, rising up into the sky, and high above them all, one Dome. I swear, that keenly as I felt the seeming absurdity of the comparison, it was so like London, at that distance, that if you could have shown it me, in a glass, I should have taken it for nothing else.

Sarah Dunant

(1950–   )

At the end of a tumultous long-term relationship, writer Sarah Dunant decided on a whim to buy an apartment near the Piazza Santa Croce in Florence. All through the first night in her new home she lay awake, listening to sounds reverberate in the narrow street below. Dunant imagined her new neighborhood during the Renaissance in her bestseller *The Birth of Venus* (2004). "The city is wealthy and colorful and confident," she said in an interview with *The New York Times*. "The early seeds of capitalism are planted and the merchant class that makes the money spends it." It is the Florence of the opposing forces of the Medicis and of the fundamentalist monk Savonarola and his Bonfire of the Vanities.

Dunant's heroine Alessandra is a passionate young woman, the fourteen-year-old daughter of a wealthy family. Although she aspires to paint and participate in the city's rich intellectual life, her fate is circumscribed by her sex. Into the history of fifteenth-century Florence, Dunant weaves issues of gender and homosexuality, race and class, religion and religiosity. This excerpt from *The Birth of Venus* details Alessandra's first meeting with a young painter, hired by her father to execute altar frescoes in the family chapel. This encounter changes both of their lives.

Dunant now divides her time between London and Florence. "I highly recommend falling in love with a city," she said. "It's more faithful and stimulating than a man. And if you pick the right one, you never have to cook again."

from THE BIRTH OF VENUS

Looking back now, I see it more as an act of pride than kindness that my father brought the young painter back with him from the North that spring. The chapel in our palazzo had recently been completed, and for some months he had been searching for the right pair of hands to execute the altar frescoes. It wasn't as if Florence didn't have artists enough of her own. The city was filled with the smell of paint and the scratch of ink on the contracts. There were times when you couldn't walk the streets for fear of falling into some pit or mire left by constant building. Anyone and everyone who had the money was eager to celebrate God and the Republic by creating opportunities for art. What I hear described even now as a golden age was then simply the fashion of the day. But I was young then, and, like so many others, dazzled by the feast.

The churches were the best. God was in the very plaster smeared across the walls in readiness for the frescoes: stories of the Gospels made flesh for anyone with eyes to see. And those who looked saw something else as well. Our Lord may have lived and died in Galilee, but his life was re-created in the city of Florence. The Angel Gabriel brought God's message to Mary under the arches of the Brunelleschian loggia, the Three Kings led processions through the Tuscan countryside, and Christ's miracles unfolded within our city walls, the sinners and the sick in Florentine dress and the crowds of witnesses dotted with public faces: a host of thick-chinned, big-nosed dignitaries staring down from the frescoes onto their real-life counterparts in the front pews.

I was almost ten years old when Domenico Ghirlandaio completed his frescoes for the Tornabuoni family in the central chapel of Santa Maria Novella. I remember it well, because my mother told me to. "You should remember this moment, Alessandra," she said. "These paintings will bring great glory to our city." And all those who saw them thought that they would.

My father's fortune was rising out of the stream of the dyeing vats in the back streets of Santa Croce then. The smell of cochineal still brings back memories of him coming home from the warehouse, the dust of crushed insects from foreign places embedded deep in his clothes. By the time the painter came to live with us in 1492—I remember the date because Lorenzo de' Medici died that spring— the Florentine appetite for flamboyant cloth had made us rich. Our newly completed palazzo was in the east of the city, between the great Cathedral of Santa Maria del Fiore and the church of Sant' Ambrogio. It rose four stories high around two inner courtyards, with its own small walled garden and space for my father's business on the ground floor. Our coat of arms adorned the outside walls, and while my mother's good taste curbed much of the exuberance that attends new money, we all knew it was only a matter of time before we too would be sitting for our own Gospel portraits, albeit private ones.

The night the painter arrived is sharp as an etching in my memory. It is winter, and the stone balustrades have a coating of frost as my sister and I collide on the stairs in our night shifts, hanging over the edge to watch the horses arrive in the main courtyard. It's late and the house has been asleep, but my father's homecoming is reason for celebration, not simply for his safe return but because, amid the panniers of samples, there is always special cloth for the family. Plautilla is already beside herself with anticipation, but then she is betrothed and thinking only of her dowry. My brothers, on the other hand, are noticeable by their absence. For all our family's good name and fine cloth, Tomaso and Luca live more like feral cats than citizens, sleeping by day and hunting by night. Our house slave Erila, the font of all gossip, says they are the reason that good women should never be seen in the streets after dark. Nevertheless, when my father finds they are gone there will be trouble.

But not yet. For now we are all caught in the wonder of the moment. Firebrands light the air as the grooms calm the horses, their snorting breath steaming into the freezing air. Father is already dismounted, his face streaked with grime, a smile as round as a cupola as he waves upward to us and then turns to my mother as she comes down the stairs to greet him, her red velvet robe tied fast across her chest and her hair free and flowing down her back like a golden river. There is noise and light and the sweet sense of safety everywhere, but not shared by everyone. Astride the last horse sits a lanky young man, his cape wrapped like a bolt of cloth around him, the cold and travel fatigue tipping him dangerously forward in the saddle.

I remember as the groom approached him to take the reins he awoke with a start, his hands clutching them back as if fearful of attack, and my father had to go to him to calm him. I was too full of my own self then to realize how strange it must have been for him. I had not heard yet how different the North was, how the damp and the watery sun changed everything, from the light in the air to the light in one's soul. Of course I did not know he was a painter then. For me he was just another servant. But my father treated him with care right from the beginning: speaking to him in quiet tones, seeing him off his horse, and picking out a separate room off the dark courtyard as his living quarters.

Later, as my father unpacks the Flemish tapestry for my mother and snaps open the bolts of milk-white embroidered lawn for us ("The women of Rennes go blind early in the service of my daughters' beauty"), he tells us how he found him, an orphan brought up in a monastery on the edge of the northern sea where the water threatens the land. How his talent with a pen overwhelmed any sense of religious vocation, so the monks had apprenticed him to a master, and when he returned, in gratitude, he painted not simply his own cell but the cells of all the other monks. These paintings so impressed my father that he decided then and there to offer him the job of glorifying our chapel. Though I should add that while he knew his cloth my father was no great connoisseur of art, and I suspect his decision was as much dictated by money, for he always had a good eye for a bargain. As for the painter? Well, as my father put it, there were no more cells for him to paint, and the fame of Florence as the new Rome or Athens of our age would no doubt have spurred him on to see it for himself.

And so it was that the painter came to live at our house.

Next morning we went to Santissima Annunziata to give thanks for my father's safe homecoming. The church is next to the Ospedale degli Innocenti, the foundling hospital where young women place their bastard babies on the wheel for the nuns to care for. As we pass I imagine the cries of the infants as the wheel in the wall turns inward forever, but my father says we are a city of great charity and there are places in the wild North where you find babies amid the rubbish or floating like flotsam down the river.

We sit together in the central pews. Above our heads hang great model ships donated by those who have survived shipwrecks. My father was in one once, though he was not rich enough at the time to command a memorial in church, and on this last voyage he suffered only common seasickness. He and my mother sit ramrod straight and you can feel their minds on God's munificence. We children are less holy. Plautilla is still flighty with the thought of her gifts, while Tomaso and Luca look like they would prefer to be in bed, though my father's disapproval keeps them alert.

When we return, the house smells of feast-day food—the sweetness of roast meat and spiced gravies curling down the stairs from the upper kitchen to the courtyard below. We eat as afternoon fades into evening. First we thank God; then we stuff ourselves: boiled capon, roast pheasant, trout, and fresh pastas followed by saffron pudding and egg custards with burned sugar coating. Everyone is on their best behavior. Even Luca holds his fork properly, though you can see his fingers itch to pick up the bread and trawl it through the sauce.

Already I am beside myself with excitement at the thought of our new houseguest. Flemish painters are much admired in Florence for their precision and their sweet spirituality. "So he will paint us all, Father? We will have to sit for him, yes?"

"Indeed. That is partly why he is come. I am trusting he will make us a glorious memento of your sister's wedding."

"In which case he'll paint me first!" Plautilla is so pleased that she spits milk pudding on the tablecloth. "Then Tomaso as eldest, then Luca, and then Alessandra. Goodness, Alessandra, you will be grown even taller by then."

Luca looks up from his plate and grins with his mouth full as if this is the wittiest joke he has ever heard. But I am fresh from church and filled with God's charity to all my family. "Still. He had better not take too long. I heard that one of the daughters-in-law of the Tornabuoni family was dead from childbirth by the time Ghirlandaio unveiled her in the fresco."

"No fear of that with you. You'd have to get a husband first." Next to me Tomaso's insult is so mumbled only I can hear it.

"What is that you say, Tomaso?" My mother's voice is quiet but sharp.

He puts on his cherubic expression. "I said, 'I have a dreadful thirst.' Pass the wine flagon, dear sister."

"Of course, brother." I pick it up, but as it moves toward him it slips out of my hands and the falling liquid splatters his new tunic.

"Ah, Mama!" he explodes. "She did that on purpose!"

"I did not!"

"She—"

"Children, children. Our father is tired and you are both too loud."

The word *children* does its work on Tomaso and he falls sullenly silent. In the space that follows, the sound of Luca's open-mouth chewing becomes enormous. My mother stirs impatiently in her seat. Our manners tax her profoundly. Just as in the city's menagerie the lion tamer uses a whip to control behavior, my mother has perfected the Look. She uses it now on Luca, though he is so engrossed in the pleasure of his food that today it takes a kick under the table from me to gain his attention. We are her life's work, her children, and there is still so much more to be done with us.

"Still," I say, when it feels as if we may talk again, "I cannot wait to meet him. Oh, he must be most grateful to you, Father, for bringing him here. As we all are. It will be our honor and duty as a Christian family to care for him and make him feel at home in our great city."

My father frowns and exchanges a quick glance with my mother. He has been away a long time and has no doubt forgotten how much his younger daughter must say whatever comes into her mind. "I think he is quite capable of caring for himself, Alessandra," he says firmly.

I read the warning, but there is too much at stake to stop me now. I take a breath. "I have heard it said that Lorenzo the Magnificent thinks so much of the artist Botticelli that he has him eat at his table."

There is a small glittering silence. This time the Look stills me. I drop my eyes and concentrate on my plate again. Next to me I feel Tomaso's smirk of triumph.

Yet it is true enough. Sandro Botticelli does sit at the table of Lorenzo de' Medici. And the sculptor Donatello used to walk the city in a scarlet robe given in honor of his contribution to the Republic by Cosimo, Lorenzo's grandfather. My mother has often told me how as a young girl she would see him, saluted by all, people making way for him—though that might have been as much to do with his bad temper as his talent. But the sad fact is that though Florence is rife with painters I have never met one. While our family is not as strict as some, the chances of an unmarried daughter finding herself in the company of men of any description, let alone artisans, are severely limited. Of course that has not stopped me from meeting them in my mind. Everyone knows there are places in the city where workshops of art exist. The great Lorenzo himself has founded such a one and filled its rooms and gardens with sculpture and paintings from his own classical collection. I imagine a building full of light, the smell of colors like a simmering stew, the space as endless as the artists' imaginations.

My own drawings up till now have been silverpoint, laboriously scratched into boxwood, or black chalk on paper when I can find it. Most I have destroyed as unworthy and the best are hidden well away (it was made clear to me early that my sister's cross-stitching would gain more praise than any of my sketches). So I have no idea whether I can paint or not. I am like Icarus without wings. But the desire to fly was very strong in me. I think I was always looking for a Daedalus.

I was young then, as you know: fourteen that same spring. The most preliminary study of mathematics would reveal that I had been conceived in the heat of the summer, an inauspicious time for the beginning of a child. During her pregnancy, when the city was in turmoil during the Pazzi conspiracy, there was a rumor that my mother had seen bloodlust and violence in the streets. I once overheard a servant suggesting that my willfulness might be the result of that transgression. Or it could have been the wet nurse they sent me to. Tomaso, who is always rigorous with the truth when it contains spite, told me she had later been arraigned for prostitution, so who knows what humors and lusts I suckled at her breasts? Though Erila says it is only his jealousy speaking, his way of paying me back for a thousand slights inflicted in the classroom.

Whatever the reasons, I was a singular child, more suited to study and argument than duty. My sister, who was sixteen months older and had begun to bleed the year before, was promised to a man of good family, and there had even been talk of a similarly illustrious liaison for me (as our fortune rose so did my father's marriage expectations), despite my emerging intractability.

In the weeks following the painter's arrival my mother was eagle-eyed on my behalf, keeping me closeted in study or helping with

Plautilla's wedding wardrobe. But then she was called away to Fiesole to her sister, who was so torn apart by the birth of an oversize baby that she was in need of female counsel. She went, leaving strict instructions that I should go about my studies and do exactly what my tutors and my elder sister told me. I of course agreed that I would.

I already knew where to find him. Like a bad republic, our house praises virtue publicly but rewards vice privately and gossip could always be had at a price, though in this case my Erila gave it for free.

"The talk is that there isn't any. Nobody knows anything. He keeps his own company, eats in his room, and speaks to no one. Though Maria says she's seen him pacing the courtyard in the middle of the night."

It is afternoon. Erila has unpinned my hair and drawn the curtains in readiness for my rest and is about to leave when she turns and looks at me directly. "We both know it is forbidden for you to visit him, yes?"

I nod, my eyes on the carved wood of the bedstead: a rose with as many petals as my small lies. There is a pause in which I would like to think she looks upon my disobedience sympathetically. "I shall be back to wake you in two hours. Rest well."

I wait till the sunshine has stilled the house, then slide down the stairs and into the back courtyard. The heat is already clinging to the stones and his door is open, presumably to let in what little breeze there might be. I move silently across the baked courtyard and slip inside.

The interior is gloomy, the shafts of daylight spinning dust particles in the air. It is a dreary little room with just a table and chair and a series of pails in one corner and a connecting door to a smaller inner chamber ajar. I push it open farther. The darkness is profound and my ears work before my eyes. His breathing is long and even. He is lying on a pallet by the wall, his hand flung out over strewn papers. The only other men I have seen sleeping are my brothers, and their snores are harsh. The very gentleness of this breath disturbs me. My stomach grows tight with the sound, making me feel like the intruder I am, and I pull the door closed behind me.

In contrast the outer room is brighter now. Above the desk are a series of tattered papers: drawings of the chapel taken from the builders' plans, torn and grimy with masonry marks. To the side hangs a wooden crucifix, crudely carved but striking, with Christ's body hanging so heavily off the cross that you can feel the weight of his flesh hanging from his nails. Beneath it are some sketches, but as I pick them up the opposite wall catches my eye. There is something drawn there, directly onto the flaking plaster: two figures, half realized, to the left a willowy Angel, feathered wings light as smoke billowing out behind him, and opposite a Madonna, her body unnaturally tall and slender, floating ghostly free, her feet lifted high off the ground. I move closer to get a better look. The floor is thick with the ends of candles stuck in puddles of melted wax. Does he sleep through the day and work at night? It might explain Mary's attenuated figure, her body lengthening in the flicker of the candlelight. But he has had enough light to enliven her face. Her looks are northern, her hair pulled fiercely back to show a wide forehead, so that her head reminds me of a perfectly shaped pale egg. She is staring wide-eyed at the Angel, and I can feel a fluttering excitement in her, like a child who has been given some great gift and cannot quite comprehend its good fortune. While perhaps she ought not to be so forward with God's messenger, there is such joy in her attention that it is almost contagious. It makes me think of a sketch I am working up on my own Annunciation and brings a flush of shame to my face at its clumsiness.

The noise is more like a growl than any words. He must have risen from his bed silently, because as I whirl around he is standing in the doorway. What do I remember of this moment? His body is long and lanky, his undershirt crumpled and torn. His face is broad under a tangle of long dark hair, and he is taller than I remember from that first night and somehow wilder. He is still half asleep, and his body has the tang of dried sweat about it. I am used to living in a house of rose- and orange-flower scented air; he smells of the street. I really think until that moment I had believed that artists somehow came directly from God and therefore had more of the spirit and less of man about them.

The shock of his physicality sluices any remaining courage out of me. He stands blinking in the light, then suddenly lurches himself toward me, wrenching the papers out of my hand.

"How dare you?" I yelp, as he shoves me to the side. "I am the daughter of your patron, Paolo Cecchi!"

He doesn't seem to hear. He rushes to the table, grabbing the remaining sketches, all the time muttering in a low voice, "*Noli tangere . . . noli tangere.*" Of course. There is one fact my father forgot to tell us. Our painter has grown up amid Latin-speaking monks, and while his eyes might work here his ears do not.

"I didn't touch anything," I bark back in terror. "I was simply looking. And if you are to be accepted here, you will have to learn to talk in our language. Latin is the tongue of priests and scholars, not painters."

My retort, or maybe it is the force of my fluent Latin, silences him. He stands frozen, his body shaking. It is hard to know which one of us was more scared at that moment. I would have fled had it not been for the fact that across the courtyard I spot my mother's bed servant coming out from the storeroom. While I have allies in the servants' quarters I also have enemies, and Angelica's loyalties have long since proved to lie elsewhere. If I am discovered now there would be no telling what outrage it would cause in the house.

"Be assured I never harmed your drawings," I say hurriedly, anxious to avoid another outburst. "I am interested in the chapel. I simply came to see how your designs were progressing."

He mutters something again. I wait for him to repeat it. It takes a long time. Finally he raises his eyes to look at me, and as I stare at him I become aware for the first time of how young he is—older than I am, yes, but surely not by many years—and how white and sallow his skin. Of course I know that foreign lands breed foreign colors. My own Erila is burned black by the desert sands of North Africa from where she came, and in those days you could find any number of shades in the markets of the city, so much was Florence a honeypot for trade and commerce. But this whiteness is different, having about it the feel of damp stone and sunless skies. A single day under the Florentine sun would surely shrivel and burn his delicate surface.

When he finally speaks he has stopped shaking, but the effort has cost him. "I paint in God's service," he says, with the air of a novitiate delivering a litany he has been taught but not fully understood, "and it is forbidden for me to talk with women."

"Really," I say, stung by the snub. "That might explain why you have so little idea of how to paint them." I cast a glance toward the elongated Madonna on the wall.

Even in the gloom I can feel how the words hurt him. For a moment I think he might attack me again, or break his own rules and answer me back, but instead he turns on his heel and, clutching the papers to his chest, stumbles back into the inner room, the door slamming closed behind him.

"Your rudeness is as bad as your ignorance, sir," I call after him, to cover my confusion. "I don't know what you have learned in the North, but here in Florence our artists are taught to celebrate the human body as an echo of the perfection of God. You would do well to study the city's art before you risk scribbling on its walls."

And in a flurry of self-righteousness I stride from the room into the sunlight, not knowing if my voice has penetrated through the door.

Lawrence Ferlinghetti

(1 9 1 9 –   )

One of the last of the Beat poets, Lawrence Ferlinghetti is a San Francisco institution. In the 1950s he founded both the City Lights bookstore in North Beach
and City Lights Publishers. Defying obscenity laws, he published Allen Ginsberg's
Howl in his Pocket Poets series. He was prosecuted, but declared innocent in a
victory for free speech.

Ferlinghetti was born in Yonkers, New York. Shortly after his birth his mother
was institutionalized and he was shipped off to live with relatives in France, not to
return to the United States until he was five. A graduate of the University of North
Carolina, Ferlinghetti served in World War II and then went to the Sorbonne for his
doctorate, financed by the GI Bill. After moving to San Francisco, he fell in with Ken-
neth Rexroth, Allen Ginsberg, Gary Snyder, and other members of the Beat movement. City Lights bookstore provided a forum for their readings and social activism.

Now well into his eighties, Ferlinghetti may be America's most popular poet,
with over one million copies of his best-known work, *A Coney Island of the
Mind*, in print. These short poems, "Canti Toscani"—lyrical snapshots of Tuscany—are from *European Poems and Transitions*, published in 1980.

CANTI TOSCANI

I
Tuscan woman with olive eyes
     (the whites milk white)
  catches the last sun in them
    and flashes back the light
Pale lamps, in the night

I I
Red sun setting
   over Toscana

through the cypresses
                    over the red tile roofs
                         and green lush vineyards
near Volterra and Piccioli
                    Paesani on old bikes
                         on straight dirt roads
and the trees turning brown
                              like a drought
          as the sun goes out
and the streetlights
                    coming on
                              in little Ponsaco
     its iron churchbell clanging—
Night falls!

I I I
Toulouse-Lautrec of Lucca
                    by the Romanesque cathedral
     selling his Sunday paintings
                              of the Duomo
          stands only four feet high
                         his hands full of sighs

I V
Sun of Lucca turning brown
                    like a ripe olive
     in olive-oil sky
                    drops its stone pit
          over the rim
                    of the town
          as olive light
                    floods the landscape

V
Tower of Pisa
                    leans away from the sun
     which turns dark red

          as its day's work
                     is done
and then falls down
              on the red tile roofs
    and pulls them down
          and pulls down the town
                  into darkness
Only the tower stands up
                as night fills
                     my cup

V I
Driving into Florence from the West
From the freeway through
the flashing cars and new
high room apartments
and glass houses
to the old city
by the old Arno
with its old bridges
We
      very gradually
              re-
                con-
                    struct
                        our
                           old old
                    illusions

Penelope Fitzgerald

(1916–2000)

Penelope Fitzgerald's delicate novels are inhabited by people she defined as "exterminatees . . . people likely to be stamped out." She sympathized with such characters, probably because she was one herself. Her literary life was improbable at best: her first novel was published when she was sixty, she struggled with an alcoholic husband, and she raised three children in often dire economic circumstances. The family's low point was living in a dilapidated houseboat on the Thames that sank—twice. Then they moved to public housing.

However, Fitzgerald's origins were in the prominent British literary and religious family, the Knoxes; her father was editor of *Punch*, her uncle, a Greek scholar, and another uncle, a monsignor. At twenty-two she married Desmond Fitzgerald, who "didn't have much luck in his life," and she held a series of jobs to supplement the family income. Fitzgerald wrote her first book, a mystery entitled *The Golden Child*, to entertain her dying husband.

Like her other novels, *Innocence* (1968), from which this excerpt is taken, is scarcely more than two hundred pages. Yet, it tells the complex tale of two widely separated generations of the Ridolfis, an Italian noble family. The sixteenth-century Ridolfis were midgets and the twentieth-century Ridolfis, of normal height, struggle with romance and the changing economic forces of postwar Italy.

In 1998 Fitzgerald said, "I have remained true to my deepest convictions, I mean to the courage of those who are born to be defeated, the weaknesses of the strong and the tragedy of misunderstandings and missed opportunities which I have done my best to treat as comedy, for otherwise how can we manage to bear it?"

from INNOCENCE

The Count, holding himself well but stiffly, walked down to the palazzo's courtyard. The ground floor was let out to shops (one of them a hairdresser's) and small offices. The cortile was thronged with parked cars and scooters. Bicycles were always carried indoors and upstairs for safety's sake by their owners. Two horses belonging to the mounted police stood patiently, for long stretches, tethered to iron stanchions let into a marble pillar. In the fourteenth century the whole area had been a graveyard for unbaptised infants, whose salvation was doubtful.

With relief the Count got into his solid old Fiat 1500 sedan. The hollowed leather of the driver's seat fitted his sharp joints. Reluctance to start, small items out of alignment, a rattle which might or might not be something to do with the ashtrays, were no trouble, rather a consolation to a driver who recognized them all.

He drove out of the city on the via Chiantigiana. In tune to the persistent rattling, he reflected that his wife, who was not dead, but preferred to live in Chicago, and Maddalena's husband, who was not dead either, though he was sometimes thought to be, but preferred to live in East Suffolk, must both receive invitations to the wedding, but would not accept them. On the other hand the Monsignore must be asked to officiate, and would officiate, though this would have to be by courtesy of the parish priest at Valsassina. The country, as the Count drove on, the gentle inclines, the olives, vines, and vegetables, suggested that the earth here was still friendly and even protective to human beings, but it had been rewarded in every vineyard with forty-five thousand white concrete posts to the hectare. This did not disturb Giancarlo, who forgave the land its changing appearance as he forgave himself his own.

Spring was very late. At Valsassina there was a bitter smell from the straw fires which had been lit at night to keep the earth warm. They were still tying up the vine shoots and taking off the bare wood. Much more noticeably, two of Cesare's little motocultivators were rolling in procession back and forth across the ridge. The Count marvelled, not for the first time, at how much of the agricultural day consists of moving things from one place to another. He passed the little stone building, once a chapel, which the farmworkers used for their midday break. The ragged roof steamed like a kettle, they were boiling something up in there. Higher up, a stone cross marked the place where Cesare's father had been shot during the

German retreat, or possibly during the Allied advance, there was no chance now of ever knowing which, or what he had been trying to protest against.

At the top of the rising ground Giancarlo parked in the front courtyard, where it was always supposed to be warmer (but this was a fiction) and as he got out of the car the autumn wind was waiting for him. A lizard which had emerged, as wrinkled as an old man's hand, into what looked like warm sunshine had retreated instantly. The whole of the right-hand wall was covered with a climbing viburnum, spreading upwards and outwards as it always had done within living memory, as far as it could reach. This plant had had the sense to begin shedding its leaves early.

Valsassina itself was somewhere between a farmhouse and a casa signorile and was sometimes admired for its original plan, but in fact it had been put up almost at random on the site of an old watchtower. Once inside, you always had the same sensation of no one being there, a cavernous emptiness, with a faint sound of something dripping, and darkness, not pitch darkness but a reddish dark between the brick floors and the terracotta tiles of the ceilings. Immediately to the right as you went in was the fermentation room for the house wine. The powerful odour of saturated wood travelled from one end of the house to the other. From here, also, came the sound of dripping. Straight ahead was the dining-room, with a massive fireplace of pietra serena.

"Cesare!" shouted Giancarlo. Then he remembered that his nephew kept Wednesdays for office work.

The dining-room was as dark as the hall, the shutters were up against the sudden cold. But the outlines of knives and forks could be made out, and two substantial white napkins on the old immovable dining-table. The napkins meant that he hadn't telephoned in vain, he was expected. A door at the farther end opened, letting in the clear autumn light, and an old man appeared, making some kind of complaint, interrupted by an old woman who asked the Count decisively what kind of pasta he wanted her to cook. "I can't hear both of you at once," said Giancarlo. The man, Bernardino Mattioli, was, he knew, subject to mild delusions of grandeur. Cesare might well be glad to be rid of him, but as Bernardino had nowhere else to go that would be impossible. How can my nephew live here like this, he thought, a young man on his own? They say that every man in his heart wants to go back to die in the place where he was born. While he was considering this—he had been born in the bedroom directly above the room where he was sitting now—Bernardino approached him.

"I have something to say which Your Excellency will find strangely interesting." The old woman interposed again. It turned out that there were only two possibilities for midday lunch, green tagliatelle or plain.

"Any decision must be in the nature of a gamble," said the Count, "we will have green." She retreated towards the kitchen, and her voice could be heard calling out to what had seemed to be a deserted house. "They want the green!" Giancarlo thought, I have to be back in Florence by half-past four for a committee meeting of the Touring Club.

At the back the two wings of the house lost their pretensions, and turned into not much more than a series of sheds. Beyond the back courtyard were deep and ancient ditches, planted with fig trees and vegetables, all cut back this year by the wind. The last shed to the left looked, from the pulley above the loft, as though it had once been a small granary. This was the office. There Cesare could be seen, sitting absolutely motionless and solid in front of two piles of papers. When a shadow fell across him and he looked up and saw who was there he rose to his feet, and fetched the only other chair, stirring up a smell of poultry and old dust. The Count lowered himself onto it, exaggerating his fragility, as a kind of insurance against ill-chance. Cesare sat down again, turning away from the desk towards his uncle.

The desk, an old walnut piece, looked abandoned and pitiful, as furniture always does once it has been put out of the house. The brass keyplates were missing and the handles had been replaced by pieces of string through the screw-holes. "That desk wasn't out here in your father's day," said the Count, almost as though he had forgotten this until now. But since in fact he had mentioned it a number of times, Cesare made no reply. He never said anything unless the situation absolutely required it. Conversation, as one of life's arts, or amusements, was not understood by him, unless silence can be counted as part of it.

For a good many years the Valsassina estate had been engaged in a legal petition to decide the exact location of its vineyards. When Cesare or his late father mentioned the tragedy of 1932, they were not thinking of the fate of the eleven university professors who refused in that year to take the Fascist oath. They meant that in 1932 the authorities had declared Valsassina to be just outside the boundary line of the Chianti area. This meant that none of the Ridolfi wines could be labelled or sold as classic, and their market value was reduced by a quarter. The calculations, however, had been made from the position of the house itself, whereas some of the outlying vineyards fell inside the boundary. They had deteriorated, it was true, and could possibly be described as abandoned, but Cesare was doggedly negotiating for a low interest loan to buy a new digger, which would make replanting with sangiovese grapes possible in a short time. Those borderline fields might then be readmitted as classic. It was a letter from the local Consorzio on this subject, and another one from the bank, that were planted on the desk in front of him now.

"It's cold in here," Cesare said.

Unquestionably it was. The high windows had been designed so that the sun would never strike through them, and there was no heating in the room except a small charcoal stove. The Count was glad that he was wearing his old military greatcoat, which still fitted him very well. In a few months' time, under the Baistrocchi army reforms, the Italian cavalry would be gone for ever. When he had heard this he had silently resolved to be buried in his coat. Cesare, however, spoke as though he had only noticed the cold for the first time. His uncle stretched himself out towards the stove and as he grew a little warmer his breath became visible.

"Cesare, I've come to talk to you about Chiara's wedding. You know, of course, that she's going to marry this doctor." The "this" wasn't quite right, he corrected himself to "marry Dr Salvatore Rossi."

There was a pause, which gave him the feeling of having spoken too quickly. Cesare then said, "Chiara came out here a month or so ago. She didn't stay long." The Count wondered if this was a complaint, although it hardly sounded like one. Chiara ought to come as often as possible, if only because a twelfth of the estate had been left to her by her uncle, Cesare's father. It wasn't that the estate business didn't interest her, it did, and she was very quick at getting the hang of the accounts.

"Life seems an eternity to a girl at school," he said.

"How do you know what it feels like to be a girl at school?" Cesare asked, apparently with deep interest.

"Well, I can imagine that now she's finished with it she wants to stay in Florence and, I suppose, to meet different kinds of people."

"That she evidently did," said Cesare.

The Count tried again. "We were a little surprised, you know, not to hear from you. We sent you the announcement of the engagement, of course, I'm sure."

He could be quite sure, since he could see the card standing all by itself on the light powdering of dust and cornmeal which covered the desk. Cesare followed his glance and said, "I don't let them disturb the things in here."

He got up, and his uncle at once understood that they were going to look at something or other on the property. Either Cesare thought this a necessary formality, or he wanted to turn over in his mind what he had just heard. The Count found that he had to check himself from making the kind of gesticulations with which people insult the deaf and the dumb. Meanwhile a section of the darkness in the far corner of the office detached itself and was seen to be a gun-dog of the old-fashioned rough-haired Italian breed. She shook and stretched herself, as a preparation for going out. It was like the action of wringing a dish-mop.

The idea that his uncle had driven out from Florence to discuss something quite else seemed not to disturb Cesare. Perhaps he gave him credit for being able, if he came to the country, to behave as if he lived there. Outside, the ragged sky burned like a blue and white fire, hard on the eyes. Everything, as though at a given signal, was leaning away from the wind or struggling against it.

They walked, not to the vineyards but along a cart track to a hillside planted as far as the horizon with olives. The ground beneath the trees had been ploughed up for potatoes, and the two of them had to go along side by side, but at a distance of a furrow apart, one foot in and one foot out; really, it would have been easier for some-one with one leg shorter than the other. The tail of the old dog could be seen moving along the furrow at Cesare's heels. For some reason the Count, who was reflecting that he was too old for such outings, felt more at ease when he was walking at a higher level than Cesare, who at last came to a halt.

"The Consorzio think we ought to get rid of the olives and sell them for timber. There's all kinds of cheap cooking oil now."

"What will you do?"

"I don't know."

The fattore, who must have been following them, now came up in absolute silence and joined Cesare between two lean old trees. Cesare bent down and picked up a handful of stones or earth or both, sorted them out in his palm and showed them to the fattore, who nodded, apparently satisfied. Then, noticing the Count, he wished everyone in general good morning, and retreated down the slope. At the bottom he got onto his bicycle, adjusting a sheet of corrugated iron which he had been carrying on the handlebars, and pedalled slowly away. The wind caught the flapping edge of the iron with a metallic note, repeated again and again, fainter and fainter. The dog, crouching, followed the sound with sharp attention, hoping that the sound might become a shot. And yet when I was a boy and lived here I was impatient for every morning, the Count thought. And Chiara was always clamouring to come out here, ever since she could totter about after Cesare.

When they got back to the house the shutters had been drawn back in the spacious lavatory which had offered its row of green marble basins and urinals to shooting parties in the days of Umberto I. The shutters were drawn, too, in the dining-room. From daily habit Bernardino had grouped the oil, the salt, the pepper, and the bread round the master's place, so that he could help himself at top speed and get back to work, while the Count's chair was drawn up in front of a barren expanse of table. When they sat down Cesare, without embarrassment, began to redistribute everything, while Bernardino, apparently propelled out of the kitchen, brought in the dish of pasta, its sauce freckled and dappled golden from the oven. The heat and fragrance seemed out of place in the astonishing cold of the room.

Cesare began to break off pieces of bread and throw them into his mouth with unerring aim, then drank a little Valsassina. The wine, in the Florentine way, was not poured out for guests, who were expected to help themselves. The Count, whose digestion was not always reliable, pecked and sipped. How large my nephew's nose is! He thought. How large his hands! From this angle he reminds me of someone quite outside the family, I think perhaps Cesare Pavese, with those brilliant eyes, not grey; not green exactly. The large nose makes him look kindly, and I know that he is kindly, but he doesn't get any easier to talk to. In the *Inferno* the only ones condemned to silence are those who had betrayed their masters, Brutus and Judas in particular. Dante must have thought of them, before their punishment, as chatterers, or even as serious conversationalists, always first with the news. But, in Cesare's case, what if he were condemned to talk!

He pulled himself up. No one knew better than himself what difficulties Cesare must have, face to face with the bank, the Consorzio, the tenants, and the stony and chalky ground, whose blood was a wine which was not permitted to be labeled classico. If his nephew were to be asked, either by divine or human authority—either on Judgment Day or by the redistribution committee of the local Communist party—whether he had made good use of his time, the answer, if Cesare could bring himself to make one, must surely be yes.

The old woman appeared, and remarking that the fire should have been lit long ago put a shovelful of hot charcoal under the dry lavender and olive roots on the hearth. The warmth of the blaze spread courageously a little way into the room and the Count lost the connection of his thoughts, found himself repeating aloud, for no apparent reason, "If we could buy children with silver and gold, without women's company! But it cannot be." At the same time the dog, who had been huddled underneath the table, sensed that the next course was coming and sprang convulsively to its feet. This jerked him back to attention.

"The point is that Chiara wants a country wedding, here at Valsassina. I came here, I'm afraid, principally to talk about money. We could have done that on the telephone, in fact money is the only thing one can talk about successfully on the telephone, but then . . . in any case, the expenses of the whole thing would of course be mine. The details, I suppose, aren't for you and me, but there are some caterers that Maddalena favours because she says they make pastries for the Vatican, such folly, we know that the Pacelli pope is looked after by German nuns who would never allow him to eat pastry from Florence." To his annoyance Bernardino, platter in hand, bent over him at this point.

"Your Excellency could not find a better place to receive your guests than Valsassina. But you will explain to them when they come that I am of better family than I seem. All the land which you have been walking round this morning, if justice were done, would belong to me."

Cesare paid no attention whatever to this interruption. He laid down his knife and fork, but this was because he wanted to know something.

"What was it you said just now about women?"

The Count repeated the line from Euripides.

"I don't read much," said Cesare.

"I expect you don't have time."

"I shouldn't read if I did have time."

Cesare used very few gestures, but one, not to be forgotten by anyone who ever knew him, was to spread both hands flat in front of him, as he was doing now. You got the impression that he had never sat at a table without enough room for him to do this. The hands weighed down firmly, as a press is screwed down, wood against wood.

"Tell me, where did she meet this man?"

"Salvatore? At a concert, it seems."

"And he's a professional man."

"A doctor is no more professional than a farmer," said the Count. "One must never underrate what a man's profession means to him." He still counted himself as an Army man, and hoped that his nephew might remember this, but Cesare was evidently under strain, perhaps from the necessity of saying so much at one time.

"He's a neurologist, he's a consultant at the S. Agostino. He's very clever, no doubt about that."

"All young doctors are supposed to be clever. How old is he?"

"Rather older than Chiara, I suppose in his late twenties."

"You mean he's thirty."

"Well."

"Why is she marrying him?"

"She could only have one reason. You know your cousin. She is in love. Please don't think that I claim to be an authority on the subject, however."

"If she wants the wedding here," said Cesare, "why didn't she ask me herself?"

"I'm sure that she will, but just at the moment you must forgive her, she hardly knows what she's doing. I would be the first to admit that it's a regrettable state of affairs."

"There's always time to telephone. There's always time even to write a letter. My father sent my mother a letter from the defence of the Carso. If someone doesn't write it means simply this, that there's something else more important to them, even if it's only the pleasure of doing nothing."

"You mustn't take it in that way, Cesare. It's not an important matter."

"You're right, of course it isn't." As they walked out to the court-yard together Cesare said: "I take it that the marriage won't make any difference to Chiara's interest here, I mean her part-share?"

In the end, his uncle thought, he doesn't care for anything but Valsassina.

E. M. Forster

(1879–1970)

At the end of the nineteenth century Edward Morgan Forster traveled to Italy and was forever changed. Exposure to Mediterranean culture provided a welcome counterbalance to his rigid upper-class upbringing. He believed that British pragmatism should be tempered with imagination, mysticism, and sensitivity to nature—attributes he found in southern Europeans.

Two of Forster's first four novels were set in Italy: *Where Angels Fear to Tread* (1905), from which this selection is taken, and *A Room with a View* (1908). Although often overlooked in comparison to its more comic successor, *Where Angels Fear to Tread* is a profound look at the British middle class. A young lawyer, Philip Herriton, travels to Tuscany to save his late brother's widow from an unsuitable romance with an Italian. There he is joined by his sister-in-law's friend and chaperone Caroline Abbott. But the rescue goes horribly awry. In scarcely one hundred pages Forster not only invokes a strong sense of place (his fictional Monteriano is based on San Gimignano), but draws a devastating comparison between the English and the Italian character.

from WHERE ANGELS FEAR TO TREAD

When the bewildered tourist alights at the station of Monteriano, he finds himself in the middle of the country. There are a few houses round the railway, and many more dotted over the plain and the slopes of the hills, but of a town, mediaeval or otherwise, not the slightest sign. He must take what is suitably termed a "*legno*"—a piece of wood—and drive up eight miles of excellent road into the middle ages. For it is impossible, as well as sacrilegious, to be as quick as Baedeker.

It was three in the afternoon when Philip left the realms of common-sense. He was so weary with travelling that he had fallen asleep in the train. His fellow-passengers had the usual Italian gift of divination, and when Monteriano came they knew he wanted to go there, and dropped him out. His feet sank into the hot asphalt of the platform, and in a dream he watched the train depart, while the porter who ought to have been carrying his bag, ran up the line playing touch-you-last with the guard. Alas! He was in no humour for Italy. Bargaining for a *legno* bored him unutterably. The man asked six lire; and though Philip knew that for eight miles it should scarcely be more than four, yet he was about to give what he was asked, and so make the man discontented and unhappy for the rest of the day. He was saved from this social blunder by loud shouts, and looking up the road saw one cracking his whip and waving his reins and driving two horses furiously, and behind him there appeared a swaying figure of a woman, holding star-fish fashion on to anything she could touch. It was Miss Abbott, who had just received his letter from Milan announcing the time of his arrival, and had hurried down to meet him.

He had known Miss Abbott for years, and had never had much opinion about her one way or the other. She was good, quiet, dull, and amiable, and young only because she was twenty-three: there was nothing in her appearance or manner to suggest the fire of youth. All her life had been spent at Sawston with a dull and amiable father, and her pleasant, pallid face, bent on some respectable charity, was a familiar object of the Sawston streets. Why she had ever wished to leave them was surprising; but as she truly said, "I am John Bull to the backbone, yet I do want to see Italy, just once. Everybody says it is marvellous, and that one gets no idea of it from books at all." The curate suggested that a year was a long time; and Miss Abbott, with decorous playfulness, answered him, "Oh, but you must let me have my fling! I promise to have it once, and once only. It will give me things to think about and talk about for the rest of my life." The curate had consented; so had Mr. Abbott. And here she was in a *legno*, solitary, dusty, frightened, with as much to answer and to answer for as the most dashing adventuress could desire.

They shook hands without speaking. She made room for Philip and his luggage amidst the loud indignation of the unsuccessful driver, whom it required the combined eloquence of the station-master and the station beggar to confute. The silence was prolonged until they started. For three days he had been considering what he should do, and still more what he should say. He had invented a dozen imaginary conversations, in all of which his logic and eloquence procured him certain victory. But how to begin? He was in the enemy's country, and everything—the hot sun, the cold air behind the heat, the endless rows of olive-trees, regular yet mysterious—seemed hostile to the placid atmosphere of Sawston in which his thoughts took birth. At the outset he made one great concession. If the match was really suitable, and Lilia were bent on it, he would give in, and trust to his influence with his mother to set things right. He would not have made the concession in England; but here in Italy, Lilia, however willful and silly, was at all events growing to be a human being.

"Are we to talk it over now?" he asked.

"Certainly, please," said Miss Abbott, in great agitation. "If you will be so very kind."

"Then how long has she been engaged?"

Her face was that of a perfect fool—a fool in terror.

"A short time—quite a short time," she stammered, as if the shortness of the time would reassure him.

"I should like to know how long, if you can remember."

She entered into elaborate calculations on her fingers. "Exactly eleven days," she said at last.

"How long have you been here?"

More calculations, while he tapped irritably with his foot. "Close on three weeks."

"Did you know him before you came?"

"No."

"Oh! Who is he?"

"A native of the place."

The second silence took place. They had left the plain now and were climbing up the outposts of the hills, the olive-trees still accompanying. The driver, a jolly fat man, had got out to ease the horses, and was walking by the side of the carriage.

"I understand they met at the hotel."

"It was a mistake of Mrs. Theobald's."

"I also understand that he is a member of the Italian nobility."

She did not reply.

"May I be told his name?"

Miss Abbott whispered, "Carella." But the driver heard her, and a grin split over his face. The engagement must be known already.

"Carella? Conte or Marchese, or what?"

"Signor," said Miss Abbott, and looked helplessly aside.

"Perhaps I bore you with these questions. If so, I will stop."

"Oh, no, please; not at all. I am here—my own idea—to give all information which you very naturally—and to see if somehow—please ask anything you like."

"Then how old is he?"

"Oh, quite young. Twenty-one, I believe."

There burst from Philip the exclamation, "Good Lord!"

"One would never believe it," said Miss Abbott, flushing. "He looks much older."

"And is he good-looking?" he asked, with gathering sarcasm.

She became decisive. "Very good-looking. All his features are good, and he is well built—though I dare say English standards would find him too short."

Philip, whose one physical advantage was his height, felt annoyed at her implied indifference to it.

"May I conclude that you like him?"

She replied decisively again, "As far as I have seen him, I do."

At that moment the carriage entered a little wood, which lay brown and sombre across the cultivated hill. The trees of the wood were small and leafless, but noticeable for this—that their stems stood in violets as rocks stand in the summer sea. There are such violets in England, but not so many. Nor are there so many in Art, for no painter has the courage. The cart-ruts were channels, the hollow lagoons; even the dry white margin of the road was splashed, like a causeway soon to be submerged under the advancing tide of spring. Philip paid no attention at the time: he was thinking what to say next. But his eyes had registered the beauty, and next March he did not forget that the road to Monteriano must traverse innumerable flowers.

"As far as I have seen him, I do like him," repeated Miss Abbott, after a pause.

He thought she sounded a little defiant, and crushed her at once.

"What is he, please? You haven't told me that. What's his position?"

She opened her mouth to speak, and no sound came from it. Philip waited patiently. She tried to be audacious, and failed pitiably.

"No position at all. He is kicking his heels, as my father would say. You see, he has only just finished his military service."

"As a private?"

"I suppose so. There is general conscription. He was in the Bersaglieri, I think. Isn't that the crack regiment?"

"The men in it must be short and broad. They must also be able to walk six miles an hour."

She looked at him wildly, not understanding all that he said, but feeling that he was very clever. Then she continued her defence of Signor Carella.

"And now, like most young men, he is looking out for something to do."

"Meanwhile?"

"Meanwhile, like most young men, he lives with his people—father, mother, two sisters, and a tiny tot of a brother."

There was a grating sprightliness about her that drove him nearly mad. He determined to silence her at last.

"One more question, and only one more. What is his father?"

"His father," said Miss Abbott. "Well, I don't suppose you'll think it a good match. But that's not the point. I mean the point is not—I mean that social differences—love, after all—not but what——"

Philip ground his teeth together and said nothing.

"Gentlemen sometimes judge hardly. But I feel that you, and at all events your mother—so really good in every sense, so really unworldly—after all, love—marriages are made in heaven."

"Yes, Miss Abbott, I know. But I am anxious to hear heaven's choice. You arouse my curiosity. Is my sister-in-law to marry an angel?"

"Mr. Herriton, don't—please, Mr. Herriton—a dentist. His father's a dentist."

Philip gave a cry of personal disgust and pain. He shuddered all over, and edged away from his companion. A dentist! A dentist at Monteriano. A dentist in fairyland! False teeth and laughing gas and the tilting chair at a place which knew the Etruscan League, and the

Pax Romana, and Alaric himself, and the Countess Matilda, and the
Middle Ages, all fighting and holiness, and the Renaissance, all fighting and beauty! He thought of Lilia no longer. He was anxious for
himself: he feared that Romance might die.

Romance only dies with life. No pair of pincers will ever pull it out
of us. But there is a spurious sentiment which cannot resist the unexpected and the incongruous and the grotesque. A touch will loosen
it, and the sooner it goes from us the better. It was going from Philip
now, and therefore he gave the cry of pain.

"I cannot think what is in the air," he began. "If Lilia was determined to disgrace us, she might have found a less repulsive way. A
boy of medium height with a pretty face, the son of a dentist at Monteriano. Have I put it correctly? May I surmise that he has got not one
penny? May I also surmise that his social position is nil? Further-
more——"

"Stop! I'll tell you no more."

"Really, Miss Abbott, it is a little late for reticence. You have
equipped me admirably!"

"I'll tell you not another word!" she cried, with a spasm of terror.
Then she got out her handkerchief, and seemed as if she would shed
tears. After a silence, which he intended to symbolize to her the
dropping of a curtain on the scene, he began to talk of other subjects.

They were among olives again, and the wood with its beauty and
wildness had passed away. But as they climbed higher the country
opened out, and there appeared, high on a hill to the right, Monteriano. The hazy green of the olives rose up to its walls, and it seemed
to float in isolation between trees and sky, like some fantastic ship
city of a dream. Its colour was brown, and it revealed not a single
house—nothing but the narrow circle of the walls, and behind them
seventeen towers—all that was left of the fifty-two that had filled the
city in her prime. Some were only stumps, some were inclining stiffly
to their fall, some were still erect, piercing like masts into the blue. It
was impossible to praise it as beautiful, but it was also impossible to
damn it as quaint.

Meanwhile Philip talked continually, thinking this to be great evidence of resource and tact. It showed Miss Abbott that he had

probed her to the bottom, but was able to conquer his disgust, and by sheer force of intellect continue to be as agreeable and amusing as ever. He did not know that he talked a good deal of nonsense, and that the sheer force of his intellect was weakened by the sight of Monteriano, and by the thought of dentistry within those walls.

The town above them swung to the left, to the right, to the left again, as the road wound upward through the trees, and the towers began to glow in the descending sun. As they drew near, Philip saw the heads of people gathering black upon the walls, and he knew well what was happening—how the news was spreading that a stranger was in sight, and the beggars were aroused from their content and bid to adjust their deformities; how the alabaster man was running for his wares, and the Authorized Guide running for his peaked cap and his two cards of recommendation—one from Miss M'Gee, Maida Vale, the other, less valuable, from an Equerry to the Queen of Peru; how some one else was running to tell the landlady of the Stella d'Italia to put on her pearl necklace and brown boots and empty the slops from the spare bedroom; and how the landlady was running to tell Lilia and her boy that their fate was at hand.

Perhaps it was a pity Philip had talked so profusely. He had driven Miss Abbott half demented, but he had given himself no time to concert a plan. The end came so suddenly. They emerged from the trees on to the terrace before the walk, with the vision of half Tuscany radiant in the sun behind them, and then they turned in through the Siena gate, and their journey was over. The Dogana men admitted them with an air of gracious welcome, and they clattered up the narrow dark street, greeted by that mixture of curiosity and kindness which makes each Italian arrival so wonderful.

He was stunned and knew not what to do. At the hotel he received no ordinary reception. The landlady wrung him by the hand; one person snatched his umbrella, another his bag; people pushed each other out of his way. The entrance seemed blocked with a crowd. Dogs were barking, bladder whistles being blown, women waving their handkerchiefs, excited children screaming on the stairs, and at the top of the stairs was Lilia herself, very radiant, with her best blouse on.

"Welcome!" she cried. "Welcome to Monteriano!" He greeted her, for he did not know what else to do, and a sympathetic murmur rose from the crowd below.

"You told me to come here," she continued, "and I don't forget it. Let me introduce Signor Carella!"

Philip discerned in the corner behind her a young man who might eventually prove handsome and well-made, but certainly did not seem so then. He was half enveloped in the drapery of a cold dirty curtain, and nervously stuck out a hand, which Philip took and found thick and damp. There were more murmurs of approval from the stairs.

"Well, din-din's nearly ready," said Lilia. "Your room's down the passage, Philip. You needn't go changing."

He stumbled away to wash his hands, utterly crushed by her effrontery.

"Dear Caroline!" whispered Lilia as soon as he had gone. "What an angel you've been to tell him! He takes it so well. But you must have had a *mauvais quart d'heure*."

Miss Abbott's long terror suddenly turned into acidity. "I've told nothing," she snapped. "It's all for you—and if it only takes a quarter of an hour you'll be lucky!"

Dinner was a nightmare. They had the smelly dining-room to themselves. Lilia, very smart and vociferous, was at the head of the table; Miss Abbott, also in her best, sat by Philip, looking, to his irritated nerves, more like the tragedy confidante every moment. That scion of the Italian nobility, Signor Carella, sat opposite. Behind him loomed a bowl of goldfish, who swam round and round, gaping at the guests.

The face of Signor Carella was twitching too much for Philip to study it. But he could see the hands, which were not particularly clean, and did not get cleaner by fidgeting amongst the shining slabs of hair. His starched cuffs were not clean either, and as for his suit, it had obviously been bought for the occasion as something really English—a gigantic check, which did not even fit. His handkerchief he had forgotten, but never missed it. Altogether, he was quite unpresentable, and very lucky to have a father who was a dentist in Monteriano. And why, even Lilia—— But as soon as the meal began it furnished Philip with an explanation.

For the youth was hungry, and his lady filled his plate with spaghetti, and when those delicious slippery worms were flying down his throat, his face relaxed and became for a moment unconscious and calm. And Philip had seen that face before in Italy a hundred times—seen it and loved it, for it was not merely beautiful, but had the charm which is the rightful heritage of all who are born on that soil. But he did not want to see it opposite him at dinner. It was not the face of a gentleman.

Conversation, to give it that name, was carried on in a mixture of English and Italian. Lilia had picked up hardly any of the latter language, and Signor Carella had not yet learnt any of the former. Occasionally Miss Abbott had to act as interpreter between the lovers, and the situation became uncouth and revolting in the extreme. Yet Philip was too cowardly to break forth and denounce the engagement. He thought he should be more effective with Lilia if he had her alone, and pretended to himself that he must hear her defence before giving judgment.

Signor Carella, heartened by the spaghetti and the throat-rasping wine, attempted to talk, and, looking politely towards Philip, said, "England is a great country. The Italians love England and the English."

Philip, in no mood for international amenities, merely bowed.

"Italy too," the other continued a little resentfully, "is a great country. She has produced many famous men—for example Garibaldi and Dante. The latter wrote the 'Inferno,' the 'Purgatorio,' the 'Paradiso.' The 'Inferno' is the most beautiful." And with the complacent tone of one who has received a solid education, he quoted the opening lines—

> *Nel mezzo del cammin di nostra vita*
> *Mi ritrovai per una selva oscura*
> *Che la diritta via era smarrita—*

a quotation which was more apt than he supposed.

Lilia glanced at Philip to see whether he noticed that she was marrying no ignoramus. Anxious to exhibit all the good qualities of her betrothed, she abruptly introduced the subject of *pallone*, in which, it appeared, he was a proficient player. He suddenly became shy and developed a conceited grin—the grin of the village yokel whose cricket score is mentioned before a stranger. Philip himself had loved to watch *pallone*, that entrancing combination of lawn-tennis and fives. But he did not expect to love it quite so much again.

"Oh, look!" exclaimed Lilia, "the poor wee fish!"

A starved cat had been worrying them all for pieces of the purple quivering beef they were trying to swallow. Signor Carella, with the brutality so common in Italians, had caught her by the paw and flung her away from him. Now she had climbed up to the bowl and was trying to hook out a fish. He got up, drove her off, and finding a large glass stopper by the bowl, entirely plugged up the aperture with it.

"But may not the fish die?" said Miss Abbott. "They have no air."

"Fish live on water, not on air," he replied in a knowing voice, and sat down. Apparently he was at his ease again, for he took to spitting on the floor. Philip glanced at Lilia but did not detect her wincing. She talked bravely till the end of the disgusting meal, and then got up saying, "Well, Philip, I am sure you are ready for bye-bye. We shall meet at twelve o'clock lunch tomorrow, if we don't meet before. They give us *caffè* later in our rooms."

It was a little too impudent. Philip replied, "I should like to see you now, please, in my room, as I have come all the way on business." He heard Miss Abbott gasp. Signor Carella, who was lighting a rank cigar, had not understood.

It was as he expected. When he was alone with Lilia he lost all nervousness. The remembrance of his long intellectual supremacy strengthened him, and he began volubly—

"My dear Lilia, don't let's have a scene. Before I arrived I thought I might have to question you. It is unnecessary. I know everything. Miss Abbott has told me a certain amount, and the rest I see for myself."

"See for yourself?" she exclaimed, and he remembered afterwards that she had flushed crimson.

"That he is probably a ruffian and certainly a cad."

"There are no cads in Italy," she said quickly.

He was taken aback. It was one of his own remarks. And she further upset him by adding, "He is the son of a dentist. Why not?"

"Thank you for the information. I know everything, as I told you before. I am also aware of the social position of an Italian who pulls teeth in a minute provincial town."

He was not aware of it, but he ventured to conclude that it was pretty low. Nor did Lilia contradict him. But she was sharp enough to say, "Indeed, Philip, you surprise me. I understood you went in for equality and so on."

"And I understood that Signor Carella was a member of the Italian nobility."

"Well, we put it like that in the telegram so as not to shock dear Mrs. Herriton. But it is true. He is a younger branch. Of course families ramify—just as in yours there is your cousin Joseph." She adroitly picked out the only undesirable member of the Herriton clan. "Gino's father is courtesy itself, and rising rapidly in his profession. This very month he leaves Monteriano, and sets up at Poggibonsi. And for my own poor part, I think what people *are* is what matters, but I don't suppose you'll agree. And I should like you to know that Gino's uncle is a priest—the same as a clergyman at home."

Philip was aware of the social position of an Italian priest, and said so much about it that Lilia interrupted him with, "Well, his cousin's a lawyer at Rome."

"What kind of 'lawyer'?"

"Why, a lawyer just like you are—except that he has lots to do and can never get away."

The remark hurt more than he cared to show. He changed his method, and in a gentle, conciliating tone delivered the following speech:—

"The whole thing is like a bad dream—so bad that it cannot go on. If there was one redeeming feature about the man I might be uneasy. As it is I can trust to time. For the moment, Lilia, he has taken you in, but you will find him out soon. It is not possible that you, a lady, accustomed to ladies and gentlemen, will tolerate a man whose position is—well, not equal to the son of the servants' dentist in Coronation Place. I am not blaming you now. But I blame the glamour of Italy—I have felt it myself, you know—and I greatly blame Miss Abbott."

"Caroline! Why blame her? What's all this to do with Caroline?"

"Because we expected her to———" He saw that the answer would involve him in difficulties, and waving his hand, continued, "So I am confident, and you in your heart agree, that this engagement will not last. Think of your life at home—think of Irma! And I'll also say think of us; for you know, Lilia, that we count you more than a relation. I should feel I was losing my own sister if you did this, and my mother would lose a daughter."

She seemed touched at last, for she turned away her face and said, "I can't break it off now!"

"Poor Lilia," said he, genuinely moved. "I know it may be painful. But I have come to rescue you, and, book-worm though I may be, I am not frightened to stand up to a bully. He's merely an insolent boy. He thinks he can keep you to your word by threats. He will be different when he sees he has a man to deal with."

What follows should be prefaced with some simile—the simile of a powder-mine, a thunderbolt, an earthquake—for it blew Philip up in the air and flattened him on the ground and swallowed him up in the depths. Lilia turned on her gallant defender and said—

"For once in my life I'll thank you to leave me alone. I'll thank your mother too. For twelve years you've trained me and tortured me, and I'll stand it no more. Do you think I'm a fool? Do you think I never felt? Ah! when I came to your house a poor young bride, how you all looked me over—never a kind word—and discussed me, and thought I might just do; and your mother corrected me, and your sister snubbed me, and you said funny things about me to show how clever you were! And when Charles died I was still to run in strings for the honour of your beastly family, and I was to be cooped up at Sawston and learn to keep house, and all my chances spoilt of marrying again. No, thank you! No, thank you! 'Bully'? 'Insolent boy'? Who's that pray, but you? But, thank goodness, I can stand up against the world now, for I've found Gino, and this time I marry for love!"

The coarseness and truth of her attack alike overwhelmed him. But her supreme insolence found him words, and he too burst forth.

"Yes! And I forbid you to do it! You despise me, perhaps, and think I'm feeble. But you're mistaken. You are ungrateful and impertinent and contemptible, but I will save you in order to save Irma and

our name. There is going to be such a row in this town that you and
he'll be sorry you came to it. I shall shrink from nothing, for my
blood is up. It is unwise of you to laugh. I forbid you to marry
Carella, and I shall tell him so now."

"Do," she cried. "Tell him so now. Have it out with him. Gino!
Gino! Come in! *Aventi!* Fra Filippo forbids the banns!"

Gino appeared so quickly that he must have been listening outside
the door.

"Fra Filippo's blood's up. He shrinks from nothing. Oh, take care
he doesn't hurt you!" She swayed about in vulgar imitation of Philip's
walk, and then, with a proud glance at the square shoulders of her
betrothed, flounced out of the room.

Did she intend them to fight? Philip had no intention of doing so;
and no more, it seemed, had Gino, who stood nervously in the middle of the room with twitching lips and eyes.

"Please sit down, Signor Carella," said Philip in Italian. "Mrs. Herriton is rather agitated, but there is no reason we should not be calm.
Might I offer you a cigarette? Please sit down."

He refused the cigarette and the chair, and remained standing in
the full glare of the lamp. Philip, not averse to such assistance, got his
own face into shadow.

For a long time he was silent. It might impress Gino, and it also
gave him time to collect himself. He would not this time fall into the
error of blustering, which he had caught so unaccountably from
Lilia. He would make his power felt by restraint.

Why, when he looked up to begin, was Gino convulsed with silent
laughter? It vanished immediately; but he became nervous, and was
even more pompous than he intended.

"Signor Carella, I will be frank with you. I have come to prevent
you marrying Mrs. Herriton, because I see you will both be unhappy
together. She is English, you are Italian; she is accustomed to one
thing, you to another. And—pardon me if I say it—she is rich and
you are poor."

"I am not marrying her because she is rich," was the sulky reply.

"I never suggested that for a moment," said Philip courteously.
"You are honourable, I am sure; but are you wise? And let me remind
you that we want her with us at home. Her little daughter will be

motherless, our home will be broken up. If you grant my request you will earn our thanks—and you will not be without a reward for your disappointment."

"Reward—what reward?" He bent over the back of a chair and looked earnestly at Philip. They were coming to terms pretty quickly. Poor Lilia!

Philip said slowly, "What about a thousand lire?"

His soul went forth into one exclamation, and then he was silent, with gaping lips. Philip would have given double: he had expected a bargain.

"You can have them tonight."

He found words, and said, "It is too late."

"But why?"

"Because——" His voice broke. Philip watched his face—a face without refinement perhaps, but not without expression—watched it quiver and re-form and dissolve from emotion into emotion. There was avarice at one moment, and insolence, and politeness, and stupidity, and cunning—and let us hope that sometimes there was love. But gradually one emotion dominated, the most unexpected of all; for his chest began to heave and his eyes to wink and his mouth to twitch, and suddenly he stood erect and roared forth his whole being into one tremendous laugh.

Philip sprang up, and Gino, who had flung wide his arms to let the glorious creature go, took him by the shoulders and shook him, and said, "Because we are married—married—married as soon as I knew you were coming. There was no time to tell you. Oh, oh! You have come all the way for nothing. Oh! And oh, your generosity!" Suddenly he became grave, and said, "Please pardon me; I am rude. I am no better than a peasant, and I——" Here he saw Philip's face, and it was too much for him. He gasped and exploded and crammed his hands into his mouth and spat them out in another explosion, and gave Philip an aimless push, which toppled him on to the bed. He uttered a horrified Oh! and then gave up, and bolted away down the passage, shrieking like a child, to tell the joke to his wife.

For a time Philip lay on the bed, pretending to himself that he was hurt grievously. He could scarcely see for temper, and in the passage he ran against Miss Abbott, who promptly burst into tears.

"I sleep at the Globo," he told her, "and start for Sawston tomorrow morning early. He has assaulted me. I could prosecute him. But shall not."

"I can't stop here," she sobbed. "I daren't stop here. You will have to take me with you!"

Laura Fraser

(1961–   )

After a year of marriage Laura Fraser's husband left her for his high school girl-friend. Devasted, she retreated from San Francisco to Florence. Even the familiar-ity of one of her favorite cities did nothing to mend her heart. "Mi hai spaccato il cuore," she recalled from her Italian class. "You have broken my heart . . . You have cloven it in two." She left Florence and went to Ischia, where she met "M.," a married aesthetics professor. Their affair spanned several cities and two continents, and when it was over she was ready to go on with her life. She chronicled their relationship, first in an article for the online magazine *Salon*, and then in a book, *An Italian Affair* (2001), from which this excerpt is taken.

Although she writes in the second person—an unusual choice for a memoir—Fraser is disarmingly candid. "The whole experience seemed like a dream and I felt like I was observing myself in that dream," she said. "So the second person gave me the sense of seeing myself from the outside." Critics said that her story is every woman's nightmare—abandonment—and every woman's fantasy—redemption through a sexy, clandestine affair.

Journalist Laura Fraser has contributed to *Vogue*, *Glamour*, *Mother Jones*, *Self*, and many other publications. She has also written a book of nonfiction, *Losing It*, about the diet industry. Fraser lives in San Francisco.

from AN ITALIAN AFFAIR

FLORENCE

When the plane touches down in Florence, it's evening. Lucia is there, waving from outside the security area, flipping her short dark hair away from her angular face. She kisses you on both cheeks and says you look great, even though that can't possibly be true. She speaks Italian faster than you can understand in your bleary condition, but you're glad to just follow along. Lucia loads your bag into her miniature car and goes careening around the perimeter of the city and into the center.

Just outside the pedestrian zone, she maneuvers into a tiny parking spot, and you walk from there along the narrow cobblestone streets until you reach a *pensione* right in the historic center, near the Piazza della Signoria. You're staying at a little hotel this visit because Lucia, an art teacher who was divorced, unhappily, in her late thirties, has a new boyfriend who stays over. So there's no more room at her place. You don't mind; Lucia seems so content, her face softer than the last time you saw her.

You ring at a massive wooden door, get buzzed in, and then squeeze into an elevator cage that barely fits the two of you and your bag. You greet the grumpy signora at the front desk, roused from her TV napping, and deposit your things. It's late, but Lucia insists you have to go out for a drink.

"*Andiamo,*" she says, and you are glad to be persuaded.

You return to the streets, which, despite the hour, are filled with couples strolling, middle-aged signoras locking arms, tourists taking flash photos, and bands of teenagers gathered on the steps of the magnificent marble Duomo. You end up at one of the cafés on the Piazza della Repubblica, taking a seat at an outdoor table, the September night air still warm. The waiter comes up in his crisp white shirt and black bow tie, and without asking, Lucia orders you both glasses of *spumante secco*.

The *spumante secco* reminds you of a moment you shared the year before, when you were vacationing together for a few days in the Cinque Terre, on the Ligurian coast, hiking from one fishing village to the next. You had arrived in Manarola, with its pastel houses stacked up around a tiny harbor, and sat down, dusty and tired, for a drink before dinner. Lucia had ordered the *spumante*, and by the time the waiter set the glasses down the sun was just setting beyond the little harbor, turning the whole sea as pink as smooth sandstone. "*La vita è un' arte,*" she'd said, clinking glasses.

You had returned to that moment in your mind many times since, to cheer you up.

When the waiter brings the drinks, Lucia clicks glasses with you again. "*Cin cin,*" she says, chin chin. Then she gets right down to business, asking what happened with your husband.

"*Raccontami tutto,*" she says. The Italians have that wonderful verb, *raccontare*, that means to tell a story. Tell me the story about everything.

She says she can't imagine how it happened. Just the year before, she reminds you, when you'd stayed with her for a few weeks, your new husband was always calling from San Francisco, just to tell you he loved you. In return, you had sent him cards you made with photo booth pictures, wearing Italian movie star sunglasses, blowing kisses, *ciao ciao*, telling him he was the only reason you didn't stay in Florence forever.

"What happened?" Lucia asks.

You say you aren't really sure, you're still in a state of shock about the whole thing. You recount, as best you can in your night-school Italian, the bare details of the breakup. You'd been married just over a year, after being together for three years before that. He had a new job as a trial attorney, and you'd just had your first book out; you were both doing what you'd always wanted to do with your lives. Everything seemed to be fine, even if you were both very busy. Then suddenly, just as mysteriously as you had fallen in love four years before, he seemed to fall out of love.

"When did it start, this falling out of love?" asks Lucia, sipping her drink.

You don't know. You had been luxuriating in your new marriage and didn't see the signs of trouble. Maybe it was in February, on your birthday, when you first became aware of a rift between you. You had driven north of San Francisco to Point Reyes National Seashore. That was the place, you tell Lucia, that had reminded her of the Sardinian coast when she visited you there. It was the place your husband and you had hiked when you were first so amazed that you'd found each other. On that day in February, on the trail back from the estuary where you had watched some sea lions lounge in the winter sun with their pups, you brought up the topic of having a child. Your husband—let's call him Jon—said he wasn't sure it was a good time. You said it's probably never a good time, but you had talked about it for a couple of years, and at thirty-six, you can't wait forever. He was quiet for a while before telling you that if you did get pregnant, it would really freak him out.

"But he wanted to have children?" Lucia asks.

"Yeah, that's why we decided to get married."

Lucia blows out smoke with a sigh.

"I was so sure we were going to have a child," you tell her, "that I even bought a set of maternity clothes." You had never confessed that to anyone before. They were still in the back of your closet, because you couldn't stand to give them away.

"You already bought maternity clothes?" asked Lucia. "*Sei pazza, cara.*" You're crazy, my dear. She takes a long look at you and shakes her head. "Well," she says, waving her cigarette, "you can always wear them if you get really fat."

"*Perfetto!*" you say, laughing for the first time in months. "Do they serve *gelato* here?" you joke, scanning the restaurant for the waiter. Then your eyes rest back on Lucia, who has stopped smiling. "I was stupid," you say.

"You weren't stupid. You wanted a *bambino*. That's natural. Go on."

That day on the hike, the conversation shifted subtly, crucially. Jon said he wasn't just freaked out about having a baby in general. He was freaked out about you having a baby together. In that one moment, the whole relationship was in question, everything was up for grabs, and he couldn't explain why.

In the weeks after that, Jon got up earlier every morning to go to work, and stayed later after work at the gym. It also turned out that he was seeing a lot of a high school girlfriend, who, after being out of touch for twenty years, had called out of the blue. That explained why Jon, who had been too tired for months to make love at nine-thirty, was now coming home sometimes at one in the morning.

"He was seeing another woman?" asks Lucia, her bright face darkening. "Did you know her?"

You had met her once. You came home from being out with a friend one evening to find the remains of a cozy dinner, with candles and flowers. You called, and no one answered. You went upstairs to the bedroom, dreading the worst, and found them out on the terrace outside. They were wrapped in sleeping bags, drinking wine, staring at the moon.

"He *knew* you were coming home and he was there with another woman? In camping bags?" asked Lucia, incredulous. "What did you do?"

"I introduced myself." She left quickly, and the rest was a blur of discussions and lies, even a broken plate (you threw it, of course). Suddenly you were in the third session with a marriage counselor where your husband said, flatly, I just want out of this relationship. He didn't even call it a marriage. He dropped you off at home with an anxious, gripping hug, both of you crying, and that was it. He left.

"That was four months ago," you tell Lucia, "in May."

"I'm so sorry," says Lucia.

You're quiet for a moment, and then she makes a gesture flicking her fingers under her chin that Italians use to say economically, forget him, he wasn't worth it, life goes on and you'll be better off.

"He seemed like he was an interesting, intelligent man," Lucia says, "but he never had the love of life you have anyway, the sense of *la bella vita*."

You nod. Lucia is right. There's nothing more to say. You drain your glass, and Lucia gestures for another round.

"You'll find someone else, someone better," Lucia says. "I never thought I would at first, but eventually, I did. It may not have been in time for a family, but . . ." She sips her *spumante*. "*Però, è così.*"

You lift your glass to Lucia. "To your new love," you say. She smiles.

"And to yours. When he comes."

The next morning, you wander around your favorite places in Florence. You stroll in the Boboli Gardens, hiking to the top, where the view of the city's spires, domes, and red-tiled roofs has always awed you. But now it just looks like another postcard.

You walk back down through the park, taking winding paths that lead to the streets, and study the windows of the boutiques near the Ponte Vecchio. You pass the men's store where the year before a charming salesman had spent half an hour helping you choose among the most beautiful ties in Italy, holding each one up under his chin, while you tried to decide which one you should send home to your husband. The tie you eventually agreed on had looked great on the Italian, and your husband had liked it, too—as much, anyway, as he ever liked a piece of clothing. When you met him, he had little regard for his appearance: aviator glasses, Grateful Dead T-shirts, bushy black hair, floodwater jeans. Beautiful smile, though. After living with you, he'd cut his hair, bought new glasses, some clothes that fit, and he'd received a lot of gorgeous ties. So now he looks great for his new girlfriend. And you look, well, older.

Next door, a boutique is just opening after lunch. You don't ordinarily go into Italian boutiques, not only because their clothes are usually made for tiny people, but because if you go inside it shows you're serious about buying something. You can't just browse the way you can in the United States. You nod hello to the shopkeeper, a stylish woman in her forties with a long black mane, and glance at the colorful shirts stacked in twos and threes on minimalist glass shelves. When you were together, your husband had definite ideas about what he liked you to wear: nothing too colorful or sexy, lots of navy blue, anything with a polo collar, sensible shoes. For a free-spirited type, he had extremely Princetonian taste in women's clothing. It was as if he'd been attracted to you for your exuberance, and then did everything he could to tone it down. You dutifully chucked your red shoes into the back of the closet and wore a lot of gray.

You ask the shopkeeper if you can try on a short magenta jacket. She looks at you doubtfully. "I don't think it will work on you," she concludes. Unlike in the United States, where clerks will sell you anything, no matter how unflattering, Italian shopkeepers don't want to be responsible for any aesthetic errors walking around on the streets.

"Why not?" you ask her.

"Signora," she says, delicately, "you have a large bottom and a small waist, and a short jacket will not look good on you. You must always wear a long jacket, fitted in here," she says, gesturing to your waist.

She was right, of course. What were you thinking? You should never deviate from that slenderizing long-jacket rule. You also never should have walked in. They have nothing your size in that store, nothing big enough for you and your big bottom.

The shopkeeper, sensing that you are out of sorts, whirls around to another rack, sifts through, and hands you a bronze knit top with tiny skin-baring stripes of crochet woven in. "This will suit you," she says. You try it on, halfheartedly, but it's a little too clingy, a little bare. You emerge from the dressing room and stand, slumped, in front of her. "It doesn't work on me."

She studies you. "The color is good for your hair, it picks up the gold, and the brown in your eyes."

"It's a little too sexy," you say doubtfully.

The shopkeeper gives you a look that suggests that nothing can ever be too sexy. "Well, you can wear a little camisole underneath it if you must," she says, pulling at the fabric here and there. "And you have to stand up, hold yourself strong." You straighten up a bit. "There," she says, "you have a beautiful bust, you should show it off."

You turn in front of the mirror. "This makes me look fat."

The *commessa* throws up her hands. "You are a woman, you have a woman's body, so what?" she says. "You should show what's nice about your body. I think your husband will like this."

He certainly wouldn't have liked it. "I don't have a husband," you tell her, fingering the fabric.

"Well, then, it's good to dress sexy for yourself," she says. "Maybe even better."

"*D'accordo.*" Yes. You could dress sexy for yourself. You walk out with a top that your husband definitely would have hated, for about the price of a really nice tie.

The next day, you wake up questioning why you're in Italy. It's September, your friends are all busy working, and you have no plans. You've been to Florence before, you've seen all the major museums and monuments already, but you distract yourself by being a tourist anyway. You wait with all the other tourists, a long line of ants, to finally get into the Uffizi, crowding around the Botticellis and Titians, trying to catch a glimpse of the paintings between all the elbows and shoulders.

You really aren't in the mood for any more museums, so you rent a bicycle and ride up to Fiesole, past villas and vineyards, past the cliff where Leonardo da Vinci made some hapless assistant test out his first flying machine, and all the way to the top of the hill. The view everywhere is stupendous—cypress trees and olive terraces,

Florence at your feet—but you can't just sit there and admire it. You're impatient to move on, to coast back down to town as fast as you can. No matter where you go, you always have the sense that something is following you close behind.

The following morning, you don't care that you're in Italy, you can't get out of bed. You're as tearful and depressed as you'd been in San Francisco; you've come all this way and all you can think about is how much you miss your husband, and how there's no one to call if you want to call home. At lunchtime, it's all you can do to finally get up and go see your friend Nina at her office near Santa Croce.

Nina is on the phone when you arrive, arguing with someone, gesturing angrily with one hand and greeting you effusively with the other. She drops the phone and runs over to embrace you, kissing you quickly on both cheeks, giving her assistant some instructions over your shoulder. Nina picks up her perfect black jacket and trim leather bag and motions you to come on, follow her out.

Nina, a sophisticated woman in her forties, stayed with you in San Francisco for a month several years ago, a friend of your Italo-American friend Cecilia, who had lived in Italy years before. At the time, you spoke no Italian, but Nina spoke a little English, and you communicated well enough that you admired her sensibility. She would make big bowls of exquisitely savory pasta, even though she swore she couldn't cook. She felt so sorry for your boyfriend then, for going out with a vegetarian, that she once made him a steak *and* a roast for dinner. She ate lunch every day at the same Italian restaurant in the neighborhood, and said she had absolutely no desire to go anywhere else, to venture out to try Thai, Cambodian, or Vietnamese food because there was always a risk of getting cilantro in a dish, and cilantro tastes like soap. A petite, dark-haired woman with a smoky voice, Nina had brought few clothes with her, but always dressed impeccably in a wool skirt, twin set, and flat Italian loafers—even just to go to her English language classes. She couldn't understand the way her American friend dressed, and once opened up your closet and demanded to know why you went around in sloppy jeans all the time when you had a wardrobe full of beautiful clothes. "*Non ha senso,*" she said. It makes no sense.

A year later, Nina's friend—and now your friend—Lucia came to

visit San Francisco with a group of her girlfriends. You had big dinner parties at your flat, everyone's cheeks red with wine and laughter.
They invited you to stay with them in a house in Monterey that they'd
managed to exchange for a week for one of their places in Italy. You
went hiking with Lucia in Big Sur—she was the only one of the Italian women who was interested in hiking—and you liked that she was
so willing to be awed by the drama of the steep coastal mountains,
and by the playful sea lions at the rocky beach. Even though you
spoke only Spanish in common, you became great friends, closer
than most friends you'd known in San Francisco for years. There was
something *simpatico* between you.

After the Italian women went home, you decided to try to learn
the language, taking one evening class after another and watching all
the Marcello Mastroianni films you could get your hands on. You
took advantage of having friends and a free place to stay and visited
Nina and Lucia in Florence a couple of times over the years. You
became familiar with Florence, knowing the bus routes and flea markets and out-of-the-way restaurants where only Italians ate. You went
to cooking school for a week in a fourteenth-century villa in Tuscany,
spending mornings making ravioli and risotto, and afternoons walking on dusty paths through vineyards, olive groves, and patches of
purple thistles. Then it was two weeks in a language school overlooking the Arno in Florence, drilling *passato remoto* verbs with young
Swiss students who were much more serious than you were, but who
managed to make the language sound guttural and stiff. You went to
a Bob Dylan concert in a medieval town square outside of Florence,
your Italian friends insisting that you translate the lyrics, and then
laughing when you tried, "all confused in a big mess of blue."

By the time Lucia's friend Giovanna came to San Francisco to stay
for a month—nothing an Italian would ever consider an imposition,
and so you didn't, either—you'd learned enough of the language to
carry on a decent conversation and slowly, slowly improved.

Now Nina leads you from her office into a busy little stand-up lunch
place, where everyone crowds around the bar trying to shout his or
her order. The guy behind the bar ignores everyone else when Nina
approaches the counter. He asks what La Nina would like today, and

she asks him what's good. They have a long, flirtatious conversation while everyone else tries to catch the waiter's attention. Finally Nina orders and steers you to a wobbly high table by the window, setting down a couple of glasses of red wine and then going back to the bar to pick up the plates of pasta. Nina tries a bite of the simple penne with fresh tomatoes and basil and exclaims about how good it is, thrilled at her choice, even though she eats at that same place every single day.

Nina says she was sorry to hear about your separation. "The first time you're heartbroken is always the worst," she assures you, dismissing the topic, and then asks about your vacation so far. You tell her about the exhibits and museums you've seen, and she is as excited talking about the art that surrounds her every day as she is about her lunch.

She shakes her head, marveling, "Laura, Laura," she says. "Last time you were here, you said you would learn Italian, and now you've learned it!"

"I need practice," you say.

"You need an Italian lover," Nina replies, matter-of-factly. "That's the only solution." Nina lights a cigarette, considering that. "To everything."

You tell her it's not such a bad idea. More than anything, you say, just realizing it, you want to put a body between yourself and your husband. You don't want him to be the last person you made love to, especially since the last time had been so horrible.

Nina asked why it had been so bad, and you tell her, because it's somehow easy to tell intimate stories in a romance language. It was during the brief period when your husband and you had been tense with each other; he was on his way out of the relationship, and you were trying to hang on, still thinking it was just a difficult time, the kind of thing couples go through that ends up making their marriages stronger. You thought maybe if you made love, things would be better, you would reconnect. You had joked about it, saying it could be just like casual sex, and he reluctantly agreed. After you'd had sex, mechanical sex, you leaned over his face to kiss him, and he turned away. "No," he'd said. "You're not supposed to kiss on the lips."

Nina gasps. "*Incredible.*"

Afterward, you got up to take a shower, pounding hot, to wash the whole thing away, and you knew that it was the last time you'd ever make love to your husband.

"That's terrible when you know it's the last time," Nina says. "But you always know." Nina drags on her cigarette and blows the smoke out the side of her mouth. "After that experience, the angels made a special note that you deserve better next time. I'm sure."

"*Speriamo di sì,*" you say. Let's hope so. You pick at your pasta and tell Nina you're glad Lucia seems happy with her new boyfriend, since Lucia had been depressed after she split up with her husband— although it's hard to read depression in someone who is always so energetic and quick to laugh. You ask Nina if she is seeing anyone herself, and Nina waves away the question, too silly to consider. Then she confesses that she's been dating a musician, and starts laughing at herself.

"He's fat!" Nina bursts out. "I've never been with a fat man before!" She leans closer and whispers. "It's like riding waves," she says. "Wonderful!"

You like that image, and the way your Italian friends appreciate sensuality in all types, forget the ideal. You tell Nina that you yourself are cursed with always having skinny men interested in you. "Opposites attract," you say.

Nina looks at your body in that frank way Italian women will size you up. "You're thinner than you were last year," she observes.

It's the divorce, you explain. For the first time in your life, you've had no interest in food.

"Eat your pasta," Nina commands, and you do, glad that your appetite is returning.

As you wait for the waiter to bring coffee, Nina asks what you intend to do for the rest of your vacation. You tell her you don't know; you realize it's a bad time to be in Italy, your friends are all busy, and you've spent enough time in Florence over the years that you don't need another week dodging tour groups and looking at church interiors. You leave out that it's too hard to be in a place where your friends are all in love. You want to visit Giovanna in Bologna, but she, too, was recently married, and so you really can't stay there long, either. You don't have a plan for cooking school or a language course. You've already been to Rome, Venice, Ravenna, Umbria, Bologna, Liguria, and Tuscany. Maybe you'll go somewhere new.

Nina slaps her elegant little hand on the table. "*Napoli!*" she says, pleased with herself. "Perfect!" She'd just been to Naples, and had a wonderful time. The old architecture, the sense of beauty amidst decay, the food—it was all wonderful.

You're surprised. You'd always heard that Naples was a dangerous city to travel in, especially for a woman alone.

Nina waves away that concern. "It's like New York," she says. "If you carry your camera in a plastic bag, keep your money close to you, and act like you know what you're doing, you'll be fine."

"Maybe," you say.

"And Ischia!" Nina exclaims, ignoring your reluctance. "Go to Naples, look around the old city—you must look around—and then get the ferry to Ischia." Nina is definite, and full of plans, describing the island. "Or you can take the ferry from Pozzuoli, if you like. You can also go to Amalfi, to Pompeii . . ." Nina ticks off the possibilities on her fingers. "Just don't go to Capri. Capri is crawling with tourists, and way too expensive. You'll pay ten thousand lire there just for a cappuccino." Nina downs her espresso in one gulp. She has solved all of your problems, so she checks her watch. She has to get back to work.

You walk back to Nina's office, half a block away, and kiss good-bye. Nina runs up the stone steps to the grand front door of her building, then turns around. "Ischia, Laura," she calls, waving. "Ischia."

And so, the next day, you set out for Ischia. Maybe you'll see Naples, Capri, Pompeii, and the Amalfi coast, too, but your sights are set on Ischia. Something about a volcanic island with natural hot baths and long pebbly beaches sounds about right. Everything will be white stucco and washed with Mediterranean light. Everything else will be far, far away.

Paul Gervais

(1946–)

"It amazes me that I have a garden I personally keep—even this need of mine to have a garden is new to me," wrote novelist Paul Gervais. "But more amazing still is the fact that my garden is not in North Tewksbury, Massachusetts, where I grew up, not in New England with its shallow horticultural roots and climatic extremes, but in Italy, in the cradle of a great garden tradition, in a light-filled, temperate landscape that seems, even now that it's mine, unattainable."

Since 1982 Gervais and his partner, Gil, have lived in the Villa Massei in the province of Lucca. Like many transplanted Americans, they bought a tumble-down villa in a romantic haze and have spent two decades restoring it. But it was the gardens that most challenged them. There were a thousand olive trees and a vineyard that needed tending, a meadow of fruit trees, 111 rose bushes, a *limonaia,* or lemon house, a grotto, and huge cypress trees. Paul and Gil knew little about gardening.

In twenty years they have become amateur horticulturists and their garden is so splendid that it was included in a prestigious international garden tour. In *A Garden in Lucca* (2000), from which this excerpt is taken, Gervais recounts buying the Villa Massei, resurrecting its grounds, learning about horticulture, and visiting some of the most famous gardens in Italy. Along the way his memoir examines the relationship of Tuscans to their beautiful land.

from A GARDEN IN LUCCA

The saucer magnolias were in bloom in Corso Garibaldi, the filled-in medieval moat. I walked along Via Vittorio Veneto to Piazza San Michele. Until the eleventh century fluted chunks of toppled colonnades must have lain here in the brambles, a playground for cats—this is the site of the ancient Roman forum. In the campanile the quarter hour struck a tonal code the Lucchesi understand, a familial dialectal phrase. I was reminded of those first few nights I had spent in Lucca in November 1979. The guest room I occupied in Leonardo's attic apartment had a single high, shuttered window. I couldn't have been more than fifteen feet away from the tower's rack of bells, the noisy medieval mechanism that ran them. And yet I remembered welcoming the disturbance; it assured me throughout the night that this extraordinary trip wasn't a dream after all.

In Via Santa Lucia, by the apse of San Michele, the flower seller threw her baritone voice to passersby. "*Duemila, mazzi belli! Duemila al mazzo!*" Two thousand lire, beautiful bunches. In this spring season they were poppy-flowered anemones, eye-catching hot pinks and pale purples. When her calls woke me those November mornings here, she was selling gladioli, which I'd buy and place in an antique brass vase in Leonardo's living room.

I dodged handsomely dressed women on bicycles who rang their tiny handlebar bells, *zing zing*, a detached, genteel shooing. A bar waiter passed, delivering breakfast, coffee, and pastries on a silvery tray to a neighboring shopkeeper. Children brought warm *focaccia* to their lips in Via Calderia, a narrow street flanked by plain-faced palaces with contrastingly opulent interiors—like Renaissance Florentines cloaked in black capes, the Lucchesi have never worn their wealth on the surface.

It had been years since I last visited the garden at Palazzo Pfanner. But at nine-thirty this morning the enormous turquoise *portone* at number 33 Via degli Angeli was closed. I scanned the simple brass *plaquette* of doorbells. Raimondi Pfanner, Virdis Pfanner, two P. Pfanners, and one A. Pfanner—names incised with niello permanence in a timeless cursive script. The only regularly pushed bell belonged to Bruscuglia Baisi (all the others were tarnished). Perhaps this was the concierge. I entertained the thought of ringing for entrance but didn't want to make a nuisance of myself.

The Pfanners, a Swiss family from Lake Constance, bought this palace in 1860. They were merchants in the beer trade. It was the local Moriconi who commissioned its construction, in 1667, but they'd go broke in their extravagance, sell everything, and move to Poland, migrant fortune seekers. Another Lucchese family, the Controni, completed the house with an enlarged, still more grandiose plan. The garden they built is the only one of any note that survives in this historically wealthy city, which once included many such *angolini verdi*.

I decided to walk up onto the city wall, where there's a view, though limited, down into the garden. Perhaps by the time I came back the great doors would be open as they promised to be, daily; the Pfanners welcomed all for a modest fee.

In front of the palace next door, high school students gathered for a break between classes at the Liceo Classico N. Machiavelli. They wore jeans, captioned sweatshirts, and friendship bracelets, but there was history in their faces, in their high-bridged noses, in the depth of their eyes: Roman, Celtic-Ligurian, Etruscan. In a group of three, one boy, blond as a Lombard, invaders of the sixth century, glanced at me and said to his friend, "We really should be speaking English." Was I part of a new invasion?

I turned left onto Via Cesere Battisti, the sharp echo of well-shod feet against cold paving stones the only sound heard here. Piazza del Collegio offered, ironically, no access to the school, but there was a narrow walk to the ramparts at Baluardo San Frediano. The path I followed was paved in gray river stones the size of pears, harvested from the Serchio. They were cut in half lengthwise and laid in mortar, rough side up, offering a secure step in wet weather. The walkway was edged in quarried stone strips from Matraia. In this city of skilled artisans and craftsmen, such finishing touches are everywhere, even underfoot.

There's a belvedere up on the wall facing the Pfanner garden below. Two young linden trees are staked straight in the clay ground, promising shade for future generations. I stood between them now and gazed down into the distant, light-filled garden with its long-shadowed statuary, its audible water jet in a central pool.

A garden doesn't fully reveal its secrets until you're there within it, but the Pfanner palace itself could be studied well from here. The great porticoed staircase, with its high arches and broad terrace landings, faces the garden like the tiered gallery of a Baroque theater. The building's volumes and schemes, seventeenth-century reinterpretations of late Florentine Mannerism, attest to the family's social standing and good taste. French doors on the *piano nobile*, the main floor, open to waist-high stone balustrades. All the windows and arches are framed with moldings in fine classical relief of *pietra serena*, the ubiquitous gray stone of Tuscany.

The future King Frederick IV of Denmark and Norway found this house palatial enough to live here in 1692 as crown prince. Lucca was the backdrop of his courtship of aristocrat Maria Maddalena Trenta, the details of which are imagined in Börge Janssen's novel, *The Girl from Lucca.*

Suddenly I was surrounded by a group of schoolchildren. The elated, piercing tones (gutsy voices), a bouquet of peculiar young smells. This was the *gita* season, when class groups make outings in huge, plushly upholstered buses with white antimacassars. A young teacher read from a guidebook and gestured toward the garden's lemon house, where there was a toppled balustrade, a statue of a lion, a twisted-necked marble eagle checking out the newly arrived disturbance behind its back. Within the garden itself two young women crossed a gravel path. Signs of life. I made my way down the way I had come up.

The *portone* was open and I entered.

To the right was a carved stone tub, cordoned off. It was decorated with a crumbling oval-shaped relief. Had I not known from guidebooks that this sarcophagus was from the third century A.D. I'd have thought its medallion depicted an eighteenth-century high-busted noblewoman, a seductive fan to her chin—Crown Prince Fredrick's paramour?

I climbed the imposing staircase to view the garden from above. On the wide banister a white marble putto rides a lion-pawed eagle whose body emerges from a triton, a conical seashell. The loggia's walls and ceiling are richly decorated in false perspective. Above Alessandro Pfanner's apartment door an ethereal Fame blows a brass horn. In another ceiling panel two plump putti admire their reflections in gilded hand mirrors.

In 1996 Hollywood descended upon Lucca for the filming of *The Portrait of a Lady*, Nicole Kidman as Isabel Archer. Palazzo Pfanner became the home of English expatriate Gilbert Osmond, played by John Malkovich. Henry James had housed his esthete/cad upon "an olive-muffled hill" near Porta Romana in Florence. With its grand Ammannati proportions, Palazzo Pfanner bears little resemblance to

Osmond's "incommunicative" weather-worn house of irregularly sized windows, but in the film's final version we're shown so little of the palace that these reinterpretations don't matter. Director Jane Campion's portrait of Italy is uncharacteristically dark, a disenchanted April. Only the keenest Lucchese eye could recognize the Pfanner garden, Victorianized as it is in the blue shadows of huge brought-in pots of flowering hydrangeas—scenic designers working overtime to justify their fees.

The view from this high terrace shows the garden's concept of inclusion: garden, nearby campanile, city walls, hilly countryside; all of a piece, all characters in a single drama true as life, veiled now in a thin mist that tumbled softly in on a seasonal shifting breeze.

I entered the garden through a cast-iron gate, a turn-of-the-century security fence. It was topped with spearheads and miniature urns, strangely empty. There were four *Cycas revoluta* in antique lemon pots; one of them was five feet tall, and so ancient. I love the dark feathery *Cycas*; neither palm nor fern, it looks like both. It's a primitive conebearing plant, in fact, a sort of conifer, and it evokes the nineteenth century, when temperate Europe went mad for the tropicals.

I was welcomed by a pair of marble statues of a "not too vulgar chisel," according to eighteenth-century garden writer Cristoforo Martelli Leonardi. Hera, goddess of conjugal love, holds a broken torch, a peacock by her side. Peacocks once roamed free here, but this is the last of them, frozen in stone, the pet of Jupiter's bride. On my left, an old, bearded Zeus holds an eagle. But for the sounds of the central basin's jetting water, the caws of gliding crows, the polite cries of classics students at the *liceo* next door, the god of storms now stood in calm.

I tried to imagine this sort of statue standing in my garden's hedge. How would it look in the context of a house that's infinitely more modest than this celebrated palace? Where do you go to find works of art like these? The Pfanners seemed to have tons of statues, but they obviously weren't selling them off. A reception line of twelve of them leads to a central octagonal pool. The four elements preside: Vulcan, Mercury, Dionysus, Oceanus. Between the statues are potted lemons and new standard roses; one still wore its identifying tag: G. FIORE.

The basin drains via a carved stone sluice to three concentric half-circle pools lined with lava rock. Its raised border is planted out in a scheme of reds: red salvia, red geraniums, red standard roses, red canna.

Red was perhaps the gardenesque motif here when Felice Pfanner, in 1848, opened his beer garden. His café is said to have evoked Paris, the outdoor *Moulin de la Galette* painted by Renoir. Beneath the porticoed staircase, marble-topped tables were once stacked thick with glass mugs of beer brewed right on the premises. Local gentlemen tipped back their boaters and sipped through the froth, their ladies clutching parasols. Felice Pfanner was shameless. Winters, he froze the central basin with chemical additives so that he could ice skate as he'd done on lake Constance when he was a child.

No coins in the fountain. I was the only visitor now, the two ladies having left. The rising mist thinned, forming low white spindly clouds; their shadows scanned the grassy quadrangle by the disused brewery buildings, where towering bamboo set its tips to the breeze. Cats scuffled under an old crepe myrtle. The only plant of any interest here is an eight-foot-tall *Buxus harlandii*, the long-leaved box that brings to mind a plangent Korea or Japan.

A formal garden's abandon is most evident at its edges: where gravel meets grass, grass meets soil, soil meets plantings. This garden's seams were splitting with the unraveled threads of neglect. The spindly plants attested to the fact that no true gardener had touched the place in years—surely not with his hands, much less with his mind or heart. The antique lemon pots are numbered in whitewash, but their positions were random now, their varied sizes of no concern when places are assigned each spring. The same sickly French geraniums, stored in the *limonaia* in winter, find their way back out each April to wrought iron étagères, their dusty potting soil ever poorer. The topiary are misshapen blobs. All lines are broken; muddled statements go misunderstood. This garden is an echo, a sunned memory of grand emotions no longer felt, but it's a real and evocative one—we must tread very respectfully in such worlds.

But what did the Pfanner garden have to teach me, the budding garden maker, what lessons did it impart? This visit threw very little light on the palimpsest of my garden proposal at home. But I did learn this: a garden lives by virtue of the gardener's presence. When that presence is felt, the visitor emerges in a state of exaltation, the gardener's love somehow assumed. When it's not, he's sadly aware of its absence. More important than filling my garden with objects, statuary and urns, fountains or topiary, I'd fill it with the presence of my commitment.

My mind was on lunch. The clock tower at San Frediano chimed twelve. I counted the tollings and looked at my watch; one of us was off.

Back up on the wall, I crossed the half-circle base of a decapitated Roman defense tower. Before me and behind me stretched Passeggiata delle Mura, a Gothic nave of plane trees—city ramparts turned public park for a belle époque of peace. If I'd continued along this route for forty-five minutes I'd have been back where I was now, having seen the city from all sides. Nottolini, architect to the Lucchese Bourbon court, was garden designer here. In 1818 he planted limes and mulberries and long double rows of sycamores by order of Duchess Maria Luisa. Some of the trees are dying now—of disease, of old age, or both. Huge low stumps, weathered gray, mark where the worst cases occurred. Newly planted replacements stand promisingly between them.

A young woman appeared following a dog. It walked with a showy swagger, its tail coiled. The woman watched the ground just ahead of her, a profoundly remote smile on her face; it was as if she were reliving a recent joy, fortune, or success. She was cradling an opera score in her arms, the printed word VERDI visible at the top. She sang a single note, then softly cleared her throat. Running through the scale in my mind, I concluded that her note was a G, and that she was adrift in the reverie of the unsung score that framed it. "What kind of a dog is that?" I asked.

"*Un incrocio,*" she said. "*Husky e chow-chow.*"

"Its tongue is black," I said.

"*Sì sì,*" she confirmed, flattered.

This section of wall I walked was the most ancient of all, thirteenth century. Some of the stones, travertine blocks laid in plumb, date back to Roman times.

I passed the old city prison: walls of detention within walls of defense. Chet Baker resided here for a hitch on drug charges back in the sixties. People still talk about his red Ferrari that sat out gathering dust on a nearby street until his release. The houses in this quarter have balconies and terraces the same height as the ramparts. Potted plants, propagated from exchanged cuttings, were lined up in rows, watered by dripping laundry.

At Baluardo di Santa Croce a gardener took a midday nap on a park bench, his municipal orange overalls rolled up as a pillow. The woman with the chow sat at a picnic table and opened her music. On the clumpy grass by the circular brick battlements an American couple dutifully ate their *salumeria* (delicatessen) lunch, washing it down with mineral water sipped from a plastic bottle. Giulio in Pelleria was more my style: not a restaurant, an institution.

Most diners were single businessmen for whom a long central table offered plenty of room for each. One by one they laid down their cigarette packs, their sunglasses, their car keys: Merit, Armani, Alfa Romeo, status symbols all, consciously chosen. They crossed their legs away from each other. They unfolded their newspapers neatly, the pink *Gazzeta dello Sport*, the least expensive fashion accessory in Italy.

The owner seated me at a separate table even though I was alone. Foreign visitors are treated like dignitaries here—we'll sing Giulio's praises upon our return to that huge potential market of ours, won't we? His cordial welcoming is so practiced it reads like utter sincerity. He opened his arms as if to embrace me. He was chewing a Toscano, the twisted little black cigar that's manufactured here within the city walls. In the old days in Boston (this according to Gil's father) Italian Americans smoked cigars that looked like these. They were called "stogies." If you say the word Toscano several times fast it comes out stogie in the end.

Wine bottles, local labels, are lined up for display on shelves, but the inferior wine everyone drinks comes in *fiaschi* wrapped in straw; you pay for what you consume. The walls are hung with lithographs and drawings by Possenti, a living Lucchese painter who's been dining out on his inventory for years. The artist is self-portraitized in his every work. To my left, he's in bed with a ring-necked duck, an invasion of mixed fowl through the window over his washstand.

An elderly woman took the table to my right. Her pearls were dark, dated by their length: long as a flapper's. Her hair was gray, luminous, in place. Instantly she was served a plate of *panzanella*, a dish easily made at home: yesterday's Tuscan bread, onion, tomato, basil, olive oil. She took out a silver pillbox and picked through it, carefully portioning her dose. Her fingers trembled; her hooded eyelids fluttered. I imagined that this was her ritual one meal a day; that she lived alone; that in the evenings she suppered on *caffèlatte* and a sweet *cornetto*.

I thought about the fact that I'd had my very first meal in Lucca at this restaurant, in 1979. Our guides led us through a maze of foggy gray streets into the still murkier darkness of a typical evening here. I felt unforgivably foreign having just come from Milan, where I'd been underdressed but otherwise in my element. I ordered squid in *zimino*: squid, Swiss chard, garlic, and tomato concentrate, sautéed quickly over a hot flame. It was so rich in complex strong flavors that I couldn't finish it. The middle-aged couples around us seemed, for the freshness of their guilty looks, to be cheating on their husbands and wives. They smoked and made vulgar sucking noises with their jagged yellow teeth. I'd just got off a train and it was late and I was jet-lagged. I went away hungry, unintentionally drunk, finding fault. A year later we tried it again. On a bright morning in late summer. I had the *maccheroni tortellati*: heaven.

The owner now sat down with a client at a table next to mine. He extended his legs in his café chair, bearing his round stomach in pride. His sweatshirt read, ORIGINAL FLYING WEAR REGISTERED MARK. He admitted to his friend that he'd been smoking for fifty years.

His wife brought me bread in a Chinese-made basket. Her hair was bleached lemon yellow to the roots. I knew enough to refuse the menu; it's only for tourists. The regulars listen to verbal suggestions, seemingly personalized. "I have fresh *porcini* mushrooms with polenta," she said. She has the sweet, plump smile of motherly warmth; if this hard life as a restaurateur has involved any sacrifice on her part, she'd never let on.

I started with a plate of *farro* in a broth of *fagioli*. *Farro* in English is "spelt," but it tastes and looks like barley. This is an antique recipe, a Lucchese specialty. You make a broth of white beans, pass it through a sieve, then add a puree of sautéed garlic, onion, celery, carrot, and tomato. The spelt is cooked apart and added to the finished broth; it makes a thick, richly flavorful soup to be eaten tepid, never hot. Here at Giulio it's served in a shallow bowl. A single ladleful is all you need, garnished with a dribble of the newest olive oil, a dusting of fresh-ground pepper over the top. It's important not to mix the oil in, or you'll lose the occasional impact of that burst of pure olive flavor.

The owner was telling his friend that male painters have more success than females do; they get better prices. The restaurateur's a collector, it seemed. I looked again at his gallery of Possentis, imagining them removed. "These days," he said, "painters are bums; they're a mess. In the old days, they killed themselves working and were poor. Now they do nothing and they're rich."

At the center table, one man smoked, did a crossword puzzle in the paper, and ate a plate of horse meat tartar, all at the same time.

The owner's wife appeared by my side. She wore the little lacy white apron of a café waitress tied tightly around her waist.

"Is that horse meat American?" I asked, pointing.

"I don't know," she said. "Why?"

"I'd once read that most of the horse meat eaten in Europe is American, shipped out of Boston, in fact."

"I don't know anything of this," she said, "but it's very very good, our tartar."

"Is it an antique dish, like *farro?*"

"Oh no," she said. "Not at all. Twenty years ago, the local football team used to dine here every day at lunch. They asked my mother if she would serve them horse meat because it makes them strong. My mother got them the horse meat and they were very thankful. They ate it grilled at first, like beef steaks. But then one day one of them said, 'Signora, why don't you serve it to us raw, ground up, like steak tartar?' We all tried it and it was delicious. It was so, so good, truly. You know, at first the idea gave me chills just to think of it, but then one day I tried it. Wonderful!"

"What's in it?"

"Garlic, olive oil, lemon, and fresh basil. And then we invented the *salsa verde* to go with it. We put parsley, onion, pickled cucumber, and capers, and just a little mayonnaise. What a success we've had. Look around you. So many eating it."

A man at the center table picked his teeth with his knife. The old lady finished her *panzanella* and drained her glass of the same red wine I was drinking, a Chianti, according to the label.

My mushrooms and polenta arrived. On its white, wide-rimmed plate this could have been the work of a sophisticated chef who contrived total simplicity. The polenta was creamy and smooth and sat up like a soufflé in a gleaming rim of the mushrooms' saucy juices: olive oil, pureed tomato, and garlic.

In 1990 this restaurant moved from its previous location, the rustic ground floor of a worker's house around the corner, to Piazza San Donato. This new space is three times as big as the old, and so the luncheon waiting lines of before have vanished. Unfortunately, they hired the wrong architect to remodel the sixteenth-century building they now occupy. He gave them an architect's statement, school of Gae Aulenti: a Quai d'Orsay of a trattoria, slick fittings of green marble and enameled steel in a pastel postmodern palette. All the furniture was moved straight over from the old locale, however: the country café chairs, the antique bread-making stand, the green-and-white-checked tablecloths, the Possentis. The end product is like Gropius's housing development in Dessau-Törten: its eventual occupants never completed the Bauhaus dream; soon they unpacked their old ways, spread doilies, and hung lace curtains. But the food here has remained the same, traditional and tasty. I barely notice the architecture anymore, these flavors so transport.

"Enjoying the mushrooms?" asked the owner's wife.

"They're wonderful," I said.

"You're American," she said, "or are you English?"

"American," I confirmed yet again. I knew she'd never remember.

"And you didn't order chicken?"

"Chicken?"

"All Americans order chicken."

"Oh?" I said.

"At night in the summer, all the Americans are here and they all want chicken. You know, for us chicken is something you never eat. You eat chicken only in a poor, poor house when the hen is too old to lay eggs. But you Americans, you eat it every day. How it makes me laugh! I can go through fifty chickens in a night. Can you imagine? Nothing but chickens for you!"

Barbara Grizzuti Harrison

(1934–2002)

Italian American writer Barbara Grizzuti Harrison wrote in the foreword to her book *Italian Days* (1989), "I did not know, when I went to Italy, the nature of my undertaking . . . I understood this more clearly as I traveled south, to the sun . . . and to my family. I discovered everything I feared and everything I loved." Like many, her journey was one of reconciliation to the bifurcated life of the hyphenated American.

Grizzuti Harrison grew up in Brooklyn. When she was a child her mother left Catholicism and embraced the Jehovah's Witnesses' faith. Barbara converted with her mother, but her father and brother did not, creating a rift in an already contentious family. She remained a Jehovah's Witness, even working at the world headquarters in Brooklyn, until her early twenties, when she renounced the faith and left. She married in 1960, had two children, and divorced in 1968.

One of the seminal writers of the women's movement, Grizzuti Harrison contributed to *Ms.* magazine; her first book, *Unlearning the Lie: Sexism in School* (1960), was based on her children's experience in their Brooklyn school. A subsequent book, *Visions of Glory: A History and Memory of Jehovah's Witnesses*, is part autobiography, part history of her former faith. In middle age Grizzuti Harrison returned to Catholicism. She said that she was influenced by interviewing the Catholic activist Dorothy Day and by the high school English teacher who first encouraged her writing.

from ITALIAN DAYS

SAN GIMIGNANO: "City of Fine Towers"

A tower is the creation of another century. Without a past it is nothing.
Indeed, a new tower would be ridiculous.

—*Gaston Bachelard*

There are places one comes home to that one has never been to: San Gimignano.

An English spinster, almost deaf, attaches herself to me on the bus to San Gimignano. She tells me of her adventures and misadventures in Spain, Portugal, Italy—all having to do with trains nearly missed, roads not taken, the kindness of strangers. I am not feeling particularly generous or kindly, except toward the green hills and the fields of yellow flowers in which I wish to lose my thoughts. "Rape, I think those flowers are," she says, "horrible name. I think they make oil of it." I think it is saffron, perhaps crocus. . . .

Butter-yellow flowers bloom from the medieval towers for which San Gimignano is famous. They are variously called wallflowers and violets (and said by townspeople to grow nowhere else on earth). The small and fragrant flowers sprang up on the coffin of St. Fina (among whose gifts was the ability to extinguish house fires) and on the town's towers on the day of her death. (On that day bells tolled; they were rung by angels.) St. Fina is sometimes called the Saint of the Wallflowers. (*Wallflower*, in addition to its botanical meaning, in colloquial Italian means, as it does in English, a "girl who is not invited to dance"—*ragazza che fa da tappezzeria*.) She died when she was fifteen. She was loved for her goodness and beauty, she had butter-yellow hair, she once accepted an orange from a young man at a well, and she died on an oak plank in penance for what seems to have been an entirely blameless life. In paintings by Ghirlandaio in San Gimignano's cathedral, she is so slender and delicate, so attenuated, as to cause one pain.

Modest St. Fina, a silent slip of a girl, might seem an odd choice for veneration in a walled city of military architecture—proud ramparts and aggressive towers built by suspicious patrician families to hide treasures and to assert the will for power. (Alberti railed against towers, regarding them as antisocial; in the sixteenth century Cosimo de' Medici ordered a halt to the expansion of San Gimignano, forbidding the commune of Florence to allocate to it "even the slightest amount for any need, be it sacred or profane.")

There is a wrinkle in time in San Gimignano. There is no such thing as a mellow or lovable skyscraper, but the towers of San

Gimignano, glibly called the skyscrapers of Tuscany, seem to have been born old . . . or at least to have anticipated the day when gentle St. Fina would, like Rapunzel, who also lived in a tower and whose hair was also gold, seem the perfect anointing presence. One imagines her—one imagines both Rapunzel and St. Fina—at the top of a steep, narrow, spiraling stone stairway, breathing silently in a slender shaft of brief light from a narrow window . . . everything military has retreated from this fairy-tale place.

There are fourteen tall towers in San Gimignano; there were once seventy-two. They are surrounded, on the narrow city streets, by palazzi and modest houses, all higgledy-piggledy, with projecting Tuscan roofs. They stretch from earth to sky and are built on shifting soil; and they speak, as Georges Duby says, two languages: "on the one hand the unreal space of courtly myth, the vertical flight of mystic ascension, the linear curve carrying composition in to the scrolls of poetic reverie. And on the other, a rigorous marquetry offering the view of a compact universe, profound and solid." They have one peculiar property: their stones remain the same color—a gray-gold with a suggestion, a faint pentimento, of black—whether wet with rain or hot with sun. The little guidebook I bought in San Gimignano is quite lyrical and accurate about the walls and towers of San Gimignano, which embody, as its author says, the contradictions of the medieval mind, a mind "reserved and hospitable, bold and fearful. Fearful of enemies, of strangers, of night-time, of treasons." The walls kept enemies out; they also kept people in; they imparted, to those within, a "sense of community, of common interests and ideals never denied." San Gimignano is formidable in its beauty; every description of it I have ever read makes it sound both forbidding and delightful. Forbidding it once was, in the days of fratricidal warfare, when families threw collapsible wooden bridges from the window of one tower-fortress to that of another (the days when it traded with Egypt, Syria, and Tunisia and men vied for great wealth); now it is simply delightful. And sheltering. The walls cup and cradle (as, in Niccolò Gerini's painting of St. Fina, she cradles the walled city in her slender young arms). The towers exist not to keep enemies—the Other—out, but to house the soul warmly; one has a sense of great bodily integrity in these spaces; one feels safe. When St. Fina drove the Devil out of San Gimignano with a gesture of her long and lovely hand, she did it for us.

Because one yields, in San Gimignano, to the fancy that the world is created anew each day, that time does not, in the way we ordinarily understand it, exist, it is exactly right, and so lovely, to find in a deserted piazza a small thirteenth-century church dedicated to St. Augustine, whose reflections on the nature and measurement of time so profoundly informed his love of God (and anticipated the existentialists):

> But if the present were always present, and would not pass into the past, it would no longer be time, but eternity. Therefore, if the present, so as to be time, must be so constituted that it passes into the past, how can we say that it is, since the cause of its being is the fact that it will cease to be? Does it not follow that we can truly say that it is time, only because it tends towards non-being? . . . How, then, can . . . the past and the future be, when the past no longer is and the future as yet does not be?

On the chancel wall of the church are lively fifteenth-century frescoes by Benozzo Gozzoli of the life of the great theologian. I am surprised to see St. Monica plump, peasant-sturdy, and careworn; I always imagined that one who prayed unceasingly, as she did, for the salvation of her son, would find one's flesh melting in the process. (I think of a life of prayer as inimical to fat.) Of all the charming frescoes, the most charming is that of Augustine chatting with the infant Jesus about the Mystery of the Trinity (that which might be remote and austere Gozzoli rendered immediate and intimate); the Child attempts to empty the sea into a puddle—much as any child might at the seashore, with a pail, or a shell—the impossibility of which convinces Augustine that the Trinity cannot be comprehended by reason alone.

Everything You have made is beautiful, Augustine said to his God, but You are more beautiful than anything You have made. In the cloister of the Church of St. Augustine, that beauty is palpable; one feels one has entered the light and peace of God. The cloister is divided by box hedges into four quadrangular plots of land in which

grow irises and tulips and palm trees and white and yellow dande-
lions and pink and blue wandering flowers. . . . How sweet, these
enclosures within an enclosed opening: open/close, close/open; a
cypress punctuates each of four corners. A loggia—pots of yellow
flowers and geraniums—looks out over a central cistern; the scent of
lilacs is pervasive, the lilacs swarm with bees. The fragrance of lilacs
mingles with the fragrance of woodsmoke. I walk beneath a tree the
leaves of which are the color of China tea; a cobweb brushes across
my forehead. A jet plane streaks across the fragrance of lilacs; an
orange-and-black cat mews piteously in the garden.

(Were mazes an outgrowth and elaboration of these enclosures
within enclosures? Why would anyone wish to complicate and con-
volute so simple, satisfying, and sweet a design?)

The sacristan plucks tenacious thorns from my coat. He is listening to a popular love song on his transistor radio in the sacristy. I light
a candle and the sacristan extinguishes the flame. Even God has a
riposo in Italy at lunch hour.

My hotel, once a palazzo, is in the Piazza della Cisterna, in the
middle of which is a thirteenth-century cistern. From the piazza,
through the battlemented archway, I can reach the square of the
cathedral with its seven towers. I like the feel of the herringbone-
patterned bricks under my thin sandals. I wander up and down steep
hills, arched alleys, passing old men and women with canes. I never
want to leave. My terraced hilltop room looks out over roofs and
towers and blessed hills to the Val d'Elsa. I am beginning to believe
the Annunciation did take place here. Art plagiarizes nature. I want
to fly, as Cellini wanted to fly, "on a pair of wings made of waxed
linen." And I want to stay here, rooted, forever.

At dinner a baby crawls through the tunneled legs of diners, to the
cooing delight of waiters. A woman lights a cigarette, over which a
British man and woman make a great disapproving fuss. "There is no
remedy for death," the smoker says, coolly addressing the room at
large. She says this in English and then in Italian.

After dinner, in a dim lounge, I watch *Two Women*, a movie with
Sophia Loren. I am joined by the Italian woman who smokes. Out of
an abundance of feeling I cry, not so much because this is the story

of a rape, not because of the girl's loss of innocence and the mother's rage and grief, but because the injured girl is singing, her voice frail, a song my grandmother used to sing: "*Vieni, c'è una strada nel bosco* . . . I want you to know it, too . . . *c'è una strada nel cuore* . . . There's a road in my heart. . . ." The woman who smokes is crying, too. I am thinking of my daughter. When she leaves, the woman kisses the crown of my head. We have exchanged no words. Men have stood on the threshold and not come in. I never see her again.

I cross the piazza to sit in a brightly lit outdoor café. It is late. I am the only woman in the café. I fend off three approaches. I won't be denied the pleasure of seeing the light and shadows of the lovely square, the purple night sky. Inside, male voices are raised in a sentimental love song; they sing to the strings of a mandolin. Their singing is saccharine, their laugher is boisterous, and there are no women here. I wonder, with some little anger, what it would be like to be part of their sentimental, prideful, tough and tender world. I put on dark glasses. A little boy eating a gelato plays hide-and-seek, covering his eyes with sticky fingers (hide), waiting for me to smile (seek). A policeman strolls by apparently without purpose. I am an anomaly. I remove my glasses, thinking that if I can't see men's faces, they can't see mine.

What pleasure does it give men to sing of the beauty of women when there are no women in the café?

I find myself thinking of the handsome guide at the Davanzati who held the elevator for me.

The bed linen smells of lilacs. The air vibrates with the aftersound of bells.

In San Gimignano the birds sing all night long.

In the morning I drink my coffee from a mug bearing the words OLD TIME TEA.

In the Piazza della Cisterna there is a *sala di giochi*—video games. Is it possible that the children who grow up here—young men with studied, languid poses—think they are living in a hick town?

On the Via San Martino, away from the cathedral and the Cisterna, there is a café peopled entirely by old men. The café is part billiard parlor; newspapers are bought and read in common. I am accepted here in the morning light of day; I would not have been accepted here last night. I am served my morning coffee with old-fashioned gallantry by a man in a shiny black suit. With great difficulty he recites something he has been taught by an English-speaking cousin: "'We shall sit upon the ground and tell sad stories of the death of Kings.' Is sad?" he asks.

To leave a walled city is to feel evicted, cast out—cast out of paradise; no matter that the countryside outside the walls is paradisical.

The bus, full of high-spirited schoolchildren, that stopped at Porta San Giovanni was the wrong bus, but the driver took me on anyway, avuncularly advised the children to be more calm in the presence of *la bella signora*, and deposited me at the right bus stop. We went by back roads, and I had the sensation, for the first time in Tuscany, not of passing but of being in the countryside, part of (not merely an observer of) a gorgeous (and calm) crazy quilt of silver-green olive trees and flowering peach and cherry trees; the yellow-and-red bus wound its way through the intricate sensual folds of hills dignified by cypress trees: "And you, O God, saw all the things that you had made, and behold, 'they were very good.' For we also see them and behold, they are all very good."*

The bus went slowly, like a swimmer who loves the water too much to race and challenge it, and the world unfolded like a child's picture book: gardeners turning over soil with gnarled, patient hands; bronzed youths of Etruscan beauty casually strolling by the roadside as if here were just anywhere and everywhere was beautiful; showers of wisteria framing old women shelling peas in doorways; lovers picnicking in a vineyard; laughing nuns pushing children on orange swings, their heavy habits floating on magnolia-scented air: "Your works praise you."†

---

*Confessions of St. Augustine 13/28; 13/33.
†Ibid.

Robert Hellenga

(1941–)

"I was twenty-nine years old when the Arno flooded its banks on Friday 4 November 1966 . . . On Tuesday I decided to go to Italy, to offer my services as a humble book conservator, to save whatever could be saved, including myself." So begins Margot Harrington's adventure working as a "mud angel," an American volunteer trying to rescue Florence's waterlogged treasures. In the process she falls in love with an older, married man, Dottor Sandro Postiglione, and finds a long-lost series of sixteenth-century erotic drawings. Robert Hellenga's novel *The Sixteen Pleasures* (1989) takes its title from Harrington's discovery. In this excerpt Dottor Postiglione tries to salvage frescoes that are literally disappearing in the wake of the flood. Under the direction of Signor Giorgio Focacci, the *soprintendente* of the Uffizi, the monks of the Lodovici Chapel trained German-made heat lamps on their priceless frescoes, causing the surface paint to disintegrate. Sandro Postiglione tries to keep the paintings from vanishing altogether.

Author Robert Hellenga teaches at Knox College in Illinois, but lived for a time in Florence. In *The New York Times* he wrote of the difficulty of plunging into life as a resident before exhausting the city's tourist potential. "After a month in Florence we still haven't been to the Uffizi or to the Pitti Palace or the Bargello or the Duomo. My children are about to start school without knowing a word of Italian . . . all the places we haven't seen, we'll see as residents; all the friends we haven't met, we'll meet as neighbors; all the adventures we haven't had, we'll have in a place where we belong." Hellenga's subsequent novel, *The Fall of the Sparrow*, is also set, in part, in Italy.

from THE SIXTEEN PLEASURES

PRAY WITHOUT CEASING

There are many frescoed chapels in Florence that could fall to the wrecking ball without eliciting tears of regret from Dottor Postiglione, but the Lodovici Chapel in the Badia Fiorentina is not one of them. Quite the opposite, in fact. Its frescoes are, in their own way, as fine as those in the Carmine, and every bit as dramatic, though a recent (and highly controversial) restoration, carried out against his advice by a charlatan from the ministry in Rome, has rather tarted it up and destroyed some of the original charm.

"The brothers are praying in the chapel."

"You're hoping for a miracle, is that it?"

"God is good, Dottore, God is good."

"But tell me, Abbot Remo, what exactly has happened? The water damage was minimal, wasn't it? And I thought the *nafta* had been removed with great success?"

Signor Giorgio intervenes. "The heat lamps are your only hope, Abbot Remo. Believe me, you're too impatient. You have to pull the moisture out from behind the walls. You can't just snap your fingers and it's done. No. It takes time and patience."

"You command my greatest respect, Signor Giorgio," says the abbot, "but the situation is desperate and I must ask Dottor Postiglione to assist me."

"Very well, Abbot Remo, I wash my hands of the matter."

Signor Giorgio, fortunately, is not a man to hold a grudge. As long as he receives a salary commensurate with his exalted position as a *soprintendente* he will not take umbrage at trifling insults.

"See what you can do, Sandro," he says good-naturedly to Dottor Postiglione to show that he is not annoyed as he leaves.

The abbot *in extremis* is more painful to Dottor Postiglione than the abbot *in furore*. It is hard to believe that this is the same man who denounced him, in a letter to *La Nazione*, as an enemy of art and of progress.

"Everything that can be done will be done, I can assure you, Abbot Remo. I shall come myself. I have already telephoned for one of the vans. You should never have used those heat lamps; they work too fast."

"But Signor Giorgio—"

"Yes, Signor Giorgio and I don't see eye to eye on this question. Remember, Signor Giorgio is an administrator. But don't give up hope. We shall find something."

The abbot groans, and continues to groan, in the taxi that takes them to the Badia.

The church of the Badia Fiorentina has undergone many reconstructions. It was enlarged by Arnolfo di Cambio, architect of the Duomo, in 1282. The ruined campanile was reconstructed in 1330. The Cloister of the Oranges was added in 1435–40 by Bernardo Rossellino, who also constructed, in 1495, the portal that opens onto the present-day Via del Proconsolo. And finally, in the seventeenth century the entire structure was remodeled in the baroque style by Matteo Segaloni, who completely changed the orientation of the church, which is in the shape of a Greek cross, so that the high altar, once on the west end of the cross, is now on the east.

The Lodovici Chapel, which one reaches through a door in the west wall, was frescoed by an unknown painter (the "Master of the Badia Fiorentina") in the early fifteenth century, miraculously survived the radical reorientation by Matteo Segaloni and (even more miraculously) the attention of the nineteenth-century restorers, the same experts who repainted the Giotto frescoes in Santa Croce.

Dottor Postiglione pays the taxi driver—the abbot carries no money—and they enter the church, which is damp and chilly, through the portico on the Via del Proconsolo, and make their way to the Lodovici Chapel. The *dottore* experiences what a sinner who has frozen to death might feel upon waking up in hell, a pleasing warmth that almost immediately becomes intolerable. Two fantastical heating machines, like diabolical engines, have been trained at the base of the dado in an effort—evidently unsuccessful—to keep the moisture from rising to the level of the frescoes. This is the first time Dottor Postiglione has actually seen one of these machines, which the Committee to Rescue Italian Art has imported from Germany. The fires roar. The flames shoot blue and orange, licking the *pietra serena* panels of the dado, like the flames that tickle the feet of Pope Boniface VIII in the *Inferno*. They provide the only light in the room. Hellish. The noise is equally infernal, a roaring, mingled with the sound of the assembled monks, who have congregated to pray for the salvation of the frescoes. One of the brothers reads from the Ordinary, and the others give the responses in unison. The smell, too, is infernal. Electric, sulfuric, human. Twenty large, sweating, unwashed monks. (Dottor Postiglione suspects that they have congregated in this small room to get warm, the way people used to go to the movie theaters to get warm.) It is impossible to think in such circumstances. The *dottore* fishes in his pocket for some change and deposits one hundred lire in a little coin box. The electric light goes on and stays on for three minutes.

Art restorers, like plastic surgeons, learn to steel themselves against the power of painful visual stimuli: harelips, cleft palates, webbed hands and feet and other deformities for the one. For the other: mutilated canvases, deteriorating marble, crumbling stone, flaking pigments. But sometimes even the most hardened professional is caught by surprise, by a visual blow, as it were, to the solar plexus. The wind is knocked out of him, and he experiences a physical convulsion that is impossible to conceal. This is what happens to Dottor Postiglione when the light comes on and he catches sight of the frescoes.

He switches off the heaters and asks the abbot to dismiss the monks, who leave the warm room reluctantly and resume their prayers in the church itself. The light goes out and he fishes in his pocket for more change.

"You have to get some light in here," he snaps at the abbot.

"Yes, right away. I'll see to it immediately."

"Isn't there a switch to turn the light on so you don't have to keep putting change in the box?"

"Brother Sacristan will know, I'm sure."

"Get those heaters out of here." The *dottore* mops his high forehead with a handkerchief.

The abbot was right. The frescoes seem to be growing off the wall. They are moving, shimmering masses, like one of those idiotic religious cards you can buy at San Lorenzo: when you shift the angle slightly the picture changes from (say) Christ on the cross to (say) Christ ascending into heaven.

Though he is not a religious man, Dottor Postiglione crosses himself in the dark, still holding the handkerchief in his hand.

The watermark in the chapel is about two meters high. Some fuel oil remains on the lower part of the frescoes and on the clear gray stone at the base. The real problem, however, is not the water damage, or the oil slick, which can be removed. The real problem is that moisture rising *through* the tremendous walls of the old building not only carries with it salts from the ground, it dissolves the soluble salts that it encounters within the walls themselves, bringing them to the surface, where the water evaporates. The salts then crystallize, forming either superficial excrescences on the surface or cryptoflorescences within the actual pores of the wall. Various types of disintegration can occur at this point, depending on the nature of the salts themselves and the nature of the surface. As the crystals expand, something has to give way. Either the pores of the wall will break, causing the surface of the paint to disintegrate, or the crystals will be extruded in crystalline threads, like cotton candy. This is what is happening now. The crystals are growing so rapidly that you can almost see them forming, like whiskers. Not dark stubble, however, but translucent filaments, so that the surface of the painting, viewed from an angle, looks like a vertical field of wildflowers, something from the brush of an impressionist. But if the pressure exerted by the growing crystals becomes too strong, the paint surface will begin to crumble, and a work of art that has ministered to the needs of rich and poor alike for six centuries will disappear. As if someone were erasing a blackboard.

You can tear up a musical score without destroying the music. You can burn a novel without destroying the story. But a painting is itself, has no soul, no essence other than itself. It is what it is, a physical object. If it is destroyed it is gone forever. *Sic transit gloria mundi.* This is why Dottor Postiglione prefers it to the other fine arts.

"Calcium nitrates," Dottor Postiglione says to the abbot. "Too many dead bodies in the crypt. Too much nitrogen in the soil. You should have installed a moisture barrier as I recommended."

"Yes, Dottore, but where were we to find the money? You yourself know how difficult and expensive . . . What were we to do?"

The *dottore* sighs. The problem at hand won't be helped by getting into another argument with the abbot.

He tries to conceal the depth of his concern from Abbot Remo, but the abbot, like an anxious father, reads the *dottore*'s mind easily and resumes his pleading: "Dottore, you must *do* something."

The *dottore* looks at his watch, an uncharacteristic gesture, for he has never been an impatient man, not a man who got into a frenzy waiting for his wife to get dressed, or to return with the car, though when his wife moved to Rome she took the car. Since then something of the balance of life has been lost. The *dottore*'s work has become too important. Great works of art in the past have been lost. There are probably too many of them anyway, just as there are too many churches in Florence. But he doesn't like to see them go, and the Badia is a special place, a nice place to slip into and sit for a while if you're in the *centro*. There's a nice quiet cloister that's difficult to find unless you know where you're going. No one's likely to wander in there, not even the monks.

The abbot, unable to locate a light or an extension cord, stations a monk by the door. The monk keeps feeding hundred-lire pieces into the box to keep the lights on until the hastily assembled restoration crew arrives with floodlights and extension cords and the chapel begins to look like the scene of the crime in a detective show. A photographer starts snapping shots; the carpenters begin assembling a scaffolding; the technicians measure the humidity and the temperature. But there is no time for careful measurements and serious photographs to document the problem and the work. No time, even, for proper analysis of the salts, which is crucial in order to determine their exact composition. Something has to be done at once to retard the capillary action that is bringing the salts to the surface. A dramatic trial of strength is being enacted before their very eyes. If the crystals prove stronger than the pores in the wall, the *intonaco* itself— the surface coat of plaster that actually holds the paint—will begin to disintegrate and the painting will be lost. Student volunteers are bringing in ladders and a portable sink from the truck, and heavy glass bottles of various solvents and gels and fixatives, and boxes of Japanese tissues.

"Calcium sulfate?" Dottor Postiglione, altering his diagnosis, ventures a tentative opinion in the form of a question to one of the students. "I'm afraid so," he says, answering his own question. The sulfates are less soluble and therefore more dangerous than the nitrates. "Look at that patch there, and there." A white, opaque film has begun to form in several places near the lower edge of the fresco, where the donor, a Renaissance merchant, Francesco Lodovici, and his wife, kneel. The patches indicate the conversion of calcium carbonate into calcium sulfate within the *intonaco* itself, a cancer growing before his very eyes.

"Where's the nearest source of water?" he asks the abbot, who has returned with a small table lamp.

"In the *gabinetto*, Dottore, behind the sacristy."

"We'll need water. Some of your men will have to carry it. You have buckets?"

"Yes, Dottore. Brother Sacristan will know."

Dottor Postiglione lights a cigarette and throws the match on the floor. Holding his cigarette at arm's length, he inspects one of the white patches. "I've never seen anything like this," he says to one of the carpenters, an older man with small wide-set eyes. "I mean happening so fast. I warned Signor Giorgio about these heating machines. They're pulling the moisture up faster than it can evaporate, so the whole process is accelerating."

The carpenter touches his cheekbone to show that he appreciates the gravity of the situation.

A monk enters the chapel with a leaky wooden bucket of water from the *gabinetto*.

Dottor Postiglione, his cigarette dangling from his lips, removes his coat, rolls up his sleeves, washes his hands. Monks, gathered around the door, still chant and respond in a repetitive tribal ritual. Their chanting reminds Dottor Postiglione of the Buddhists who congregate in the apartment beneath him twice a day to chant wordlessly and meditate.

He measures thirty grams of ammonium bicarbonate into a wide-mouthed beaker. One of the carpenters drops a wrench and curses. A monk pours another bucket of water into the portable sink. The student volunteers watch in silence. Fifty grams of sodium bicarbonate. The bicarbonates form a base that will, if all goes well, dissolve the newly formed crystals. Twenty-five grams of Desogen (10 percent strength). The Desogen will "wet" the solution so that it will not form into droplets (like water droplets on a newly waxed car) and run down the surface of the painting. Six grams of carboxymethyl cellulose. To retain moisture.

Dottor Postiglione tears a sheet of Japanese tissue into small pieces, which he dips into the solution and applies to different areas of the painting, like small Band-Aids. The abbot, who has joined the monks in prayer, keeps popping back into the small chapel to see what's going on.

"How does it look, Dottore?"

Dottor Postiglione holds out his hand, palm down, and moves it from side to side, like a man trilling an octave on the piano, but slowly.

"I was too proud," the abbot says, "to listen to you before. I've learned something from—"

"Please, Abbot Remo. Let's forget the past."

"If I can help in any way . . ."

Dottor Postiglione puts an arm around the abbot and gently leads him to the door. "You belong here," he says, "with your children. Pray without ceasing, Abbot Remo, pray without ceasing."

William Dean Howells

(1 8 3 7 – 1 9 2 0)

Compared to his two great friends, Henry James and Mark Twain, William Dean Howells is little remembered, but in his time he was America's foremost critic and one of its most esteemed writers, considered a leading proponent of American realism. He worked for both *The Atlantic* and *Harper's* magazines and was the president of the American Academy of Arts and Letters. Howells promoted the work of many writers, including Stephen Crane, Emily Dickinson, and Paul Laurence Dunbar.

In 1860 Howells wrote a campaign biography of Abraham Lincoln and was rewarded with the post of consul to Venice. He lived in Italy for four years and several of his novels, including *Indian Summer* (1886), from which this excerpt is taken, are set there. *Indian Summer* is the story of three Americans in Florence: Theodore Colville, a middle-aged bachelor from Des Vaches, Indiana, who has come to Italy to take stock of his life; Lina Bowen, a comely widow with a nine-year-old daughter; and Mrs. Bowen's charge, Imogene Graham, a twenty-year-old beauty who sets her sights on Colville. The novel is a nineteenth-century comedy of manners, but gives an accurate portrait of the American community in Florence. This selection takes place during Carnival.

from INDIAN SUMMER

In that still air of the Florentine winter time seems to share the arrest of the natural forces, the repose of the elements. The pale blue sky is frequently overcast, and it rains two days out of five; sometimes, under extraordinary provocation from the north, a snowstorm whirls along under the low gray dome, and whitens the brown roofs, where a growth of spindling weeds and grass clothes the tiles the whole year round, and shows its delicate green above the gathered flakes. But for the most part the winds are laid, and the sole change is from quiet sun to quiet shower. This at least is the impression which remains in the senses of the sojourning stranger, whose days slip away with so little difference one from another that they seem really not to have passed, but, like the grass that keeps the hill-sides fresh round Florence all the winter long, to be waiting some decisive change of season before they begin.

The first of the Carnival sights, that marked the lapse of a month since his arrival, took Colville by surprise. He could not have believed that it was February yet if it had not been for the straggling maskers in armor whom he met one day in Via Borgognissanti, with their visors up for their better convenience in smoking. They were part of the chorus at one of the theatres, and they were going about to eke out their salaries with the gifts of people whose windows the festival season privileged them to play under. The silly spectacle stirred Colville's blood a little, as any sort of holiday preparation was apt to do. He thought that it afforded him a fair occasion to call at Palazzo Pinti, where he had not been so much of late as in the first days of his renewed acquaintance with Mrs. Bowen. He had at one time had the fancy that Mrs. Bowen was cool toward him. He might very well have been mistaken in this; in fact, she had several times addressed him the politest reproaches for not coming; but he made some evasion, and went only on the days when she was receiving other people, and when necessarily he saw very little of the family.

Miss Graham was always very friendly, but always very busy, drawing tea from the samovar, and looking after others. Effie Bowen dropped her eyes in re-established strangeness when she brought the basket of cake to him. There was one moment when he suspected that he had been talked over in family council, and put under a certain regimen. But he had no proof of this, and it had really nothing to do with his keeping away, which was largely accidental. He had taken up, with as much earnestness as he could reasonably expect of himself, that notion of studying the architectural expression of Florentine character at the different periods. He had spent a good deal of money in books, he had revived his youthful familiarity with the city, and he had made what acquaintance he could with people interested in such matters. He met some of these in the limited but very active society in which he mingled daily and nightly. After the first strangeness to any sort of social life had worn off, he found himself very fond of the prompt hospitalities which his introduction at Mrs. Bowen's had opened to him. His host—or more frequently it was his hostess—had sometimes merely an apartment at a hotel; perhaps the family was established in one of the furnished lodgings which stretch the whole length of the Lung' Arno on either hand, and abound in all the new streets approaching the Cascine, and had set up the simple and facile housekeeping of the sojourner in Florence for a few months; others had been living in the villa or the palace they had taken for years.

The more recent and transitory people expressed something of the prevailing English and American aestheticism in the decoration of their apartments, but the greater part accepted the Florentine drawing-room as their landlord had imagined it for them, with furniture and curtains in yellow satin, a cheap ingrain carpet thinly covering the stone floor, and a fire of little logs ineffectually blazing on the hearth, and flickering on the carved frames of the pictures on the wall and the nakedness of the frescoed allegories in the ceiling. Whether of longer or shorter stay, the sojourners were bound together by a common language and a common social tradition; they all had a Day, and on that day there was tea and bread and butter for every comer. They had one another to dine; there were evening parties, with dancing and without dancing. Colville even went to a fancy ball, where he was kept in countenance by several other Florentines of the period of Romola. At all these places he met nearly the same people, whose alien life in the midst of the native community struck him as one of the phases of modern civilization worthy of note, if not particular study; for he fancied it destined to a wider future throughout Europe, as the conditions in England and America grow more tiresome and more onerous. They seemed to see very little of Italian society, and to be shut out from practical knowledge of the local life by the terms upon which they had themselves insisted. Our race finds its simplified and cheapened London or New York in all its Continental resorts now, but nowhere has its taste been so much studied as in Italy, and especially in Florence. It was not, perhaps, the real Englishman or American who had been considered, but a *forestiere* conventionalized from the Florentine's observation of many Anglo-Saxons. But he had been so well conjectured that he was

hemmed round with a very fair illusion of his national circumstances.

It was not that he had his English or American doctor to prescribe
for him when sick, and his English or American apothecary to com-
pound his potion; it was not that there was an English tailor and an
American dentist, an English book-seller and an English baker, and
chapels of every shade of Protestantism, with Catholic preaching in
English every Sunday. These things were more or less matters of
necessity, but Colville objected that the barbers should offer him an
American shampoo; that the groceries should abound in English bis-
cuit and our own canned fruit and vegetables, and that the grocers'
clerks should be ambitious to read the labels of the Boston baked
beans. He heard—though he did not prove this by experiment—that
the master of a certain trattoria had studied the doughnut of New
England till he had actually surpassed the original in the qualities that
have undermined our digestion as a people. But above all it interested him to see that intense expression of American civilization, the
horse-car, triumphing along the magnificent avenues that mark the
line of the old city walls; and he recognized an instinctive obedience
to an abstruse natural law in the fact that whereas the omnibus,
which the Italians have derived from the English, was not filled
beyond its seating capacity, the horse-car was overcrowded without
and within at Florence just as it is with us who invented it.

"I wouldn't mind even that," he said one day to the lady who was
drawing him his fifth or sixth cup of tea for that afternoon, and with
whom he was naturally making this absurd condition of things a
matter of personal question; "but you people here pass your days in
a round of unbroken English, except when you talk with your servants. I'm not sure you don't speak English with the shop people. I
can hardly get them to speak Italian to me."

"Perhaps they think you can speak English better," said the lady.

This went over Florence; in a week it was told to Colville as something said to some one else. He fearlessly reclaimed it as said to himself, and this again was told. In the houses where he visited he had
the friendly acceptance of any intelligent and reasonably agreeable
person who comes promptly and willingly when he is asked, and
seems always to have enjoyed himself when he goes away. But

besides this sort of general favor, he enjoyed a very pleasing little personal popularity which came from his interest in other people, from his good-nature, and from his inertness. He slighted no acquaintance, and talked to every one with the same apparent wish to be entertaining. This was because he was incapable of the cruelty of open indifference when his lot was cast with a dull person, and also because he was mentally too lazy to contrive pretenses for getting away; besides, he did not really find anybody altogether a bore, and he had no wish to shine. He listened without shrinking to stories that he had heard before, and to things that had already been said to him; as has been noted, he had himself the habit of repeating his ideas with the recklessness of maturity, for he had lived long enough to know that this can be done with almost entire safety.

He haunted the studios a good deal, and through a retrospective affinity with art, and a human sympathy with the sacrifice which it always involves, he was on friendly terms with sculptors and painters who were not in every case so friendly with one another. More than once he saw the scars of old rivalries, and he might easily have been an adherent of two or three parties. But he tried to keep the freedom of the different camps without taking sides; and he felt the pathos of the case when they all told the same story of the disaster which the taste for bric-à-brac had wrought to the cause of art; how people who came abroad no longer gave orders for statues and pictures, but spent their money on curtains and carpets, old chests and chairs, and pots and pans. There were some among these artists whom he had known twenty years before in Florence, ardent and hopeful beginners; and now the backs of their gray or bald heads, as they talked to him with their faces toward their work, and a pencil or a pinch of clay held thoughtfully between their fingers, appealed to him as if he had remained young and prosperous, and they had gone forward to age and hard work. They were very quaint at times. They talked the American slang of the war days and of the days before the war; without a mastery of Italian, they often used the idioms of that tongue in their English speech. They were dim and vague about the country, with whose affairs they had kept up through the newspapers. Here and there one thought he was going home very soon; others had finally relinquished all thoughts of return. These had, perhaps without knowing it, lost the desire to come back; they cowered before the expensiveness of life in America, and doubted of a future with which, indeed, only the young can hopefully grapple. But in spite of their accumulated years, and the evil times on which they had fallen, Colville thought them mostly very happy men, leading simple and innocent lives in a world of the ideal, and rich in the inexhaustible beauty of the city, the sky, the air. They all, whether they were ever going back or not, were fervent Americans, and their ineffaceable nationality marked them, perhaps, all the more strongly for the patches of something alien that overlaid it in places. They knew that he was or had been a newspaper man; but if they secretly cherished the hope that he would bring them to the *dolce lume* of print, they never betrayed it; and the authorship of his letter about the American artists in Florence, which he printed in the *American Register* at Paris, was not traced to him for a whole week.

Colville was a frequent visitor of Mr. Waters, who had a lodging in Piazza San Marco, of the poverty which can always be decent in Italy. It was bare, but for the books that furnished it; with a table for his writing, on a corner of which he breakfasted, a wide sofa with cushions in coarse white linen that frankly confessed itself a bed by night, and two chairs of plain Italian walnut; but the windows, which had no sun, looked out upon the church and the convent sacred to the old Socinian for the sake of the meek, heroic mystic whom they keep alive in all the glory of his martyrdom. No two minds could well have been farther apart than the New England minister and the Florentine monk, and no two souls nearer together, as Colville recognized with a not irreverent smile.

When the old man was not looking up some point of his saint's history in his books, he was taking with the hopefulness of youth and the patience of age a lesson in colloquial Italian from his landlady's daughter, which he pronounced with a scholarly scrupulosity and a sincere atonic Massachusetts accent. He practiced the language wherever he could, especially at the trattoria where he dined, and where he made occasions to detain the waiter in conversation. They humored him, out of their national good-heartedness and sympathy, and they did what they could to realize a strange American dish for him on Sundays—a combination of stockfish and potatoes boiled, and then fried together in small cakes. They revered him as a foreign gentleman of saintly amiability and incomprehensible preferences; and he was held in equal regard at the next green-grocer's, where he spent every morning five centesimi for a bunch of radishes and ten for a little pat of butter to eat with his bread and coffee: he could not yet accustom himself to mere bread and coffee for breakfast, though he conformed as completely as he could to the Italian way of living. He respected the abstemiousness of the race; he held that it came from a spirituality of nature to which the North was still strange, with all its conscience and sense of individual accountability. He contended that he never suffered in his small dealings with these people from the dishonesty which most of his countrymen complained of; and he praised their unfailing gentleness of manner: this could arise only from goodness of heart, which was perhaps the best kind of goodness, after all.

None of these humble acquaintances of his could well have accounted for the impression they all had that he was some sort of ecclesiastic. They could never have understood—nor, for that matter, could any one have understood through European tradition—the sort of sacerdotal office that Mr. Waters had filled so long in the little deeply book-clubbed New England village where he had outlived most of his flock, till one day he rose in the midst of the surviving dyspeptics and consumptives and, following the example of Mr. Emerson, renounced his calling forever. By that time even the pale Unitarianism thinning out into paler doubt was no longer tenable with him. He confessed that while he felt the Divine goodness more and more, he believed that it was a mistake to preach any specific creed or doctrine, and he begged them to release him from their service. A young man came to fill his place in their pulpit, but he kept his place in their hearts. They raised a subscription of seventeen hundred dollars and thirty-five cents, and this being submitted to the new button manufacturer, who had founded his industry in the village, he promptly rounded it out to three thousand, and Mr. Waters came to Florence. His people parted with him in terms of regret as delicate as they were awkward, and their love followed him. He corresponded regularly with two or three ladies, and his letters were sometimes read from his pulpit.

Colville took the Piazza San Marco in on his way to Palazzo Pinti on the morning when he had made up his mind to go there, and he stood at the window looking out with the old man when some more maskers passed through the place—two young fellows in old Florentine dress, with a third habited as a nun.

"Ah," said the old man, gently, "I wish they hadn't introduced the nun! But I suppose they can't help signalizing their escape from the domination of the Church on all occasions. It's a natural reaction. It will all come right in time."

"You preach the true American gospel," said Colville.

"Of course. That *is* the gospel."

"Do you suppose that Savonarola would think it had all come out right," asked Colville, a little maliciously, "if he could look from the window with us here and see the wicked old Carnival, that he tried so hard to kill four hundred years ago, still alive? And kicking?" he added, in cognizance of the caper of one of the maskers.

"Oh yes; why not? By this time he knows that his puritanism was all a mistake, unless as a thing for the moment only. I should rather like to have Savonarola here with us; he would find these costumes familiar; they are of his time. I shall make a point of seeing all I can of the Carnival, as part of my study of Savonarola, if nothing else."

"I'm afraid you'll have to give yourself limitations," said Colville, as one of the maskers threw his arm round the mock-nun's neck. But the old man did not see this, and Colville did not feel it necessary to explain himself.

The maskers had passed out of the piazza now, and "Have you seen our friends at Palazzo Pinti lately?" said Mr. Waters.

"Not very," said Colville. "I was just on my way there."

"I wish you would make them my compliments. Such a beautiful young creature."

"Yes," said Colville, "she is certainly a beautiful girl."

"I meant Mrs. Bowen," returned the old man, quietly.

"Oh; I thought you meant Miss Graham. Mrs. Bowen is my contemporary, and so I didn't think of her when you said young. I should have called her pretty rather than beautiful."

"No; she's beautiful. The young girl is good-looking—I don't deny that; but she is very crude yet."

Colville laughed. "Crude in looks? I should have said Miss Graham was rather crude in mind, though I'm not sure I wouldn't have stopped at saying *young*."

"No," mildly persisted the old man; "she couldn't be crude in mind without being crude in looks."

"You mean," pursued Colville, smiling, but not wholly satisfied, "that she hasn't a lovely nature?"

"You never can know what sort of nature a young girl has. Her nature depends so much upon that of the man whose fate she shares."

"The woman is what the man makes her? That is convenient for the woman, and relieves her of all responsibility."

"The man is what the woman makes him, too, but not so much so. The man was cast into a deep sleep, you know—"

"And the woman was what he dreamed her. I wish she were!"

"In most cases she is," said Mr. Waters.

They did not pursue the matter. The truth that floated in the old minister's words pleased Colville by its vagueness, and flattered the man in him by its implication of the man's superiority. He wanted to say that if Mrs. Bowen were what the late Mr. Bowen had dreamed her, then the late Mr. Bowen, when cast into his deep sleep, must have had Lina Ridgely in his eye. But this seemed to be personalizing the fantasy unwarrantably, and pushing it too far. For like reason he forbore to say that if Mr. Waters's theory were correct, it would be better to begin with some one whom nobody else had dreamed before; then you could be sure at least of not having a wife to somebody else's mind rather than your own. Once on his way to Palazzo Pinti, he stopped, arrested by a thought that had not occurred to him before in relation to what Mr. Waters had been saying, and then pushed on with the sense of security which is the compensation the possession of the initiative brings to our sex along with many responsibilities. In the enjoyment of this, no man stops to consider the other side, which must wait his initiative, however they mean to meet it.

In the Por San Maria, Colville found masks and dominoes filling the shop windows and dangling from the doors. A devil in red and a clown in white crossed the way in front of him from an intersecting street; several children in pretty masquerading dresses flashed in and out among the crowd. He hurried to the Lung' Arno, and reached the palace where Mrs. Bowen lived with these holiday sights fresh in his mind. Imogene turned to meet him at the door of the apartment, running from the window where she had left Effie Bowen still gazing.

"We saw you coming," she said, gaily, without waiting to exchange formal greetings. "We didn't know at first but it might be somebody else disguised as you. We've been watching the maskers go by. Isn't it exciting?"

"Awfully," said Colville, going to the window with her, and putting his arm on Effie's shoulder, where she knelt in a chair looking out. "What have you seen?"

"Oh, only two Spanish students with mandolins," said Imogene; "but you can see they're *beginning* to come."

"They'll stop now," murmured Effie, with gentle disappointment; "it's commencing to rain."

"Oh, too bad!" wailed the young girl. But just then two mediaeval men-at-arms came in sight, carrying umbrellas. "Isn't that too delicious? Umbrellas and chain armor!"

"You can't expect them to let their chain armor get rusty," said Colville. "You ought to have been with me—minstrels in scale armor, Florentines of Savonarola's times, nuns, clowns, demons, fairies—no end to them."

"It's very well saying we ought to have been with you; but we can't go anywhere alone."

"I didn't say alone," said Colville. "Don't you think Mrs. Bowen would trust you with me to see these Carnival beginnings?" He had not meant at all to do anything of this kind, but that had not prevented his doing it.

"How do we know, when she hasn't been asked?" said Imogene, with a touch of burlesque dolor, such as makes a dignified girl enchanting, when she permits it to herself. She took Effie's hand in hers, the child having faced round from the window, and stood smoothing it, with her lovely head pathetically tilted on one side.

"What haven't I been asked yet?" demanded Mrs. Bowen, coming lightly toward them from a door at the side of the salon. She gave her hand to Colville with the prettiest grace, and a cordiality that brought a flush to her cheek. There had really been nothing between them but a little unreasoned coolness, if it were even so much as that; say rather a dryness, aggravated by time and absence, and now, as friends do, after a thing of that kind, they were suddenly glad to be good to each other.

"Why, you haven't been asked how you have been this long time," said Colville.

"I have been wanting to tell you for a whole week," returned Mrs. Bowen, seating the rest in taking a chair for herself. "Where have you been?"

"Oh, shut up in my cell at Hôtel d'Atene, writing a short history of the Florentine people for Miss Effie."

"Effie, take Mr. Colville's hat," said her mother. "We're going to make you stay to lunch," she explained to him.

"Is that so?" he asked, with an effect of polite curiosity.

"Yes." Imogene softly clapped her hands, unseen by Mrs. Bowen, for Colville's instruction that all was going well. If it delights women to pet an undangerous friend of our sex, to use him like one of themselves, there are no words to paint the soft and flattered content with which his spirit purrs under their caresses. "You must have nearly finished the history," added Mrs. Bowen.

"Well, I could have finished it," said Colville, "if I had only begun it. You see, writing a short history of the Florentine people is such quick work that you have to be careful how you actually put pen to paper, or you're through with it before you've had any fun out of it."

"I think Effie will like to read that kind of history," said her mother.

The child hung her head, and would not look at Colville; she was still shy with him; his absence must have seemed longer to a child, of course.

At lunch they talked of the Carnival sights that had begun to appear. He told of his call upon Mr. Waters and of the old minister's purpose to see all he could of the Carnival in order to judge intelligently of Savonarola's opposition to it.

"Mr. Waters is a very good man," said Mrs. Bowen, with the air of not meaning to approve him quite, nor yet to let any notion of his be made fun of in her presence. "But for my part I wish there were not going to be any Carnival; the city will be in such an uproar for the next two weeks."

"Oh, Mrs. Bowen!" cried Imogene, reproachfully. Effie looked at her mother in apparent anxiety lest she should be meaning to put forth an unquestionable power and stop the Carnival.

"The last Carnival, I thought there was never going to be any end to it; I was so glad when Lent came."

"Glad when *Lent* came!" breathed Imogene, in astonishment; but she ventured upon nothing more insubordinate, and Colville admired to see this spirited girl as subject to Mrs. Bowen as her own child. There is no reason why one woman should establish another woman over her, but nearly all women do it in one sort or another, from love of a voluntary submission, or from a fear of their own ignorance, if they are younger and more inexperienced than their lieges. Neither the one passion nor the other seems to reduce them to a like passivity as regards their husbands. They must apparently have a fetich of their own sex. Colville could see that Imogene obeyed Mrs. Bowen not only as a protégée but as a devotee.

"Oh, I suppose *you* will have to go through it all," said Mrs. Bowen, in reward of the girls' acquiescence.

"You're rather out of the way of it up here," said Colville. "You had better let me go about with the young ladies—if you can trust them to the care of an old fellow like me."

"Oh, I don't think you're so very old, at all times," replied Mrs. Bowen, with a peculiar look, whether indulgent or reproachful he could not quite make out.

But he replied, boldly, in his turn: "I have certainly my moments of being young still; I don't deny it. There's always a danger of their occurrence."

"I was thinking," said Mrs. Bowen, with a graceful effect of not listening, "that you would let me go too. It would be quite like old times."

"Only too much honor and pleasure," returned Colville, "if you will leave out the old times. I'm not particular about having them along." Mrs. Bowen joined in laughing at the joke, which they had to themselves. "I was only consulting an explicit abhorrence of yours in not asking you to go at first," he explained.

"Oh yes; I understand that."

The excellence of the whole arrangement seemed to grow upon Mrs. Bowen. "Of course," she said, "Imogene ought to see all she can of the Carnival. She may not have another chance, and perhaps if she had, *he* wouldn't consent."

"I'll engage to get *his* consent," said the girl. "What I was afraid of was that I couldn't get yours, Mrs. Bowen."

"Am I so severe as that?" asked Mrs. Bowen, softly.

"Quite," replied Imogene.

"Perhaps," thought Colville, "it isn't always silent submission."

For no very good reason that any one could give, the Carnival that year was not a brilliant one. Colville's party seemed to be always meeting the same maskers on the street, and the maskers did not greatly increase in numbers. There were a few more of them after night-fall, but they were then a little more bacchanal, and he felt it was better the ladies had gone home by that time. In the pursuit of the tempered pleasure of looking up the maskers he was able to make the reflection that their fantastic and vivid dresses sympathized in a striking way with the architecture of the city, and gave them an effect of Florence which he could not otherwise have had. There came by-and-by a little attempt at a *corso* in Via Cerratani and Via Tornabuoni. There were some masks in carriages, and from one they actually threw plaster *confetti*; half a dozen bare-legged boys ran before and beat one another with bladders. Some people, but not many, watched the show from the windows, and the footways were crowded.

Having proposed that they should see the Carnival together, Colville had made himself responsible for it to the Bowen household. Imogene said, "Well, is *this* the famous Carnival of Florence?"

"It certainly doesn't compare with the Carnival last year," said Mrs. Bowen.

"Your reproach is just, Mrs. Bowen," he acknowledged. "I've managed it badly. But you know I've been out of practice a great while there in Des Vaches."

"Oh, poor Mr. Colville!" cried Imogene. "He isn't altogether to blame."

"I don't know," said Mrs. Bowen, humoring the joke in her turn. "It seems to me that if he had consulted us a little earlier, he might have done better."

He drove home with the ladies, and Mrs. Bowen made him stay to tea. As if she felt that he needed to be consoled for the failure of his Carnival, she was especially indulgent with him. She played to him on the piano some of the songs that were in fashion when they were in Florence together before. Imogene had never heard them; she had heard her mother speak of them. One or two of them were negro songs, such as very pretty young ladies used to sing without harm to themselves or offense to others; but Imogene decided that they were rather rowdy. "Dear me, Mrs. Bowen! Did *you* sing such songs? You wouldn't let Effie!"

"No, I wouldn't let Effie. The times are changed. I wouldn't let Effie go to the theatre alone with a young gentleman."

"The times are changed for the worse," Colville began. "What harm ever came to a young man from a young lady's going alone to the theatre with him?"

He staid till the candles were brought in, and then went away only because, as he said, they had not asked him to stay to dinner.

He came nearly every day, upon one pretext or another, and he met them oftener than that at the teas and on the days of other ladies in Florence; for he was finding the busy idleness of the life very pleasant, and he went everywhere. He formed the habit of carrying flowers to the Palazzo Pinti, excusing himself on the ground that they were so cheap and so abundant as to be impersonal. He brought violets to Effie and roses to Imogene; to Mrs. Bowen he always brought a bunch of the huge purple anemones which grow so abundantly all winter long about Florence. "I wonder why *purple* anemones?" he asked her one day in presenting them to her.

"Oh, it is quite time I should be wearing purple," she said, gently.

"Ah, Mrs. Bowen!" he reproached her. "Why do I bring purple violets to Miss Effie?"

"You must ask Effie!" said Mrs. Bowen, with a laugh.

After that he staid away forty-eight hours, and then appeared with a bunch of the red anemones, as large as tulips, which light up the meadow grass when it begins to stir from its torpor in the spring. "They grew on purpose to set me right with you," he said, "and I saw them when I was in the country."

It was a little triumph for him, which she celebrated by putting them in a vase on her table, and telling people who exclaimed over them that they were some Mr. Colville gathered in the country. He enjoyed his privileges at her house with the futureless satisfaction of a man. He liked to go about with the Bowens; he was seen with the ladies, driving and walking, in most of their promenades. He directed their visits to the churches and the galleries; he was fond of strolling about with Effie's daintily gloved little hand in his. He took her to Giacosa's and treated her to ices; he let her choose from the confectioner's prettiest caprices in candy; he was allowed to bring the child presents in his pockets. Perhaps he was not as conscientious as he might have been in his behavior with the little girl. He did what he could to spoil her, or at least to relax the severity of the training she had received; he liked to see the struggle that went on in the mother's mind against this, and then the other struggle with which she overcame her opposition to it. The worst he did was to teach Effie some picturesque Western phrases, which she used with innocent effectiveness; she committed the crimes against convention which he taught her with all the conventional elegance of her training. The most that he ever gained for her were some concessions in going out in weather that her mother thought unfit, or sitting up for half-hours after her bedtime. He ordered books for her from Goodban's, and it was Colville now, and not the Rev. Mr. Morton, who read poetry aloud to the ladies on afternoons when Mrs. Bowen gave orders that she and Miss Graham should be denied to all other comers.

It was an intimacy; and society in Florence is not blind, and especially it is not dumb. The old lady who had celebrated Mrs. Bowen to him the first night at Palazzo Pinti led a life of active question as to what was the supreme attraction to Colville there, and she referred her doubt to every friend with whom she drank tea. She philosophized the situation very scientifically, and if not very conclusively, how few are the absolute conclusions of science upon any point!

"He is a bachelor, and there is a natural affinity between bachelors and widows—much more than if he were a widower too. If he were a widower, I should say it was undoubtedly mademoiselle. If he were a little *bit* younger, I should have no doubt it was madame; but men of that age have such an ambition to marry young girls! I suppose that they think it proves they are not so very old, after all. And certainly he isn't too old to marry. If he were wise—which he probably isn't, if he's like other men in such matters—there wouldn't be any question about Mrs. Bowen. Pretty creature! And so much sense! Too much for him. Ah, my dear, how we are wasted upon that sex!"

Mrs. Bowen herself treated the affair with masterly frankness. More than once in varying phrase she said: "You are very good to give us so much of your time, Mr. Colville, and I won't pretend I don't know it. You're helping me out with a very hazardous experiment. When I undertook to see Imogene through a winter in Florence, I didn't reflect what a very gay time girls have at home, in Western towns especially. But I haven't heard her breathe Buffalo once. And I'm sure it's doing her a great deal of good here. She's naturally got a very good mind; she's very ambitious to be cultivated. She's read a good deal, and she's anxious to know history and art; and your advice and criticism are the greatest possible advantage to her."

"Thank you," said Colville, with a fine, remote dissatisfaction. "I supposed I was merely enjoying myself."

He had lately begun to haunt his banker's for information in regard to the Carnival balls, with the hope that something might be made out of them. But either there were to be no great Carnival balls, or it was a mistake to suppose that his banker ought to know about them. Colville went experimentally to one of the people's balls at a minor theatre, which he found advertised on the house walls. At half past ten the dancing had not begun, but the masks were arriving; young women in gay silks and dirty white gloves; men in women's dresses, with enormous hands; girls as pages; clowns, pantaloons, old women, and the like. They were all very good-humored; the men, who far outnumbered the women, danced contentedly together. Colville liked two cavalry soldiers who waltzed with each other for an hour, and then went off to a battery on exhibition in the pit, and had as much electricity as they could hold. He liked also two young citizens who danced together as long as he staid, and did not leave off even for electrical refreshment. He came away at midnight, pushing out of the theatre through a crowd of people at the door, some of whom were tipsy. This certainly would not have done for the ladies, though the people were civilly tipsy.

Henry James

(1843–1916)

Henry James and Edith Wharton were great friends, American expatriates who chose to settle in Europe—James in England and Wharton in France. Although personally close (Wharton once wrote to him of her unhappy marriage and James responded simply, "Keep making the movements of life"), their work was stylistically and temperamentally quite different. He drew sensitive portraits of women; her heroines were calculating and successful. James wrote probably the two greatest novels about the clash between European sensibilities and American wealth in *Daisy Miller* (1879) and *The Portrait of a Lady* (1881). His novel *Confidence* (also published in 1879), from which this selection is excerpted, is set in Siena.

Henry James traveled relentlessly, oftentimes with Wharton, who drove her Panhard-Levassor. He never tired of revisiting his favorite places and wrote, "There are times and places that come back yet again, but that when the brooding tourist puts out his hand to them, meet it a little slowly, or even seem to recede a step, as if in slight fear of some liberty he may take. Surely they should know by this time that he is capable of taking none." In his nomadic life he became friends with almost all of the literary and political giants of the nineteenth century: Thoreau, Emerson, Hawthorne, Mark Twain, Teddy Roosevelt, William Dean Howells, John Singer Sargent, Robert Louis Stevenson, Robert Browning, Oliver Wendell Holmes, Alfred Lord Tennyson, James McNeill Whistler. Ironically, James, arguably one of the greatest writers of all, made little money. Toward the end of his life he got a literary advance of eight thousand dollars, although in fact Wharton had secretly arranged for the money to come from her account. In 1915 James decided to become a British citizen and on New Year's Day 1916 the king gave him the Order of Merit. Henry James died two months later on February 28 and is buried in England.

from CONFIDENCE

It was in the early days of April; Bernard Longueville had been spending the winter in Rome. He had travelled northward with the consciousness of several social duties that appealed to him from the further side of the Alps, but he was under the charm of the Italian spring, and he made a pretext for lingering. He had spent five days at Siena, where he had intended to spend but two, and still it was impossible to continue his journey. He was a young man of a con- templative and speculative turn, and this was his first visit to Italy, so that if he dallied by the way he should not be harshly judged. He had a fancy for sketching, and it was on his conscience to take a few pic- torial notes. There were two old inns at Siena, both of them very shabby and very dirty. The one at which Longueville had taken up his abode was entered by a dark, pestiferous arch-way, surmounted by a sign which at a distance might have been read by the travellers as the Dantean injunction to renounce all hope. The other was not far off, and the day after his arrival, as he passed it, he saw two ladies going in who evidently belonged to the large fraternity of Anglo-Saxon tourists, and one of whom was young and carried herself very well. Longueville had his share—or more than his share—of gallantry, and this incident awakened a regret. If he had gone to the other inn he might have had charming company: at his own establishment there was no one but an aesthetic German who smoked bad tobacco in the dining-room. He remarked to himself that this was always his luck, and the remark was characteristic of the man; it was charged with the feeling of the moment, but it was not absolutely just; it was the result of an acute impression made by the particular occasion; but it failed in appreciation of a providence which had sprinkled Longueville's career with happy accidents—accidents, especially, in which his characteristic gallantry was not allowed to rust for want of exercise. He lounged, however, contentedly enough through these bright, still days of a Tuscan April, drawing much entertainment from the high picturesqueness of the things about him. Siena, a few years since, was a flawless gift of the Middle Ages to the modern imagination. No other Italian city could have been more interesting to an observer fond of reconstructing obsolete manners. This was a taste of Bernard Longueville's, who had a relish for serious literature, and at one time had made several lively excursions into mediaeval history. His friends thought him very clever, and at the same time had an easy feeling about him which was a tribute to his freedom from pedantry. He was clever indeed, and an excellent companion; but the real measure of his brilliancy was in the success with which he entertained himself. He was much addicted to conversing with his own wit, and he greatly enjoyed his own society. Clever as he often was in talking with his friends, I am not sure that his best things, as the phrase is, were not for his own ears. And this was not on account of any cynical contempt for the understanding of his fellow-creatures: it was simply because what I have called his own society was more of a stimulus than that of most other people. And yet he was not for this reason fond of solitude; he was, on the contrary, a very sociable animal. It must be admitted at the outset that he had a nature which seemed at several points to contradict itself, as will probably be perceived in the course of this narration.

He entertained himself greatly with his reflections and meditations upon Sienese architecture and early Tuscan art upon Italian street-life and the geological idiosyncrasies of the Apennines. If he had only gone to the other inn, that nice-looking girl whom he had seen passing under the dusky portal with her face turned away from him might have broken bread with him at this intellectual banquet. Then came a day, however, when it seemed for a moment that if she were disposed she might gather up the crumbs of the feast. Longueville, every morning after breakfast, took a turn in the great square of Siena—the vast piazza, shaped like a horse-shoe, where the market is held beneath the windows of that crenellated palace from whose overhanging cornice a tall, straight tower springs up with a movement as light as that of a single plume in the bonnet of a captain. Here he strolled about, watching a brown *contadino* disembarrass his donkey, noting the progress of half an hour's chaffer over a bundle of carrots, wishing a young girl with eyes like animated agates would let him sketch her, and gazing up at intervals at the beautiful, slim tower, as it played at contrasts with the large blue air. After he had spent the greater part of a week in these grave considerations, he made up his mind to leave Siena. But he was not content with what he had done for his portfolio. Siena was eminently sketchable, but he had not been industrious. On the last morning of his visit, as he stood staring about him in the crowded piazza, and feeling that, in spite of its picturesqueness, this was an awkward place for setting up an easel, he bethought himself, by contrast, of a quiet corner in another part of the town, which he had chanced upon in one of his first walks—an angle of a lonely terrace that abutted upon the city-wall, where three or four superannuated objects seemed to slumber in the sunshine—the open door of an empty church, with a faded fresco exposed to the air in the arch above it, and an ancient beggar-woman sitting beside it on a three-legged stool. The little terrace had an old polished parapet, about as high as a man's breast, above which was a view of strange, sad-colored hills. Outside, to the left, the wall of the town made an outward bend, and exposed its rugged and rusty complexion. There was a smooth stone bench set into the wall of the church, on which Longueville had rested for an hour, observing the composition of the little picture of which I have indicated the elements, and of which the parapet of the terrace would form the foreground. The thing was what painters call a subject, and he had promised himself to come back with his utensils. This morning he returned to the inn and took possession of them, and then he made his way through a labyrinth of empty streets, lying on the edge of the town, within the wall, like the superfluous folds of a garment whose wearer has shrunken with old age. He reached his little grass-grown terrace, and found it as sunny and as private as before. The old mendicant was mumbling petitions, sacred and profane, at the church door; but save for this the stillness was unbroken. The yellow sunshine warmed the brown surface of the city-wall, and lighted the hollows of the Etruscan hills. Longueville settled himself on the empty bench, and, arranging his little portable apparatus, began to ply his brushes. He worked for some time smoothly and rapidly, with an agreeable sense of the absence of obstacles. It seemed almost an interruption when, in the silent air, he heard a distant bell in the town strike noon. Shortly after this, there was another interruption. The sound of a soft footstep caused him to look up; whereupon he saw a young woman standing there and bending her

eyes upon the graceful artist. A second glance assured him that she
was that nice girl whom he had seen going into the other inn with her
mother, and suggested that she had just emerged from the little
church. He suspected, however—I hardly know why—that she had
been looking at him, for some moments before he perceived her. It
would perhaps be impertinent to inquire what she thought of him;
but Longueville, in the space of an instant, made two or three reflections upon the young lady. One of them was to the effect that she
was a handsome creature, but that she looked rather bold; the burden
of the other was that—yes, decidedly—she was a compatriot. She
turned away almost as soon as she met his eyes; he had hardly time to
raise his hat, as, after a moment's hesitation, he proceeded to do. She
herself appeared to feel a certain hesitation; she glanced back at the
church door, as if under the impulse to retrace her steps. She stood
there a moment longer—long enough to let him see that she was a
person of easy attitudes—and then she walked away slowly to the
parapet of the terrace. Here she stationed herself, leaning her arms
upon the high stone ledge, presenting her back to Longueville, and
gazing at rural Italy. Longueville went on with his sketch, but less
attentively than before. He wondered what this young lady was doing
there alone, and then it occurred to him that her companion—her
mother, presumably—was in the church. The two ladies had been in
the church when he arrived; women liked to sit in churches; they had
been there more than half an hour, and the mother had not enough
of it even yet. The young lady, however, at present preferred the view
that Longueville was painting; he became aware that she had placed
herself in the very centre of his foreground. His first feeling was that
she would spoil it; his second was that she would improve it. Little by
little she turned more into profile, leaning only one arm upon the
parapet, while the other hand, holding her folded parasol, hung down
at her side. She was motionless; it was almost as if she were standing
there on purpose to be drawn. Yes, certainly she improved the picture. Her profile, delicate and thin, defined itself against the sky, in
the clear shadow of a coquettish hat; her figure was light; she bent
and leaned easily; she wore a gray dress, fastened up as was then the
fashion, and displaying the broad edge of a crimson petticoat. She

kept her position; she seemed absorbed in the view. "Is she *posing*— is she attitudinizing for my benefit?" Longueville asked of himself. And then it seemed to him that this was a needless assumption, for the prospect was quite beautiful enough to be looked at for itself, and there was nothing impossible in a pretty girl having a love of fine landscape. "But posing or not," he went on, "I will put her into my sketch. She has simply put herself in. It will give it a human interest. There is nothing like having a human interest." So, with the ready skill that he possessed, he introduced the young girl's figure into his foreground, and at the end of ten minutes he had almost made something that had the form of a likeness. "If she will only be quiet for another ten minutes," he said, "the thing will really be a picture." Unfortunately, the young lady was not quiet; she had apparently had enough of her attitude and her view. She turned away, facing Longueville again, and slowly came back, as if to re-enter the church. To do so she had to pass near him, and as she approached he instinc- tively got up, holding his drawing in one hand. She looked at him again, with that expression that he had mentally characterized as "bold," a few minutes before—with dark, intelligent eyes. Her hair was dark and dense; she was a strikingly handsome girl.

"I am so sorry you moved," he said, confidently, in English. "You were so—so beautiful."

She stopped, looking at him more directly than ever; and she looked at his sketch, which he held out toward her. At the sketch, however, she only glanced, whereas there was observation in the eye that she bent upon Longueville. He never knew whether she had blushed; he afterward thought she might have been frightened. Nev- ertheless, it was not exactly terror that appeared to dictate her answer to Longueville's speech.

"I am much obliged to you. Don't you think you have looked at me enough?"

"By no means. I should like so much to finish my drawing."

"I am not a professional model," said the young lady.

"No. That's my difficulty," Longueville answered, laughing. "I can't propose to remunerate you."

The young lady seemed to think this joke in indifferent taste. She turned away in silence; but something in her expression, in his feeling at the time, in the situation, incited Longueville to higher play. He felt a lively need of carrying his point.

"You see it will be pure kindness," he went on,—"a simple act of charity. Five minutes will be enough. Treat me as an Italian beggar."

She had laid down his sketch and had stepped forward. He stood there, obsequious, clasping his hands and smiling.

His interruptress stopped and looked at him again, as if she thought him a very odd person; but she seemed amused. Now, at any rate, she was not frightened. She seemed even disposed to provoke him a little.

"I wish to go to my mother," she said.

"Where is your mother?" the young man asked.

"In the church, of course, I didn't come here alone!"

"Of course not; but you may be sure that your mother is very contented. I have been in that little church. It is charming. She is just resting there; she is probably tired. If you will kindly give me five minutes more, she will come out to you."

"Five minutes?" the young girl asked.

"Five minutes will do. I shall be eternally grateful." Longueville was amused at himself as he said this. He cared infinitely less for his sketch than the words appeared to imply; but, somehow, he cared greatly that this graceful stranger should do what he had proposed.

The graceful stranger dropped an eye on the sketch again.

"Is your picture so good as that?" she asked.

"I have a great deal of talent," he answered, laughing. "You shall see for yourself, when it is finished."

She turned slowly toward the terrace again.

"You certainly have a great deal of talent, to induce me to do what you ask." And she walked to where she had stood before. Longueville made a movement to go with her, as if to show her the attitude he meant; but, pointing with decision to his easel, she said—

"You have only five minutes." He immediately went back to his work, and she made a vague attempt to take up her position. "You must tell me if this will do," she added, in a moment.

"It will do beautifully," Longueville answered, in a happy tone, looking at her and plying his brush. "It is immensely good of you to take so much trouble."

For a moment she made no rejoinder, but presently she said—

"Of course if I pose at all I wish to pose well."

"You pose admirably," said Longueville.

After this she said nothing, and for several minutes he painted rapidly and in silence. He felt a certain excitement, and the movement of his thoughts kept pace with that of his brush. It was very true that she posed admirably; she was a fine creature to paint. Her prettiness inspired him, and also her audacity, as he was content to regard it for the moment. He wondered about her—who she was, and what she was—perceiving that the so-called audacity was not vulgar boldness, but the play of an original and probably interesting character. It was obvious that she was a perfect lady, but it was equally obvious that she was irregularly clever. Longueville's little figure was a success—a charming success, he thought, as he put on the last touches. While he was doing this, his model's companion came into view. She came out of the church, pausing a moment as she looked from her daughter to the young man in the corner of the terrace; then she walked straight over to the young girl. She was a delicate little gentlewoman, with a light, quick step.

Longueville's five minutes were up; so, leaving his place, he approached the two ladies, sketch in hand. The elder one, who had passed her hand into her daughter's arm, looked up at him with clear, surprised eyes; she was a charming old woman. Her eyes were very pretty, and on either side of them, above a pair of fine dark brows, was a band of silvery hair, rather coquettishly arranged.

"It is my portrait," said her daughter, as Longueville drew near. "This gentleman has been sketching me."

"Sketching you, dearest?" murmured her mother. "Wasn't it rather sudden?"

"Very sudden—very abrupt!" exclaimed the young girl with a laugh.

"Considering all that, it's very good," said Longueville, offering his picture to the elder lady, who took it and began to examine it. "I can't tell you how much I thank you," he said to his model.

"It's very well for you to thank me now," she replied. "You really had no right to begin."

"The temptation was so great."

"We should resist temptation. And you should have asked my leave."

"I was afraid you would refuse it; and you stood there, just in my line of vision."

"You should have asked me to get out of it."

"I should have been very sorry. Besides, it would have been extremely rude."

The young girl looked at him a moment.

"Yes, I think it would. But what you have done is ruder."

"It is a hard case!" said Longueville. "What could I have done, then, decently?"

"It's a beautiful drawing," murmured the elder lady, handing the thing back to Longueville. Her daughter, meanwhile, had not even glanced at it.

"You might have waited till I should go away," this argumentative young person continued.

Longueville shook his head.

"I never lose opportunities!"

"You might have sketched me afterwards, from memory."

Longueville looked at her, smiling.

"Judge how much better my memory will be now!"

She also smiled a little, but instantly became serious.

"For myself, it's an episode I shall try to forget. I don't like the part I have played in it."

"May you never play a less becoming one!" cried Longueville. "I hope that your mother, at least, will accept a memento of the occasion." And he turned again with his sketch to her companion, who had been listening to the girl's conversation with this enterprising stranger, and looking from one to the other with an air of earnest confusion. "Won't you do me the honor of keeping my sketch?" he said. "I think it really looks like your daughter."

"Oh, thank you, thank you; I hardly dare," murmured the lady, with a deprecating gesture.

"It will serve as a kind of amends for the liberty I have taken,"

Longueville added; and he began to remove the drawing from its paper block.

"It makes it worse for you to give it to us," said the young girl.

"Oh, my dear, I am sure it's lovely!" exclaimed her mother. "It's wonderfully like you."

"I think that also makes it worse!"

Longueville was at last nettled. The young lady's perversity was perhaps not exactly malignant; but it was certainly ungracious. She seemed to desire to present herself as a beautiful tormentress.

"How does it make it worse?" he asked, with a frown.

He believed she was clever, and she was certainly ready. Now, however, she reflected a moment before answering.

"That you should give us your sketch," she said at last.

"It was to your mother I offered it," Longueville observed.

But this observation, the fruit of his irritation, appeared to have no effect upon the young girl.

"Isn't it what painters call a study?" she went on. "A study is of use to the painter himself. Your justification would be that you should keep your sketch, and that it might be of use to you."

"My daughter is a study, sir, you will say," said the elder lady in a little, light, conciliating voice, and graciously accepting the drawing again.

"I will admit," said Longueville, "that I am very inconsistent. Set it down to my esteem, madam," he added, looking at the mother.

"That's for you, mamma," said his model, disengaging her arm from her mother's hand and turning away.

The mamma stood looking at the sketch with a smile which seemed to express a tender desire to reconcile all accidents.

"It's extremely beautiful," she murmured, "and if you insist on my taking it—"

"I shall regard it as a great honor."

"Very well, then; with many thanks, I will keep it." She looked at the young man a moment, while her daughter walked away. Longueville thought her a delightful little person; she struck him as a sort of transfigured Quakeress—a mystic with a practical side. "I am sure you think she's a strange girl," she said.

"She is extremely pretty."

"She is very clever," said the mother.

"She is wonderfully graceful."

"Ah, but she's good!" cried the old lady.

"I am sure she comes honestly by that," said Longueville expressively, while his companion, returning his salutation with a certain scrupulous grace of her own, hurried after her daughter.

Longueville remained there staring at the view but not especially seeing it. He felt as if he had at once enjoyed and lost an opportunity. After a while he tried to make a sketch of the old beggar-woman who sat there in a sort of palsied immobility, like a rickety statue at a church-door. But his attempt to produce her features was not gratifying, and he suddenly laid down his brush. She was not pretty enough—she had a bad profile.

Erica Jong

(1942 –   )

"I've been in love with Italy since I was nineteen," says Erica Jong. "I love the Mediterranean landscape. I love olive trees. I love cypress trees. If I could be in any landscape I wanted, it would be a Mediterranean landscape."

Jong was born in New York City to an iconoclastic Jewish family. Her mother was a painter whose talent was thwarted. "My mother's frustrations powered both my feminism and my writing," Jong says. Erica painted and wrote from an early age and her first collection of poetry, *Fruits and Vegetables*, was published in 1971. Her next book forever changed American literature. Thirty years after its publication, Erica Jong is inextricably linked to her autobiographical novel *Fear of Flying*, its exploration of uncharted feminist territory, and the life and lust of its protagonist, Isadora Wing. Although John Updike, Henry Miller, and Philip Roth had written of male sexuality, few authors had examined women's lives with such candor. In the process Jong coined a phrase for uncomplicated, spontaneous, shameless sex. "I used to worry that they would put 'zipless fuck' on my tombstone," she confessed. "I don't anymore though. I know it's rare for a book to touch so many lives and I am really humbled by it."

Since *Fear of Flying*, Jong has published poetry, essays, novels, and a midlife memoir, *Fear of Fifty*, in which she wrote, "I have written openly about sex, appropriated male picaresque adventures for women, poked fun at the sacred cows of our society. I have lived as I chose, married, divorced, remarried, divorced, remarried and divorced again . . . this is the most heinous of my sins—not having done these things, but confessed to them in print."

"Ritratto," a candid, poignant look at the Italian Romeo, is from *Becoming Light: Poems New and Selected* (1991).

RITRATTO

He was a two-bit Petrarchist who lounged
Near the Uffizi in the ochre afternoons
Surveying the girls. A certain insolence
In how he moved his hips, his stony eyes,
His hands which seemed to cup their breasts like fruit
As they slid by, pretending blank disdain,
Won him a modest reputation in a place
Where sad-eyed satyrs of an ageless middle age
Are seldom scarce.
                On rainy days he stalked
The galleries. Between the Giottos
And Masaccios, he slithered hissing
In his moccasins, and whistling low.

His metaphors were old; the girls were young.
Their eyes (he said) were little lakes of blue
(Rolling the *bella lingua* off his tongue).
Their hair was gold, their lips like flowers that grew
Within his *bel' giardino* on the hill,
(Although he had no garden on the hill,
In summer the young girls grew thick as weeds.)

Blonds were his passion but (like Tacitus) he thought
The German fräuleins blowzy, rugged, rough
And yet inevitable: August brought
Such hordes as might have sacked another Rome.
He always sent the fair barbarians home
With something Burckhardt hardly hinted at.
(He kept his assignations in a Fiat.)

You should have seen his little pied-à-terre—
Two blocks from where his mother lived; there
He kept his treasures: blonds of every nation—
(Two dozen half-undressed U.N. legations)—

Were photographically ensconced along his wall.
Beside the crucifix and Virgin was a small
Photo of *la Mamma*—which surveyed,
With madamely aplomb, the girls he'd laid.
(Note also: right below the feet of God,
A shelf with hair oil and *Justine* by Sade.)

D. H. Lawrence

(1885–1930)

David Herbert Lawrence and his wife Frieda were true nomads—perpetual travelers or houseguests. Born in England, Lawrence was the fourth child of battling parents. He once said, "I was born hating my father, as early as ever I can remember." His mother encouraged his interest in art and he briefly taught in South London. After his first novel, *The White Peacock*, was published, Lawrence met Frieda von Richthofen, a married mother of three children. Two months later they eloped and their gypsy lives began.

Over the next years the Lawrences lived in France, Italy, Ceylon, Australia, New Mexico, and Mexico. D. H. Lawrence is most famous for the publication of *Lady Chatterley's Lover*, the story of a well-off woman, the wife of a paralyzed veteran, who has an affair with a gardener and becomes pregnant with his child. One of the models for the cuckolder-gardener was a young Italian soldier, Angelino Ravagli. Banned in both the United States and England, *Lady Chatterley* was published privately in 1928, but not released in an unexpurgated version until 1960 after an obscenity trial. One of the witnesses for the defense was E. M. Forster.

In 1925 Lawrence discovered that he had tuberculosis and he and Frieda returned from New Mexico to Europe. Lawrence died in Vence, France, and his ashes were buried in New Mexico. *Etruscan Places*, from which this selection is excerpted, was published posthumously in 1932. In 1950 Frieda married Angelino Ravagli, with whom she had had an affair in 1925.

from ETRUSCAN PLACES

VOLTERRA

Volterra is the most northerly of the great Etruscan cities of the west. It lies back some thirty miles from the sea, on a towering great bluff of rock that gets all the winds and sees all the world, looking out down the valley of the Cecina to the sea, south over vale and high land to the tips of Elba, north to the imminent mountains of Carrara, inward over the wide hills of the Pre-Apennines, to the heart of Tuscany.

You leave the Rome–Pisa train at Cecina, and slowly wind up the valley of the stream of that name, a green, romantic, forgotten sort of valley, in spite of all the come-and-go of ancient Etruscans and Romans, medieval Volterrans and Pisans, and modern traffic. But the traffic is not heavy. Volterra is a sort of inland island, still curiously isolated, and grim.

The small, forlorn little train comes to a stop at the Saline de Volterra, the famous old salt works now belonging to the State, where brine is pumped out of deep wells. What passengers remain in the train are transferred to one old little coach across the platform, and at length this coach starts to creep like a beetle up the slope, up a cog-and-ratchet line, shoved by a small engine behind. Up the steep but round slope among the vineyards and olives you pass almost at walking-pace, and there is not a flower to be seen, only the beans make a whiff of perfume now and then, on the chill air, as you rise and rise, above the valley below, coming level with the high hills to the south, and the bluff of rock with its two or three towers, ahead.

After a certain amount of backing and changing, the fragment of a train eases up at a bit of a cold wayside station, and is finished. The world lies below. You get out, transfer yourself to a small ancient motor-omnibus, and are rattled up to the final level of the city, into a cold and gloomy little square, where the hotel is.

The hotel is simple and somewhat rough, but quite friendly, pleasant in its haphazard way. And what is more, it has central heating, and the heat is on, this cold, almost icy, April afternoon. Volterra lies only 1800 feet above the sea, but it is right in the wind, and cold as any Alp.

The day was Sunday, and there was a sense of excitement and fussing, and a bustling in and out of temporarily important persons, and altogether a smell of politics in the air. The waiter brought us tea, of a sort, and I asked him what was doing. He replied that a great banquet was to be given this evening to the new *podestà* who had come from Florence to govern the city, under the new regime. And evidently he felt that this was such a hugely important "party" occasion we poor outsiders were of no account.

It was a cold, grey afternoon, with winds round the hard dark corners of the hard, narrow medieval town, and crowds of black-dressed, rather squat little men and pseudo-elegant young women pushing and loitering in the streets, and altogether that sense of furtive grinning and jeering and threatening which always accompanies a public occasion—a political one especially—in Italy, in the more out-of-the-way centres. It is as if the people, alabaster-workers and a few peasants, were not sure which side they wanted to be on, and therefore were all the more ready to exterminate anyone who was on the other side. This fundamental uneasiness, indecision, is most curious in the Italian soul. It is as if the people could never be wholeheartedly anything: because they can't trust anything. And this inability to trust is at the root of the political extravagance and frenzy. They don't trust themselves, so how can they trust their "leaders" or their "party"?

Volterra, standing sombre and chilly alone on her rock, has always, from Etruscan days on, been grimly jealous of her own independence. Especially she has struggled against the Florentine yoke. So what her actual feelings are, about this new-old sort of village tyrant, the *podestà*, whom she is banqueting this evening, it would be hard, probably, even for the Volterrans themselves to say. Anyhow the cheeky girls salute one with the "Roman" salute, out of sheer effrontery: a salute which has nothing to do with me, so I don't return it. Politics of all sorts are anathema. But in an Etruscan city which held out so long against Rome I consider the Roman salute unbecoming, and the Roman *imperium* unmentionable.

It is amusing to see on the walls, too, chalked fiercely up: *Morte a Lenin!* though that poor gentleman has been long enough dead, surely even for a Volterran to have heard of it. And more amusing still is the legend permanently painted: *Mussolini ha sempre ragione!* Some are born infallible, some achieve infallibility, and some have it thrust upon them.

But it is not for me to put even my little finger in any political pie. I am sure every post-war country has hard enough work to get itself governed, without outsiders interfering or commenting. Let those rule who can rule.

We wander on, a little dismally, looking at the stony stoniness of the medieval town. Perhaps on a warm sunny day it might be pleasant, when shadow was attractive and a breeze welcome. But on a cold, grey, windy afternoon of April, Sunday, always especially dismal, with all the people in the streets, bored and uneasy, and the stone buildings peculiarly sombre and hard and resistant, it is no fun. I don't care about the bleak but truly medieval piazza: I don't care if the Palazzo Pubblico has all sorts of amusing coats of arms on it: I don't care about the cold cathedral, though it is rather nice really, with a glow of dusky candles and a smell of Sunday incense: I am disappointed in the wooden sculpture of the taking down of Jesus, and the bas-reliefs don't interest me. In short, I am hard to please.

The modern town is not very large. We went down a long, stony street, and out of the Porta dell'Arco, the famous old Etruscan gate. It is a deep old gateway, almost a tunnel, with the outer arch facing the desolate country on the skew, built at an angle to the old road, to catch the approaching enemy on his right side, where the shield did not cover him. Up handsome and round goes the arch, at a good height, and with that peculiar weighty richness of ancient things; and three dark heads, now worn featureless, reach out curiously and inquiringly, one from the keystone of the arch, one from each of the arch bases, to gaze from the city and into the steep hollow of the world beyond.

Strange, dark old Etruscan heads of the city gate, even now they are featureless they still have a peculiar, out-reaching life of their own. Ducati says they represented the heads of slain enemies hung at the city gate. But they don't hang. They stretch with curious eagerness forward. Nonsense about dead heads. They were city deities of some sort.

And the archaeologists say that only the doorposts of the outer arch, and the inner walls, are Etruscan work. The Romans restored the arch, and set the heads back in their old positions. (Unlike the Romans to set anything back in its old position!) While the wall above the arch is merely medieval.

But we'll call it Etruscan still. The roots of the gate, and the dark heads, these they cannot take away from the Etruscans. And the heads are still on the watch.

The land falls away steeply, across the road in front of the arch. The road itself turns east, under the walls of the modern city, above the world: and the sides of the road, as usual outside the gates, are dump-heaps, dump-heaps of plaster and rubble, dump-heaps of the white powder from the alabaster works, the waste edge of the town.

The path turns away from under the city wall, and dips down along the brow of the hill. To the right we can see the tower of the church of Santa Chiara, standing on a little platform of the irregularly-dropping hill. And we are going there. So we dip downwards above a Dantesque, desolate world, down to Santa Chiara, and beyond. Here the path follows the top of what remains of the old Etruscan wall. On the right are little olive-gardens and bits of wheat. Away beyond is the dismal sort of crest of modern Volterra. We walk along, past the few flowers and the thick ivy, and the bushes of broom and marjoram, on what was once the Etruscan wall, far out from the present city wall. On the left the land drops steeply, in uneven and unhappy descents.

The great hilltop or headland on which Etruscan "Volterra," *Velathri, Vlathri,* once stood spreads out jaggedly, with deep-cleft valleys in between, more or less in view, spreading two or three miles away. It is something like a hand, the bluff steep of the palm sweeping in a great curve on the east and south, to seawards, the peninsulas of fingers running jaggedly inland. And the great wall of the Etruscan city swept round the south and eastern bluff, on the crest of steeps and cliffs, turned north and crossed the first finger, or peninsula, then started up hill and down dale over the fingers and into the declivities, a wild and fierce sort of way, hemming in the great crest. The modern town occupies merely the highest bit of the Etruscan city site.

The walls themselves are not much to look at, when you climb down. They are only fragments, now, huge fragments of embankment, rather than wall, built of uncemented square masonry, in the grim, sad sort of stone. One only feels, for some reason, depressed. And it is pleasant to look at the lover and his lass going along the top of the ramparts, which are now olive-orchards, away from the town. At least they are alive and cheerful and quick.

On from Santa Chiara the road takes us through the grim and depressing little suburb-hamlet of San Giusto, a black street that emerges upon the waste open place where the church of San Giusto rises like a huge and astonishing barn. It is so tall, the interior should be impressive. But no! It is merely nothing. The architects have achieved nothing, with all that tallness. The children play around with loud yells and ferocity. It is Sunday evening, near sundown, and cold.

Beyond this monument of Christian dreariness we come to the Etruscan walls again, and what was evidently once an Etruscan gate: a dip in the wall-bank, with the groove of an old road running to it.

Here we sit on the ancient heaps of masonry and look into weird yawning gulfs, like vast quarries. The swallows, turning their blue backs, skim away from the ancient lips and over the really dizzy depths, in the yellow light of evening, catching the upward gusts of wind, and flickering aside like lost fragments of life, truly frightening above those ghastly hollows. The lower depths are dark grey, ashy in colour, and in part wet, and the whole thing looks new, as if it were some enormous quarry all slipping down.

This place is called *Le Balze*—the cliffs. Apparently the waters which fall on the heights of Volterra collect in part underneath the deep hill and wear away at some places the lower strata, so that the earth falls in immense collapses. Across the gulf, away from the town, stands a big, old, picturesque, isolated building, the *Badia* or Monastery of the Camaldolesi, sad-looking, destined at last to be devoured by *Le Balze*, its old walls already splitting and yielding.

From time to time, going up to the town homewards, we come to the edge of the walls and look out into the vast glow of gold, which is sunset, marvellous, the steep ravines sinking in darkness, the farther valley silently, greenly gold, with hills breathing luminously up, passing out into the pure, sheer gold gleams of the far-off sea, in which a shadow, perhaps an island, moves like a mote of life. And like great guardians the Carrara mountains jut forward, naked in the pure light like flesh, with their crests portentous: so that they seem to be advancing on us: while all the vast concavity of the west roars with gold liquescency, as if the last hour had come, and the gods were smelting us all back into yellow transmuted oneness.

But nothing is being transmuted. We turn our faces, a little frightened, from the vast blaze of gold, and in the dark, hard streets the town band is just chirping up, brassily out of tune as usual, and the populace, with some maidens in white, are streaming in crowds towards the piazza. And, like the band, the populace also is out of tune, buzzing with the inevitable suppressed jeering. But they are going to form a procession.

When we come to the square in front of the hotel, and look out from the edge into the hollow world of the west, the light is sunk red, redness gleams up from the far-off sea below, pure and fierce, and the hollow places in between are dark. Over all the world is a low red glint. But only the town, with its narrow streets and electric light, is impervious.

The banquet, apparently, was not till nine o'clock, and all was hubbub. B. and I dined alone soon after seven, like two orphans whom the waiters managed to remember in between whiles. They were so thrilled getting all the glasses and goblets and decanters, hundreds of them, it seemed, out of the big chiffonnier-cupboard that occupied the back of the dining-room and whirling them away, stacks of glittering glass, to the banquet-room: while out-of-work young men would poke their heads in through the doorway, black hats on, overcoats hung over one shoulder, and gaze with bright inquiry through the room, as though they expected to see Lazarus risen, and not seeing him, would depart again to the nowhere whence they came. A banquet is a banquet, even if it is given to the devil himself; and the *podestà* may be an angel of light.

Outside was cold and dark. In the distance the town band tooted spasmodically, as if it were short-winded this chilly Sunday evening. And we, not bidden to the feast, went to bed. To be awakened occasionally by sudden and roaring noises—perhaps applause—and the loud and unmistakable howling of a child, well after midnight.

Morning was cold and grey again, with a chilly and forbidding country yawning and gaping and lapsing away beneath us. The sea was invisible. We walked the narrow cold streets, where high, cold, dark stone walls seemed almost to press together, and we looked in at the alabaster workshops, where workmen, in Monday-morning gloom and half-awakedness, were turning the soft alabaster, or cutting it out, or polishing it.

Everybody knows Volterra marble—so called—nowadays, because of the translucent bowls of it which hang under the electric lights, as shades, in half the hotels of the world. It is nearly as transparent as alum, and nearly as soft. They peel it down as if it were soap, and tint it pink or amber or blue, and turn it into all those things one does not want: tinted alabaster lampshades, light-bowls, statues, tinted or untinted, vases, bowls with doves on the rim, or vine-leaves, and similar curios. The trade seems to be going strong. Perhaps it is the electric-light demand: perhaps there is a revival of interest in "statuary." Anyhow there is no love lost between a Volterran alabaster worker and the lump of pale Volterran earth he turns into marketable form. Alas for the goddess of sculptured form, she has gone from here also.

But it is the old alabaster jars we want to see, not the new. As we hurry down the stony street the rain, icy cold, begins to fall. We flee through the glass doors of the museum, which has just opened, and which seems as if the alabaster inside had to be kept at a low temperature, for the place is dead-cold as a refrigerator.

Cold, silent, empty, unhappy the museum seems. But at last an old and dazed man arrives, in uniform, and asks quite scared what we want. "Why, to see the museum!" "*Ah! Ah! Ah sì—sì!*" It just dawns upon him that the museum is there to be looked at. "*Ah sì, sì, Signori!*"

We pay our tickets, and start in. It is really a very attractive and pleasant museum, but we had struck such a bitter cold April morning, with icy rain falling in the courtyard, that I felt as near to being in the tomb as I have ever done. Yet very soon, in the rooms with all those hundreds of little sarcophagi, ash-coffins, or urns, as they are called, the strength of the old life began to warm one up.

Urn is not a good word, because it suggests, to me at least, a vase, an amphora, a round and shapely jar: perhaps through association with Keats's "Ode to a Grecian Urn"—which vessel no doubt wasn't an urn at all, but a wine-jar—and with the "tea-urn" of children's parties. These Volterran urns, though correctly enough used for storing the ashes of the dead, are not round, they are not jars, they are small alabaster sarcophagi. And they are a peculiarity of Volterra. Probably because the Volterrans had the alabaster to hand.

Anyhow here you have them in hundreds, and they are curiously alive and attractive. They are not considered very highly as "art." One of the latest Italian writers on Etruscan things, Ducati, says: "If they have small interest from the artistic point of view, they are extremely valuable for the scenes they represent, either mythological or relative to the beliefs in the after-life."

George Dennis, however, though he too does not find much "art" in Etruscan things, says of the Volterran ash-chests: "The touches of Nature on these Etruscan urns, so simply but eloquently expressed, must appeal to the sympathies of all—they are chords to which every heart must respond: and I envy not the man who can walk through this museum unmoved without feeling a tear rise in his eye"

> And recognizing ever and anon
> The breeze of Nature stirring in his soul.

The breeze of Nature no longer shakes dewdrops from our eyes, at least so readily, but Dennis is more alive than Ducati to that which is alive. What men mean nowadays by "art" it would be hard to say. Even Dennis said that the Etruscans never approached the pure, the sublime, the perfect beauty which Flaxman reached. Today, this makes us laugh: the Greekified illustrator of Pope's *Homer*! But the same instinct lies at the back of our idea of "art" still. Art is still to us something which has been well cooked—like a plate of spaghetti. An ear of wheat is not yet "art." Wait, wait till it has been turned into pure, into perfect macaroni.

For me, I get more real pleasure out of these Volterran ash-chests than out of—I had almost said, the Parthenon frieze. One wearies of the aesthetic quality—a quality which takes the edge off everything, and makes it seem "boiled down." A great deal of pure Greek beauty has this boiled-down effect. It is too much cooked in the artistic consciousness.

In Dennis's day a broken Greek or Greekish amphora would fetch thousands of crowns in the market, if it was the right "period," etc.

These Volterran urns fetched hardly anything. Which is a mercy, or they would be scattered to the ends of the earth.

As it is, they are fascinating, like an open book of life, and one has no sense of weariness with them, though there are so many. They warm one up, like being in the midst of life.

The downstairs rooms of ash-chests contain those urns representing "Etruscan" subjects: those of sea-monsters, the sea-man with fish-tail, and with wings, the sea-woman the same: or the man with serpent-legs, and wings, or the woman the same. It was Etruscan to give these creatures wings, not Greek.

If we remember that in the old world the centre of all power was at the depths of the earth, and at the depths of the sea, while the sun was only a moving subsidiary body: and that the serpent represented the vivid powers of the inner earth, not only such powers as volcanic and earthquake, but the quick powers that run up the roots of plants and establish the great body of the tree, the tree of life, and run up the feet and legs of man, to establish the heart: while the fish was the symbol of the depths of the waters, whence even light is born: we shall see the ancient power these symbols had over the imagination of the Volterrans. They were a people faced with the sea, and living in a volcanic country.

Then the powers of the earth and the powers of the sea take life as they give life. They have their terrific as well as their prolific aspect.

Someone says the wings of the water-deities represent evaporation towards the sun, and the curving tails of the dolphin represent torrents. This is part of the great and controlling ancient idea of the come-and-go of the life-power, the surging up, in a flutter of leaves and a radiation of wings, and the surging back, in torrents and waves and the eternal downpour of death.

Other common symbolic animals in Volterra are the beaked griffins, the creatures of the powers that tear asunder and, at the same time, are guardians of the treasure. They are lion and eagle combined, of the sky and of the earth with caverns. They do not allow the treasure of life, the gold, which we should perhaps translate as consciousness, to be stolen by thieves of life. They are guardians of the treasure: and then, they are the tearers asunder of those who must depart from life.

It is these creatures, creatures of the elements, which carry men away into death, over the border between the elements. So is the dolphin, sometimes; and so the hippocampus, the sea-horse; and so the centaur.

The horse is always the symbol of the strong animal life of man: and sometimes he rises, a sea-horse, from the ocean: and sometimes he is a land creature, and half-man. And so he occurs on the tombs, as the passion in man returning into the sea, the soul retreating into the death-world at the depths of the waters: or sometimes he is a centaur, sometimes a female centaur, sometimes clothed in a lion-skin, to show his dread aspect, bearing the soul back, away, off into the other-world.

It would be very interesting to know if there were a definite connexion between the scene on the ash-chest and the dead whose ashes it contained. When the fish-tailed sea-god entangles a man to bear him off, does it mean drowning at sea? And when a man is caught in the writhing serpent-legs of the Medusa, or of the winged snake-power, does it mean a fall to earth; a death from the earth, in some manner; as a fall, or the dropping of a rock, or the bite of a snake? And the soul carried off by a winged centaur: is it a man dead of some passion that carried him away?

But more interesting even than the symbolic scenes are those scenes from actual life, such as boar-hunts, circus-games, processions, departures in covered wagons, ships sailing away, city gates being stormed, sacrifice being performed, girls with open scrolls, as if reading at school; many banquets with man and woman on the banqueting couch, and slaves playing music, and children around: then so many really tender farewell scenes, the dead saying good-bye to his wife, as he goes on the journey, or as the chariot bears him off, or the horse waits; then the soul alone, with the death-dealing spirits standing by with their hammers that gave the blow. It is as Dennis says, the breeze of Nature stirs one's soul. I asked the gentle old man if he knew anything about the urns. But no! no! He knew nothing at all. He had only just come. He counted for nothing. So he protested. He was one of those gentle, shy Italians too diffident even to look at the chests he was guarding, but when I told him what I thought some of the scenes meant he was fascinated like a child, full of wonder, almost breathless. And I thought again, how much more Etruscan than Roman the Italian of today is: sensitive, diffident, craving really for symbols and mysteries, able to be delighted with true delight over small things, violent in spasms, and altogether without sternness or natural will-to-power. The will-to-power is a secondary thing in an Italian, reflected on to him from the Germanic races that have almost engulfed him.

The boar-hunt is still a favourite Italian sport, the grandest sport of Italy. And the Etruscans must have loved it, for they represent it again and again, on the tombs. It is difficult to know what exactly the boar symbolized to them. He occupies often the centre of the scene, where the one who dies should be: and where the bull of sacrifice is. And often he is attacked, not by men, but by young winged boys, or by spirits. The dogs climb in the trees around him, the double axe is swinging to come down on him, he lifts up his tusks in a fierce wild pathos. The archaeologists say that it is Meleager and the boar of Calydon, or Hercules and the fierce brute of Erymanthus. But this is not enough. It is a symbolic scene: and it seems as if the boar were himself the victim this time, the wild, fierce fatherly life hunted down by dogs and adversaries. For it is obviously the boar who must die: he is not, like the lions and griffins, the attacker. He is the father of life running free in the forest, and he must die. They say too he represents winter: when the feasts for the dead were held. But on the very oldest archaic vases the lion and the boar are facing each other, again and again, in symbolic opposition.

Fascinating are the scenes of departures, journeyings in covered wagons drawn by two or more horses, accompanied by driver on foot and friend on horseback, and dogs, and met by other horsemen coming down the road. Under the arched tarpaulin tilt of the wagon reclines a man, or a woman, or a whole family: and all moves forward along the highway with wonderful slow surge. And the wagon, as far as I saw, is always drawn by horses, not by oxen.

This is surely the journey of the soul. It is said to represent even the funeral procession, the ash-chest being borne away to the cemetery, to be laid in the tomb. But the *memory* in the scene seems much deeper than that. It gives so strongly the feeling of a people who have trekked in wagons, like the Boers, or the Mormons, from one land to another.

They say these covered-wagon journeys are peculiar to Volterra, found represented in no other Etruscan places. Altogether the feeling of the Volterran scenes is peculiar. There is a great sense of *journeying*: as of a people which remembers its migrations, by sea as well as land. And there is a curious restlessness, unlike the dancing surety of southern Etruria: a touch of the Gothic.

In the upstairs rooms there are many more ash-chests, but mostly representing Greek subjects: so called. Helen and the Dioscuri, Pelops, Minotaur, Jason, Medea fleeing from Corinth, Oedipus, and the Sphinx, Ulysses and the Sirens, Eteocles and Polynices, Centaurs and Lapithae, the Sacrifice of Iphigenia—all are there, just recognizable. There are so many Greek subjects that one archaeologist suggested that these urns must have been made by a Greek colony planted there in Volterra after the Roman conquest.

One might almost as well say that *Timon of Athens* was written by a Greek colonist planted in England after the over-throw of the Catholic Church. These "Greek" ash-chests are about as Grecian as *Timon of Athens* is. The Greeks would have done them so much "better."

No, the "Greek" scenes are innumerable, but it is only just recognizable what they mean. Whoever carved these chests knew very little of the fables they were handling: and fables they were, to the Etruscan artificers of that day, as they would be to the Italians of this. The story was just used as a peg upon which the native Volterran hung his fancy, as the Elizabethans used Greek stories for their poems. Perhaps also the alabaster cutters were working from old models, or the memory of them. Anyhow, the scenes show nothing of Hellas.

Most curious these "classic" subjects: so unclassic! To me they hint at the Gothic which lay unborn in the future, far more than at the Hellenistic past of the Volterran Etruscan. For, of course, all these alabaster urns are considered late in period, after the fourth century B.C. The Christian sarcophagi of the fifth century A.D. seem much more nearly kin to these ash-chests of Volterra than do contemporary Roman chests: as if Christianity really rose, in Italy, out of Etruscan soil, rather than out of Greco-Roman. And the first glimmering of that early, glad sort of Christian art, the free touch of

Gothic within the classic, seems evident in the Etruscan scenes. The Greek and Roman "boiled" sort of form gives way to a raggedness of edge and a certain wildness of light and shade which promises the later Gothic, but which is still held down by the heavy mysticism from the East.

Very early Volterran urns were probably plain stone or terra-cotta. But no doubt Volterra was a city long before the Etruscans penetrated into it, and probably it never changed character profoundly. To the end, the Volterrans burned their dead: there are practically no long sarcophagi of Lucumones. And here most of all one feels that the *people* of Volterra, or Velathri, were not Oriental, not the same as those who made most show at Tarquinia. This was surely another tribe, wilder, cruder, and far less influenced by the old Aegean influences. In Caere and Tarquinia the aborigines were deeply overlaid by incoming influences from the East. Here not! Here the wild and untamable Ligurian was neighbour, and perhaps kin, and the town of wind and stone kept, and still keeps, its northern quality.

So there the ash-chests are, an open book for anyone to read who will, according to his own fancy. They are not more than two feet long, or thereabouts, so the figure on the lid is queer and stunted. The classic Greek or Asiatic could not have borne that. It is a sign of barbarism in itself. Here the northern spirit was too strong for the Hellenic or Oriental or ancient Mediterranean instinct. The Lucumo and his lady had to submit to being stunted, in their death-effigy. The head is nearly life-size. The body is squashed small.

But there it is, a portrait-effigy. Very often, the lid and the chest don't seem to belong together at all. It is suggested that the lid was made during the lifetime of the subject, with an attempt at real portraiture: while the chest was bought ready-made, and apart. It may be so. Perhaps in Etruscan days there were the alabaster workshops as there are today, only with rows of ash-chests portraying all the vivid scenes we still can see: and perhaps you chose the one you wished your ashes to lie in. But more probably, the workshops were there, the carved ash-chests were there, but you did not select your own chest, since you did not know what death you would die. Probably you only had your portrait carved on the lid, and left the rest to the survivors.

So maybe, and most probably, the mourning relatives hurriedly *ordered* the lid with the portrait-bust, after the death of the near one, and then chose the most appropriate ash-chest. Be it as it may, the two parts are often oddly assorted: and so they were found with the ashes inside them.

But we must believe that the figure on the lid, grotesquely shortened, is an attempt at a portrait. There is none of the distinction of the southern Etruscan figures. The heads are given the "imperious" tilt of the Lucumones, but here it becomes almost grotesque. The dead nobleman may be wearing the necklace of office and holding the sacred patera or libation-dish in his hand; but he will not, in the southern way, be represented ritualistically as naked to below the navel; his shirt will come to his neck: and he may just as well be holding the tippling wine-cup in his hand as the sacred patera; he may even have a wine-jug in his other hand, in full carousal. Altogether the peculiar "sacredness," the inveterate symbolism of the southern Etruscans, is here gone. The religious power is broken.

It is very evident in the ladies: and so many of the figures are ladies. They are decked up in all their splendour, but the mystical formality is lacking. They hold in their hands wine-cups or fans or mirrors, pomegranates or perfume-boxes, or the queer little books which perhaps were the wax tablets for writing upon. They may even have the old sexual and death symbol of the pine-cone. But the *power* of the symbol has almost vanished. The Gothic actuality and idealism begins to supplant the profound *physical* religion of the southern Etruscans, the true ancient world.

In the museum there are jars and bits of bronze, and the pateras with the hollow knob in the middle. You may put your two middle fingers in the patera, and hold it ready to make the last libation of life, the first libation of death, in the correct Etruscan fashion. But you will not, as so many of the men on these ash-chests do, hold the symbolic dish upside down, with the two fingers thrust into the *mundus*. The torch upside down means the flame has gone below, to the underworld. But the patera upside down is somehow shocking. One feels the Volterrans, or men of Velathri, were slack in the ancient mysteries.

At last the rain stopped crashing down icily in the silent inner courtyard; at last there was a ray of sun. And we had seen all we could look at for one day. So we went out, to try to get warmed by a kinder heaven.

There are one or two tombs still open, especially two outside the Porta a Selci. But I believe, not having seen them, they are of small importance. Nearly all the tombs that have been opened in Volterra, their contents removed, have been filled in again, so as not to lose two yards of the precious cultivable land of the peasants. There were many tumuli: but most of them are leveled. And under some were curious round tombs built of unsquared stones, unlike anything in southern Etruria. But then, Volterra is altogether unlike southern Etruria.

One tomb has been removed bodily to the garden of the archaeological museum in Florence: at least its contents have. There it is built up again as it was when discovered in Volterra in 1861, and all the ash-chests are said to be replaced as they stood originally. It is called the Inghirami tomb, from the famous Volterran archaeologist Inghirami.

A few steps lead down into the one circular chamber of the tomb, which is supported in the centre by a square pillar, apparently supposed to be left in the rock. On the low stone bed that encircles the tomb stand the ash-chests, a double row of them, in a great ring encircling the shadow.

The tomb belongs all to one family, and there must be sixty ash-chests, of alabaster, carved with the well-known scenes. So that if this tomb is really arranged as it was originally, and the ash-chests progress from the oldest to the latest counter-clockwise, as is said, one ought to be able to see certainly a century or two of development in the Volterran urns.

But one is filled with doubt and misgiving. Why, oh why, wasn't the tomb left intact as it was found, where it was found? The garden of the Florence museum is vastly instructive, if you want object-lessons about the Etruscans. But who wants object-lessons about vanished races? What one wants is a contact. The Etruscans are not a theory or a thesis. If they are anything, they are an *experience*.

And the experience is always spoilt. Museums, museums, museums, object-lessons rigged out to illustrate the unsound theories of archaeologists, crazy attempts to coordinate and get into a fixed order that which has no fixed order and will not be coordinated! It is sickening! Why must all experience be systematized? Why must even the vanished Etruscans be reduced to a system? They never will be. You break all the eggs, and produce an omelette which is neither Etruscan nor Roman not Italic nor Hittite, nor anything else, but just a systematized mess. Why can't incompatible things be left incompatible? If you make an omelette out of a hen's egg, a plover's, and an ostrich's, you won't have a grand amalgam or unification of hen and plover and ostrich into something we may call "oviparity." You'll have that formless object, an omelette.

So it is here. If you try to make a grand amalgam of Cerveteri and Tarquinia, Vulci, Vetulonia, Volterra, Chiusi, Veii, then you won't get the essential *Etruscan* as a result, but a cooked-up mess which has no life-meaning at all. A museum is not a first-hand contact: it is an illustrated lecture. And what one wants is the actual vital touch. I don't want to be "instructed"; nor do many other people.

They could take the more homeless objects for the museums, and still leave those that *have* a place in their own place: the Inghirami tomb here at Volterra.

But it is useless. We walk up the hill and out of the Florence gate, into the shelter under the walls of the huge medieval castle which is now a State prison. There is a promenade below the ponderous walls, and a scrap of sun, and shelter from the biting wind. A few citizens are promenading even now. And beyond, the bare green country rises up in waves and sharp points, but it is like looking at the choppy sea from the prow of a tall ship; here in Volterra we ride above all.

And behind us, in the bleak fortress, are the prisoners. There is a man, an old man now, who has written an opera inside those walls. He had a passion for the piano: and for thirty years his wife nagged him when he played. So one day he silently and suddenly killed her. So, the nagging of thirty years silenced, he got thirty years of prison, and *still* is not allowed to play the piano. It is curious.

There were also two men who escaped. Silently and secretly they carved marvellous likenesses of themselves out of the huge loaves of hard bread the prisoners get. Hair and all, they made their own effigies lifelike. Then they laid them in the bed, so that when the warder's light flashed on them he should say to himself: "There they lie sleeping, the dogs!"

And so they worked, and they got away. It cost the governor, who loved his household of malefactors, his job. He was kicked out. It is curious. He should have been rewarded, for having such clever children, sculptors in bread.

David Leavitt

(1961–   )

and Mark Mitchell

David Leavitt and his partner, Mark Mitchell, went to Tuscany in 1993 and never left. They bought a house, restored it, and puzzled out how to be gay American writers in Italy. Leavitt said, "I find that being abroad and out of my own language is a benefit to me as a writer. I think more creatively."

Leavitt's literary life has been marked by controversy. His novel *While England Sleeps* was pulled from the shelves because the poet Stephen Spender claimed its plot was plagiarized from his memoir. It was reissued only after Leavitt agreed to rewrite it. In 1996 *Esquire* magazine stopped the publication of one novella in his book *Arkansas*, objecting to its sexual content. Leavitt said that his fiction defies one of the tenets of modern publishing—gay characters are accepted as long as they stay in their place, "the sort of friendly maternal drag queens, the sort of effeminate, but warm and cuddly brother figure." Leavitt used E. M. Forster, one of his literary heroes, as an example. Forster, he theorized, did not write another novel after *A Passage to India* because "he knew that if he were to publish that kind of novel, he could possibly be prosecuted."

Leavitt and Mitchell now divide their time between Tuscany and Florida, where Leavitt has taken a teaching job. "There's a lot I enjoy about being back, like the incredible ease of doing practical things . . . When we got to Florida we needed to get Florida driver's licenses. It took seven minutes. I know because I timed it." This excerpt from *In Maremma* (2001), a memoir of their life in Tuscany, describes the process of getting an Italian license.

from IN MAREMMA

"THE DOCUMENTS MUST AGREE"

In March 2000, the following item appeared in the *Italy Daily*, a supplement to *The International Herald Tribune*. It says much about the poetry and madness of Italian bureaucracy:

> Highway police arrested 10 people late Wednesday in Pescara, charging them with running a fraudulent drivers' school that sold drivers' licenses for up to five million lire each. Another 32 people were accused of participating in what authorities described as a cooperative that drew clients from around Italy, some of whom were reportedly almost blind. Italians frequently complain that obtaining a drivers' license in Italy is difficult without attending costly schools. Foreign residents in Italy for more than one year are also expected to attend the schools and obtain a national license, regardless of their driving record.

For us, the long process of getting licenses began shortly after we bought Podere Fiume. To live in the countryside one has to have a car, and to own a car in Italy one has to have an Italian driver's license. This is simply the law. If you don't have an Italian driver's license, your only options are to ask an Italian friend to buy a car for you, then sign a document giving you the right to drive it, or to bring in a car from another country—yet if you do this, after four months you will still be obliged to replace the foreign license plates with Italian ones, which requires an Italian license.

Many countries have reciprocity agreements for licenses with Italy; the United States, unfortunately, is not one of them, since there is no federal driver's license and it would be bureaucratically untenable for Italy to make separate agreements with each of the fifty states. As a result, even drivers who, like us, have had licenses for almost a quarter of a century are compelled to take the driving test here. In Italian.

Wanting advice, we called Elizabeth, since we knew she had gotten an Italian license several years earlier. "Oh, it was easy," she said. "I just paid someone to take the test for me."

"But how can someone take it for you?"

"Only the oral part. What you do is you pretend you don't speak Italian and explain that you've brought along a translator. Of course he isn't really a translator. You mumble to him, and he answers all the questions. It costs about two million lire."

Neither of us was particularly keen to pay two million lire to a "translator." Nor did we believe that we needed one, even if Elizabeth had. After all, we both spoke Italian. We were good drivers. Also, Mark had managed to survive orals in graduate school: could a driving test be so much worse than that?

A lawyer we knew now explained to us how to proceed. In order to circumvent the notorious driving schools, we would need to get in touch with an *agente*. In Italy, an *agente* is basically someone who makes his living mediating between bureaucracies and human beings. Little of a practical nature can be done without an *agente*, since the system is so baroque that learning to negotiate even a small region of it requires years of study.

The *agente* the lawyer recommended was named Bruno. He drove a motorcycle and wore a cashmere coat. To obtain licenses, he said, we would first have to complete a form (*pratica*). This would cost 200,000 lire. After that we would have to take an eye exam from a doctor who would also affirm that we were in good health. This would cost 150,000 lire. After that Bruno would make an appointment for us to take the *oral* exam. If we passed it, he would make an appointment for us to take the driving test—the one behind the wheel.

Now the comedy begins. First we go to take the eye exam. To our amazement, the doctor who administers it turns out to be, to all intents and purposes, blind. (Perhaps he got *his* license in Pescara.) So far as we can tell, he is able to give the exam only because he has memorized the chart. Indeed, he can barely read our passports through his thick glasses and the clouds of smoke from his cigar.

Once we receive the necessary certificates, Bruno makes an appointment for us to take the oral exam—the *teoria*. When? we ask. In just two months, he tells us. Two months! He smiles, and explains that in France the wait is usually four months. Then he gives us some small pink slips of paper (*foglie rosse*) permitting us to drive during the interval. He also gives us a manual of road regulations to study, along with a book of sample written tests. These tests have a reputation for being almost sadistically difficult, mostly because they exalt the principle of the trick question. An example:

When encountering this sign,

1. One must decrease speed.   TRUE   FALSE
2. One must drive with prudence.   TRUE   FALSE
3. It is forbidden to pass.   TRUE   FALSE

One and two are true. Three, however, is false. When driving through a dip in the road (*cunetta*) it is, in fact, legal to pass, although obviously unwise to do so.

Fortunately, we are not going to have to take the written test—a fact that does not in any way mitigate our anxiety over the oral test that we will have to take. So we study. Both of us, by nature, are studiers, and indeed the exercise proves to be well worth it. After years of driving in Italy, we finally learn the meaning of certain road signs we had previously found to be enigmas:

Obviously it is important to know what signs mean, just as it is important to know the basics of giving first aid to an injured driver or passenger after an accident. On the other hand, the many pages of the manual devoted to right-of-way (*precedenza*) demonstrated amply why this part of the exam is known as "theory." After all, a drawing such as this one,

illustrating an intersection of five streets in which there is neither a stop sign nor a stoplight nor a yield sign, and requiring the testee to adduce the sequence in which the various cars should give way to one another, has little to do with reality. Intersections of this sort quite simply do not exist, and even if they did, the truth is that in Italy "right-of-way" belongs to the speediest, the most aggressive, the driver "with balls" (*con palle*).

Even so, we are determined to master the theory of *precedenza*, not only because we have to but because, as theory, it has its own mysterious allure. We memorize the rules of passing (the most ignored of all on Italian roads), the basic mechanical principles of the car engine, the guidelines on where it is and isn't permissible to park. We learn what the *croce di Sant'Andrea* means and what distinguishes railroad crossings *con barriere* from those without.

The morning of the test, we drive out very early to the *Motorizzazione*—the Motor Vehicles Authority—the offices of which are located far from the center of Rome, on the Via Salaria. Like many municipal buildings in Italy, the *Motorizzazione* is an imposing, ugly structure, its very architecture intended to bully and subdue. The walls are of dirty stone; there are NO DOGS signs posted everywhere. Inside, the light is greasy. The testing room itself, when we peer into it, proves to be a large and windowless trapezoid cluttered with chair-desks of the sort more commonly found in high schools. In a sort of antechamber, a United Nations of examinees sits waiting. Most of them are accompanied by instructors from their driving schools, who quiz them on *precedenza* even as they wait.

David is summoned first to the exam room, along with another American, a language teacher from Chicago who has already failed the test once. They speak in English while the examiner, a prematurely elderly young man rather resembling a stoat, reads through the language teacher's *pratica*. In his case, all appears to be in order. Then the examiner opens David's file, placing his medical certificate alongside his passport. For several minutes he looks from the certificate to the passport, the passport to the certificate. Then he pushes them back across the desk.

"The medical certificate says that you were born in 1971," he says. "The passport says that you were born in 1961."

David laughs. "Oh, that's a mistake. I'm not surprised—you see, the doctor who gave me the eye exam was blind."

No laughter. No even a smile.

"Also, your passport says that you were born in Pennsylvania USA."

"True."

"But your medical certificate says that you were born in Pittsburgh USA."

"Also true. Pittsburgh is the city. Pennsylvania is the state."

"But they don't agree. They must agree."

Here the language teacher enters the fray, assuring the examiner that David is not lying: Pittsburgh really is a city in Pennsylvania. He goes on to explain, with the remarkable calm of a teacher, that in the United States the state of birth is always given on passports, just as in Italy the city of birth is given. No doubt the doctor put down the city in order to remain in accordance with Italian rules.

"But they don't agree," the examiner repeats. "The documents must agree."

"Pittsburgh is the second-largest city in Pennsylvania," David throws in hopefully.

It is no use. The examiner is intractable. David is ordered out and told to make a new appointment.

When he tells Mark what has happened, Mark looks at his own documents and discovers the same discrepancy: his medical certificate says that he was born in Biloxi, while his passport says that he was born in Mississippi.

In a white rage, we hunt down Bruno. He is as unflappable as the examiner was intractable. First he looks at the medical forms. Then he looks at the passports. "Well, he was right," he says after a moment. "This is the doctor's fault. The documents must agree."

We think about it. We grow calmer. Of course the documents must agree, we acknowledge. There is no reason to be angry with the examiner. He had *ragione*. He was just doing his job.

Only hours later, once we are back at Podere Fiume, do we realize what really happened that morning: for a few moments we had been thinking like Italians.

Six weeks later, we return to the *Motorizzazione* and this time actually take the test. Mark goes first, along with an Arab and an Albanian. For forty-five minutes David watches through an open door while the candidates sit hunched across the desk from the examiner, who makes diagrams in the air with his hands. Not a word can be heard, though if one watches carefully one can see, intermittently, that Mark is laughing.

"Did you pass?" David asks when the three men emerge.

"I am promoted," he says. (*Sono promosso*.)

It is now David's turn. While he and two other candidates—both Romanian—respond to questions in the trapezoid-shaped room, Mark takes on the role of the ancient mariner for those who have yet to be tested. As is common in such situations, tension fosters an atmosphere of intimacy. For a time Mark and the Tunisian woman who works at the Saudi Arabian embassy and the elegant lady from Bangladesh form a little community. Worriedly they listen while he tells them what has been asked (Why is it dangerous to drive quickly on a curve?) as well as what has not (nothing about *precedenza*; a sigh of collective relief is heard).

A quarter of an hour passes. All at once one of the Romanians comes flying out of the room as if he has quite literally been ejected. "He fucked up," a driving teacher murmurs darkly. (*Ha bocciato*.)

"It's the second time, too," says another.

A quarter of an hour after that, his countryman storms out. He, too, has fucked up. David is now alone with the examiner. Another quarter of an hour passes—by now the women are beside themselves with panic—when at last he comes out.

"*Anch'io sono promosso*," he says. Which means only that he, too, has won the right to take another test.

*   *   *

A few days later, we were talking with Pina and Giampaolo, who run our favorite restaurant in Maremma—Il Mulino in Semproniano—about the driving test. "Why do they make it so hard to pass?" we asked.

"It goes back to Fascism," Giampaolo said. "The *fascisti* wanted to make the ordinary citizen fearful and dependent on the state."

"And to encourage corruption," Pina added. "Bribery. This way, people who worked for the state could get rich."

The Fascist attitude also led to the invention of a whole industry: the industry of the *agente*.

How odd that we were having this conversation in Tuscany, on a hilltop not far from the sea, on that lovely peninsula that was for centuries quite literally the mother of invention! After all, Italy gave us Leonardo da Vinci and Galileo and Marconi. Now most of that energy has been eaten up by the exigencies of contending with bureaucracy—contending with it, or evading it. If there are no longer poets in Italy, it is because bureaucracy has slayed or absorbed them.

Another month later and the comedy was finished. (So sings the clown.)

To take the "practical" driving exam, we first had to meet someone called Signor Antonio in the Olympic Village in Rome. Since we had to be there at 8:00 AM, we left home at 5:00 AM. (How pointless it all seemed, driving to Rome in the dark to take a driving exam!)

Although we had never been there before, getting to the proper piazza in the *Villaggio Olimpico* proved to be a piece of cake. Since we arrived at 7:30, there was time for us to have a coffee before meeting up with Signor Antonio. Light was beginning to creep into the sky, which had an orange cast, later than it seemed it should have. This was the scirocco, the African wind that carries with it the sand of the Sahara; it would worsen as the morning progressed, so that by the time we took the exam it would be necessary to use headlights.

Having had our coffee, and not finding Signor Antonio, we walked around. The architecture of the Olympic Village answered every idea

one had of hell. It was in the summer of 1960 that the XVII
Olympic Games were held in Rome, and in addition to the dormito-
ries for the athletes, which are now depressing apartments for the
down-at-heel (according to a placard, one building had recently been
"deratted and disinfested"), other reminders of the event include an
unmown park strewn with hypodermics; a granite obelisk bearing
the five interlocking rings; streets named for the participating nations,
many of which (Yugoslavia, the Soviet Union) no longer exist. There
was also a grimly lit pharmacy with a gigantic sign in its front window
announcing a special on "Incontinence Diapers." (The Italians do
not use euphemisms for this sort of thing. In the United States, by
contrast, advertisers prefer phrases like "Adult Hygiene System.")

Presently Signor Antonio arrived in a white Fiat 600. We exchanged
pleasantries, after which Mark drove, then David. After half an hour,
we were through—or so we thought—for we had been given to
understand that Signor Antonio was the examiner. But he was not. As
he explained, he worked for one of the more than five hundred driving schools in Rome; his function was not to conduct the exam but to
give us a quick "lesson"—which we thought was the exam—and to
provide the car for the real exam. In Italy one cannot legally take the
exam in one's own car; instead one has to take it in a car specially out-
fitted with two sets of brakes—one for the driver and one for the forward passenger.

And now the examiner himself arrives. He is a short, misshapen,
corrupt-looking man with hair like steel wool. In his arms he carries
a thick briefcase that, we soon learn from Signor Antonio, contains
the licenses for all the examinees who have been waiting for him.
Before beginning his work, though, he must first be taken to the bar
for coffee by Signor Antonio and all the other instructors from the
driving schools. While they are in the bar, an order for the exams is
worked out. There are twelve examinees. We are to go seventh and
eighth.

The long and short of the exam is that one of us passed, the other
failed. The one who failed (Mark) was the first one of us to go, and
the first American of the day as well. (All of the Asians had already
failed.) Halfway into the exam, the misshapen examiner began deliv-

ering himself of anti-American invective to Signor Antonio, who was in the car to man the second set of brakes. "Americans think they can come into Italy and get whatever they want," he said. Mark did his best to maintain his cool. "They have to be taught," the examiner continued ominously. Mark indicated two cars that had just run a stop sign, and was ignored. "This American," the examiner said, then broke off to call Signor Antonio's attention to a poster for a female candidate in the upcoming election called Monica Ciccolini and made a rude remark about her person, as well as about the similarity of her name to that of the Italian porn actress Cicciolina. Signor Antonio, meanwhile, had joined the cause with the examiner and put in his oar about Americans—even though we had each paid him one hundred thousand lire to advocate for us.

Why one of us passed and the other failed was a caprice (Mark is a much better driver than David), for the system is designed so that the examiner does not have to be accountable for his decisions. If a passing surge of antipathy toward Americans was his reason for failing Mark, the examiner will face no reprisals. We recalled once again what Pina and Giampaolo had said about the Fascists; for all its rhetoric about "us" (*noi*), Fascism was deeply divisive. The populace was to be made anxious and insecure, even tyrannized, with the state transformed into an almost Homeric god. In the person of the driving examiner, we met that same sadism: a false and repellent pride in being Italian—and in *not* being Japanese, or Indian, or African, or Canadian—the implications of which were given weight by the recent movement of some citizens in the rich northern part of the country to secede and form a new nation called Padania, by the rise of neo-Fascism in the raiments of Forza Italia, and by the constant pressure of the Catholic Church to sustain a culture of conformism. Nor was the irony of this scene being enacted in the Olympic Village, a forty-year-old monument to an ideal of fraternity, lost on us. For though the Italians are vocal in criticizing their government, the fact remains that Italians have more or less the system they have chosen, and perhaps even want.

There is no charm in any of this. The cloud has no silver lining. One is not made a better person for having had the experience. But cynicism is not the answer; nor, for that matter, is the romanticizing of bureaucracy—a thing to look at unflinchingly, and to be made angry by, and finally to grieve for.

Postscript: One month later Mark took the *pratica* again; he passed.

Robert Lowell

(1917–1977)

Poet Robert Lowell spent four tumultuous years living in Italy. While there he suffered recurrent mental breakdowns and episodes of manic depression, and his marriage to his second wife, Elizabeth Hardwick, foundered. But then Lowell's entire life was tumultuous.

Born to a patrician Boston family, Lowell attended Harvard (as did most of the men in his family), but left after two years. He eventually graduated from Kenyon College. During World War II Lowell was a conscientious objector and served several months in jail. His opposition to service was, in part, motivated by a conversion to Catholicism, a further repudiation of his elite background. He moved to Italy after the war, but returned to the United States in 1954 following the death of his mother. Then Lowell suffered a complete breakdown and was committed to McLean, a mental hospital in Massachusetts.

In the sixties and seventies Lowell's life alternated between periods of psychosis, literary productivity, and political activism. He became friends with the Kennedys and Eugene McCarthy, participated in the antiwar demonstrations of the Vietnam era, and produced volumes of confessional poetry. His marriage to Hardwick finally ended in the early 1970s, and he married for a third time. Robert Lowell died in 1977 in New York City on his way to see Elizabeth Hardwick, with whom he was trying to reconcile.

"Florence," from *Selected Poems* (1976), is dedicated to Mary McCarthy.

FLORENCE

(For Mary McCarthy)

I long for the black ink,
cuttlefish, April, Communists
and brothels of Florence—

everything, even the British
fairies who haunted the hills,
even the chills and fever
that came once a month
and forced me to think.
The apple was more human there than here,
but it took a long time for the blinding
golden rind to mellow.

How vulnerable the horseshoe crabs
dredging the bottom like flat-irons
in their antique armor,
with their swordgrass blackbone tails,
made for a child to grab
and throw strangling ashore!

Oh Florence, Florence, patroness
of the lovely tyrannicides!
Where the tower of the Old Palace
pierces the sky
like a hypodermic needle,
Perseus, David and Judith,
lords and ladies of the Blood,
Greek demi-gods of the Cross,
rise sword in hand
above the unshaven,
formless decapitation
of the monsters, tubs of guts,
mortifying chunks for the pack.
Pity the monsters!
Pity the monsters!
Perhaps, one always took the wrong side—
Ah, to have known, to have loved
too many Davids and Judiths!
My heart bleeds black blood for the monster.
I have seen the Gorgon.
The erotic terror

of her helpless, big bosomed body
lay like slop.
Wall-eyed, staring the despot to stone,
her severed head swung
like a lantern in the victor's hand.

Frances Mayes

Frances Mayes, a Georgia-born creative writing teacher from San Francisco, bought Bramasole, her Tuscan home, in 1990. As Mayes's legions of fans know, she and her partner, Ed, renovated their villa outside of Cortona. Her long-lived marriage had disintegrated and her daughter was grown when she and Ed, a poet several years her junior, embarked on their new life. *Under the Tuscan Sun* (1996), from which this excerpt is taken, chronicles their struggles with Italian workmen and bureaucrats, search for potable water, and battles with mosquitoes and scorpions—while eating gourmet meals with ingredients from local markets.

It is the late-in-life reinvention of oneself that attracts readers to Mayes's books, *Under the Tuscan Sun*, *Bella Tuscany*, and *In Tuscany*. In the years since the publication of *Under the Tuscan Sun*, thousands of tourists have made a pilgrimage to Cortona; in high season thirty or forty may be standing outside of Bramasole hoping to catch a glimpse of the author. With over a million copies in print, the book has been translated into more than fourteen languages and made into a movie starring Diane Lane. For the film a grand fountain was constructed in Cortona's Piazza Signorelli—and then taken down after the shoot ended. The people of Cortona seem to take their new celebrity in stride. In *The New York Times* the mayor was quoted as saying, "Bramasole is a nice house, but it has no real architectural significance . . . I haven't read Mrs. Mayes's book, but I am told it discusses very nicely the atmosphere here, our people and our way of life."

Under the Tuscan Sun is dedicated to Ann Cornelisen, another Georgia native who immigrated to Tuscany, where she befriended Frances and Ed Mayes.

from UNDER THE TUSCAN SUN

I am about to buy a house in a foreign country. A house with the beautiful name of Bramasole. It is tall, square, and apricot-colored with faded green shutters, ancient tile roof, and an iron balcony on the second level, where ladies might have sat with their fans to watch some spectacle below. But below, overgrown briars, tangles of roses, and knee-high weeds run rampant. The balcony faces southeast, looking into a deep valley, then into the Tuscan Apennines. When it rains or when the light changes, the facade of the house turns gold, sienna, ocher; a previous scarlet paint job seeps through in rosy spots like a box of crayons left to melt in the sun. In places where the stucco has fallen away, rugged stone shows what the exterior once was. The house rises above a *strada bianca*, a road white with pebbles, on a terraced slab of hillside covered with fruit and olive trees. Bramasole: from *bramare*, to yearn for, and *sole*, sun: something that yearns for the sun, and yes, I do.

The family wisdom runs strongly against this decision. My mother has said "Ridiculous," with her certain and forceful stress on the second syllable, "RiDICulous," and my sisters, although excited, fear I am eighteen, about to run off with a sailor in the family car. I quietly have my own doubts. The upright seats in the *notaio*'s outer office don't help. Through my thin white linen dress, spiky horsehairs pierce me every time I shift, which is often in the hundred-degree waiting room. I look over to see what Ed is writing on the back of a receipt: Parmesan, salami, coffee, bread. How can he? Finally, the signora opens her door and her torrential Italian flows over us.

The *notaio* is nothing like a notary; she's the legal person who conducts real-estate transactions in Italy. Ours, Signora Mantucci, is a small, fierce Sicilian woman with thick tinted glasses that enlarge her green eyes. She talks faster than any human I have ever heard. She reads long laws aloud. I thought all Italian was mellifluous; she makes it sound like rocks crashing down a chute. Ed looks at her raptly; I know he's in thrall to the sound of her voice. The owner, Dr. Carta, suddenly thinks he has asked too little; he *must* have, since we have agreed to buy it. We think his price is exorbitant. We *know* his price is exorbitant. The Sicilian doesn't pause; she will not be interrupted by anyone except by Giuseppe from the bar downstairs, who suddenly swings open the dark doors, tray aloft, and seems surprised to see his *Americani* customers sitting there almost cross-eyed in confusion. He brings the signora her midmorning thimble of espresso, which she downs in a gulp, hardly pausing. The owner expects to claim that the house cost one amount while it really cost much more. "That is just the way it's done," he insists. "No one is fool enough to declare the real value." He proposes we bring one check to the *notaio*'s office, then pass him ten smaller checks literally under the table.

Anselmo Martini, our agent, shrugs.

Ian, the English estate agent we hired to help with the translation, shrugs also.

Dr. Carta concludes, "You Americans! You take things so seriously. And, *per favore*, date the checks at one-week intervals so the bank isn't alerted to large sums."

Was that the same bank I know, whose sloe-eyed teller languidly conducts a transaction every fifteen minutes, between smokes and telephone calls? The signora comes to an abrupt halt, scrambles the papers into a folder, and stands up. We are to come back when the money and papers are ready.

A window in our hotel room opens onto an expansive view over the ancient roofs of Cortona, down to the dark expanse of the Val di Chiana. A hot and wild wind—the *scirocco*—is driving normal people a little crazy. For me, it seems to reflect my state of mind. I can't sleep. In the United States, I've bought and sold a few houses before—loaded up the car with my mother's Spode, the cat, and the ficus for the five- or five-thousand-mile drive to the next doorway where a new key would fit. You *have* to churn somewhat when the roof covering your head is at stake, since to sell is to walk away from a cluster of memories and to buy is to choose where the future will take place. And the place, never neutral of course, will cast its influence. Beyond that, legal complications and contingencies must be worked out. But here, absolutely everything conspires to keep me staring into the dark.

Italy always has had a magnetic north pull on my psyche. Houses have been on my mind for four summers of renting farmhouses all over Tuscany. In the first place Ed and I rented with friends, we started calculating on the first night, trying to figure out if our four pooled savings would buy the tumbled stone farm we could see from the terrace. Ed immediately fell for farm life and roamed over our neighbors' land looking at the work in progress. The Antolinis grew tobacco, a beautiful if hated crop. We could hear workers shout "*Vipera!*" to warn the others of a poisonous snake. At evening, a violet blue haze rose from the dark leaves. The well-ordered farm looked peaceful from the vantage point of our terrace. Our friends never came back, but for the next three vacations, the circuitous search for a summer home became a quest for us—whether we ever found a place or not, we were happening on places that made pure green olive oil, discovering sweet country Romanesque churches in villages, meandering the back roads of vineyards, and stopping to taste the softest Brunello and the blackest Vino Nobile. Looking for a house gives an intense focus. We visited weekly markets not just with the purchase of picnic peaches in mind; we looked carefully at all the produce's quality and variety, mentally forecasting birthday dinners, new holidays, and breakfasts for weekend guests. We spent hours sitting in piazzas or sipping lemonade in local bars, secretly getting a sense of the place's ambiance. I soaked many a heel blister in a hotel bidet, rubbed bottles of lotion on my feet, which had covered miles of stony streets. We hauled histories and guides and wildflower books and novels in and out of rented houses and hotels. Always we asked local people where they liked to eat and headed to restaurants our many guidebooks never mentioned. We both have an insatiable curiosity about each jagged castle ruin on the hillsides. My idea of heaven still is to drive the gravel farm roads of Umbria and Tuscany, very pleasantly lost.

Cortona was the first town we ever stayed in and we always came back to it during the summers we rented near Volterra, Florence, Montisi, Rignano, Vicchio, Quercegrossa, all those fascinating, quirky houses. One had a kitchen two people could not pass in, but there was a slice of a view of the Arno. Another kitchen had no hot water and no knives, but the house was built into medieval ramparts overlooking vineyards. One had several sets of china for forty, countless glasses and silverware, but the refrigerator iced over every day and by four the door swung open, revealing a new igloo. When the weather was damp, I got a tingling shock if I touched anything in the kitchen. On the property, Cimabue, legend says, discovered the young Giotto drawing a sheep in the dirt. One house had beds with back-crunching dips in the middles. Bats flew down the chimney and buzzed us, while worms in the beams sent down a steady sifting of sawdust onto the pillows. The fireplace was so big we could sit in it while grilling our veal chops and peppers.

We drove hundreds of dusty miles looking at houses that turned out to be in the floodplain of the Tiber or overlooking strip mines. The Siena agent blithely promised that the view would be wonderful again in twenty years; replanting stripped areas was a law. A glorious medieval village house was wildly expensive. The saw-toothed peasant we met in a bar tried to sell us his childhood home, a windowless stone chicken house joined to another house, with snarling dogs lunging at us from their ropes. We fell hard for a farm outside Montisi; the *contessa* who owned it led us on for days, then decided she needed a sign from God before she could sell it. We had to leave before the sign arrived.

As I think back over those places, they suddenly seem preposterously alien and Cortona does, too. Ed doesn't think so. He's in the piazza every afternoon, gazing at the young couple trying to wheel their new baby down the street. They're halted every few steps. Everyone circles the carriage. They're leaning into the baby's face, making noises, praising the baby. "In my next life," Ed tells me, "I want to come back as an Italian baby." He steeps in the piazza life: the sultry and buffed man pushing up his sleeve so his muscles show when he languidly props his chin in his hand; the pure flute notes of Vivaldi drifting from an upstairs window; the flower seller's fan of bright flowers against the stone shop; a man with no neck at all unloading lambs from his truck. He slings them like flour sacks over his shoulder and the lambs' eyeballs bulge out. Every few minutes, Ed looks up at the big clock that has kept time for so long over this piazza. Finally, he takes a stroll, memorizing the stones in the street.

Across the hotel courtyard a visiting Arab chants his prayers toward dawn, just when I finally can fall asleep. He sounds as though he is gargling with salt water. For hours, he rings the voice's changes over a small register, over and over. I want to lean out and shout, "Shut up!" Now and then I have to laugh. I look out, see him nodding in the window, a sweet smile on his face. He reminds me so much of tobacco auctioneers I heard in hot warehouses in the South as a child. I am seven thousand miles from home, plunking down my life savings on a whim. Is it a whim? It feels very close to falling in love and that's never really whimsical but comes from some deep source. Or does it?

Mary McCarthy

(1912 – 1989)

"Was she savage because she was serious," asked one critic of the writer Mary McCarthy, "or serious because she needed an excuse to be savage?" McCarthy loathed sentimentality, hypocrisy, and dishonesty, and when she turned her writing skills on an enemy, her typewriter turned into a skewer. She is most famous for her novel *The Group*, a roman à clef about Vassar and her graduating class, which included the writers Elizabeth Bishop and Muriel Rukeyser.

Born in Seattle, Mary McCarthy was orphaned at six. Raised by strict grandparents (an upbringing recalled in her memoir *Memories of a Catholic Girlhood*), McCarthy rebelled and after college became active in the American left. She married four times and cut a wide sexual swath through the New York literary community (her second husband was Edmund Wilson—whom she called "a monster"—and one lover was editor of the *Partisan Review*).

One of McCarthy's enduring affairs was with Italy. In the 1950s she was part of the American community of writers who moved there. Her two books of nonfiction, *Venice Observed* (1956) and *The Stones of Florence* (1959), from which this selection is taken, are love letters to those cities. But she does not forsake her tart tongue or lapse into sentimental reverie. In *The Stones of Florence* she complains of the heat and the traffic, decries the Italians' lack of civic-mindedness, and is shocked at the disorganization of the museums. She concludes that Florence is "a terrible city, in many ways, uncomfortable and dangerous to live in, a city of drama, argument and struggle." A perfect place for Mary McCarthy.

from THE STONES OF FLORENCE

"How can you stand it?" This is the first thing the transient visitor to Florence, in summer, wants to know, and the last thing too—the eschatological question he leaves echoing in the air as he speeds on to Venice. He means the noise, the traffic, and the heat, and something else besides, something he hesitates to mention, in view of former raptures: the fact that Florence seems to him dull, drab, provincial. Those who know Florence a little often compare it to Boston. It is full of banks, loan agencies, and insurance companies, of shops selling place mats and doilies and tooled-leather desk sets. The Raphaels and Botticellis in the museums have been copied a thousand times; the architecture and sculpture are associated with the schoolroom. For the contemporary taste, there is too much Renaissance in Florence: too much *David* (copies of Michelangelo's gigantic white nude stand on the Piazza della Signoria and the Piazzale Michelangelo; the original is in the Academy), too much rusticated stone, too much glazed terracotta, too many Madonnas with Bambinos. In the lacklustre cafés of the dreary main piazza (which has a parking lot in the middle), stout women in sensible clothing sit drinking tea, and old gentlemen with canes are reading newspapers. Sensible, stout, countrified flowers like zinnias and dahlias are being sold in the Mercato Nuovo, along with straw carryalls, pocketbooks, and marketing baskets. Along the Arno, near Ponte Vecchio, ugly new buildings show where the German bombs fell.

Naples is a taste the contemporary traveller can understand, even if he does not share it. Venice he can understand . . . Rome . . . Siena. But Florence? "Nobody comes here any more," says the old Berenson, wryly, in his villa at Settignano, and the echoing sculpture gallery of the Bargello bears him out; almost nobody comes here. The big vaulted main hall seems full of marble wraiths: San Giorgio, San Giovanni, San Giovannino, the dead gods and guardians of the city. The uniformed modern guards standing sentinel over the creations of Donatello, Desiderio, Michelozzo, Luca della Robbia, Agostino di Duccio have grown garrulous from solitude, like people confined in prison: they fall on the rare visitor (usually an art historian) and will scarcely let him go. The Uffizi, on the contrary, is invaded by barbarian hordes from the North, squadrons of tourists in shorts, wearing sandals or hiking shoes, carrying metal canteens and cameras, smelling of sweat and sun-tan oil, who have been hustled in here by their guides to contemplate *Venus on the Half-Shell.*

"*Il Diluvio Universale,*" observes a Florentine, sadly, punning on the title of Paolo Uccello's fresco (now in the Belvedere). There is no contradiction. "Nobody comes here any more" is simply the other side, the corollary, of the phenomenon of mass tourism—the universal deluge. The masses rush in where the selective tourist has fled. Almost nobody comes to see Donatello's *David* in the Bargello, the first nude statue of the Renaissance, or San Giorgio or San Giovannino, Donatello's also, or the *cantorias* of dancing children in the Museum of the Works of the Duomo, but Michelangelo and Cellini, partly, no doubt, because of vaguely sensed "off-colour" associations, draw crowds of curiosity-seekers. Florence is scraping the bottom of the tourist barrel. And the stolid presence of these masses with their polyglot guides in the Uffizi, in the Pitti, around the Baptistery doors and the Medici Tombs, in the cell of Savonarola and the courtyard of Palazzo Vecchio is another of the "disagreeables," as the Victorians used to call them, that have made Florence intolerable and, more than that, inexplicable to the kind of person for whom it was formerly a passion. "How can you stand it?"

Florence is a manly town, and the cities of art that appeal to the current sensibility are feminine, like Venice and Siena. What irritates the modern tourist about Florence is that it makes no concession to the pleasure principle. It stands four-square and direct, with no air of mystery, no blandishments, no furbelows—almost no Gothic lace or baroque swirls. Against the green Arno, the ochre-and-dun file of hotels and palazzi has the spruce, spare look of a regiment drawn up in drill order. The deep shades of melon and of tangerine that you see in Rome, the pinks of Venice, the rose of Siena, the red of Bologna have been ruled out of Florence as if by municipal decree. The eye turns from mustard, buff, écru, pale yellow, cream to the severe black-and-white marbles of the Baptistery and of Santa Maria Novella's façade or the dark green and white and flashing gold of San Miniato. On the Duomo and Giotto's bell tower and the Victorian façade of Santa Croce there are touches of pink, which give these buildings a curious festive air, as though they alone were dressed up for a party. The general severity is even echoed by the Florentine bird, which is black and white—the swallow, a bachelor, as the Florentines say, wearing a tail coat.

The great sculptors and architects who stamped the outward city with its permanent image or style—Brunelleschi, Donatello, Michelangelo—were all bachelors. Monks, soldier-saints, prophets, hermits were the city's heroes. Saint John the Baptist, in his shaggy skins, feeding on locusts and honey, is the patron, and, except for the Madonna with her boy-baby, women saints count for little in the Florentine iconography. Santa Reparata, a little Syrian saint, who once was patron of the Cathedral, was replaced by the Madonna (Santa Maria del Fiore) early in the fifteenth century. The Magdalen as a penitent and desert-wanderer was one of the few female images, outside of the Madonna, to strike the Florentine imagination; Donatello's gaunt sculpture of her stands in the Baptistery: fearsome brown figure, in wood, clad in a shirt of flowing hair that surrounds her like a beard, so that at first glance she appears to be a man and at second glance almost a beast. Another of these hairy wooden Magdalens, by Desiderio, is in the church of Santa Trinita. Like these wild creatures of the desert, many of the Florentine artists were known for their strange ascetic habits: Paolo Uccello, Donatello, Piero di Cosimo, Michelangelo, Pontormo. When he was doing a statue of Pope Julius II in Bologna, Michelangelo, though an unsociable person, slept four to a bed with his workmen, and in Rome, so he wrote his relations, his quarters were too squalid to receive company.

Many Florentine palaces today are quite comfortable inside and possess pleasant gardens, but outside they bristle like fortresses or dungeons, and, to the passing tourist, their thick walls and bossy surfaces seem to repel the very notion of hospitality. From the Grand Canal, the Venetian palaces, with their windows open to the sun, offer glimpses of sparkling chandeliers and painted ceilings, and it is not hard for the most insensitive tourist to summon up visions of great balls, gaming, love-making in those brilliant rooms. The Florentine palaces, on the contrary, hide their private life like misers, which in fact the Florentines are reputed to be. Consumption is not conspicuous here; an unwritten sumptuary law seems to govern outward display. The famous Florentine elegance, which attracts tourists to the shops on Via Tornabuoni and Via della Vigna Nuova, is characterized by austerity of line, simplicity, economy of effect. In this spare city, the rule of *nihil nimis* prevails. A beggar woman who stands soliciting in front of Palazzo Strozzi, when offered alms a second time in the same day, absently, by another Florentine, refuses: "No. You gave me before." Poverty has its own decorum; waste is frowned on. This is a city of endurance, a city of stone. A thing often noticed, with surprise, by foreigners is that the Florentines love their poor, for the poor are the quintessence of Florence—dry in speech, frugal, pessimistic, "queer," disabused. "*Pazienza!*" is their perpetual, shrugging counsel, and if you ask them how they are, the answer is "*Non c'è male.*" "Not so bad." The answer to a favourable piece of tidings is "*Meno male,*" literally, "less bad." These people are used to hardship, which begins with a severe climate and overcrowding.

The summers are the worst. The valley of the Arno is a natural oven, in which the city bakes, almost without relief, throughout July and August. Venice has the sea; Rome has a breeze and fountains; Bologna has arcades; Siena is high. But the stony heat of Florence has no extenuation. Some people pretend that it is cooler in Fiesole or near the Boboli Garden, but this is not true, or at least not true enough. For the populace and the tourists, the churches are the only refuge, except for UPIM, the local five-and-ten (a Milanese firm), which is air-cooled, and for an icy swimming pool, surrounded by a flower garden, in the Tennis Club of the Cascine that few tourists hear about and that the native population, on the whole, cannot afford. The Boboli Garden is too hot to walk in until sunset, which is the time it closes. In some Italian cities, the art galleries are cool, but the Uffizi, with its small rooms and long glassed-in corridors, is stifling, and the Pitti stands with wings extended in a glaring gravel courtyard, like a great brown flying lizard, basking in the terrible sun. Closed off, behind blinds and shutters, the city's inhabitants live a nocturnal life by day, like bats, in darkened rooms, wanly lit for the noon meal by electricity. At seven o'clock in the evening, throughout the city, there is a prolonged rumble that sounds as if it were thunder; the blinds are being rolled up to let in the exhausted day. Then the mosquitoes come.

For the tourist, it is too hot, after ten o'clock in the morning, to sight-see, too close, with the windows shut and the wooden blinds lowered, to sleep after lunch, too dark to read, for electricity is expensive, and the single bulb provided for reading in most Florentine hotels and households is no brighter than a votive candle. Those who try to sight-see discover the traffic hazard. The sidewalks are mere tilted rims skirting the building fronts; if you meet a person coming towards you, you must swerve into the street; if you step backward onto the pavement to look up at a palace, you will probably be run over. "Rambles" through Florence, such as the old guidebooks talk of, are a funny idea under present conditions. Many of the famous monuments have become, quite literally, invisible, for lack of a spot from which they can be viewed with safety. Standing (or trying to stand) opposite Palazzo Rucellai, for example, or Orsanmichele, you constitute a traffic obstruction, to be bumped by pedestrians, honked at by cars, rammed by baby carriages and delivery carts. Driving a car, you are in danger of killing; walking or standing, of being killed. If you walk, you curse the automobiles and motor-scooters; if you drive, you curse the pedestrians—above all, old women, children, and tourists with their noses in maps or guidebooks.

A "characteristic" Florentine street—that is, a street which contains points of touristic interest (old palaces, a Michelozzo portal, the room where Dostoievski finished *The Idiot*, et cetera)—is not only extremely narrow, poor, and heavily populated, lined with florists and greengrocers who display their wares on the strip of sidewalk, but it is also likely to be one of the principal traffic arteries. The main route today from Siena and Rome, for example, is still the old Roman "way," the Via Romana, which starts at the old arched gate, the Porta Romana (1326; Franciabigio fresco in the archway), bends northeast, passing the gardens of the Annalena (suppressed convent) on the left and the second gate of the Boboli on the right, the church of San Felice (Michelozzo façade) on the left again, to the Pitti Palace, after which it changes its name to Via Guicciardini, passes Palazzo Guicciardini (birthplace of the historian), the ancient church of Santa Felicita (*Deposition* by Pontormo inside, in a Brunelleschi chapel), and continues to Ponte Vecchio, which it crosses, changing its name again to Por Santa Maria and again to Calimala before reaching the city centre. The traffic on Via Romana is highly "characteristic." Along the narrow sidewalk, single file, walks a party of Swiss or German tourists, barelegged, with cameras and other equipment hanging bandoleer-style from various leather straps on their persons; clinging to the buildings, in their cleated shoes, they give the effect of a scaling party in the Alps. They are the only walkers, however, who are not in danger of death. Past them flows a confused stream of human beings

and vehicles: baby carriages wheeling in and out of the Boboli Garden, old women hobbling in and out of church, grocery carts, bicycles, Vespas, Lambrettas, motorcycles, *topolino*s, Fiat *seicento*s, a trailer,
a donkey cart from the country delivering sacks of laundry that has
been washed with ashes, in the old-fashioned way, Cadillacs, Alfa
Romeos, *millecento*s, Chevrolets, a Jaguar, a Rolls-Royce with a chauf-
feur and a Florence licence plate, bands of brawny workmen carrying bureaus, mirrors, and credenzas (for this is the neighbourhood of
the artisans), plumbers tearing up the sidewalk, pairs of American
tourists with guidebooks and maps, children, artists from the Pensione Annalena, clerks, priests, housemaids with shopping baskets
stopping to finger the furred rabbits hanging upside down outside
the poultry shops, the sanitation brigade (a line of blue-uniformed
men riding bicycles that propel wheeled platforms holding two or
three garbage cans and a broom made of twigs), a pair of boys transporting a funeral wreath in the shape of a giant horseshoe, big tourist
buses from abroad with guides talking into microphones, trucks full
of wine flasks from the Chianti, trucks of crated lettuces, trucks of
live chickens, trucks of olive oil, the mail truck, the telegraph boy on
a bicycle, which he parks in the street, a tripe-vendor, with a glassed-
in cart full of smoking-hot entrails, outsize Volkswagen station wagons marked "U.S. Forces in Germany," a man on a motorcycle with
an overstuffed armchair strapped to the front of it, an organ-grinder,
horse-drawn fiacres from the Pitti Palace. It is as though the whole
history of Western locomotion were being recapitulated on a single
street; an airplane hums above; missing only is the Roman litter.

But it is a pageant no one can stop to watch, except the gatekeeper
at the Boboli, who sits calmly in his chair at the portal, passing the
time of day. In his safe harbour, he appears indifferent to the din,
which is truly infernal, demonic. Horns howl, blare, shriek; gears
rasp; brakes squeal; Vespas sputter and fart; tyres sing. No human
voice, not even the voice of a radio, can be distinguished in this
mechanical babel, which is magnified as it rings against the rough
stone of the palaces. If the Arno valley is a natural oven, the palaces
are natural amplifiers. The noise is ubiquitous and goes on all day and
night. Far out, in the suburbs, the explosive chatter of a Vespa min-

gles with the cock's crow at four in the morning; in the city an early worker, warming up his scooter, awakens a whole street.

Everyone complains of the noise; with the windows open, no one can sleep. The morning paper reports the protests of hotel-owners, who say that their rooms are empty: foreigners are leaving the city; something must be done; a law must be passed. And within the hotels, there is a continual shuffling of rooms. Number 13 moves to 22, and 22 moves to 33, and 33 to 13 or to Fiesole. In fact, all the rooms are noisy and all are hot, even if an electric fan is provided. The hotel-managers know this, but what can they do? To satisfy the client, they co-operate with polite alacrity in the make-believe of room-shuffling. If the client imagines that he will be cooler or quieter in another part of the hotel, why destroy his illusions? In truth, short of leaving Florence, there is nothing to be done until fall comes and the windows can be shut again. A law already exists forbidding the honking of horns within city limits, but it is impossible to drive in a city like Florence without using your horn to scatter the foot traffic.

As for the Vespas and the Lambrettas, which are the plague of the early hours of the morning, how can a law be framed that will keep their motors quiet? Readers of the morning newspaper write in with suggestions; a meeting is held in Palazzo Vecchio, where more suggestions are aired: merit badges to be distributed to noiseless drivers; state action against the manufacturers; a special police night squad, equipped with radios, empowered to arrest noisemakers of every description; an ordinance that would make a certain type of muffler mandatory, that would make it illegal to race a motor "excessively," that would prohibit motor-scooters from entering the city centre. This last suggestion meets with immense approval; it is the only one Draconian enough to offer hope. But the motor-scooterists' organization at once enters a strong protest ("undemocratic," "discriminatory," it calls the proposal), and the newspaper, which has been leading the anti-noise movement, hurriedly backs water, since Florence is a democratic society, and the scooterists are the *popolo minuto*— small clerks and artisans and factory workers. It would be wrong, the paper concedes, to penalize the many well-behaved scooterists for the sins of a few "savages," and unfair, too, to consider only the city centre and the tourist trade; residents on the periphery should have the right to sleep also. The idea of the police squad with summary powers and wide discretion is once again brought forward, though the city's finances will hardly afford it. Meanwhile, the newspaper sees no recourse but to appeal to the *gentilezza* of the driving public.

This, however, is utopian: Italians are not civic-minded. "What if *you* were waked up at four in the morning?"—this plea, so typically Anglo-Saxon, for the other fellow as an imagined self, elicits from an Italian the realistic answer: "But I *am* up." A young Italian, out early on a Vespa, does not project himself into the person of a young Italian office worker in bed, trying to sleep, still less into the person of a foreign tourist or a hotel-owner. As well ask the wasp, after which the Vespa is named, to think of itself as the creature it is about to sting. The *popolo minuto*, moreover, *likes* noise, as everyone knows. "*Non fa rumore*," objected a young Florentine workman, on being shown an English scooter. "It doesn't make any noise."

All ideas advanced to deal with the Florentine noise problem, the Florentine traffic problem, are utopian, and nobody believes in them, just as nobody believed in Machiavelli's Prince, a utopian image of the ideally self-interested despot. They are dreams, to toy with: the dream of prohibiting *all* motor traffic in the city centre (on the pattern of Venice) and going back to the horse and the donkey; the dream that someone (perhaps the Rockefellers?) would like to build a subway system for the city. . . . Professor La Pira, Florence's Christian Democratic mayor, had a dream of solving the housing problem, another of the city's difficulties: he invited the homeless poor to move into the empty palaces and villas of the rich. This Christian fantasy collided with the laws of property, and the poor were turned out of the palaces. Another dream succeeded it, a dream in the modern idiom of a "satellite" city that would arise southeast of Florence, in a forest of parasol pines, to house the city's workers, who would be conveyed back and forth to their jobs by special buses that would pick them up in the morning, bring them home for lunch, then back to work, and so on. This plan, which had something of science fiction about it, was blocked also; another set of dreamers—

professors, architects, and art historians—rose in protest against the defacement of the Tuscan countryside, pointing to the impracticalities of the scheme, the burdening of the already overtaxed roads and bridges. A meeting was held, attended by other professors and city-planners from Rome and Venice; fiery speeches were made; pamphlets distributed; the preservers won. La Pira, under various pressures (he had also had a dream of eliminating stray cats from the city), had resigned as mayor meanwhile.

But the defeat of Sorgane, as the satellite city was to be called, is only an episode in the factional war being fought in the city, street by street, building by building, bridge by bridge, like the old wars of the Blacks and Whites, Guelphs and Ghibellines, Cerchi and Donati. It is an uncertain, fluctuating war, with idealists on both sides, which began in the nineteenth century, when a façade in the then-current taste was put on the Duomo, the centre of the city was modernized, the old walls along the Arno were torn down. This first victory, of the forces of progress over old Florence, is commemorated by a triumphal arch in the present Piazza della Repubblica with an inscription to the effect that new order and beauty have been brought out of ancient squalor. Today the inscription makes Florentines smile, bitterly, for it is an example of unconscious irony: the present Piazza, with its neon signs advertising a specific remedy against uric acid, is, as everyone agrees, the ugliest in Italy—a folly of nationalist grandeur committed at a time when Florence was, briefly, the capital of the new Italy. Those who oppose change have only to point to it, as an argument for their side, and because of it the preservers have won several victories. Nevertheless, the parasol pines on the hill of Sorgane may yet fall, like the trees in the last act of *The Cherry Orchard*, unless some other solution is found for the housing problem, for Florence is a modern, expanding city—that is partly why the selective tourist dislikes it.

H. V. Morton

(1892–1979)

H. V. Morton was one of the twentieth century's first great travel writers. Reading Morton is like traveling with a learned, curious, convivial companion. He meanders across the landscape, digresses into history, stops to introduce a chance acquaintance, quotes a bit of Shakespeare. Devoid of pedantry, he respects the intellect of his readers while informing and entertaining them. *A Traveller in Italy* is not the "ten-day, five-city bus tour," but a leisurely guided stroll through ancient places.

Henry Vollam Morton was born in Lancashire and came to travel writing through journalism. He worked first on the *Birmingham Gazette* and then on the *Daily Mail*, where he had a popular column about life in London. That column became the bestseller *Heart of London* (1925), and four more London volumes followed. Eventually, he expanded his travel series to the rest of Europe and the Middle East. After World War II he and his wife moved to South Africa, although they often returned to Italy. *A Traveller in Italy*, published in 1964, was one of Morton's last books. When he finished it the manuscript was nearly one thousand pages, and he told his publisher that it would break his heart to cut it. The publisher cut not a word.

from A TRAVELLER IN ITALY

12

The Tiber and the Arno rise in the mountains north of Arezzo and flow south on parallel courses for some way, then the Arno, instead of flowing through Arezzo, turns a "scornful snout," as Dante put it, and, swinging west in a great loop, makes for Florence, Pisa, and the Tyrrhenian Sea. The Tiber flows on steadfastly southwards to Rome.

The valleys through which these rivers flow are among the greatest beauties of Italy, indeed it is almost impossible to decide which of the two is the more attractive. I suppose many people would prefer the wilder upper reaches of the Arno, known as the Casentino, where among the mountains and the falling streams are towns and villages whose history goes back to Rome. Their modern names all carry an echo in Latin: Subbiano—*Sub Janum*; Campogialli—*Campus Gallorum*; Pieve al Bagnoro—*Plebs Balnei Aurei*; Cincelli—*Centum Cellae*; Traiana—*Trajanus*; Campoluci—*Campus Lucii*; Capolona—*Caput Leonis*; and so on. Upon the highest points of the Central Apennines in the Casentino are two monasteries, Camaldoli, and La Verna, where S. Francis received the Stigmata.

To me the Tiber Valley appealed quite as much as the Casentino. It delighted me to see the youthful Tiber babbling over its stones on its long journey to Rome. I thought the peasants in these two rich valleys different from those round Florence and Siena, and wondered whether the old way of life was stronger here. In the Valley of the Tiber I really did see the haughty type of young woman painted by Piero della Francesca.

In a maze of side-roads that twist in all directions three or four miles west of the young Tiber, a hill covered with the white, red roofed buildings of a small town rises from the plain. Its name is Monterchi, which is the modern corruption of *Mons Herculis*; and it was the birthplace of Piero's mother. The view from its ramparts is magnificent. I looked north across the Tiber Valley to the Alpe della Luna and south into Umbria. It was wonderful to stand there on a summer's morning and to follow the white threads of the lanes between the vineyards and the orchards, and to hear, borne up upon the hot and lazy air, such country sounds as the barking of farm dogs, the song of some invisible worker in the fields, and the creak of an ox-wagon as it wound its way round the hill up to the quiet, pretty little town.

On the flat land at the foot of Monterchi a double line of cypress trees leads up to the cemetery on the hillside opposite the town, and in its tiny mortuary chapel Piero della Francesca painted one of his most famous frescoes—*Madonna del Parto*—the Pregnant Madonna. The chapel contains only an altar below the fresco. When I entered there was no one there but a peasant girl who had just lit a lamp on the altar and, turning, revealed herself to be in the same condition as

the Madonna. Above the altar Piero has painted a dome-shaped
pavilion, much the same kind of circular tent in which Constantine is
sleeping in the Arezzo frescoes, but richer and more ornate. Two
winged angels gracefully lift the entrance to this tent to reveal inside
a young woman in a light blue gown of fifteenth-century cut, evidently a maternity gown of the period, unbuttoned down the front,
accentuating her condition.

She is one of the most beautiful of Piero della Francesca's women.
Like all of this artist's pictures, this lingers in the memory, and afterwards I was haunted by it and wanted to see it again, as I was to do
on three occasions. Every time I returned to see the fresco, it
refreshed my mind like a great poem one has committed to memory.

The second time I was there two pregnant women came up the
cypress avenue and placed on the altar two little tins which they filled
with olive oil, then, having placed a wick in the oil and set it alight,
they prayed and went out. The village girls for miles around make
this offering to the *Madonna del Parto*, asking her for an easy delivery.

How strange to see this procession of life to a cemetery. Quite
often birth and death must meet at the door of this chapel; and that
is probably what Piero della Francesca intended.

A few miles from Monterchi I crossed the infant Tiber and, travelling
through a rich land of vines, olives, and fat, white cattle, came to
Sansepolcro, the artist's birthplace. I found a small town gathered,
with its ridged red roofs, within crumbling ramparts. It was market
day and a number of booths had been set up where vegetables, secondhand clothes, and agricultural tools were being sold. When I
asked a passer-by to direct me to the *Resurrezione*, he pointed to an
old building approached by a double flight of steps, which turned
out to be the Law Court. Through an open door I saw a lawsuit in
progress: a policeman was standing by, an advocate was arguing a
case, while the magistrate was solemnly writing notes, wearing what
looked like an undergraduate's gown. I thought I had come to the
wrong building until the caretaker, uttering that hissing sound made
by Italians on such occasions and scratching the air with the fingers
of one hand, signed for me to follow him. In the next room, a large

gaunt hall, I saw, facing me upon the end wall, t̶
Piero della Francesca.

It is early morning. The rising sun has touched wit̶
thin clouds that lie in a blue sky. Four Roman soldiers ̶
asleep beside a marble sarcophagus. They have watched all n̶
now, with the dawn, have dozed off in awkward attitudes: th̶e of
them have not even removed their helmets. Above them rises a tremendous revelation of strength. Christ has emerged from the grave
and stands above the four figures, gazing straight ahead, with his bare
left foot upon the marble. A pink cloak, touched with the morning
light, falls in thick folds over His left shoulder, leaving His right arm
and the right side of His body bare. He holds a banner bearing a
red cross and on His body, below the breast, is a red lance wound.
His figure appears real, yet it belongs to the other world: if one were
ever to have a vision, I thought, it would have this startling impact
upon one.

The expression of suppressed strength in the Saviour's attitude
and face is like no other painting of Christ I have ever seen. He is
nearer in appearance to the Pantokrator with wide searching eyes
who gazes straight at you from the semi-dome of Byzantine churches,
than to the gentle, compassionate Christ of Christian Art. The contrast between the relaxed figures of the sleeping men and the taut,
upright figure, so wide-awake, is like the culminating moment in a
drama. How can those men continue to sleep with that stupendous
apparition above them? And as I looked at the bearded face of this
powerful, unsentimental Christ, the words ran through my mind: "He
descended into hell; the third day he rose again from the dead."

13

Two or three years ago I happened to go into a secondhand book-
shop in Cape Town to buy a fairly scarce book on Florence. The
bookseller, whose name is Anthony Clarke, spoke of Italy as he had
seen it as a gunner officer in the last war.

"I always like to think," he said, surprisingly, "that I am responsible for the safety of Piero della Francesca's *Resurrection* in Sansepol-

ɔ.' I asked him to tell me the story, which he later put into writing. "It was sometime in 1944," wrote Mr. Clarke. "I was then a troop commander in the Chestnut Troop 'A' Battery, 1st Regiment, R.H.A. Our regiment was the artillery support for the independent 9th Armoured Brigade, and 'Chestnuts' were supporting the 3rd Hussars. For a while, I recall, we were based around Città di Castello and then moved north. It was during this move that I was ordered to establish an observation post overlooking Sansepolcro.

"At first light I moved forward in my tank on the eastward slopes of the hills on the east, and then, with a signaller and a portable wireless, walked over the crest onto the forward slopes. We cleared out the inside of a large bush, made ourselves as comfortable as possible—for we were going to be there all day—and settled down to watch and wait. We were not in direct communication with our guns (this might have some bearing on what took place later) as our wireless had not the range. We were in communication with our tank, and the tank's wireless was in touch with the Battery.

"I ordered one round of fire from one gun on a particular range and bearing somewhere in the middle of the valley, so should I need gunfire in a hurry I would have a fair idea what order to give without having to fuss around with a map and protractor. Our guns were about two to three miles south.

"Then we waited. The sun came up in a cloudless sky and Sansepolcro lay clearly before us. I was told over the wireless that the enemy were suspected of being in the town and that I was to shell it prior to our troops moving in. So I ranged on the town and put down two or three rounds of troop fire (4 guns). My battery commander, Marcus Linton, M.C., R.H.A., informed me over the wireless that ammunition was plentiful and that I could go ahead and use as much as I liked. An attack was going to be launched the next morning and it was up to us to clear the town first. So I shelled Sansepolcro. In the meantime I was scanning the town almost yard by yard and was unable to see any sign of the enemy anywhere, though, of course, that did not mean they were not there! At the back of my mind a small question kept nagging. Why did I know the name of Sansepolcro? Somewhere I had heard the name and it must have been in connection with something important for me to remember it. But when or where I could not remember.

"Then my signaller and I had a visitor. He was a ragged youngster with a dog. We said, '*Tedeschi*—Sansepolcro?' and pointed to the town. He shook his head and grinned and pointed to the hills. The Germans had vacated the town, a further support of my own opinion. Then I remembered why I knew the name of Sansepolcro— ('the Greatest Painting in the World!'). I must have been about eighteen when I read that essay of Aldous Huxley's. I recalled clearly his description of the tiring journey from Arezzo and how it was worth it for at the end of it lay Francesca's *Resurrection*, 'the greatest painting in the world!'

"I estimated the number of shells I had fired and was sure that if I had not destroyed the greatest painting I had done considerable damage. So I fired no more . . . We sat, the signaller and I, under our covering bush watching for, but never seeing, any enemy. When it was dark we withdrew and returned to the gun position.

"The next day we entered Sansepolcro unmolested. I asked immediately for the picture. The building was untouched. I hurried inside and there it was, secure and magnificent. The townsfolk had started to sandbag it, but the sandbags were only about waist-high. I looked up at the roof: one shell, I knew, would have been sufficient to undo the admiration of centuries. And that is that. Sometimes I wonder how I would be feeling now if I had happened to destroy the *Resurrection*. At one time I thought of writing to Aldous Huxley. The incident might, I suppose, be a fine illustration of the power of literature, and that the pen is mightier than the sword!"

I went to see the picture again with Alberto, who took a camera and a flash-gun with him. It was an unusual experience, remembering the reverent atmosphere of the Uffizi, to observe the homely casualness with which the masterpiece is treated in its native town. When Alberto said he wished to take a photograph, a stout table was immediately produced for him to stand on, and helpers emerged on every hand; I think I recognized even the magistrate.

In the afternoon we went to visit one of Alberto's many friends, who has a house on the ramparts of Sansepolcro. He happened to be out, but his wife insisted that we should drink a glass of vermouth as we walked about the garden, gazing on one side over the ridged roofs and chimney-pots of Sansepolcro to the silver thread of the Tiber in the valley beyond, and, on the other, into the Buitoni factory. Miles of macaroni and spaghetti now carry the name of Sansepolcro to all parts of the world. We were shown over the model factory and admired shining machines which pressed out the pasta and passed it on to others, which packed it. All this began in the last century with Grandmother Buitoni, whose primitive, cast-iron spaghetti machines are to be admired in the factory's museum.

Some of the small towns in the Casentino and the Tiber Valleys are visible from miles away, seated proudly upon their hills; others, like Anghiari, you see when high above them on a winding road which gives an eagle's view into their streets—you can even see if it is market day—then, as you wind your way down, the view changes and you can no longer see within the walls but, with every bend of the road and each new vista, the walls grow higher until, as you descend into the valley, you look up and see the town high above you on its rock.

The smallest of these places would not be embarrassed to entertain pope or king. Though the inhabitants may be small farmers, and the most important people are the priest, the chemist, and the *Maresciallo die Carabinieri*, who know how affairs are conducted in the great world. It is surprising what splendour can be unearthed for a special occasion, maybe even a theatre, as in Anghiari. This is an unexpected little Scala to find in a small mountain fastness, and the inscription *Teatro di Anghiari del l'Accademia de' Ricomposti* links the little place, if not perhaps with Plato, at least with the age of academies. Now, of course, times have changed. I noticed a florid poster showing a woman cowering before a revolver, an advertisement for a film called *La Morsa si Chiude*.

I remember Anghiari for having sheltered me during a heavy downpour when the piazza became a lake into which every hilly street poured its torrent. Water shot in the most graceful curves from every roof and blocked-up gutter. I took refuge in an antique shop into which I had to creep sideways, so full was it of old chestnut and mahogany chests-of-drawers, washstands, copper pans, basins and jugs, old pictures in battered frames, chairs, tables, and the rest. I discovered the owner seated with a couple of friends among piles of chairs and tables, eating a water melon. Moving aside a few armchairs and a card-table or two, they smiled pleasantly and welcomed me with a scarlet segment. There was an old inlaid chestnut writing-table that I could have had for almost nothing, but it was heavy and in these days there are no warships waiting to take a traveller's purchases to his native land.

My favourite town is Poppi, which I think of as the capital of the Casentino. One meets mediaevalism all over the north of Italy, but this town seemed to me to be a living fragment of a remote past. It is a town of enchanters, knights, and maidens with long hair at castle windows. Even the small bus that links Poppi with Arezzo might, by a small stretch of the imagination, be an enchanted dragon, or a dragon condemned by a sorcerer to imitate a diesel engine with its groans and its shrieks and its sudden jets of smoke. It is a town of stone arcades which lead up to a castle, clearly a relative of the Palazzo Vecchio in Florence. After dark, when the lamps are lit, Poppi becomes quite sinister, and a couple of amiable citizens, as they play a game of dominoes in a wine shop, might be the first and second murderers. The centre of the town is not large enough to be called a piazza, but is at the top of a hilly street where several roads meet. In the centre an octagonal baroque oratory is dedicated to Our Lady of the Plague, and the story is that during a visitation of the plague centuries ago, the priest walked round the town with the image of the Virgin, whereupon the plague instantly ceased. The words *Ave Maria* are written over the altar. Ten o'clock is past bedtime in Poppi, and at that late hour a little group of people sometimes waits in the darkness for the last bus to arrive from Arezzo. It can be heard some way off in the valley, as it gnashes its teeth and snorts along from Bibbiena, then it growls menacingly and seems to pause and gather strength for its uphill pull to the town, where it arrives fuming. It almost exactly fits some of the narrow streets, and as it comes to a stop with a belch of rage and draconian puffs of diesel oil, those inside, led by the village priest, stand up and, as if performing the same physical exercise, or some religious act, stretch their arms in unison and lift down suitcases, wicker-baskets, and brown paper parcels. The priest is the first to descend, his steel spectacles gleaming, his shovel hat like a ruffled cat, a large parcel beneath his arm. There is much kissing of children and cries of welcome; relatives and friends, thank God, are safe within the walls of Poppi again!

The caretaker of the castle of Poppi is Leonido Gatteschi, who is eighty years old. He wears a black beret and carries a cane with a gold knob. He will tell you, as he stands on the ramparts above the plain, looking out to the mountains where you can see La Verna and Camaldoli, that he has looked after the castle for sixty-five years and his chief worry is that no one will take over from him. He is inclined to blame the younger generation—striplings of forty and fifty—for having no sense of responsibility. If the Counts of Guidi ever had a devoted seneschal, his spirit must have been reborn in Leonido Gatteschi.

It is an impressive castle and in such good condition that you could move in tomorrow with your men-at-arms and serving wenches, and make it quite comfortable with a few tapestries. I don't think I have ever seen a more decorative and dramatic courtyard, with its picturesque staircase emblazoned with coats-of-arms and a balustrade of nearly a hundred miniature stone columns. Signor Gatteschi led me over the castle, talking all the time and waving the gold-topped cane, which in his hands became a wand of office. I saw a chapel where ghostly frescoes of the Giotto School were struggling through the whitewash; I saw gaunt halls in which the knights of the Middle Ages managed to make themselves massively comfortable; and, most interesting of all, I saw the bedroom of the Guidi Counts, a large room notable for some excellent mediaeval plumbing. The water, which was laid on, was filtered through charcoal, and I noticed above a stone wash-basin the name Panosco Ridolfi and the date was 1469. The town library is kept in this room. How incredible it is, and how typical of Italy, that a library of twenty thousand volumes, including nearly eight hundred incunabula and six hundred illuminated manuscripts, also town records that go back to 1330, should be seen incidentally as one rambles over a mediaeval castle.

When we were on the ramparts, we looked to the north and saw in the valley beneath us the site of the battle of Campaldino, in which

Dante fought, when the Ghibellines of Arezzo were beaten by the Florentine Guelphs on a summer's day in 1289. So began Arezzo's long history as a colony or subject city of Florence.

We turned away from that depressing sight and looked to the south. Seeing the old man on the ramparts waving his gold-topped cane above the distant valleys, one might have imagined that he was seeking some flash of the sun on helmet or lance-point, a sign that his lord would not be late for dinner.

15

"I wish to introduce you to a beautiful lady," said Alberto one morning. "Please don't ask me any questions, but just come with me." We motored north from Arezzo into the Casentino, where the Arno advances and retreats from the road, sometimes, as at Subbiano, flowing beside it for miles, dark and reed-fringed. At a little place called Rassina, we turned into a side road and were soon approaching a mountain called the Pratomagno. Such roads are one of the surprises of the Casentino. They often expire, as if from sheer fatigue, upon the flanks of the mountains, where mule tracks continue up to hill villages which appear to be as remote, though only a few miles from Florence or Arezzo, as if they were still in the Middle Ages.

We met nothing on our road but mules loaded with wood, moving in single file. Suddenly, rounding a bend, we saw that the road went no farther. When Alberto cut off the engine, we heard the rush of water tumbling from a wooded ravine and, looking up, we saw a white village above us.

"That is Carda," said Alberto. "We shall have to leave the car and climb up by the path." We could see this track winding round between immense boulders. "But first let us see whether my friend is about."

There were some brick buildings surrounded by a high fence at the foot of the mountain. We entered the enclosure and saw a man in waders feeding ravenous trout. The long, concrete channels of a trout hatchery boiled with fish as the man cast chopped liver into the water. In some channels the fish were little fingerlings which looked, as they fought for their food, as if someone had thrown a bowl of silver into the water; others were about a pound in weight, while some were enormous.

"Those are the ones the trout fishermen buy if they cannot catch anything in the mountains!" remarked Alberto. "Oh yes, of course," he added, noting my look of surprise, "no fisherman would face his wife with an empty basket!"

The man locked up the trout hatchery, and together we climbed up the mule track to Carda. We arrived at a picturesque group of stone houses built on various levels, with a tiny church and its bell-tower on the highest point, facing a small, open space, the so-called piazza, from whose boundary wall I looked into a valley far below. Everything was granite-grey, and there was not a tree or shrub in sight. Hens and geese ran in and out of the houses, and on every side were ravines and precipices and a view of the Protomagno rolling away into the distance. It was astonishing to think that Florence was less than thirty miles to the north-west as the crow flies, and Arezzo about twenty miles to the south, yet we might have been in Tibet.

The inhabitants gathered round, the men talkative and interested, the women standing inquisitively in the doorways, the hostile geese lengthening their necks at us and hissing.

"You are now going to see the beautiful lady," whispered Alberto.

We entered the little church where, above the altar, I was shown the Madonna of Carda.

"She is said to be the work of Andrea della Robbia," said Alberto, "but you will find no picture of her in any book on art or on the della Robbias, and she is one of the most beautiful Madonnas ever made by Andrea. The people of Carda believe that the lost secret of the della Robbia glaze is concealed in her head, but, of course, that is a story you hear of other della Robbia masterpieces."

The villagers glanced at us, delighted with our interest in their treasure. They all talked at once, anxious to tell us the epic of Carda: how the Madonna came to the mountain village. The story is that in 1554, when Florence was at war with Siena, two men of Carda were fighting with the Florentine army. One day they came to a ruined church in that part of the Chiana Valley which then belonged to Siena, and, entering this church, they saw the Madonna above the ruined altar and fell on their knees. They promised that should she bring them safely through the war, they would carry her away from her ruined church and install her in their own church in Carda. First carefully hiding the statue where they could find it again, they rejoined their troop; and when the war was over, they recovered the Madonna and, in spite of its weight, took it in turns to carry it on their backs to Carda. It is life-size and of white glaze, and one of the most beautiful works of this master that I have seen. She has been attractively mounted in a niche against a blue background.

The manager of the trout farm invited us to his house, which was built on the hillside in such a way that the door was at roof level and we went downstairs to the kitchen. Here his wife brewed coffee while he produced a bottle of vermouth and some local cheese, which was the best I have ever tasted. This sheep's milk cheese varies from town to town throughout Italy; in some towns it is as hard as parmesan, in others it has the texture of gruyère, and it can also be soft, though I think perhaps the right name for this kind of cheese is *cacio pecorino*. When I said that I had seen no sheep on the mountain, our host told me that the village owned a large communal flock which was pastured on the other side of the hill. There was a shepherds' rota in the village so that everyone took his turn in looking after the flock. "It is worth while to come back to Carda in the evening," he said, "to see the sheep flowing like a river in the lanes and each one finding its own way home."

Alberto chaffed him about Carda's annual carnival, which must also be a sight worth witnessing. A competition is held for original ways to eat spaghetti; the winner last year had eaten it out of a shoe! Anyone found at work on carnival morning is tied up and carried to the space in front of the church, where he is obliged to empty glass after glass of wine until he can hardly stand, and at that moment is elected King of the Carnival.

"Did I keep my promise?" asked Alberto on the way back.

"You did," I replied. "She is one of the beauties of Tuscany."

16

A few miles to the north-west of Sansepolcro, upon the mountains that slope down to the valley of the Tiber, a narrow winding road of the kind described as *non carrozzabile* leads to the hamlet of Caprese. Later ages have added to Caprese the name of Michelangelo. It was here, upon the sixth of March in the year 1475, that an unexplainable miracle occurred when a nice, commonplace couple brought a genius down to earth. And the little heart that began to beat that day on the hilltop of Caprese was to go on beating for eighty-nine years, at the end of which time a sad, tired, disillusioned old man with burning eyes, a broken nose, and a long white beard, one who felt that he had failed and had been frustrated by the vanity of popes, caught a cold and died in Rome.

On the way up to the village I saw nobody except a gang of road workers who were removing a rock fall, then I came to a few houses and, after several more hairpin bends, arrived at the top of the hill and to a group of old stone buildings which stood deserted, with a locked-up air about them. It was a strange place in which to find a monument. I walked to it and saw in bronze relief the infant Michelangelo starting up from his cradle in surprise at the sight of a vision of his *Night* from the Medici Tombs and, in the background, the *Moses*. This extraordinary conception is perhaps a little too dramatic. What is so appealing about the infancy of genius is that there is nothing to distinguish it from ordinary infancy. It is only in later childhood that the first of those signs appear which indicates that a human being may have been set apart to achieve more, and to sorrow more, than ordinary men. Remembering Michelangelo's troubles with Julius II, I thought it a little unfair to give him such an early vision of the *Moses*!

Upon the side of a double-storey building erected on the edge of the mountain, and approached by way of an outside stair, I read an inscription which said that Michelangelo had been born there. The building was locked and the houses opposite appeared to be empty. I was about to leave when a small car arrived containing a young man and an old one whose face might have been carved out of walnut shell. The young man was the village schoolmaster, with a roll call of sixteen, he told me; the old man produced some keys and we unlocked the birthplace and opened the windows.

The house has been transformed since Ludovico Buonarroti and his wife Francesca dei Neri went to live there. It is now a gaunt hall with some photographs of Michelangelo's work on the walls and a few books and magazines in an adjoining room called the library. Next to the birthplace is a chapel in which Michelangelo was christened, a humble, barnlike place which has recently been restored. These two buildings, and the foundations of an ancient castle which had just been discovered a few paces away, were all there was to be seen.

It is not possible to imagine the young Michelangelo crawling about this hilltop, or learning to walk there, since, while still an infant in arms, he was taken to the family property at Settignano, a few miles from Florence, and put out to nurse with a stonecutter's wife. "If there is anything good in me," he once said to Vasari, "it comes from the pure air of your Arezzo hills where I was born, and perhaps also from the milk of my nurse with which I sucked in the chisels and hammers with which I used to carve my figures." Certainly there was nothing in his family history to explain his genius. His father was an impoverished man of good family who thought it beneath his dignity to be a merchant or a mechanic and preferred to haunt the Medici and beg for odd jobs. That the temporary post of magistrate at Chiusi and Caprese had fallen vacant for six months, and had been accepted by Ludovico Buonarroti, is the reason why Michelangelo happened to be born there. Though the elder Buonarroti declined to soil his own hands, he had no compunction at all in receiving the proceeds of Michelangelo's handiwork when his son became famous; indeed as long as his father and brothers lived, Michelangelo sent them money to maintain their farm, but was never able to satisfy their needs.

We closed the windows and locked up the house, and as I went off down the hill, the idea that appealed to me was not that of an infant haunted by future greatness, but of two infants: Michelangelo on the hill, and the Tiber in the valley below, both at the beginning of their journey to Rome.

I had arranged to meet Alberto on another hilltop, at Sigliano, for a picnic with the *Associazione Amici della Musica di Arezzo*. There was a scene of bustle and excitement on this hilltop. Motor coaches had arrived with the musicians and their friends, and they were now strolling about admiring the view of the vineyards as they sloped down to the infant Tiber and inspecting the only building on the hill, a venerable little church which contained an early fresco of S. Christopher and the infant Jesus.

Most of the excitement was caused by about thirty young women, all of them, I was told, aspiring professional pianists, who had come from various countries to a musical finishing-school, and as they tripped over the hilltop in their high heels, they vied with each other in winning a smile from their host, a celebrated musician. It was delightful to watch so much international charm in action, but, alas, the maestro, who was accustomed to it, wore the air of a languid god.

The old priest stood beaming in his worn cassock, delighted by the invasion and by the smell of grilled steak which rose from a corner of the west wall of his church, where waiters in dinner-jackets— incredible touch!—were busy with a charcoal grill. The old man took me into his house to wash in a tin basin. The building was as bleak and lonely as a hermit's cell. I could see few books, but the vegetable garden was admirable. We stood above the sun-drenched world, looking down the hillside where the olive trees stood, each with its little circle of shade, towards the valley where the Tiber was sliding over its pebbles.

Tables, their white cloths held down by stones, had been set out in the shade of the olive trees, and the waiters carried round casks of red and white Chianti and filled the carafes. Some of the more robust spirits, including Alberto, proposed many toasts before the meal began, so that when eventually we sat down to gigantic Florentine steaks, the party had reached the state of exhilaration which usually occurs much later. On my left was an American woman who seemed to have no connection at all with the Society, but she was a distinct acquisition to it.

"Have you noticed," she asked, "the number of country people around here who have steel dentures?"

"No, I haven't."

"Well, just watch out," she said, "and don't say you haven't been warned! I guess there was some shortage of porcelain, or whatever it is, during the war, so they fitted them out with steel instead. It's terrific! When they smile at you, you want to run for your life!"

The meal ended with pears and *pecorino*, then came the speeches, so full of flourishes, tributes, and compliments which had to be delivered to the last syllable. We were grateful to the priest's dog for chasing a cat up a tree and driving the hens under the main table round the feet of the maestro himself; but the speeches continued.

What a picture it was. Beyond the shade in which we sat, the white world blazed with heat, and we could hear the drowsy sounds of afternoon coming up from the valley. The pretty girls leaning on their elbows at their table in the dappled shadow, making eyes above their wine glasses, lighting their cigarettes, and adopting in the spattered light a dozen relaxed attitudes that would have delighted Renoir, turned the mind away from the speeches to other times. Nothing is new in Tuscany, we were merely the latest of those who had laughed and joked upon that hilltop under the same blue sky.

Eric Newby

(1919–)

In 1942 veteran travel writer Eric Newby, then a British soldier, was captured and imprisoned in a Nazi POW camp in the Apennine Mountains. A year later he escaped and hid among the remote communities of the Po Valley near Parma. One of the locals who aided him was a bank clerk of Slovenian extraction named Wanda. They fell in love, were reunited after the war, and married. Wanda not only became Eric Newby's wife, but also his literary foil in their adventures throughout the world. The story of their wartime affair became Newby's *Love and War in the Apennines* (1971).

After the war the couple settled in England, but returned to Italy in the 1960s and bought a dilapidated farmhouse, I Castagni (The Chestnuts), near the town of Fosdinovo. Their obstacles are familiar to readers of this genre—rats as big as cats, a house that lacks even rudimentary essentials like a roof, a balky septic tank that was an epidemic waiting to happen—but Eric and Wanda's affection for this land and its history, coupled with their own memories of war, make a compelling story. Unlike many other British and American expatriates who colonized Tuscany, the Newbys bonded with their neighbors.

In 1991 Eric and Wanda sold I Castagni. The life of the *contadini* had changed; tractors and cars roared on the small hillside roads. Many of their neighbors died and no one wanted to do the hard labor of maintaining the *vigneto* and the olive trees. "It has taken us a long time even to begin to realize that we aren't part of the life of I Castagni any more," wrote Newby in his memoir *A Small Place in Italy* (1999), from which this selection is excerpted, "and I don't think we ever will realize it completely as long as we live."

from A SMALL PLACE IN ITALY

Easter Sunday fell almost as late as it possibly could, and when we set off for Italy on the Tuesday of Easter week, it was in a Land Rover crammed with everything we could think of that might help us to survive in what was little more than the shell of a house.

All the way across France and Northern Italy it poured and poured, except at the Mont Blanc Tunnel where it was snowing at both ends, as it had been the previous time. As Wanda said, "When it comes to travelling we are some pickers!"

We eventually reached the eighteenth, twenty-first or twenty-second bend, or whatever it was, in the early afternoon of Good Friday, Venerdì Santo. The weather was much too bad to attempt to open up the house and we decided to stay the night in a hotel up at Fosdinovo. We had had enough of camping.

So we continued on up another lot of bends until we reached the town of Fosdinovo, which up to now we had not seen except once in passing through it, and there we put up at one of the two hotels.

The town was situated on a steep-sided spur, more than five hundred metres above the sea, and much of it was almost completely hidden from view behind its mediaeval walls and ramparts. The hotel we had chosen to stay in stood just outside the lower of the two principal gates. To the east and west the ramparts terminated in a series of precipices, falling away on the eastern side to dense forests. To the west they fell, equally steeply, to the same sort of terraced hill country in which I Castagni was situated. Through it ran a deep gorge, carved out by a torrent that had its origin higher up the mountainside, and eventually emptied itself, that is when there was any water to empty, into the Magra near Sarzana. All in all, Fosdinovo would have been a difficult place for a besieging army to take. The only possible way would have been to attack it from the top of the spur but this was effectively defended by the vast Castello Malaspina.

The Castello was an ideal residence for the Malaspina who spent much of the time over many centuries, in common with other members of the local aristocracy, plotting. From the fourteenth century onwards, they were a power in the region, reinforced by judicious couplings with such famous families as the Gambacorti of Pisa, the Doria, the Centurione, the Pallavicini of Genoa, the Orsucci of Lucca, the Santelli of Pesaro and the Cangrande della Scala, a union recorded by a marble relief over the entrance to the Castello, depicting a dog with a flowering hawthorn in its mouth. And they remained a power until 1796 when Carlo Emanuele Malaspina was deprived of his domains by the French.

The hotel was of a sort that had already long since become a rarity in most parts of Italy, even the most remote, and although we neither of us knew it at the time, its days in its present form were numbered.

Old, if not ancient, dark, cavernous, rambling were just some of the epithets that could be applied to it without being offensive. In fact it was lovely. Its rooms were full of good rustic furniture of the mid-nineteenth century and of later date, of a sort that we would have been only too happy to acquire for I Castagni: presses and chests of drawers in mahogany and chestnut which could swallow up heaps of clothes; cylindrical marble-topped bedside tables of the sort that Attilio possessed which also secreted within them massive *vasi da notte* with floral embellishments, receptacles of which, judging by the sanitary arrangements obtaining at I Castagni, we were going to stand in constant need.

But most desirable of all were the beautiful bedsteads, of all shapes and sizes, built of wood or wrought iron with tin-plate panels painted with flowers and Arcadian landscapes, or decorated with mother-of-pearl, or very simple ones constructed entirely of wrought iron with no embellishment at all.

The hotel was owned by a local butcher who had a shop a few yards up the road, inside what had been one of the gates of the town. He also made excellent *salami*. He was a good butcher, but he always gave the impression of being on the point of falling asleep, like the Dormouse in *Alice in Wonderland*. Even shaking hands with him was an enervating experience.

His wife was of an entirely different disposition: large but not fat, black-haired, full of energy, what the Italians call *slancio*, and with a voice that made the rafters ring, and she was as adept at cutting meat or boning hams as her husband.

She was also extremely generous. The morning of Easter Saturday when we left the hotel to go down to I Castagni and paid our bill she gave us an entire *salame* as if it were an arrival present, and whenever thereafter we bought anything in the shop and she was there she always gave us something extra, which meant that we couldn't use it as much as we might otherwise have done.

There were two daughters of marriageable age, both of whom had fiancés. They were personable girls and were a good catch for any young men, with an hotel, a *ristorante*, a *caffè/bar* and butcher's shop as visible future assets. Meanwhile they acted as waitresses and chambermaids and ran the bar, all of which was enough to be getting on with, while the Signora's elderly mother did the cooking for the *ristorante* with some outside help in the season, which had not yet begun. Both subsequently married.

After we had signed in and had been consigned to one of the cavernous bedrooms which by now, with the awful weather prevailing outside, was almost totally dark, the two girls invited us to take part in the *Processione del Venerdì Santo*.

This procession, which had to end in the afternoon, at the hour of Christ's death, was due to start in a couple of minutes from the Oratorio dei Bianchi, an old church in the middle of the town. In the course of this procession the participants would make an almost complete tour of it. They themselves were going to take part. Would we like to go with them? We said yes.

Swathed in the warmest clothes we had at our disposal, but still inadequately clad—the wind was coming straight off the Apuan Alps, which were newly snow-covered—we set off with the girls for the piazza in which the Oratorio was situated and in which the procession would be assembling.

The piazza was about the size of a squash court and one side of it was entirely taken up by one façade of the Oratorio, an austere and beautiful construction of what appeared to be almost translucent marble. It had been built in 1600 by Pasquale Malaspina and a great marble escutcheon over the entrance displayed the coat of arms of the Malaspina, a flowering hawthorn. Below it there was an Annunciation carved in the same material. Inside the building, hidden behind the high altar, was a wooden statue of the Madonna, carved in 1300 and lodged here when the church was built, after the original one was destroyed by fire.

Normally the doors of the Oratorio were kept closed but this afternoon they were wide open to allow an effigy of the Crucified

Christ to be taken out from it into the piazza on a wooden float carried by a band of porters, who supported the weight on their shoulders. Two other men also emerged from it bearing a funereal-looking black and silver banner which was now giving trouble in the wind that was swirling around the piazza.

At the head of the procession was the rather elderly priest of Fosdinovo and Caniparola, dressed in black vestments. He was accompanied by a couple of acolytes, who were without their censers, because they were not used in such processions, and a good thing too, in the wind that was blowing, they might easily have set themselves on fire, or some other participant.

They were followed by the main body of the faithful, among whom we found ourselves. Altogether there were not many more than fifty people and most of them were women. There were also a few children; but it was not surprising that there was a poor turn-out. It was terrible weather for a procession. Already at around two in the afternoon it was growing dark.

Conspicuous among the few men present in the piazza, apart from those who would be carrying the images, looking benevolently at all and sundry, was Attilio who, we later learned, was not only *molto religioso* but also a *grande appassionato* of religious feasts and processions. He had walked up from I Castagni in the appalling weather in order to attend this one and, in spite of the buffering he must have received on the way, was very smart in a long, dark navy-blue, fur-collared overcoat of antique cut which almost reached to his ankles, and an article of clothing without which neither of us saw him, except when, later on, he had to go to hospital, his cap.

As soon as he saw us he came shooting across the piazza as if it was ice—in fact it was wet marble and equally slippery. Then, after paying his respects to the girls in a formal manner, he took our hands in his, first Wanda's, then mine, and pumped them up and down as if he expected water to come gushing out of our mouths, at the same time saying, so far as either of us could understand, how happy he was to see us.

But what was more extraordinary, so far as I was concerned, was that, when he began the pumping treatment he said, perfectly audibly, after having more or less cut me dead up to now, "*Adesso ricordo!*" ("Now I remember!")

What he said was mysterious, if not ambiguous. Unless I knew, which I now did without a shadow of doubt, that he, Attilio, and the old man in the mountains of twenty-odd years ago were not one and the same, I would have thought that when he said, "*Adesso ricordo!*" he was remembering that time, whereas what he was presumably referring to was our brief encounter five months ago. I gave up. Two storytellers, both of whom could make things, both of whom were *religioso*, one of whom, possibly both of whom, prayed by their bedsides, although there must be, I realized, whole hordes of little old men in Italy who do just that, were more than I could cope with. Eventually the whole thing was resolved when I asked Signora Angiolina if Attilio had ever gone away from home during the war. She said categorically no, he hadn't. I was sorry I asked. Perhaps it would have been better if it had remained a mystery but short of having a sphinx on the premises at I Castagni I could hardly complain.

Anyway I didn't care. What he had just said to me gave me the same feelings of pleasure that I would experience in the future when Signora Angiolina said to me "*Hai fatto bene!*" To be remembered by Attilio was different from being remembered by any Tom, Dick or Harry, or even General de Gaulle. He never enlarged on what he meant again. Now, however, to show where his sympathies lay, he attached himself, as it were, to our suite and prepared to walk with us in the procession.

It was at this moment that the priest gave some kind of inconspicuous signal, but one that was sufficient to set the whole thing in motion, and we all began to move uphill with the priest in the van, flanked by the acolytes, followed by Christ nailed to the Cross and the two men carrying the black and silver banner flapping madly in the wind, and behind them the main body of whom I was certainly the only Protestant present, snuffling and sneezing, for a number of them had already contracted nasty colds, sometimes chanting, sometimes reciting the rosary or saying various Lenten prayers, but somehow contriving not to do all these at the same time, which would have resulted in pandemonium.

The priest, although he looked rather old, was fearfully fit. He led us at what amounted to a trot into the teeth of the freezing wind and zoomed us through the winding streets and alleys, flanked by secretive-looking houses that made up Fosdinovo, mediaeval streets and alleys in which, this Friday afternoon, almost every house had at least one window with a candle burning in it, to welcome the procession.

Some windows were draped in funereal Lenten black, others were less lugubrious with white lace curtains and some were positively jolly with flowers displayed in them. We passed an ancient Malaspina theatre that was no longer a theatre and a Malaspina mint that was no longer a mint. It only minted fifty genuine coins in its entire history. The rest, which were exported to Genova and France, were all false.

And there were shops, some of them minute, also illuminated with candles. Shops that sold wine, spades, handsaws and other iron-ware, hand-knitted socks with the natural grease still in them, and magazines giving the latest low-down on what was currently going on with the Grimaldis in the Principality of Monaco, events on which all Italy was hooked.

And we passed a *caffè* from the windows of which some of the male occupants looked out on the procession with the curious, slightly derisory air with which men in Italy look out of the windows of *caffès* at religious processions. That is if they are agnostic, commu-nist, or simply not taking part in the procession for their own private reasons, keeping, as it were, their cards close to their chests.

That is also if they hadn't got wives or mothers or grandmothers taking part in the processions. If they had, and if they had any sense and wanted a quiet life, they would keep a much lower profile and get on with watching TV, or playing *briscola*, a sort of whist, and not start looking out the window with that superior expression on their faces.

By now the wind was tremendous. At one point we came out on some ramparts below the Castello and there a savage blast caught the crucifix, bringing the bearers to their knees and almost throwing it to the ground, which would have been a *malaugurio*—and forcing the men carrying the banner to furl it.

Now we were rounding the foot of the keep of the Castello, a huge fortress in which Dante had been put up in 1306, while he wrote some stanzas of the *Inferno*, as he had apparently been, that same year, in the castle at Castelnuovo di Magra, the one we had seen the first time we had driven up the road from Caniparola, before making one of his mysterious disappearances from circulation. And as we were following this trench-like alley which ran between the dwellings and the walls, we could see the castle domestics looking down on us from overhead.

From now on most of the processional route was downhill. The first and last stop was at the Church of San Remigio in the middle of the town, the principal church of Fosdinovo.

Here the Crucified Christ was taken in, together with the now unfurled banner and followed by the rest of us, for the Adoration of the Cross.

Now the priest sang *Ecce Lignum Crucis* (Behold the Wood of the Cross), removed his shoes and adored it, prostrating himself three times and finally bending down and kissing the feet on the crucifix. Immediately after this the rest of the congregation went up to the crucifix two by two and prostrated themselves, while a number of *Improperia*, tender reproaches of Christ to his people, were sung, such as *Popule meus, quid feci tibi? aut in quo contristavi te? Respondi mihi.* (My people, what have I done to thee? or in what have I grieved thee? Answer me.)

The interior of the church was painted in a cold, bluish-grey colour, as cold as the air inside the church, and our breath smoked. Originally a Romanesque church, it had been destroyed by fire in 1600 and rebuilt as a baroque church by the Marchese Pasquale Malaspina with large numbers of magnificent side chapels, ornamented with alternating smooth and twisted Corinthian columns. It also had a barrel roof decorated with an abundance of frescoes but these were all destroyed in the fighting for the Gothic Line in the last year of the war when the town was bombarded.

In it under a Gothic arch, high up to the left of the altar, near the presbytery, was the tomb of Galeotto Malaspina, feudal lord of the region—the Malaspina acquired the castle in 1340—and he died in 1367. Wearing armour his effigy reclined on a marble tomb chest, its panels ornamented with bas-reliefs.

Much higher still above the altar there was another marble effigy, carved by an unknown sculptor in the fourteenth century, the seated figure of San Remigio, patron saint of Fosdinovo, otherwise St Remigius, Bishop of Reims. Said to be the greatest orator of his age, on Christmas Day AD 496, he baptized Clovis, King of the Franks in the cathedral there, with the greatest imaginable pomp and ceremony, and the words, "Bow thy head meekly, O Sicambrian. Adore what thou hast burnt and burn what thou hast adored." (The Sicambrian cohort of the Franks was raised by the Romans on the spot where Budapest now stands.) Some of the bones of the saint were kept in the church at Fosdinovo in a silver reliquary ornamented with branching candlesticks.

For us this was the end of the procession. Now Christ was dead. We were all wet and cold but when I turned to offer Attilio a lift down the hill to I Castagni, he was nowhere to be seen and although I drove down several bends looking for him I failed to find him. He had simply melted away.

Iris Origo

(1902–1988)

Iris Origo was born in England into both nobility and wealth. Her maternal grandparents were a prominent Anglo-Irish family and her paternal grandparents were the rich Cuttings of New York. After her father's death when she was eight, Iris and her mother moved to the lavish Villa Medici in Fiesole. Her childhood was a lonely one, as her hypochondriac mother alternately took to her bed for months or was off on exotic travels. At twenty-two Iris married Antonio Origo, an Italian landowner ten years her senior, and they moved to La Foce, a rural Tuscan estate. Origo's early life and marriage are chronicled in *Images and Shadows* (1970), from which this excerpt is taken.

Life was hard at La Foce as the Origos tried to manage a large estate and bring prosperity to a barren land and its impoverished inhabitants. During World War II, La Foce came under assault by the German army. Origo kept a secret diary of those years and in its understated prose is a model of bravery. Origo and her husband fed and sheltered the hungry and buried the dead. She once said that she was simply too busy to be afraid. Finally, the Germans occupied La Foce and Iris Origo marched sixty children eight miles through a mined road under shell fire. Corpses lined their route as they straggled to safety in nearby Montepulciano. Origo's wartime diary was published as *War in Val d'Orcia* (1984).

A respected biographer and historian, Origo wrote a study of the Italian poet Leopardi and edited the letters of Lord Byron and his lover Teresa Guiccioli. La Foce is now run as an inn.

from IMAGES AND SHADOWS

LA FOCE

... superata tellus Sidera donat.

Boethius

It was on a stormy October afternoon in 1923, forty-seven years ago, that we first saw the Val d'Orcia and the house that was to be our home. We were soon to be married and had spent many weeks looking at estates for sale, in various parts of Tuscany, but as yet we had found nothing that met our wishes.

We knew what we were looking for: a place with enough work to fill our lifetime, but we also hoped that it might be in a setting of some beauty. Privately I thought that we might perhaps find one of the fourteenth- or fifteenth-century villas which were then almost as much a part of the Tuscan landscape as the hills on which they stood or the long cypress avenues which led up to them: villas with an austere façade broken only by a deep loggia, high vaulted rooms of perfect proportions, great stone fireplaces, perhaps a little courtyard with a well, and a garden with a fountain and an overgrown hedge of box. (Many such houses are empty now, and crumbling to decay.) What I had not realised, until we started our search, was that such places were only likely to be found on land that had already been tilled for centuries, with terraced hillsides planted with olive-trees, and vineyards that were already fruitful and trim in the days of the Decameron. To choose such an estate would mean that we would only have to follow the course of established custom, handing over all the hard work to our *fattore*, and casting an occasional paternal eye over what was being done, as it always had been done. This was not what we wanted.

We still had, however, one property upon our list: some 3,500 acres on what we were told was very poor farming-land in the south of the province of Siena, about five miles from a new little watering-place which was just springing up at Chianciano. It was from there that we drove up a stony, winding road, crossed a ford, and then, after skirt-

ing some rather unpromising-looking farm buildings, drove yet farther up a hill on a steep track through some oak coppices. From the
top, we hoped to obtain a bird's-eye view of the whole estate. The
road was nothing more than a rough cart-track up which we thought
no car had surely ever been before; and the woods on either side had
been cut down or neglected. Up and up we climbed, our spirits sinking. Then suddenly we were at the top. We stood on a bare, windswept
upland, with the whole of the Val d'Orcia at our feet.

It is a wide valley, but in those days it offered no green welcome,
no promise of fertile fields. The shapeless rambling river-bed held
only a trickle of water, across which some mules were picking their
way through a desert of stones. Long ridges of low, bare clay hills—
the *crete senesi*—ran down towards the valley, dividing the landscape
into a number of steep, dried-up little water-sheds. Treeless and shrub-
less but for some tufts of broom, these corrugated ridges formed a
lunar landscape, pale and inhuman; on that autumn evening it had
the bleakness of the desert, and its fascination. To the south, the
black boulders and square tower of Radicofani stood up against
the sky—a formidable barrier, as many armies had found, to an
invader. But it was to the west that our eyes were drawn: to the summit of the great extinct volcano which, like Fujiyama, dominated and
dwarfed the whole landscape around it, and which appeared, indeed,
to have been created on an entirely vaster, more majestic scale—
Monte Amiata.

The history of that region went back very far. There had already
been Estrucan villages and burial-grounds and health-giving springs
there in the fifth century B.C.; the chestnut-woods of Monte Amiata
had supplied timber for the Roman galleys during the second Punic
war, while, from the eighth to the eleventh century, both Lombards
and Carolingians had left their traces in the great Benedictine abbeys
of S. Antimo and Abbadia San Salvatore, in the *pieve* of S. Quirico
d'Orcia and in innumerable minor Romanesque churches and
chapels—some still in use, some half-ruined or used as granaries or
storehouses—and the winding road we could just see across the valley still followed almost the same track as one of the most famous
mediaeval pilgrims' roads to Rome, the *via francigena*, linking this desolate valley with the whole of Christian Europe. Then came the period

of castle-building, of violent and truculent nobels—in particular, the Aldobrandeschi, Counts of Santa Fiora, who boasted that they could sleep in a different castle of their own on each night in the year—and who left as their legacy to the Val d'Orcia the half-ruined towers, fortresses, and battlements that we could see on almost every hilltop. And just across the valley—its skyline barely visible from where we stood—lay one of the most perfect Renaissance cities, the creation of that worldly, caustic man of letters, Aeneas Silvius Piccolomini, Pope Pius II, the first man of taste in Italy to enjoy with equal discrimination the works of art and those of nature, who would summon, in the summer heat, his Cardinals to confer with him in the chestnut woods of Monte Amiata, "under one tree or another, by the sweet murmur of the stream."

But of all this we knew nothing then, and still less could we foresee that, within our lifetime, those same woods on Monte Amiata, as well as those in which we stood, which for centuries had been a hiding-place for the outlawed and the hunted, would again be a refuge for fugitives: this time for anti-Fascist partisans and for Allied prisoners of war. We only knew at once that this vast, lonely, uncompromising landscape fascinated and compelled us. To live in the shadow of that mysterious mountain, to arrest the erosion of those steep ridges, to turn this bare clay into wheat-fields, to rebuild these farms and see prosperity return to their inhabitants, to restore the greenness of these mutilated woods—that, we were sure, was the life that we wanted.

In the next few days, as we examined the situation more closely, we were brought down to earth again. The estate was then of about 3,500 acres, of which the larger part was then woodland (mostly scrub-oak, although there was one fine beech-wood at the top of the hill) or rather poor grass, while only a small part consisted of good land. Even of this, only a fraction was already planted with vineyards or olive-groves, while much of the arable land also still lay fallow. The buildings were not many: besides the villa itself and the central farm-buildings around it, there were twenty-five outlying farms, some very inaccessible and all in a state of great disrepair and, about a mile away, a small castle called Castelluccio Bifolchi. This was originally the site of one of the Etruscan settlements belonging to the great

lucomony of Clusium (as is testified by the fine Estruscan vases
found in the necropolis close to the castle, and which now lie in the
museum of Chiusi), but the first mention of it in the Middle Ages as
a "fortified place" dates only from the tenth century, and we then
hear no more about it until the sixteenth, when it played a small part
in the long drawn-out war between Siena and Florence for the possession of the Sienese territory—a war which gradually reduced the
Val d'Orcia to the state of desolation and solitude in which we found
it. In this war Siena was supported by the troops of Charles V and
Florence by those of François I of France, and Pope Clement VII
(who was secretly allied with the French) made his way one day by a
secondary road from the Val d'Orcia to Montepulciano and, on
arriving at the Castelluccio, expressed a wish to lunch there. But the
owner of the castle, a staunch Ghibelline, refused him admittance,
"so that the Pope was obliged, with much inconvenience and hunger
to ride on to Montepulciano."*

This castle, which held within its walls our parish church, dedicated to San Bernardino of Siena, and which owned some 2,150
acres, had once formed a single estate with La Foce; when we first
saw it it was still inhabited by an old lady who (even if we had had the
money) did not wish to sell. It was not until 1934 that we were able
to buy it and thus bring the whole property together again.

As for the villa of La Foce itself, it is believed to have served as a
post-house on the road up which Papa Clemente passed, but this is
unconfirmed, and the only thing certain is that in 1557 its lands,
together with those of the Castelluccio, were handed over to the
Sienese hospital of Santa Maria della Scala, as is testified by a shield
on the villa and on the older farms, bearing this date, with the stone
ladder surmounted by a cross which is the hospital's emblem. The
home itself was certainly not the beautiful villa I had hoped for, but
merely a medium-sized country-house of quite pleasant proportions,
adorned by a loggia on the ground floor, with arches of red brick and
a façade with windows framed in the same material. Indoors it had no

*Verdiani Bandi, *I Castelli della Val d'Orcia*, p. 120, quoting the chronicler Malavolti.
Subsequently the castle was occupied in turn by the troops of the Emperor and of
the French and after the fall of Montalcino passed, like all the rest of this territory,
into the hands of Cosimo de' Medici, Grand Duke of Tuscany.

especial character or charm. A steep stone staircase led straight into a dark central room, lit only by red and blue panes of Victorian glass inserted in the doors, and the smaller rooms leading out of it were papered in dingy, faded colours. The doors were of deal or yellow pitch-pine, the floors of unwaxed, half-broken bricks, and there was a general aroma of must, dust, and decay. There was no garden, since the well was only sufficient for drinking-water, and of course no bath-room. There was no electric light, central heating, or telephone.

Beneath the house stood deep wine-cellars, with enormous vats of seasoned oak, some of them large enough to hold 2,200 gallons, and a wing connected the villa with the *fattoria* (the house inhabited by the agent or *fattore* and his assistants) while just beyond stood the build-ing in which the olives were pressed and the oil made and stored, the granaries and laundry-shed and wood-shed and, a little farther off, the carpenter's shop, the blacksmith's, and the stables. The small, dark room which served for a school stood next to our kitchen; the ox-carts which carried the wheat, wine, and grapes from the various scattered farms were unloaded in the yard. Thus villa and *fattoria* formed, according to old Tuscan tradition, a single, closely-connected little world.

When, however, we came to ask the advice of the farming experts of our acquaintance, they were not encouraging. To farm in the Sienese *crete*, they said, was an arduous and heart-breaking enterprise: we would need patience, energy—and capital. The soil-erosion of centuries must first be arrested, and then we would at once have to turn to re-afforestation, road-building, and planting. The woods, as we have already seen, had been ruthlessly cut down, with no attempt to establish a regular rotation; the olive-trees were ill-pruned, the fields ill-ploughed or fallow, the cattle underfed. For thirty years practically nothing had been spent on any farm implements, fertilis-ers, or repairs. In the half-ruined farms the roofs leaked, the stairs were worn away, many windows were boarded up or stuffed with rags, and the poverty-stricken families (often consisting of more than twenty souls) were huddled together in dark, airless little rooms. In one of these, a few months later, we found, in the same bed, an old man dying and a woman giving birth to a child. There was only the single school in the *fattoria*, and in many cases the distances were so great and the tracks so bad in winter, that only a few children could attend regularly. The only two roads—to Chianciano and Montepulciano—converged at our house (which stood on the water-shed between the Val d'Orcia and Val di Chiana, and thence derived its name), and also ended there. The more remote farms could only be reached by rough cart-tracks and, if we wished to attempt intensive farming, their number should at least be doubled. We would need government subsidies, and also the collaboration of our neighbours, in a district where few landowners had either capital to invest, or any wish to adopt newfangled methods, and we would certainly also meet with opposition from the peasants themselves—illiterate, stubborn, suspicious, and rooted, like countrymen all the world over, in their own ways.

We had no lack of warnings. Was it courage, ignorance, or mere youth that swept them all away? Five days after our first glimpse of the Val d'Orcia, in November 1923, we had signed the deed of purchase of La Foce. In the following March we were married and, immediately after our honeymoon, we returned to the Val d'Orcia to start our new life.

How can I recapture the flavour of our first year? After a place has become one's home, one's freshness of vision becomes dimmed; the dust of daily life, of plans and complications and disappointments, slowly and inexorably clogs the wheels. But sometimes, even now, some sudden trick of light or unexpected sound will wipe out the intervening years and take me back to those first months of expectation and hope, when each day brought with it some new small achievement, and when we were awaiting, too, the birth of our first child.

For the first time, in that year, I learned what every country child knows: what it is to live among people whose life is not regulated by artificial dates, but by the procession of the seasons: the early spring ploughing before sowing the Indian corn and clover; the lambs in March and April and then the making of the delicious sheep's-milk cheese, *pecorino*, which is a specialty of this region, partly because the pasture is rich in thyme, called *timo sermillo* or *popolino*. ("*Chi vuol buono il caciolino*," goes a popular saying, "*mandi le pecore al sermolino*.")* Then came the hay-making in May, and in June the harvest and the thresh-ing; the vintage in October, the autumn ploughing and sowing; and finally, to conclude the farmer's year, the gathering of the olives in December, and the making of the oil. The weather became some-thing to be considered, not according to one's own convenience but the farmer's needs: each rain-cloud eagerly watched in April and May as it scudded across the sky and rarely fell, in the hope of a kindly wet day to swell the wheat and give a second crop of fodder for the cat-tle before the long summer's drought. The nip of late frosts in spring became a menace as great as that of the hot, dry summer wind, or, worse, of the summer hail-storm which would lay low the wheat and destroy the grapes. And in the autumn, after the sowing, our prayers were for soft sweet rain. "*Il gran freddo di gennaio*," said an old proverb, "*il mal tempo di febbraio, il vento di marzo, le dolci acque di aprile, le guazze di maggio, il buon mietere di giugno, il buon battere di luglio, e le tre acque di agosto, con la buona stagione, valgon più che il tron di Salmone*."†

Some of the farming methods which we saw in those first years became obsolete in Tuscany a long time ago. Then, the reaping was still done by hand and in the wheat-fields, from dawn to sunset, the long rows of reapers moved slowly forwards, chanting rhythmically to follow the rise and fall of the sickle, while behind the binders and gleaners followed, bending low in a gesture as old as Ruth's. The wine and water, with which at intervals the men freshened their parched throats, were kept in leather gourds in a shady ditch, and several times in the day, besides, the women brought down baskets of bread and cheese and home-cured ham (these snacks were called *spuntini*) from the farms, and at midday steaming dishes of *pastasciutta* and meat. A few weeks ago, one of the oldest *contadini* still left at La Foce, a man of ninety—*laudator temporis acti*—was reminiscing with my husband about those days. "We worked from dawn to dusk, and sang

---

*"The man who wants good cheese, will feed his sheep on thyme."
†"Great cold in January, bad weather in February, March winds, sweet rain in April, showers in May, good reaping in June, good threshing in July, and the three rains of August—all with good weather—these are worth more than Solomon's throne."

as we worked. Now the machines do the work—but who feels like singing?"

An even greater occasion than the reaping, was the threshing—the crowning feast-day of the farmer's year. Threshing, until very recently, had been done by hand with wooden flails on the grass or brick threshing-floor beside each farm, but in our time there was already a threshing-machine worked by steam, and all the neighbouring farmers came to lend a hand and to help in the fine art of building the tall straw ricks, so tightly packed that, later on, slices could be cut out of them, as from a piece of cake. The air was heavy with fine gold dust, shimmering in the sunlight, the wine-flasks were passed from mouth to mouth, the children climbed on to the carts and stacks, and at noon, beside the threshing-floor, there was a banquet. First came soup and smoke-cured hams, then piled-up dishes of spaghetti, then two kinds of meat—one of which was generally a great gander, *l'ocio*, fattened for weeks beforehand—and then platters of sheep's-cheese, made by the *massaia* herself, followed by the *dolce*, and an abundance of red wine. These were occasions I shall never forget—the handsome country girls bearing in the stacks of yellow pasta and flask upon flask of wine; the banter and the laughter; the hot sun beating down over the pale valley, now despoiled of its riches; the sense of fulfillment after the long year's toil.

Then came the vintage. The custom of treading grapes beneath the peasants' bare feet—often pictured by northern writers, perhaps on the evidence of Etruscan frescoes, as a gay Bacchanalian scene—was already then a thing of the past. At that time, the bunches of grapes were brought by ox-cart to the *fattoria* in tall wooden tubs (called *bigonci*) in which they were vigorously squashed with stout wooden poles, and the mixture of stems, pulp, and juice was left to ferment in open vats for a couple of weeks, before being put into barrels, to complete the fermentation during the winter. Now, the stems are separated from the grapes by a machine (called a *diraspatrice*), *before* the pressing, and then the juice flows directly into the vats, while for the pale white wine called "virgin" the grapes are skinned before the fermentation (since it is the skin that gives the red wine its colour).

Last, in the farmer's calendar, came the making of the oil. Unlike

Greece and Spain, and some parts of southern Italy, where the olives are allowed to ripen until they fall to the ground (thus producing a much fatter and more acid oil) olives in Tuscany are stripped by hand from the boughs as soon as they reach the right degree of ripeness. Then, when the olives have been brought in by ox-cart to the *fattoria* and placed on long flat trays, so as not to press upon each other, the oil-making takes place with feverish speed, going on all day and night. When first we arrived, we found that the olives were being ground by a large circular millstone, about two metres in diameter, which was worked by a patient blindfold donkey, walking round and round. The pulp which was left over was then placed into rope baskets and put beneath heavy presses, worked by four strong men pushing at a wooden bar. This produced the first oil, of the finest quality. Then again the whole process was repeated, with a second and stronger press, and the oil was then stored in huge earthenware jars, large enough to contain Ali Baba's thieves, while the pulp (for nothing is wasted on a Tuscan farm) was sold for the 10 per cent of oil which it still contained. (During the war, we even used the kernels for fuel.) The men worked day and night, in shifts of eight hours, naked to the waist, glistening with sweat. At night, by the light of oil lamps, the scene—the men's dark glistening torsos, their taut muscles, the big grey millstone, the toiling beast, the smell of sweat and oil—had a primeval, Michelangelesque grandeur. Now, in a white-tiled room, electric presses and separators do the same work in a tenth of the time, with far greater efficiency and less human labour, and clients bring their olives to us to be pressed from all over the district. One can hardly deplore the change; yet it is perhaps at least worthwhile to record it.

One other sight, too, has already almost disappeared from the Val d'Orcia: the big grey *maremmano* oxen first brought from the Hungarian steppes to northern Italy, according to tradition, by Attila, and thence to the plains of the Maremma. In our first years in the Val d'Orcia, it was they that were used for ploughing the heavy soil, but then the day came when we bought our first tractor. Never shall I forget escorting it down the valley with a little crowd of admirers, Antonio at their head, to watch it plough its first furrow in a field near the river. Deep, deep went the shining blade into the rich black earth, deeper than a plough had ever sunk before. The children ran behind, laughing and shouting; the pigs followed, thrusting their long black snouts deep into the moist earth. It was an exciting day—but it was, for the oxen (and though we could not then foresee it, for a whole way of life) the beginning of a great change. The first tractor was followed by others, then by a reaper-and-binder and a combine, and after the war, by two bulldozers, to bring under cultivation the parts of the property which still lay fallow. Some oxen continued to be used for ploughing the steeper hillsides, but gradually they were interbred with the finer white oxen from the Val di Chiana, the *chianini*, while after the war Antonia imported, for beef, the brown and white Simmenthal cattle. You may still sometimes meet a pair of *chianini*—"gentle as evening moths"—drawing an ox-cart up a road or driving a plough on a steep hillside; but if you wish to see the grey oxen you must go to those remote hills of the Maremma (and very few are left) where tractors have not yet arrived, or to the few plains by the sea on which they still roam in their pristine freedom or stand on summer days in the deep shade of spreading cork-trees. When all those plains, too, have been handed over to the tractors—and this is swiftly happening—we shall have to go to zoos to find the kings of the Maremma.

I was fascinated in those early days by the survival of some pagan ceremonies and customs, often incorporated, as the Church has sometimes wisely done, into Christian rites. Among the most beautiful ceremonies of the year were the services, after a day of fasting, of the *quattro tempora*, which were held at the beginning of each of the four seasons, and the "rogation" processions, in which the priest, carrying a crucifix and holy relics, followed by the congregation chanting litanies, walked through the fields, imploring a blessing upon the crops—the women, with black veils upon their heads, joining in the responses, the children straggling in and out and picking wild flowers among the wheat. Both these rites dated back to the days of ancient Rome and were still being practised during our first years at La Foce, but they have now come to an end as part of the Church ritual, though I am told that some of the older peasants still hold a brief procession in the fields, and leave a rough wooden cross standing among the ripening wheat.

Other customs, too, linking pagan and Christian piety, were still practised during our first years in the Val d'Orcia, and some of them still survive. On St. Anthony's Day (St. Anthony the Abbot, patron of animals, not his namesake of Padua) the farmers would bring an armful of hay to church to be blessed by the saint, so that for the whole year their beasts might not lack fodder, and a few older men still do so today. On Monte Amiata, on the Eve of the Ascension, some women used to put milk on their window-sills which they would drink the next day, in the hope that swallows would come to bless it. This is perhaps somehow connected with the custom, still observed on this side of the valley, of not milking any sheep on Ascension Day. And even now, however deeply imbued with Communism a family may be, each one of them will bring a bunch of olive-branches to be blessed by the priest on Palm Sunday.

On Monte Amiata, too, at Abbadia San Salvatore—where chestnuts form a large part of the poor man's diet—a procession used to walk through the streets on St. Mark's Day singing:

> *San Marcu, nostru avvucatu,*
> *fa che nella castagna non c'entri il bacu.*
> *Trippole e lappole, trippole e lappole, ora pro nobis.**

And only a few years ago a peasant of Rocca d'Orcia, after saying the rosary with his family, used to add an Our Father and a Hail Mary to a saint whom you will find in no calendar, called "San Fisco Fosco," a terrible saint who lived in the middle of the sea and hated the poor, and therefore had to be propitiated.

Some other practises, too, were quite frankly pagan in origin. There are still both witch-doctors and witches in the villages across the valley, and to one of these, a few years ago, two of our workmen took the bristles of some of our swine, which the vet had not been able to cure of swine-fever. The bristles were examined, a "little powder" was strewn over them, and some herbs were given, to be

---

*"St. Mark, our advocate, see that no worm enters our chestnuts, and that each kernel bears three nuts; pray for us."

burnt in their sites—after which the pigs did recover. The same was sometimes done for cattle. There was also a very efficient witch at Campiglia d'Orcia (now dead, but I believe she has a successor) to whom one could take a garment or a hair of anyone suffering from some affliction that the doctor had been unable to heal, and which was presumed to be caused by the evil eye, and she—with the help of some card-reading and some potions—would cure him. Sometimes, however, trouble would be caused by her prescriptions, since two of our tenants' families embarked on a long feud, merely owing to the fact that she had told the daughter of one of them, that one of her neighbours "wished her ill." For all such cures, it was pointed out to me, faith was necessary: those who came to mock went away unhealed.

Divining of the future, too, was done by some of our older peasants. One of them, an old man who is still alive, specialised in foretelling, in winter, the weather for each month of the following year, by placing in twelve onion skins, named for each month of the year, little heaps of salt. These he would then carefully examine: the skins in which the salt had remained, represented the months of drought; those in which it had dissolved, those of rain.

The most interesting of our local superstitious practises, however—and probably the oldest, since it presumably had its origins in a very primitive form of nature-worship—was one that I myself have seen, that of the *poccie lattaie* (literally, milk-bearing udders). This took place in a secluded cave on our land, half way up a very steep ravine, surrounded by dry clay cliffs, but in which a hidden spring, oozing down the walls of the cave, had formed something like stalactites, which had the shape of cows' and goats' udders or women's breasts, each gently dripping a few drops of water. Here the farmers would bring their sterile cows and here, too, came nursing mothers who were losing their milk—and always, after they had tasted the water, their wish was granted. They brought with them, as gifts, seven fruits of the earth: a handful of wheat, barley, corn, rye, vetch, dried peas, and sometimes a saucer of milk.

After nearly half a century, distance has perhaps lent enchantment to these memories, but I must honestly admit that I can also recollect moments of great discouragement. I remember one grey autumn

afternoon on which, having ridden on a small grey donkey to visit
some remote farms (for there was as yet no road to the valley) I
waited alone in a hollow, while Antonio and the *fattore* walked on to
another farm. The cone-shaped clay hillocks in the midst of which I
sat were so steep, and worn so bare by centuries of erosion, that even
now no attempt has been made to grow anything upon them. Seated
beside a tuft of broom—the only plant that will grow there—on
ground as hard as a bone after the summer's drought, I was entirely
surrounded by these desolate hillocks: no tree, no patch of green, no
trace of human habitation, except against the sky a half-ruined watchtower, standing where perhaps an Etruscan tower had stood before
it, and then a Lombard, rebuilt in the Middle Ages to play its part in
a series of petty wars, and now inhabited only by a half-witted shepherd who sat at its foot, beside his ragged flock. Below me lay the
fields beside the river—land potentially fertile, but then fallow, which
would be flooded when the rains came by the encroaching river-bed.
Against the sky, behind the black rocks of Radicofani, dark clouds
were gathering for a storm, and, as the wind reached the valley, it
raised little whirpools of dust. Suddenly an overwhelming wave of
longing came over me for the gentle, trim Florentine landscape of my
childhood or for green English fields and big trees—and most of all,
for a pretty house and garden to come home to in the evening. I felt
the landscape around me to be alien, inhuman—built on a scale fit
for demi-gods and giants, but not for us. How could we ever succeed
in taming it, I asked myself, and bring fertility to this desert? Would
our whole life go by in a struggle against insuperable odds?

Perhaps my early discouragement was also partly caused by the
fact that our own house was not yet habitable. During our absence
on our honeymoon, under the direction of our architect and old
friend Cecil Pinsent, some indispensable work had been done. A sky-
light had been opened in the ceiling of the central room, to let in
some light; another room had been lined with bookshelves; all had
been cleaned and distempered and some open fireplaces, with chim-
neypieces of travertine from local quarries of Rapolano, had been
added in the library and dining-room; there was even a bathroom,
although, as yet, in the dry season, very little water. But that was all.
The cases and crates containing all our furniture and belongings were

piled up in the dining-room, unlabelled, so that when we began to look for such necessities as sheets or cooking-pans, we would come instead upon a dinner-set of fine Sèvres or a large group of bronze buffaloes, sculpted by Antonio's father. We settled temporarily in a maid's room upstairs, and set to work. In a few weeks the house was more or less habitable: the red bricks on the floor had been polished and waxed, the furniture was in place (I did not like all of it, but it was what we had), the windows were hung with chintz or linen curtains, the bookshelves were half filled. (This was the only year of my life in which I have had more than enough book-space.) But there was still, of course, no electric light or telephone, and my greatest wish, a garden, was plainly unattainable till we could get some more water, which was far more urgently needed for the farms. We both agreed that any plans for the house and garden must give way, for the present, to the needs of the land and the tenants. Anything that the crops brought in, as well as any gifts from relations, went straight into the land, and I remember that my present to Antonio, on the first anniversary of our wedding-day, was a pair of young oxen which were led under his window, adorned with gilded horns and with silver stars pasted on their flanks. It is sad to have to add that they were such a bad buy that they had to be sold again as soon as possible.

If there was much satisfaction in these efforts, there was also a certain sense of frustration, which was increased (as our advisers had foreseen) by the passive resistance of our *contadini* to any innovation. Our land worked on the system which had been almost universal in Tuscany for nearly six centuries, the *mezzadria*,—a profit-sharing contract by which the landowner built the farmhouses, kept them in repair, and supplied capital for the purchase of half the livestock, seed, fertilisers, machinery, etc., while the tenant—called *mezzadro, colono*, or *contadino*—contributed, with the members of his family, the labour. When the crops were harvested, owner and tenant (the date I am writing about is 1924) shared the profits in equal shares. In bad years, however, it was the landowner who bore the losses and lent the tenant what was needed to buy his share of seed, cattle, and fertilisers, the tenant paying back his loan when a better year came.

In larger estates, such as La Foce, which consisted of a number of farms, there was generally a central home-farm, the *fattoria*, usually adjoining the landowner's house, where the estate manager, the *fattore*, lived with his family and assistants, and from which the whole place was run. It was the owner (or his *fattore*) who established the rotations, deciding what was to be grown on each farm, what new livestock or machinery should be purchased, and what repairs were necessary, and it was in the *fattoria* office that the complicated ledgers and account-books were kept, one for each farm, in which the *contadino*'s share of all profits and expenses was set down, and also the loans made to him, in bad years, by the central administration. It was in the *fattoria* cellars and granaries that the owner's share of the produce was stored; it was there that the wine and oil were made, that the peasants came to unload the ox-carts, to go over their accounts, and to air their requests and grievances—and only those who have lived in Tuscany can know what a slow, repetitive business this can be. The *fattoria* was, in short, the hub of the life of the estate.

John Ormond

(1923-1990)

John Ormond is more closely associated with Wales than Tuscany. Considered one of his country's most popular writers, Ormond was a journalist, filmmaker, and poet. After World War II he wrote for the *Picture Post* and then was a news editor for the BBC in London. That led to writing television scripts and eventually to filmmaking. After a lapse of several decades he resumed writing poetry in the 1960s and often probed his Welsh roots through verse.

Critic Neil Corcoran wrote in *The Times Literary Supplement* that Ormond's poetry had "a tentative, unshowy art, solidly draftsmanlike, suspicious of rhetoric, but willing to push beyond its usual limits when the material seems to demand it." In this poem, "Tuscan Cypresses" from *Selected Poems* (1987), Ormond finds the history of Tuscany in the characteristic trees of the region. "They are trees, but they are more than trees, / They go deeper than that . . ."

TUSCAN CYPRESSES

Black-green, green-black, unbending intervals
On far farm boundaries; all years are one to them.
Their noon stillness is beyond decipherment.
They are at the beginning and end of the heart's quandaries.

On the darkest night roadside they judge the earth's turning,
On hills the brightness of stars is the brightness of day.
Each like a young bride is awake at too-soon dawn and hurrying
    midnight,
Yet each, like every death, is uncaring, each unknown.

They stand like heretics over long-decayed churches.
Some single as lepers are doomed to keep watch alone.

Fell those single ones, blast out their roots and detonate
Your only certainty; the curse upon you is whole.

They are the silences between the notes Carlatti left unwritten,
The silence after the last of Cimarosa's fall.
They are all seasons, they are every second of time.
They do not improvise, all is in strict measure.

Though they reach to the impossible they never outgrow
Or deceive themselves, being nothing but what they are;
They know nothing of angels only of the enticement of hills.
They look down on lakes, the persuasive sea's vainglory.

They have seen the waters divide for divinities
But that was long ago so now peace possesses them;
Their only restlessness is the need for great annexations;
They would come into their inheritance by black growth and stealth.

They march over the border down into Umbria;
Their uniform gives no glint of the sunlight back.
As the gun-carriages threaten by they are the darkness
Of future suicides and firing-squads ahead.

Their solemnity is of Umbria, of burnt earth.
Even they do not know the bottom of it all, the last
Throw of the dice, the black rejoicing, the dying,
The vegetable lie, the audacity of bright flowers.

They barely respond to the stark invention of storms.
Enemies of the living light, they are Dido's lament.
They grow in the mind, haunting, the straight flames
Of fever, black fire possessing the blood.

They have stood at the edges of all events, rehearsed
Vergil's poems before he was born, awaited his death
In another country. Only the oldest of oaks can converse with them
In the tentative syllables of their patient language.

Lorenzo stood among them as the black-scarved women
Buried a child under cold, motionless candlelight,
The red banners of death and the white surplices.
Lorenzo would die soon, wasted, his wife gripping his ankle.

Are they the world's memorial, its endless throng
Of tombstones? Are they the existence of light before it was born?
That aloofness, that uncaring of what is and what is not:
Are they all spent grief at knowing no knowing?

They do not recognise this given world from another,
Having watched Adam and Eve limp from the Garden,
The serpent ingratiate itself into the world's only apple tree,
The silver rivers of Eden begin their grey tarnish.

They are the trustees and overseers of absentee landlords,
Keeping a black account of the generations of thin, uneasy
    labourers.
They withhold judgements and watch traditions die,
Are unrejoicing over the wedding party dances.

They have watched man and woman lie down in their vows, and
    wake
Into happiness made new by morning,
And observed the *contadini* setting out for the yellow fields,
Not caring whether they should return or not return.

They watched the Great Death blacken the land,
Agnolo di Tura del Grasso, sometimes called The Fat,
Bury his five children with his own two hands,
And many another likewise, the grave-diggers dying

Or running, knowing of more than death, into the hills.
There death stood waiting between the cypresses.
The terraces of vine and olive retched with the weight of
    their dying.
The terraces crumbled and the new famine began.

The cypresses stood over it all in the putrefaction
Of silence; silence of chantings dead in the priests' throats;
Silence of merchant and beggar, physician and banker,
Of silversmith and wet-nurse, mason and town-crier.

The cypresses stood over it all and watched and watched;
You could not call this enmity, it is the world's way.
Their stance seems set as though by ordinance and yet it is not.
It is merely the circumstance of the mystery, the reason for churches.

They are not everything, but they are trees.
They watch the pulse in heaven of cold stars
And the common smoke gone up from the body's burning,
They know the sourness of vinegar,

The sweetness and smiling of holy wine,
But they partake of neither in spirit;
Cannot be bribed into turning away, not even briefly.
There is no buying off their vigilance.

They are the melancholy beyond explaining,
Beyond belief. Accepting this, they are not tempted
To put on more than their little green.
Theirs is the dark of the unbelieving, the unknowing, the
    darkness of pits.

Some few are deformed, though fewer
That in their multitudes and assembling legions
Their particles might have been heir to.
From birth their spines are erect, their outlines the essence of
    given symmetry.

Departure from this is brief aberration;
They must look down from their own escarpments of air, the
    wild lilies beneath them,
The wild mignonette, the dog-rose unheeded.
If they could smile a gale would storm south over Africa.

Each one is the containment of every one there was,
A compounding of all cypresses, of all their stillness.
They are the elegant dancers who never dance,
Preferring to watch the musicians, the bustling ones.

They are trees, but they are more than trees,
They go deeper than that. They are at the heart
Of the ultimate music; the poor loam and Roman melody of
    Keats's body
Sings silently beneath them.

What will there be of them when all men are gone?
No one to witness the seed of their secret cones,
The deep black seed, the seed beginning in Eden, coming
    from nothing,
From the beginning falling in Eden.

Only they can tell of that old story and they are silent
For all the long wisdoms have passed into them;
So silence, since it all comes to nothing.
See how it all burns, all, in the black flames of their silence,
    their silence, untelling.

Elizabeth Romer

Elizabeth Romer and her husband, John, a renowned archaeologist, chose to live in Tuscany because it is halfway between England and Egypt. Elizabeth had already fallen in love with Italy as a student at London's Royal College of Art. She wrote that she was dazzled by the art, but even more by the Italian lifestyle. "I loved the noisy market women of Rome who pressed bunches of cherries into my hands to taste before buying; the impressive arrays of cheeses in the food shops, the vast loaves of rough bread and the wine with which we filled our bottles from the big barrels kept in the dark depths of the tiny shops."

When Elizabeth and John finally bought a house, they settled in the valley between Tuscany and Umbria. They became fast friends with the owners of the *fattoria*, Silvana and Orlando Cerotti, who figure prominently in Elizabeth Romer's diary of a year in Tuscany—from January through December. *The Tuscan Year* (1984), from which this selection is excerpted, is a combination memoir, cookbook, and sociological study of the Tuscan people. It describes a way of life still governed by the seasons, the demands of farm life, and the vagaries of weather. "The days begin early, end late and there are no holidays," she wrote in the introduction to *The Tuscan Year*. Her observations are interspersed with detailed traditional recipes, many bean-based, which earn Tuscans their nickname, "*mangiafagioli*."

from THE TUSCAN YEAR

During this beautiful month of June, when the corn is ripening to a pale greeny gold, and scarlet poppies spread across the roadsides and meadows, an important event is taking place in the Cerotti family; one of Orlando's nephews is getting married to a young girl from a neighbouring village. The village, however, is over the border and the girl is Umbrian.

There is a great deal of usually good-natured rivalry between Tuscans and Umbrians, especially when it comes to the question of food. The Tuscans chide the Umbrians for being too hedonistic, drinking too much wine and not taking life seriously enough, and they distrust the richer Umbrian cooking. The Umbrians, on the other hand, maintain that the Tuscans have no sense of humour, are too severe and prone to keeping their money well tucked away under the mattress; they deride the plainness of Tuscan cooking. Where a Tuscan uses just toasted bread, olive oil, salt and garlic to make the delicious *bruschetta*, an Umbrian will add a few slices of truffle to his if at all possible. However this regional rivalry which makes Italy the fascinating mixture that it is should not be exaggerated and both families are delighted with the forthcoming wedding.

Weddings in Italy are tremendously important and invariably lavish affairs. Engagements are long and the wedding date is usually set by the bride's father; it probably very much depends on the state of the family finances. The guest list can run into hundreds—on this occasion there will be three hundred people, the entire population of at least three villages—and everyone of course expects a gargantuan feast. On the wedding day, a beautiful clear June morning, with the hills covered in brilliant yellow *ginestra* whose heavy scent fills the air and wafts down into the valley, the guests of the bride's family all assemble at her home at about eleven o'clock in the morning, wearing their best dresses and suits; they crowd around the house and chat. The large double front doors are wide open and in the huge hallway at the foot of the stairs which lead to the main part of the house a buffet is laid. The festivities commence before anyone has set foot in the church. Two long trestle tables are laid with damask cloths and are loaded with all sorts of savouries and sweet cakes. There are soft rolls filled with *prosciutto* and *salame*, open sandwiches of hard boiled egg and mayonnaise topped with stuffed olives, rolls filled with slices of herb-filled *frittata*, plates piled with home-baked cakes and of course huge flasks of wine. There is also beer, and orangeade for the children. The bride's brothers and sisters ply the guests with food but only the occasional privileged elderly guest is allowed upstairs to greet the bride. Eventually she is ready and comes down the wide staircase on the arm of her father. Already the photographer is snapping away. Italian girls are usually lovely; their wedding days are something that they treasure and their dresses are often amazingly beautiful. Brunella's is no exception and she stuns the eager crowd with her voile gown with its long pleated train. Framing her face she wears white silk flowers in her hair that cascade to her shoulders. Her father Alberto, the stocky strong village blacksmith, is very elegant in his dark serge suit. They are both rather stiff and nervous.

The tiny church where the marriage is to take place is only a few steps away from the house so everyone sets out on foot in a procession, the bride and her father leading, followed by her mother and grandmother and the rest of the numerous family and friends. At the church the groom and his family and guests are waiting; a young cousin of the bride's had been delegated to watch for his arrival. The couple are married by the bride's uncle, Don Luigi. During the ceremony Brunella's sister sings the "Ave Maria" and a very young guest has to be persuaded that it is not a good idea for him to hold the bride's hand. Afterwards everyone has their photograph taken with the new couple.

Silvana enjoyed the wedding service and sat in the congregation with her sisters-in-law. Orlando, however, preferred to stand outside in the sun with some of his cronies and chat about farming and such matters. As there are so many guests the wedding reception is to be held in a nearby country restaurant which can provide for up to five hundred people.

After all the photographs have been taken and everyone has piled into the cars there follows a hair-raising drive, a seemingly endless procession of Fiats, from the humble *cinque cento* to something far grander, careering around the twisting country road all intent on reaching the feast as soon as possible and making an uproarious din with their horns all the way. At the pretty country inn an *al fresco* bar is arranged on a large lawn where *aperitivi*, wine and small salted biscuits and nuts, are served. Eventually everyone in the huge crowd settles down at the long white-clothed tables. Since Orlando is an important uncle, he and Silvana sit at the top table with the bride and groom and the close family. There is a promising array of knives and forks and already the tables are laden with quantities of wine. Before each plate there is a menu, showing all eleven courses.

To begin there are the *antipasti*. The band of waiters bring round vast silver platters containing tiny pizzas filled with mushrooms and tomato, canapés of smoked salmon and stuffed olives, not those that appear in jars for cocktails, but large green *ascolano* olives which are stoned, stuffed with a delicate forcemeat then rolled in fine bread-crumbs and deep fried. There are also tiny veal sausages wrapped in silver foil, *crostini* of chicken liver paté, piquant tomato *crostini* with liberal doses of chili, the thinnest slices of parma ham and stuffed eggs flavoured with anchovy and capers. The waiters go round the tables several times, bringing the hot *antipasti* first, then the cold. The guests are encouraged to help themselves to wine and there are already calls for the bottles to be replenished. After the *antipasti* it is the turn of the *pasta*. This comes in three separate courses: first the restaurant's own *tagliatelle* with a rich *ragù*, then *cannelloni*, the large round tubes filled with meat and tomato covered in béchamel and parmesan and baked in the oven, lastly *tagliatelle verde*, *tagliatelle* made with the addition of finely pounded spinach to give a delightful green colour; this is served with a sauce of cream and *prosciutto cotto*. Silvana, although faintly scandalised by the extravagance of the dishes, is thoroughly enjoying herself. Good food cooked by somebody else is a real treat for her. Orlando is swapping jokes with his brothers and making short work of the excellent Umbrian wine.

Everyone having done justice to the pasta, the waiters bring the first main course which is *Piccione in Salmi*, pigeons roasted briefly then finished in a rich sauce based on brandy, *soffrito* of carrots, onions and celery, enriched with concentrated stock from the crushed pigeon bones, then thickened with butter and flour. Great dishes of *fagiolini verdi* and potatoes roasted with meat juices, whole cloves of garlic and rosemary are passed around with the pigeons. Then comes aromatic roast lamb and roast pork; these are served with *sformati* of *piselli* and *carciofi*, pureés of peas and artichokes mixed with eggs and grated parmesan and baked in moulds in the oven. After the lamb and pork come large dishes of spit-roasted duck, guinea fowl and chicken and with them a refreshing green salad. All through the meal guests propose toasts to the bride and groom or their parents, and the chant of "*bacio, bacio, bacio*" goes round the room, everyone insisting that the groom should kiss his bride. In the interval between the main courses and the *dolci* the young parish priest and his choir sing a cheeky song that they have composed all about Alberto and his family, who are very popular in their village. There are no stilted formal speeches.

The wedding cake is carried in to loud applause and there is a fusillade of *spumante* corks flying through the air. As well as the wedding cake there is a great iced chocolate cake with *vin santo* to go with it. Finally baskets of fruit are circulated, then coffee and much-needed *digestivi* or brandy. The feast has been going on for five hours and the end is signalled by the bringing in of decorative baskets of *confetti*, small mementoes of the day, one for each guest. Brunella has chosen miniature straw hats trimmed with flowers which are attached to wisps of veiling holding sugared almonds and a little card inscribed with the names of the bridal couple.

After the majority of the guests have taken their leave the hard core of revellers, mainly from the close family, set off in procession in their cars to install the bride in her new home. The line of cars, now much smaller, drives up through the mountains and branching off onto tiny unmade roads the procession eventually arrives at the groom's home, a rambling grey stone farmhouse with an old-fashioned *torre* or tower for drying chestnuts. The new couple will live with the groom's parents, who are farmers in a small way. Brunella will help her mother-in-law in the house and Fabio will continue to work on the farm, a traditional arrangement. Girls move to their in-laws' house when they marry but the eldest son at least remains in the family home with his wife. Very many of these old farmhouses are rambling structures because they consist of many stages of building; for each new bride at least one room is added on to the house. However this way of life is on the decline as most modern Italian girls want homes of their own with central heating and all the trimmings.

The cheerful party arrives at the house and there is yet more wine, liqueurs and sweet cake to be consumed. Brunella's new room has been furnished with great care. She had chosen traditional country furniture and the vast *letto matrimoniale* has an elaborate bedstead of curved brass with a lacquered plaque at the head decorated with flowers. The coverlet is made of exquisite handmade cream lace; these lovely covers are still to be found in some country markets. The photographer is still of the party and takes pictures of the pretty room in all its new splendour. Later the couple will have a lavish memento of their wedding day in the shape of an enormous album packed with hundreds of excellent colour prints. The album itself is magnificent. It is shaped like a beech leaf and the cover is of hand-worked pewter, the veins of the leaf carefully formed in the metal. The lining of the cover is made of heavy watered silk and is the colour of the inside of a cobnut shell. It is hard to believe that such workmanship still exists in this century.

John Ruskin

(1 8 1 9 – 1 9 0 0)

John Ruskin, one of the most formidable Victorian architecture and art critics, was quite mad for much of his life. Born into a wealthy merchant family, Ruskin traveled widely with his parents and published his first articles when he was just seventeen. The multivolume series *Modern Painters* and *The Seven Lamps of Architecture*, and the three volumes of *The Stones of Venice*, a comprehensive analysis of the development of Byzantine and Gothic architecture and a study of the city's moral and political history, earned him fame. *Mornings in Florence*, from which this selection is excerpted, was written in 1875.

Ruskin's political philosophy evolved from his theories about art and architecture. He felt that faith and morality were prerequisites to producing good art and that good art revealed the attributes of God. In midlife he examined the economic and political conditions of the poor and was deeply influenced by the Socialist movement. His restless intellect eventually encompassed botany and ornithology.

As his interests expanded, Ruskin's mental health declined. His only marriage was annulled for reason of "non-consummation" after six years, and his wife married one of his best friends the following year. At nearly forty he fell in love with a young Irish woman half his age. She died, insane, in 1875. Ruskin's mental health, always precarious, deteriorated, and for the rest of his life he alternated between periods of insanity and lucidity. He died in England twenty days into the twentieth century.

from MORNINGS IN FLORENCE

THE FIRST MORNING

SANTA CROCE

If there is one artist, more than another, whose work it is desirable that you should examine in Florence, supposing that you care for old art at all, it is Giotto. You can, indeed, also see work of his at Assisi; but it is not likely you will stop there, to any purpose. At Padua there is much; but only of one period. At Florence, which is his birthplace, you can see pictures by him of every date and every kind. But you had surely better see, first, what is of his best time and of the best kind. He painted very small pictures and very large—painted from the age of twelve to sixty—painted some subjects carelessly which he had little interest in—some carefully with all his heart. You would surely like, and it would certainly be wise, to see him first in his strong and earnest work—to see a painting by him, if possible, of large size, and wrought with his full strength, and of a subject pleasing to him. And if it were, also, a subject interesting to yourself—better still.

Now, if indeed you are interested in old art, you cannot but know the power of the thirteenth century. You know that the character of it was concentrated in, and to the full expressed by, its best king, St. Louis. You know St. Louis was a Franciscan, and that the Franciscans, for whom Giotto was continually painting under Dante's advice, were prouder of him than of any other of their royal brethren or sisters. If Giotto ever would imagine anybody with care and delight, it would be St. Louis, if it chanced that anywhere he had St. Louis to paint.

Also, you know that he was appointed to build the Campanile of the Duomo, because he was then the best master of sculpture, painting, and architecture in Florence, and supposed to be without superior in the world. And that this commission was given him late in life (of course he could not have designed the Campanile when he was a boy); so therefore, if you find any of his figures painted under pure campanile architecture, and the architecture by his hand, you know, without other evidence, that the painting must be of his strongest time.

So if one wanted to find anything of his to begin with, especially, and could choose what it should be, one would say, "A fresco, life size, with campanile architecture behind it, painted in an important place; and if one might choose one's subject, perhaps the most interesting saint of all saints—for *him* to do for us—would be St. Louis."

Wait then for an entirely bright morning; rise with the sun, and go to Santa Croce, with a good opera-glass in your pocket, with which

you shall for once, at any rate, see an opus; and, if you have time, several opera. Walk straight to the chapel on the right of the choir ("k"
in your Murray's Guide). When you first get into it, you will see nothing but a modern window of glaring glass, with a red-hot cardinal in
one pane—which piece of modern manufacture takes away at least
seven-eighths of the light (little enough before) by which you might
have seen what is worth sight. Wait patiently till you get used to the
gloom. Then, guarding your eyes from the accursed modern window
as best you may, take your opera-glass and look to the right, at the
uppermost of the two figures beside it. It is St. Louis, under campanile architecture, painted by—Giotto? or the last Florentine
painter who wanted a job—over Giotto? That is the first question
you have to determine; as you will have henceforward, in every case
in which you look at a fresco.

Sometimes there will be no question at all. These two gray frescos
at the bottom of the walls on the right and left, for instance, have
been entirely got up for your better satisfaction, in the last year or
two—over Giotto's half-effaced lines. But that St. Louis? Repainted
or not, it is a lovely thing—there can be no question about that; and
we must look at it, after some preliminary knowledge gained, not
inattentively.

Your Murray's Guide tells you that this chapel of the Bardi della
Libertà, in which you stand, is covered with frescos by Giotto; that
they were whitewashed, and only laid bare in 1853; that they were
painted between 1296 and 1304; that they represent scenes in the life
of St. Francis; and that on each side of the window are paintings of
St. Louis of Toulouse, St. Louis, king of France, St. Elizabeth, of
Hungary, and St. Claire,—"all much restored and repainted." Under
such recommendation, the frescos are not likely to be much sought
after; and accordingly, as I was at work in the chapel this morning,
Sunday, 6th September, 1874, two nice-looking Englishmen, under
guard of their *valet de place*, passed the chapel without so much as
looking in.

You will perhaps stay a little longer in it with me, good reader, and
find out gradually where you are. Namely, in the most interesting and
perfect little Gothic chapel in all Italy—so far as I know or can hear.
There is no other of the great time which has all its frescos in their

place. The Arena, though far larger, is of earlier date—not pure Gothic, nor showing Giotto's full force. The lower chapel at Assisi is not Gothic at all, and is still only of Giotto's middle time. You have here, developed Gothic, with Giotto in his consummate strength, and nothing lost, in form, of the complete design.

By restoration—judicious restoration, as Mr. Murray usually calls it—there is no saying how much you have lost. Putting the question of restoration out of your mind, however, for a while, think where you are, and what you have got to look at.

You are in the chapel next the high altar of the great Franciscan church of Florence. A few hundred yards west of you, within ten minutes' walk, is the Baptistery of Florence. And five minutes' walk west of that is the great Dominican church of Florence, Santa Maria Novella.

Get this little bit of geography and architectural fact well into your mind. There is the little octagon Baptistery in the middle; here, ten minutes' walk east of it, the Franciscan church of the Holy Cross; there, five minutes' walk west of it, the Dominican church of St. Mary.

Now, that little octagon Baptistery stood where it now stands (and was finished, though the roof has been altered since) in the eighth century. It is the central building of Etrurian Christianity,—of European Christianity.

From the day it was finished, Christianity went on doing her best, in Etruria and elsewhere, for four hundred years,—and her best seemed to have come to very little,—when there rose up two men who vowed to God it should come to more. And they made it come to more, forthwith; of which the immediate sign in Florence was that she resolved to have a fine new cross-shaped cathedral instead of her quaint old little octagon one; and a tower beside it that should beat Babel:—which two buildings you have also within sight.

But your business is not at present with them, but with these two earlier churches of Holy Cross and St. Mary. The two men who were the effectual builders of these were the two great religious Powers and Reformers of the thirteenth century;—St. Francis, who taught Christian men how they should behave, and St. Dominic, who taught Christian men what they should think. In brief, one the Apostle of

Works; the other of Faith. Each sent his little company of disciples to teach and to preach in Florence: St. Francis in 1212; St. Dominic in 1220.

The little companies were settled—one, ten minutes' walk east of the old Baptistery; the other, five minutes' walk west of it. And after they had stayed quietly in such lodgings as were given them, preaching and teaching through most of the century, and had got Florence, as it were, heated through, she burst out into Christian poetry and architecture, of which you have heard much talk:—burst into bloom of Arnolfo, Giotto, Dante, Orcagna, and the like persons, whose works you profess to have come to Florence that you may see and understand.

Florence then, thus heated through, first helped her teachers to build finer churches. The Dominicans, or White Friars, the Teachers of Faith, began their church of St. Mary's in 1279. The Franciscans, or Black Friars, the teachers of Works, laid the first stone of this church of the Holy Cross in 1294. And the whole city laid the foundations of its new cathedral in 1298. The Dominicans designed their own building; but for the Franciscans and the town worked the first great master of Gothic art, Arnolfo; with Giotto at his side, and Dante looking on, and whispering sometimes a word to both.

And here you stand beside the high altar of the Franciscans' church, under a vault of Arnolfo's building, with at least some of Giotto's color on it still fresh; and in front of you, over the little altar, is the only reportedly authentic portrait of St. Francis, taken from life by Giotto's master. Yet I can hardly blame my two English friends for never looking in. Except in the early morning light, not one touch of all this art can be seen. And in any light, unless you understand the relations of Giotto to St. Francis, and of St. Francis to humanity, it will be of little interest.

Observe, then, the special character of Giotto among the great painters of Italy is his being a practical person. Whatever other men dreamed of, he did. He could work in mosaic; he could work in marble; he could paint; and he could build; and all thoroughly: a man of supreme faculty, supreme common sense. Accordingly, he ranges himself at once among the disciples of the Apostle of Works, and spends most of his time in the same apostleship.

Now the gospel of Works, according to St. Francis, lay in three things. You must work without money, and be poor. You must work without pleasure, and be chaste. You must work according to orders, and be obedient.

Those are St. Francis's three articles of Italian opera. By which grew the many pretty things you have come to see here.

And now if you will take your opera-glass and look up to the roof above Arnolfo's building, you will see it is a pretty Gothic cross vault, in four quarters, each with a circular medallion, painted by Giotto. That over the altar has the picture of St. Francis himself. The three others, of his Commanding Angels. In front of him over the entrance arch, Poverty. On his right hand, Obedience. On his left, Chastity.

Poverty, in a red patched dress, with gray wings, and a square nimbus of glory above her head, is flying from a black hound, whose head is seen at the corner of the medallion.

Chastity, veiled, is imprisoned in a tower, while angels watch her.

Obedience bears a yoke on her shoulders, and lays her hand on a book.

Now, this same quatrefoil, of St. Francis and his three Commanding Angels, was also painted, but much more elaborately, by Giotto, on the cross vault of the lower church of Assisi, and it is a question of interest which of the two roofs was painted first.

Your Murray's Guide tells you the frescos in this chapel were painted between 1296 and 1304. But as they represent, among other personages, St. Louis of Toulouse, who was not canonized till 1317, that statement is not altogether tenable. Also, as the first stone of the church was only laid in 1294, when Giotto was a youth of eighteen, it is little likely that either it would have been ready to be painted, or he ready with his scheme of practical divinity, two years later.

Farther, Arnolfo, the builder of the main body of the church, died in 1310. And as St. Louis of Toulouse was not a saint till seven years afterwards, and the frescos therefore beside the window not painted in Arnolfo's day, it becomes another question whether Arnolfo left the chapels, or the church at all, in their present form.

On which point—now that I have shown you where Giotto's St. Louis is—I will ask you to think awhile, until you are interested: and then I will try to satisfy your curiosity. Therefore, please leave the little chapel for the moment, and walk down the nave, till you come to two sepulchral slabs near the west end, and then look about you and see what sort of a church Santa Croce is.

Without looking about you at all, you may find, in your Murray, the useful information that it is a church which "consists of a very wide nave and lateral aisles, separated by seven fine pointed arches." And as you will be—under ordinary conditions of tourist hurry—glad to learn so much, *without* looking, it is little likely to occur to you that this nave and two rich aisles required also, for your complete present comfort, walls at both ends, and a roof on the top. It is just possible, indeed, you may have been struck, on entering, by the curious disposition of painted glass at the east end;—more remotely possible that, in returning down the nave, you may this moment have noticed the extremely small circular window at the west end; but the chances are a thousand to one that, after being pulled from tomb to tomb round the aisles and chapels, you should take so extraordinary an additional amount of pains as to look up at the roof,—unless you do it now, quietly. It will have had its effect upon you, even if you don't, without your knowledge. You will return home with a general impression that Santa Croce is, somehow, the ugliest Gothic church you ever were in. Well, that is really so; and now, will you take the pains to see why?

There are two features, on which, more than on any others, the grace and delight of a fine Gothic building depends; one is the springing of its vaultings, the other the proportion and fantasy of its traceries. *This* church of Santa Croce has no vaultings at all, but the roof of a farm-house barn. And its windows are all of the same pattern,—the exceedingly prosaic one of two pointed arches, with a round hole above, between them.

And to make the simplicity of the roof more conspicuous, the aisles are successive sheds, built at every arch. In the aisles of the Campo Santo of Pisco, the unbroken flat roof leaves the eye free to look to the traceries; but here, a succession of up-and-down sloping beam and lath gives the impression of a line of stabling rather than a church aisle. And lastly, while, in fine Gothic buildings, the entire perspective concludes itself gloriously in the high and distant apse, here the nave is cut across sharply by a line of ten chapels, the apse being only a tall recess in the midst of them, so that, strictly speaking, the church is not of the form of a cross, but of a letter *T*.

Can this clumsy and ungraceful arrangement be indeed the design of the renowned Arnolfo?

Yes, this is purest Arnolfo-Gothic; not beautiful by any means; but deserving, nevertheless, our thoughtfulest examination. We will trace its complete character another day; just now we are only concerned with this pre-Christian form of the letter *T*, insisted upon in the lines of chapels.

Respecting which you are to observe, that the first Christian churches in the catacombs took the form of a blunt cross naturally; a square chamber having a vaulted recess on each side; then the Byzantine churches were structurally built in the form of an equal cross; while the heraldic and other ornamental equal-armed crosses are partly signs of glory and victory, partly of light, and divine spiritual presence.

But the Franciscans and Dominicans saw in the cross no sign of triumph, but of trial. The wounds of their Master were to be their inheritance. So their first aim was to make what image to the cross their church might present, distinctly that of the actual instrument of death.

And they did this most effectually by using the form of the letter *T*, that of the Furca or Gibbet,—not the sign of peace.

Also, their churches were meant for use; not show, nor self-glorification, nor town-glorification. They wanted places for preaching, prayer, sacrifice, burial; and had no intention of showing how high they could build towers, or how widely they could arch vaults. Strong walls, and the roof of a barn,—these your Franciscan asks of his Arnolfo. These Arnolfo gives,—thoroughly and wisely built; the succession of gable roof being a new device for strength, much praised in its day.

This stern humor did not last long. Arnolfo himself had other notions; much more Cimabue and Giotto; most of all, Nature and Heaven. Something else had to be taught about Christ than that He was wounded to death. Nevertheless, look how grand this stern form would be, restored to its simplicity. It is not the old church which is in itself unimpressive. It is the old church defaced by Vasari, by

Michael Angelo, and by modern Florence. See those huge tombs on
your right hand and left, at the sides of the aisles, with their alternate
gable and round tops, and their paltriest of all possible sculpture, trying to be grand by bigness, and pathetic by expense. Tear them all
down in your imagination; fancy the vast hall with its massive pillars,—not painted calomel-pill color, as now, but of their native
stone, with a rough, true wood for roof,—and a people praying
beneath them, strong in abiding, and pure in life, as their rocks and
olive forests. That was Arnolfo's Santa Croce. Nor did his work
remain long without grace.

That very line of chapels in which we found our St. Louis shows
signs of change in temper. *They* have no pent-house roofs, but true
Gothic vaults: we found our four-square type of Franciscan Law on
one of them.

It is probable, then, that these chapels may be later than the rest—
even in their stonework. In their decoration, they are so, assuredly;
belonging already to the time when the story of St. Francis was
becoming a passionate tradition, told and painted everywhere with
delight.

And that high recess, taking the place of apse, in the center,—see
how noble it is in the colored shade surrounding and joining the glow
of its windows, though their form be so simple. You are not to be
amused here by patterns in balance stone, as a French or English
architect would amuse you, says Arnolfo. "You are to read and think,
under these severe walls of mine; immortal hands will write upon
them." We will go back, therefore, into this line of manuscript
chapels presently; but first, look at the two sepulchral slabs by which
you are standing. That farther of the two from the west end is one of
the most beautiful pieces of fourteenth-century sculpture in this
world; and it contains simple elements of excellence, by your understanding of which you may test your power of understanding the
more difficult ones you will have to deal with presently.

It represents an old man, in the high deeply folded cap worn by
scholars and gentlemen in Florence from 1300–1500, lying dead,
with a book in his breast, over which his hands are folded. At his feet
is this inscription: "Temporibus hic suis phylosophye atq. medicine
culmen fuit Galileus de Galileis olim Bonajutis qui etiam summo in

magistratu miro quodam modo rempublicam dilexit, cujus sancte memorie bene acte vite pie benedictus filius hune tumulum patri sibi suisq. posteris edidit."

Mr. Murray tells you that the effigies "in low relief" (alas, yes, low enough now—worn mostly into flat stones, with a trace only of the deeper lines left, but originally in very bold relief), with which the floor of Santa Croce is inlaid, of which this by which you stand is characteristic, are "interesting from the costume," but that, "except in the case of John Ketterick, Bishop of St. David's, few of the other names have any interest beyond the walls of Florence." As, however, you are at present within the walls of Florence, you may perhaps condescend to take some interest in this ancestor or relation of the Galileo whom Florence indeed left to be externally interesting, and would not allow to enter in her walls.

I am not sure if I rightly place or construe the phrase in the above inscription, "cujus sancte memorie bene acte"; but, in main purport, the legend runs thus: "This Galileo of the Galilei was, in his times, the head of philosophy and medicine; who also in the highest magistracy loved the republic marvelously; whose son, blessed in inheritance of his holy memory and well-passed and pious life, appointed this tomb for his father, for himself, and for his posterity."

There is no date; but the slab immediately behind it, nearer the western door, is of the same style, but of later and interior work, and bears date—I forget now of what early year in the fifteenth century.

But Florence was still in her pride; and you may observe, in this epitaph, on what it was based. That her philosophy was studied *together with useful arts*, and as a part of them; that the masters in these became naturally the masters in public affairs; that in such magistracy they loved the State, and neither cringed to it nor robbed it; that the sons honored their fathers, and received their fathers' honor as the most blessed inheritance. Remember the phrase "vite pie benedictus filius," to be compared with the "nos nequiores," of the declining days of all states,—chiefly now in Florence, France, and England.

Thus much for the local interest of name. Next for the universal interest of the art of this tomb.

It is the crowning virtue of all great art that, however little is left of it by the injuries of time, that little will be lovely. As long as you can see anything, you can see—almost all;—so much the hand of the master will suggest of his soul.

And here you are well quit, for once, of restoration. No one cares for this sculpture; and if Florence would only thus put all her old sculpture and painting under her feet and simply use them for grave-stones and oilcloth, she would be more merciful to them than she is now. Here, at least, what little is left is true.

And, if you look long, you will find it is not so little. That worn face is still a perfect portrait of the old man, though like one struck out at a venture, with a few rough touches of a master's chisel. And that falling drapery of his cap is, in its few lines, faultless, and subtle beyond description.

And now, here is a simple but most useful test of your capacity for understanding Florentine sculpture or painting. If you can see that the lines of that cap are both right and lovely; that the choice of the folds is exquisite in its ornamental relations of line; and that the soft-ness and ease of them is complete,—though only sketched with a few dark touches,—then you can understand Giotto's drawing, and Botticelli's;—Donatello's carving, and Luca's. But if you see nothing in *this* sculpture, you will see nothing in theirs, *of* theirs. Where they choose to imitate flesh, or silk, or to play any vulgar modern trick with marble—(and they often do)—whatever, in a word, is French, or American, or Cockney, in their work, you can see; but what is Flor-entine, and forever great—unless you can see also the beauty of this old man in his citizen's cap,—you will see never.

There is more in this sculpture, however, than its simple portrai-ture and noble drapery. The old man lies on a piece of embroidered carpet; and, protected by the high relief, many of the finer lines of this are almost uninjured; in particular, its exquisitely-wrought fringe and tassels are nearly perfect. And if you will kneel down and look long at the tassels of the cushion under the head, and the way they fill the angles of the stone, you will—or may—know, from this example alone, what noble decorative sculpture is, and was, and must be, from the days of earliest Greece to those of latest Italy.

"Exquisitely sculptured fringe!" and you have just been abusing sculptors who play tricks with marble! Yes, and you cannot find a better example, in all the museums of Europe, of the work of a man who does *not* play tricks with it—than this tomb. Try to understand the difference: it is a point of quite cardinal importance to all your future study of sculpture.

I *told* you, observe, that the old Galileo was lying on a piece of embroidered carpet. I don't think, if I had not told you, that you would have found it out for yourself. It is not so like a carpet as all that comes to.

But had it been a modern trick-sculpture, the moment you came to the tomb you would have said, "Dear me! how wonderfully that carpet is done,—it doesn't look like stone in the least—one longs to take it up and beat it to get the dust off."

Now whenever you feel inclined to speak so of a sculptured drapery, be assured, without more ado, the sculpture is base, and bad. You will merely waste your time and corrupt your taste by looking at it. Nothing is so easy as to imitate drapery in marble. You may cast a piece any day; and carve it with such subtlety that the marble shall be an absolute image of the folds. But that is not sculpture. That is mechanical manufacture.

No great sculptor, from the beginning of art to the end of it, has ever carved, or ever will, a deceptive drapery. He has neither time nor will to do it. His mason's lad may do that if he likes. A man who can carve a limb or a face never finishes inferior parts, but either with a hasty and scornful chisel, or with such grave and strict selection of their lines as you know at once to be imaginative, not imitative.

But if, as in this case, he wants to oppose the simplicity of his central subject with a rich background,—a labyrinth of ornamental lines to relieve the severity of expressive ones,—he will carve you a carpet, or a tree, or a rose thicket, with their fringes and leaves and thorns, elaborated as richly as natural ones; but always for the sake of the ornamental form, never of the imitation; yet, seizing the natural character in the lines he gives, with twenty times the precision and clearness of sight that the mere imitator has. Examine the tassels of the cushion, and the way they blend with the fringe, thoroughly; you cannot possibly see finer ornamental sculpture. Then, look at the same tassels in the same place of the slab next the west end of the church, and you will see a scholar's rude imitation of a master's hand, though in a fine school. (Notice, however, the folds of the drapery at the feet of this figure: they are cut so as to show the hem of the robe within as well as without, and are fine.) Then, as you go back to Giotto's chapel, keep to the left, and just beyond the north door in the aisle is the much celebrated tomb of C. Marsuppini, by Desiderio of Settignano. It is very fine of its kind; but there the drapery is chiefly done to cheat you, and chased delicately to show how finely the sculptor could chisel it. It is wholly vulgar and mean in cast of fold. Under your feet, as you look at it, you will tread another tomb of the fine time, which, looking last at, you will recognize the difference between the false and true art, as far as there is capacity in you at present to do so. And if you really and honestly like the low-lying stones, and see more beauty in them, you have also the power of enjoying Giotto, into whose chapel we will return to-morrow;—not to-day, for the light must have left it by this time; and now that you have been looking at these sculptures on the floor you had better traverse nave and aisle across and across; and get some idea of that sacred field of stone. In the north transept you will find a beautiful knight, the finest in chiseling of all these tombs, except one by the same hand in the south aisle just where it enters the south transept. Examine the lines of the Gothic niches traced above them; and what is left of arabesque on their armor. They are far more beautiful and tender in chivalric conception than Donatello's St. George, which is merely a piece of vigorous naturalism founded on these older tombs. If you will drive in the evening to the Chartreuse in Val d'Ema, you may see there an uninjured example of this slab-tomb by Donatello himself: very beautiful; but not so perfect as the earlier ones on which it is founded. And you may see some fading light and shade of monastic life, among which if you stay till the fireflies come out in the twilight, and thus get to sleep when you come home, you will be better prepared for to-morrow morning's walk—if you will take another with me—than if you go to a party, to talk sentiment about Italy, and hear the last news from London and New York.

Mary Shelley

(1797–1851)

Mary Wollstonecraft Shelley's life is divided into two parts: before the death of her husband, the poet Percy Bysshe Shelley, in 1822, and after. Their notorious love affair began in 1814, when she was seventeen. Shelley was twenty-two and already married to Harriet Westbrook, who was pregnant with their second child. Harriet gave birth in November 1814 to a son, and Mary gave birth in February 1815, although her tiny daughter lived but a few weeks. The lovers' families (including Mary's father, William Godwin, a leading radical of his time) tried to convince Mary and Percy to part—to no avail.

After Harriet's suicide the lovers fled to Italy, but could not escape the tragedies that consumed the rest of their lives: all but one of their children died, Percy was depressed and in ill health, and they were alienated from their families. Their marriage was strained by Percy's belief in free love. He had affairs with other women (including possibly Mary's stepsister Claire) and encouraged Mary to take lovers as well. Even the success of Mary's gothic novel *Frankenstein* (1818), written in response to a challenge from her husband, Byron, and other friends, did not ease their suffering.

After Shelley's death, Mary plunged into despair and poverty and returned to England. She devoted herself to preserving her husband's memory and gaining legitimacy for her only remaining child, Percy Florence. Mary wrote romantic potboilers, published invaluable annotated editions of her husband's work (including volumes of his letters), and penned travel memoirs like *Travel Writing* (1843), from which this selection is excerpted. She never remarried because she wanted "Mary Shelley" on her grave.

from TRAVEL WRITING

Letter XV.

TUSCANY.

February, 1843

Nothing is more difficult than for a foreigner to give a correct account of the state of a country—its laws, manners, and customs;—the first often so different in their operation from what outwardly appears; the latter, never fully understood, Proteus-like, assume a thousand contradictory appearances, and elude investigation. A stranger can only glance at the surface of things—often deceptive—and put down the results of conversations, which, after all, if carefully examined, by no means convey the whole truth, even if they are free from some bias, however imperceptible, either in speaker or hearer, the result of which is a false impression—a false view.

An English person, accustomed to the gigantic fortunes and well-ordered luxury,—to the squalid penury, hard labour, and famine,—which mark the opposite orders of society in his own country, is struck by the appearance of ease and equality that reigns in Tuscany, and especially at Florence. There is poverty of course—but penury cannot be said to exist; there is work—but there is also rest: nay, there is no lack of enjoyment for the poor—while the nobility, for the most part, scarcely rise above the middling orders; bankers and foreigners being those who make most figure in society, and that, except on particular and infrequent occasions, on no magnificent scale.

Many reasons may be assigned for this equality. During the flourishing days of the republic of Florence, a blow was given to the nobility of the city and surrounding country, from which it never recovered. Those nobles who still preserved their titles and fortunes, were obliged to conceal all pride in the former, in order to preserve the influence naturally resulting from the latter. The Medici were merchants, and when an Austrian prince succeeded to the extinct family, no change was operated. On the contrary, it was, I believe, one of them, Leopold I, who abolished the law of primogeniture in Tuscany. It is true, that the usual result of the prohibition against entails in subdividing estates, is frequently eluded. A father possesses absolute power over his property, with the exception of a tenth or twelfth, which is called the *quota legitima*, which must descend to his children, and be divided among them in equal portions. The same law appertains even to the mother's dowry—which becomes her husband's property. A man may, therefore, accumulate and leave the whole of his possessions to his eldest son, with the exception of the above-named *quota*; and, when this has been done for some generations, large fortunes are preserved. But it seldom is: and as a man has absolute propriety in his estates, a spendthrift can alienate the whole for ever. The nobles of Tuscany being for the most part without pride of order, have readily yielded to the spirit of their country, which absorbs them in the democracy. At the same time, the feeling of accumulation being extinct, no barrier exists to prevent the dissipation of property: in the hands of a young heir, extravagance and play (the bane of Italy), soon bring to an end the fortunes of an ancient name. Thus, I am assured, many of the noblest families in Tuscany are reduced to poverty: the capital of the country has fallen into the hands of bankers, the majority of whom are of Jewish origin. A number of illustrious names, consecrated in the pages of history, have almost disappeared. They only mark the walls of palaces, empty of the impoverished descendants of their former possessors.

This absence of accumulated riches, of course, checks the arts of luxury, mechanical improvements, and all progress in the framework of society; it multiplies the numbers of those who are just raised above poverty; while the benignant nature of the climate, and the abstemious habits of the Italians, prevent the poor from suffering want. The country is, for the most part, divided into small farms (*podere*), cultivated by the family of the countryman (*contadino*) who holds them—he giving his labour, the crops, and tools—the owner the land, dwellings, and substantial repairs; the profits are divided, and the rent, for the most part, paid in kind—a circumstance which aids the farmer, and limits the fortune of the owner. The country-people labour hard—very hard, and live poorly, but they do not suffer want; and if there are no farmers so rich as with us, there is no absolute agricultural distress.

In Florence itself the common people are well to do. They are, perhaps, the least agreeable people to deal with in Italy; self-opinionated, independent, and lazy, they can often scarcely be brought to work at all; and, when they do, it is in their own way and at their own time. They love their ease, and they enjoy it: they are full of humour and intelligence, though their conceit too often acts as a drawback on the latter. I speak especially of the Florentines, as they are represented to me; for conceit is not a usual fault among the Italians.

As I have said, an English person, accustomed to heart-piercing accounts of suffering, hard labour, and starvation among our poor, gladly hails a sort of golden age in this happy country. We must look on the state of society from a wholly different point of view—we must think of the hunger of the mind; of the nobler aspirations of the soul, held in check and blighted—of the tendency of man to improve, here held down—of the peculiar and surpassing gifts of genius appertaining to this people, who are crushed and trod under foot by the jealousy of government—to understand, with how dead and intolerable a weight King Log hangs round the necks of those among them, who regret the generous passions and civic virtues of bygone times. The Florentine reads of Filippo Strozzi, of Ferruccio Ferruccini, of Michael Angelo. He remembers the pure and sacred spirit that Savanarola lighted up among the free and religious citizens; he thinks of the slavery that followed, when genius and valour left the land indignant, and

> "For deeds of violence
> Done in broad day; and more than half redeemed
> By many a great and generous sacrifice of self to others,"

what has come? The poet speaks of—

> "the unpledged bowl,
> The stab of the stiletto."*

But those days, too, are gone; there has come such life as the flocks lead on the mountain sides—such life as the idle, graceful fallow-

*Rogers's "Italy."

deer may spend, from spring-tide to rainy autumn, under the noble trees of some abundant park; but where is the soul of man? In the hands of those who teach him to fast and tell his beads—to bend the neck to the yoke—to obey the church, not God.

Nor is this all; especially among the rich; far—far from it; for men, unless tamed by labour, can never lead the innocent lives of the beasts of the field: if darker crimes are infrequent, yet vice flourishes, rank and unchecked: the sense of honour is destroyed; the nobler affections are crushed; mental culture is looked on with jealousy, and dies blighted. In the young may be found gleams of inextinguishable genius—a yearning for better things, which terrifies the parents, who see in such the seeds of discontent and ruin: they prefer for their sons the safer course of intrigue, play, idleness—the war of the passions, rather than the aspirations of virtue.

To do nothing has been long the motto of the Tuscan government; had it been strictly observed, still much might be said against it. Leopold I was a good sovereign, a clever and liberal man; Ferdinand, who succeeded to him, suffered many vicissitudes of fortune during the period of the empire of Napoleon; but he was not, like his namesake of Naples, driven by adversity to cruelty and arbitrary violence. When he was restored to his throne, still it was his wish to keep his people happy and contented. It is his praise, that if authority sheathed its sword and veiled its terrors, nor even used the wholesome restraint of the law to punish crime, it acted simply as a torpedo on the energies of the land, nor used any concealed weapons Ferdinand constantly and resolutely refused to institute a *secret police* in Tuscany. It was a story I remember, told at the time, during the revolutionary period of 1821, that the Austrian minister at Florence presented a list of sixty Carbonari to the Grand Duke, and begged that they might be arrested. "I do not know whether these men are Carbonari," said Ferdinand: "but I am sure, if I imprison them, I shall make them such," and rejected the list. His successor, Leopold II, has not had the wisdom to pursue the same course. The bane of Italy is the absence of truth, of honour, of straightforwardness; the vices opposite to these nobler virtues have now the additional culture which must ensue from the circulation of a system of *secret police*, of spies, of traitors.

Yet still the government is mild. In 31–32, the throne of Leopold

II was shaken by several conspiracies; and the revolutionary spirit of Romagna, which tended to unite all Italy in one bond, had numerous proselytes in Tuscany. But for a traitor, it is supposed, that on one occasion the person of the Grand Duke would have fallen into the hands of the conspirators: at the eleventh hour the leader took fright, and discovered all. On this, and on other occasions, the arrests were not numerous; the sentences (to us to whom treason and the gallows are quick following cause and effect), mild; and these even, after a few months, softened. Leopold wishes his people to be quiet and happy—he hates violence: to pay a traitor to betray, and so to crush a conspiracy noiselessly, appears to him wise and judicious policy. In all respects he is averse to strong measures. For many years no capital punishment has been inflicted in Tuscany; a fact, which of itself demands our admiration, and must be replete with good effects.

"All this is true," said an Italian to me; "and yet I, who wish my countrymen to cultivate manly habits of thought and action, regard our state as almost worse than any other. Tyranny is, with us, a serpent hid among flowers; and I, for one, sympathise with the sentiment of a Florentine poet—*odio il tiranno che col sonno uccide*. There are other evils besides those which press upon the *material* part of our nature, and the new generation in Tuscany feels wrongs of another description. The better spirits of our country pine for the intellectual food of which they are deprived. Thus they tend towards a new and better order of things, the more difficult to realise, because a timid and absurd policy endeavours to throw every obstacle in the way to its attainment."

Percy Bysshe Shelley

(1792–1822)

Percy Bysshe Shelley moved to Italy in 1817. The young English Romantic poet claimed that the warmer climate improved his fragile health, but he also wanted to escape outrage over his love affair and the dissolution of his marriage. Shelley left his wife Harriet and two infants for Mary Godwin, daughter of the radical thinker William Godwin. The despondent Harriet later committed suicide. Percy and Mary married and set up an unconventional household in Italy that included, at times, her stepsister Claire, Byron, and their assorted children.

Like many expatriates the Shelleys did not consort with Italians. In one letter Percy wrote, "The modern Italians seem a miserable people—without sensibility or imagination or understanding. Their outside is polished & an intercourse with them seems to proceed with much facility—tho it ends in nothing & produces nothing."

Mary and Percy moved frequently, and their tenure in Italy was marked by tragedy. Two of their three children and both of Claire's daughters (one fathered by Byron and one rumored to be fathered by Shelley) died. The Shelleys' marriage foundered, and Percy went into a deep depression expressed in his poem "Stanzas Written in Dejection, near Naples"—"Alas, I have nor hope nor health, nor peace within nor calm around." In July 1822 Shelley drowned while sailing on the Bay of Lerici when a sudden storm sank his boat, the *Ariel*. His ashes are buried in the Protestant Cemetery in Rome, but Mary returned his heart to England for burial.

These letters are excerpted from *The Letters of Percy Bysshe Shelley,* written between 1818 and 1822, edited by Frederick L. Jones.

from THE LETTERS OF PERCY BYSSHE SHELLEY

TO THOMAS MEDWIN, *GENEVA*

Florence, Jan 17, 1820.

My dear Medwin

The winter at Florence has been, for the climate, unusually severe, &
yet I imagine you must have suffered enough in Switzerland to make
you regret that you did not come further South—At least I confidently expect that we shall see you in the Spring. We are fixed for the
ensuing year in Tuscany & you will always find me by addressing me
at Leghorn.—

Perhaps you belong to the tribe of the hopeless & nothing shocks
or surprises you in politics—I have enough of unrebuked hope
remaining to be struck with horror at the proceedings in England.
Yet I reflect, as a last consolation that oppressi{ons} which author-
ize, often produce resistance—These are not times in which one has
much spirit for writing Poetry; although there is a keen air in them
that sharpens the wits of men and makes them imagine vividly even
in the midst of despondence.—

I dare say the lake before you is a plain of solid ice bounded by the
snowy hills, whose white mantles contrast with the aerial rose colour
of the eternal glaciers—a scene more grand, yet like the recesses of
the Antarctic circle—If your health allows you to skait, this plain is
the floor of your Paradise, & the white world seems spinning backwards as you fly—The thaw may have arrived, or you may have
departed & this letter reach you in a very different scene—.

This Italy, believe me, is a pleasant place, especially Rome &
Naples. Tuscany is delightful eight months of the year, but nothing
reconciles me to the slightest indication of winter; much less such
infernal cold as my nerves have been racked upon for the last ten
days.—At Naples, all the worst is over in three weeks.— When you
come hither you must take up your abode with me, & I will give you
all the experience which I have bought, at the usual market price,
during the last year & an half residence in Italy.—

You used, I remember, to paint very well; & you were remarkable, if I do not mistake, for a peculiar taste in, & knowledge of the *belle arti*—Italy is the place for you—the very place—The Paradise of exiles—the retreat of Pariahs—but I am thinking of myself rather than of you—

If you will be glad to see an old friend who will be very glad to see you—if {this} is any inducement—come to Italy—

TO THOMAS JEFFERSON HOGG, *LONDON*

Pisa, April 20, 1820.

My dear Friend,

It is some time since I heard from or of you. Peacock is metamorphosed by his Indian preferment into a very laconic correspondent; he seems persuaded of the truth of the Christian maxim, "let your communications be yea, yea, nay, nay, for whatever is more than this cometh of evil." Hunt writes to me sometimes, and tells me that, when in town, you spend the Sundays with him frequently; more he says not. *Wherefore* I resolved to write to you, so that even if you are one of the atoms of the fame-getting, money-getting whirlwind, you might know that I at least wished to hear of you.

I think it is since I last wrote that Mary has given me a little boy, whom I call Percy. He is now five months old, a lovely child, and very healthy; but you may conceive after the dreadful events of last year how great our anxiety is about him.

We spent the severity of the winter at Florence, and are now at Pisa, where we are on the point of taking a very pleasant house just outside the walls. I have been fortunate enough to make acquaintance here with a most interesting woman, in whose society we spend a great part of our time. She is married, and has two children; her husband is, what husbands too commonly are, far inferior to her, but not in the proportion of Mrs. Gisborne's. You will have some idea of the sort of person, when I tell you that I am now reading with her the "Agamemnon" of Æschylus.

I hope you have received a copy of the "Cenci" from Ollier. I told him to send you one, but as he is very negligent, I think it possible that he may not have adverted to it. In that case, whenever you pass his shop ask him for it from me. You will see that it is studiously written in a style very different from any other compositions; how far it may be better or worse will be decided according to the various judgments of those who read it. I have dedicated it to Hunt. Hunt, perhaps, is the only man among my friends whom a dedication from so unpopular a person as myself would not injure.

This winter, even in Italy, has been extremely severe, and I have suffered in proportion; but I revive with the return of spring. I spent the winter at Florence, and dedicated every sunny day to the study of the gallery there; the famous Venus, the Minerva, the Apollino—and more than all, the Niobe and her children, are there. No production of sculpture, not even the Apollo, ever produced on me so strong an effect as this Niobe. Doubtless you have seen casts of it. We are now at Pisa, where (with the exception of a few weeks, in the midst of summer, which we propose to spend at the Bagni di Lucca) we shall remain some indefinite time.

You know that some time since we talked of visiting Italy together. At that time, as at many others, an unfortunate combination of circumstances which have now ceased to exist prevented me from enjoying your society. There is no person for whom I feel so high an esteem and value as for you, or from whom I expected to receive so great a portion of the happiness of my life; and there is none of whose society I have been so frequently deprived by the unfortunate and almost inexplicable complexity of my situation. At this very moment perhaps when it is practicable, on my part, to put into execution the plan to which I allude, perhaps it is impossible on yours.

But let me dwell for a moment on the other side of the question. What say you to making us a visit in Italy? How would it consist with your professional engagements?

You could *see* but little of Italy in June and July on account of the heat, and we *must* then be at the Bagni di Lucca, which though a spot of enchanting beauty, contains none of those objects of art for which Italy is principally worth visiting. But if you are inclined seriously to think of this proposal, I would impose no other law on you than to come as soon, and return as late, as you can. Term begins, I know, in the middle of November, but how far does your business require you to be present on the first day of term? The mode of coming would be to cross France to Marseilles, from whence to Livorno there is a passage sometimes of 36 hours, but the average 3 days. Or you might engage in London for the whole journey over the Alps, but this is a very tedious and much more expensive method.

I ought to add that Mary unites with me in wishing that we may have the pleasure of seeing you. Of course, none of my other friends will join you, but I need not say that Peacock will be welcome.

Do you ever see the Boinvilles now? Or Newton? If so, tell them, especially Mrs. Boinville, that I have not forgotten them. I wonder none of them stray to this Elysian climate, and, like the sailors of Ulysses, eat the lotus and remain as I have done.

TO HORACE SMITH, *PARIS*

Pisa, September 14, 1821.

My dear Smith

I cannot express the pain and disappointment with which I learn the change in your plans, no less than the afflicting cause of it. Florence will no longer have any attraction for me this winter, and I shall contentedly sit down in this humdrum Pisa, and refer to hope and to chance the pleasure I had expected from your society this winter. What shall I do with your packages, which have now, I believe, all arrived at Guebhard's at Leghorn? Is it not possible that a favourable change in Mrs. Smith's health might produce a corresponding change in your determinations, and would it, or would it not, be premature to forward the packages to your present residence, or to London? I will pay every possible attention to your instructions in this regard.

I had marked down several houses in Florence, and one especially on the Arno, a most lovely place, though they asked rather more than perhaps you would have chosen to pay—yet nothing approaching to an English price.—I do not yet entirely give you up.—Indeed, I should be sorry not to hope that Mrs. Smith's state of health would not [*sic*] soon become such, as to remove your principal objection to this delightful climate. I have not, with the exception of three or four days, suffered in the least from the heat this year. Though, it is but fair to confess, that my temperament approaches to that of the salamander.

We expect Lord Byron here in about a fortnight. I have just taken the finest palace in Pisa for him, and his luggage, and his horse, and all his train, are, I believe, already on their way hither. I dare say you have heard of the life he led at Venice, rivalling the wise Solomon almost, in the number of his concubines. Well, he is now quite reformed, and is leading a most sober and decent life, as cavaliere servente to a very pretty Italian woman, who has already arrived at Pisa, with her father and her brother, (such are the manners of Italy,) as the jackals of the lion. He is occupied in forming a new drama, and, with views which I doubt not will expand as he proceeds, is determined to write a series of plays, in which he will follow the French tragedians and Alfieri, rather than those of England and Spain, and produce something new, at least, to England. This seems to me the wrong road; but genius like his is destined to lead and not to follow. He will shake off his shackles as he finds they cramp him. I believe he will produce something very great; and that familiarity with the dramatic power of human nature, will soon enable him to soften down the severe and unharmonising traits of his "Marino Faliero." I think you know Lord Byron personally, or is it your brother? If the latter, I know that he wished particularly to be introduced to you, and that he will sympathise, in some degree, in this great disappointment which I feel in the change, or, as I yet hope, in the prorogation of your plans.

I am glad you like "Adonais," and, particularly, that you do not think it metaphysical, which I was afraid it was. I was resolved to pay some tribute of sympathy to the unhonoured dead, but I wrote, as usual, with a total ignorance of the effect that I should produce.—I have not yet seen your pastoral drama; if you have a copy, could you favour me with it? It will be six months before I shall receive it from England. I have heard it spoken of with high praise, and I have the greatest curiosity to see it.

The Gisbornes promised to buy me some books in Paris, and I had asked you to be kind enough to advance them what they might want to pay for them. I cannot conceive why they did not execute this little commission for me, as they knew how very much I wished to receive these books by the same conveyance as the filtering-stone. Dare I ask you to do me the favour to buy them? *A complete edition of the works of Calderon*, and the French translation of Kant, a German Faust, and to add the Nympholept?—I am indifferent as to a little more or less expense, so that I may have them immediately. I will send you an order on Paris for the amount, together with the thirty-two francs you were kind enough to pay for me.

All public attention is now centred on the wonderful revolution in Greece. I dare not, after the events of last winter, hope that slaves can become freemen so cheaply; yet I know one Greek of the highest qualities, both of courage and conduct, the Prince Mavrocordato, and if the rest be like him, all will go well.—The news of this moment is, that the Russian army has orders to advance.

Mrs. S[helley] unites with me in the most heartfelt regret, and I remain, my dear Smith,

Most faithfully yours,

P.B.S.

TO JOHN GISBORNE, *LONDON*

Pisa, Octr 22, 1821.

My dear Gisborne

At length the post brings a welcome letter from you, & I am pleased to be assured of your health & safe arrival. I expect with interest & anxiety the intelligence of your progress in England, & how far the advantages there compensate the loss of Italy. I hear from Hunt that he is determined upon emigration, and if I thought this letter would arrive in time I should beg you to suggest some advice to him—such as the sending of beds linen &c. which would greatly diminish his expenses here.—But you ought to be incapable of forgiving me the fact of depriving England of what it must lose when Hunt departs.—

Did I tell you that Lord Byron comes to settle at Pisa, & that he has a plan of writing a periodical work in conjunction with Hunt? His house—Madame Felichi's, is already taken and fitted up for him—and he has been expected every day these six weeks.—La

Guiccioli his cara sposa who attends him impatiently, is a very pretty sentimental, [stupid *deleted*] innocent, superficial Italian, who has sacrifized an immense fortune to live [with *deleted*] for Lord Byron; and who, if I know any thing of my friend or her, or of human nature will hereafter have plenty of leisure & opportunity to repent of her rashness.—Lord B. is however quite cured of his gross habits—as far as habits—the perverse ideas on which they were founded are not yet eradicated.

We have furnished a house in Pisa, & mean to make it our headquarters.—I shall get all my books out, & intrench myself—like a spider in a web. If you can assist Peacock in sending them to Leghorn you would do me an especial favour—but do not buy me Calderon Faust or Kant, as H[orace] S[mith] promises to send me them from Paris, where I suppose you had not time to procure them.—Any other books you or Henry think would accord with my design Ollier will furnish you with.—

I should like very much to hear what is said of my Adonais, & you would oblige me by cutting out, or making Ollier cut out any respectable criticism on it, & sending it me. You know I don't mind a crown or two in postage.—The Epipsychidion is a mystery—As to real flesh & blood, you know that I do not deal in those articles,—you might as well go to a ginshop for a leg of mutton, as expect any thing human or earthly from me. I desired Ollier not to circulate this piece except to the Σύνετοι [cognoscenti], and even they it seems are inclined to approximate me to the circle of a servant girl & her sweetheart.—But I intend to write a Symposium of my own to set all this right. I am just finishing a dramatic poem called *Hellas* upon the contest now raging in Greece—a sort of imitation of the Persæ of Æschylus, full of lyrical poetry. I try to be what I might have been, but am not successful. I find that (I dare say I shall quote wrong,)

> "Den herrlichsten, den sich der Geist emprängt
> Drängt immer femd und fremder Stoff sich an."

The Edinburgh Review lies. Godwin's answer to Malthus is victorious and decisive; and that it should not be generally acknowledged as such, is full evidence of the influence of successful evil and tyranny.

What Godwin is, compared to Plato and Lord Bacon, we well know; but compared with these miserable sciolists, he is a vulture to a worm.

I read the Greek dramatists and Plato for ever. You are right about Antigone; how sublime a picture of a woman! and what think you of the choruses, and especially the lyrical complaints of the godlike victim? and the menaces of Tiresias, and their rapid fulfilment? Some of us have, in a prior existence, been in love with an Antigone, and that makes us find no full content in any mortal tie. As to books, I advise you to live near the British Museum, and read there. I have read, since I saw you, the "Jungfrau von Orleans" of Schiller,—a fine play, if the fifth act did not fall off. Some Greeks, escaped from the defeat in Wallachia, have passed through Pisa to re-embark at Leghorn for the Morea; and the Tuscan Government allowed them, during their stay and passage, three lire each per day and their lodging; that is good. Remember me and Mary most kindly to Mrs. Gisborne and Henry, and believe me,

Yours most affectionately,

P.B.S.

TO MRS. SHELLEY, *(CASA MAGNI.)*

Pisa, July 4, 1822.

My dearest Mary,

I have received both your letters, and shall attend to the instructions they convey. I did not think of buying the Bolivar; Lord B. wishes to sell her, but I imagine would prefer ready money. I have as yet made no inquiries about houses near Pagnano—I have no moment of time to spare from Hunt's affairs; I am detained unwillingly here, and you will probably see Williams in the [b]oat before me,—but that will be decided tomorrow.—Things are in the worst possible situation with respect to poor Hunt. I find Marianne in a desperate state of health, & on our arrival at Pisa sent for Vaccà—He decides that her case is hopeless, & that although it will be lingering must inevitably end fatally.—This decision he thought proper to communicate to Hunt,— indicating at the same time, with great judgement & precision, the treatment necessary to be observed for availing himself of the chance of his being deceived. This intelligence has extinguished the last spark of poor Hunt's spirits, low enough before—the children are well & much improved.—Lord Byron is at this moment on the point of leaving Tuscany. The Gambas have been exiled, & he declares his intention of following their fortunes. His first idea was to sail to America, which was changed to Switzerland, then to Genoa, & at last to Lucca.—Every body is in despair & every thing in confusion. Trelawny was on the point of sailing to Genoa for the purpose of transporting the Bolivar overland to the lake of Geneva, & had already whispered in my ear his desire that I should not influence Lord Byron against this terrestrial navigation.—He next received *orders* to weigh anchor & set sail for *Lerici*. He is now without instructions moody & disappointed. But it is the worst for poor Hunt, unless the present storm should blow over. He places his whole dependence upon this scheme of a Journal, for which every arrangement had been mad{e} & arri{ved} with no other remnant of his £4{00} than a debt of 60 crowns.—Lord Byron must of course furnish the requisite funds at present, as I cannot; but he seems inclined to depart without the necessary explanations & arrangements due to such a situation as Hunt's. These in spite of delicacy I must procure; he offers him the copyright of the Vision of Judgement for his first number. This offer if sincere is *more* than enough to set up the Journal, & if sincere will set every thing right.—

How are you my best Mary? Write especially how is your health & how your spirits are, & whether you are not more reconciled to staying at Lerici at least during the summer.

You have no idea how I am hurried & occupied—I have not a moments leisure—but will write by next post—Ever dearest Mary

Yours affectionately

S.

[P.S.] I have found the translation of the Symposium.

Kate Simon

(1 9 1 2 – 1 9 9 0)

Kate Simon was a woman ahead of her time. She traveled solo, producing a series of guidebooks and travel articles that are still as fresh as when they were written more than forty years ago. Simon was born in Poland to a working-class family that immigrated to New York in 1917. In 1959 her first book, *New York Pleasures and Places*, was published. An idiosyncratic look at her hometown, it proved so popular that four more "Pleasures and Places" followed: Paris, London, Rome, and Mexico. In addition to her travel writing, Simon published two well-received memoirs, *Bronx Primitive* and *A Wider World*.

Italy: The Places in Between (1970), from which this excerpt is taken, examines the out-of-the-way spots that tourists often miss. Again, her itinerary is unconventional and her observations pointed. She cautions her female readers, "A woman may be told repeatedly, with fine Italian tact, that young girls are dull little sprigs of grass; it takes care and time to make the perfect, full rose. For a woman whose native society considers five pounds of avoirdupois the equivalent of five pounds of leprosy, it is a warm boon to hear a man say that he likes a buona forchetta, a joyous eater . . ." Simon is beguiled by Italy and calls the country "a Circe in silken landscapes."

from ITALY: THE PLACES IN BETWEEN

LUCCA

Lucca might begin in the tourist office of Pisa, where the mood of gay oddities is set by the fact that information on Lucca is sometimes available only in Dutch. (The office in Lucca is, however, better supplied.) Then, in only twenty minutes by bus or car, through orchards and vines, along canals and yawning quarries, under crushed fortresses and above spunky small industrial plants, past tunnels and bright new gas stations, one reaches the talkative world of Lucca, its

ebullience enhanced by contrast with subdued—one almost writes
"submerged"—Pisa.

Behind the Pinacoteca off the grand Piazza Napoleone there is a
small street, that of the spinners (dei Filatori), which leads to the
treed walk on the city walls, both echoes of the apex of Lucca's history, the twelfth and thirteenth centuries, when her power was as
great as that of Florence and Pisa, when Lucchese silk and banking
found their way throughout Europe. So famous was Lucca and its
wonders that a sacred oath, used by William II of England, it is said,
was "per sanctum Vultum de Luca," referring to an image in the
Duomo. The mood of Lucca is no longer of ancient might, though
relics of rich piety remain to enhance the town; the wall, a specter of
sieges and famine, burning and bloodletting elsewhere, has been
pleasingly fleshed out as a broad esplanade. It is the longest of its
kind in Europe, the city's park for taking the air and views, built
through the sixteenth into the mid-seventeenth century, when the
struggles for supremacy over other Tuscan cities were long over and
the silk industry still prosperous.

The aura of lightness may be attributable to the fact that the city
was under the control of women at various times, first the Longo-
bard Matilda, early in the twelfth century, and much later, two ladies
seriously concerned with uplift, public works and the cultivation of
the arts: the sister of Napoleon, Maria Anna Elisa Bacciocchi, and
shortly after, Maria Luisa the Bourbon. Add to that the innumerable
minute piazze and engaging *vicoli*, each with its bar or trattoria—
three tables on the street and groups of men playing cards, reading
newspapers, arguing mildly.

And Lucca offers the people-watching pleasures of an almost
interminable *passeggiata* on its shopping streets. The boys stroll
together, as do the girls, except for an engaged or extremely enlightened pair. Fluffy baby carriages act as a prow for a family cutting its
way through the crowd. A girl in a smock, carrying a pile of shoe
boxes, a boy with a tray of cakes, still in his white work coat, press
purposefully through this leisured world of which they are not yet
part. Small gangs of adolescents wander through the crowd like desperate lost sheep and always, enlacing and releasing groups of
strollers, little boys who push and pommel each other. The city is for

outside, for the mélange of its periods, for the wild joy of decoration on its churches, for the extravagances of ironwork in street lamps and the painted ceilings in shops. A few of the churches are justly famous, and there is an impressive museum that absorbs the treasures of those decayed and abandoned, but with Florence nearby and Pisa around the corner and Siena not too far away, these don't call for studious attention, and that can be a great relief and Lucca's greatest asset.

Wherever one turns there is an invitation: to the vivid piazza that hums around the splendors of Saint Michael's church, to the distinguished museum, to medieval towers and Renaissance palaces. It might be reasonable to start at one of Lucca's earliest monuments and one of the city's prime delights. Carrying the map supplied by the tourist office on via Vittorio Veneto 13, cast a dazzled eye on San Michele (the time for concentration will come later) and go behind it to the via Buia. Pondering the mystery of why this is called the "dark" street in a townful of narrow medieval paths, looking into shopwindows, examining one brilliant display of door handles in a diversity of materials and contortions, you should come to the Piazza dei Mercanti, an outdoor living room filled with tables and umbrellas, flower boxes, potted trees and well-dressed, well-padded people. The toy square opens to the shopping street of Fillungo, which curves and turns easily, almost voluptuously, in its free-of-traffic hours. It shows an impressive number of jewelry shops, one of which is dignified by two sets of triple windows in carved dark wood, like sections of choir stall from a Baroque church; perhaps they are. A modern shop of glass and cool order faces a beribboned, ladylike old sweetshop; here and there, glass eaves and biddable iron and suggestions of galleries, in the well-fed, optimistic late-nineteenth-century French style.

The widening of the street as Piazza Scarpellini presents a proletarian face of inexpensive clothing, baskets, bird cages, bellows, plastic auto seats and an arch that says "Anfiteatro Romano Sec. II" and "Mercato." Roman amphitheaters and markets are hardly rarities in Italy, but there are few, if any, like this combination of Roman oval circled by medieval houses of fairly uniform height, interrupted by small arches and four tall portals that must have been the entrances to the theater. Although the soft yellow brick wears an occasional balcony dripping varicolored blankets and sports the ubiquitous lines of sheets, the effect is of a smooth-surfaced antique ring—unlike many pieces of antiquity, devoid of sadness, even when the lusty wholesale market is finished. That is, actually, the best time to go, undistracted by the market noise and color, accompanied only by a few parked cars, a pile of crates, six mashed peaches and tomatoes, a few spirals of orange peel and lettuce leaves that eluded the garbage sacks, and one lone, stubborn vendor who insists on sitting with his remaining watermelons and tomatoes.

Vestiges of the theater also cling to the outer circle of streets and houses, but vestiges of Rome are inescapable and better seen elsewhere. Return, instead, to the via Fillungo, which ends at the Virgin and Child over the arch of the Portone dei Borghi, a doorway to the large Piazza Santa Maria, crowded with souvenir stalls among its bars and trees. Having shopped or rejected, turn back toward the arch to find the via dei Carozzieri and then left, to a sight of Ghibelline swallow-tailed turret cheek by jowl with an ignoble red-brick building of international "Victorian" style, past a lost street which contents itself with auto-repair caves, to the apse end of the church of San Frediano. The balustrade of the wall-esplanade launches two lions and eagles of stone who stare down on the superb tower of the church, and below, following the columns on the apse, flows a shining stream of copper ewers, kettles, lamps, andirons, braziers, candlesticks and bells that comes to rest at the patient flank of the church. On a wall above the brass and copper, a piece of unabashed Italian prose in stone: "Here Niccolo Paganini was a guest in 1809 of the family Bucchianeri. Love and poetry tormented the genius but the musical city gave his magical violin the wings of glory." It could have been a less florid strophe, but it wouldn't have been Italian.

The majesty of the twelfth-century Basilica of San Frediano draws from its isolation on this edge of the town, fairly quiet as the rest of Lucca is not, and the plain façade, which cedes all attention to the large thirteenth-century mosaic that rises at the top. It depicts Christ's Ascension with two large angels at either side and, below, the twelve apostles, six and six, arranged on either side of a glistening lancet window. The columns that divide the three dignified naves bear, as one has come to expect in very old churches, interestingly varied capitals. The reconstructed twelfth-century baptismal font, whose templelike upper section is crammed with biblical scenes, is a good example of mixtures of influences from the north, from the southeast and, strongly, from the Roman sarcophagus. The most rewarding objects, however, are several sure, vigorous works of the Sienese sculptor, Jacopo della Quercia.

The via Anguillara has nothing to offer but a short walk through a bit of Luccan charm; simple houses, a piece of thirteenth-century overhang, a strip of sixteenth-century grating and one tree, a green balloon soaring out of a yard. The via Fontana is laden with Renaissance window cages; the via degli Angeli and the via Battisti bulge handsomely with palazzi, mainly of the seventeenth and eighteenth centuries, breeders of great doors and huge knockers, ornate ironwork balconies hung with graceful lanterns and strong stone frames around the windows. One doorway finds room for masks, urns, trumpets, shields and fruits and a baby riding a sea monster on a recessed plaque, rather like a baby's tub floating in a sea of late-Renaissance stylishness. Although a number of these palazzi are their own climax in style, the superclimax is the Palazzo Pfanner of the late seventeenth century, on the via degli Asili, quite large and fronted by a vestibule that leads to an extraordinary complexity of arches and colonnades surrounding diverse sweeps of stairs in a confusion of perspectives that only the Baroque could create or sort out. At the corner of the via degli Asili and the via San Giorgio stands the house where the composer Catalani was born, and off San Giorgio (near the via Moro) is the mighty Palazzo Santini, now the Municipal Building, originally of the fifteenth century.

From the windows of houses and the Teatro Comunale del Giglio and from record shops, you will have heard, wherever the banshee cars and motorbikes permitted, strains of good music, worthy of the place that sheltered Paganini and gave birth to Boccherini, Catalani and, above all, Puccini. You can pay your respects to him by sauntering through the bowed shapes of wood and glass usually called "Dickensian" and bolder Empire ornaments on the via Calderia to its meeting with the via di Poggio (Number 28–30), where a swan and lyre enwreathed in laurel speak the city's homage. According to the tourist-office map, the house of Boccherini should be on the via Roma, but whether they are mistaken or the plaque was taken down, at least one visitor couldn't find it.

Lucca's second major piece of sorcery is the façade of San Michele, too tall for its church, which was meant, centuries ago, to be enlarged and heightened. The thirteenth-century ornamentation of the façade was added and added to, until now it is an overlarge, irrepressible giggling thing, and enchanting. It has no caution or restraint or modesty but, like a child dressing up out of a trunkful of clothing and costume jewelry, puts on everything. The base is fairly sober, a matter of tall blind arches in which are imbedded the commonly seen recessed stone diamonds. Then, the soaring of four orders of slender columns, each determinedly different from its neighbors; some writhe, a few are knotted, some swirl, a few limit themselves to geometric patterns in zigzags or diagonals, others take on zoosful of animals in singles, doubles and heaps, and when there seems to be no room left for the thinnest breeze to enter, a few columns shed forms like bark dripping from trees. Saint Michael and two angels stand at the summit to call a stern halt to the dervish dance of decoration.

In the middle of the endless Piazza Napoleone there looms a heroic, effulgently sentimental goddess, crowned and appropriately draped, holding a scroll and a flower-tipped staff, casting her large maternal shadow on an adoring young Apollo. The monument erected in MDCCCXXXXIII (a pedant has penciled in a correction, substituting XL for the four X's) was an act of gratitude to Maria Luisa, who brought *acqua salubre* to Lucca, water which is still salubrious but doesn't taste particularly good. The goddess faces a long stretch of yellow palace, which grew and grew from its beginnings as a fortress designed by Giotto, some fifty years later demolished by the local citizens because it was occupied by enemy Pisans. In the early fifteenth century it was the site of the fortress-palace of the powerful family of Guinigi (of whom we shall hear again), battered down by an explosion when lightning ignited the gunpowder storage. The present building, the Prefettura (police matters), is of more recent themes on a late-sixteenth-century plan. Its interest to the general public, not specifically involved with the police, or the society for the prevention of TB, which shares some of the abundant space, is the general lordliness and the Pinacoteca, reached by way of an arcaded court and a stairway crammed with nineteenth-century coffering, griffins and wreaths and Lillian Russell angels in peplums threatened by Corinthian jungles on the pilasters. Having come this far, one might as well see the collection, which includes a few attractive "unknowns," several extraordinary portraits by Bronzino and Sustermans, the work of Beccafumi, Andrea del Sarto, Pontormo, Tintoretto and Titian, but by no means in profusion. This collection of the art treasures of Maria Luisa was once much richer, depleted for selling by her Apollo, her son.

The Pinacoteca is open from 9:30 to 4:00, closed Mondays and open only until 1:00 on Sundays, but you might prefer to spend limited museum time in the recently reorganized Museo Civico, off the Piazza San Francesco, on the via della Quarquonia as it meets the street "of the bastard." The restored fifteenth-century villa was that of the governor–war lord–dictator Paolo Guinigi and is now being filled, skillfully and intelligently, with examples of antique arts and decorations, spiced up by the presence of passionate, neoclassic ladies who grace the garden at the side of a graceful arcade. Sarcophagi? Of course, and Etruscan jewelry and Greek vases and bronze figurines, most effectively spaced, and a Roman mosaic that shows a poised lady who had the presence of mind to bring along her umbrella before being happily carried off by a sea monster. The range stretches over several centuries, to include the early, naïve pieces of church ornament often too high to see properly on their native walls: curly lions and docile bulls surrounded by circlets of stone braid, birds and trees on a Celtic cross, stone inlays carrying little monsters, lissome lady saints and rigid apostles. (And notice, as you go, the considerate structures that support the art and the details and design of the villa itself.) Of the fifteenth century there is a fresco, marked "Tuscan," that shows a style close to that of Filippo Lippi, and of the seventeenth, a particularly winsome tapestry angel. A Civitali Annunciation in high relief is so skillfully made that a magically carved vase takes the eye from the great event and its personages. In quite another style are the quick, small figures by another native son, Urbano Lucchesi, who lived and worked in the nineteenth century.

An interesting section—and one must keep insisting on the taste and appeal of the arrangements—deals with vats and measuring cups of copper and wood and yardsticks (one measures the *braccia lucchese* used for the famous silks), and on an upper floor, luxurious house furnishings and ecclesiastical garments, and yet more church art. It is here, as in other Italian museums, that the incurably repetitious sets in, conducive to an open-eyed blindness that sends one speedily through and out, having seen nothing. Try to stop for a few exceptions; for example, a Christ by one of the Civitali, a tender and earthy fifteenth-century Madonna whose Child embraces the large, high breast like an eager young Oedipus. Another work, steeped in the mannerisms of the late sixteenth century and completely diverting, shows David sitting on a white horse, wearing a plumed hat and bearing on his standard the head of Goliath; around him a bevy of garlanded maidens in flowing Renaissance-classic gowns dance and tootle on recorders, more nymph than nice Jewish girls.

Along the green string of canal and its miniature bridge on via del Fosso to the esplanade and a stroll among the trees, or southwestward, now, to the via Guinigi, engaged in the difficult job of maintaining its historic elements while offering hospitality to baby carriages, window boxes and kitchen curtains draped around chatting neighbors. The family palazzi absorbed not only this strip but most of the surrounding neighborhood in the thirteenth and fourteenth centuries, not necessarily out of love; mutual protection was the primary purpose of medieval clannishness. The red-brick structures, which might be dour were they not pierced by rows of trilobed gothic windows for a lighthearted Venetian effect, must have supplanted clumps of medieval tower. Now there is only one conspicuous tower left, older than the house it leans on, a jaunty old knight with great plumes of trees waving from his scalloped cap. (The best view of the tower can be had from the via Mordini at its meeting with the via delle Chiavi d'Oro—street of the golden keys—which must have been a reference to the rich family.) At the corner of the via Sant'Andrea, across from the tower, you might identify the shape of a medieval loge, where members of the family gathered to witness marriage processions and funerals, and near the top of the street of the Guinigi, the small church of Santi Simone e Giuda, stripped and almost derelict, which needn't hold you except for its unusual saint in polychrome wood.

At 21 on the via Mordini, there is another, gayer memorial to Puccini, a café called the "Fanciulla del West" in opulent golden letters fitting for her time and the composer's. A neighboring barbershop is fringed with gorgeous chenille ropes; other, earlier, gorgeousnesses are the door knockers of the via Fillungo where it takes an angle for a run southward. Along with its shops the street carries tangents into clusters of Lucchese specialties: on and near the parallel street of the Moro, well-preserved medieval houses and the church of San Salvatore; around the corner from the roaring pizza establishment on the via Buia (you are back on Fillungo), the thirteenth-century Torre del Ore, which stopped striking the hours five hundred years ago; the ponderous medieval palace once inhabited by a Barletti family and, at its side, the Chiasso Barletti. It is a gaudy alley swelled with inexpensive, basic shops that favor lengths of pink plastic tubing, small restaurants and cafés, noisy card players and comfortably padded ladies billowing over kitchen chairs set among eel-like swarms of children.

Out of the Chiasso (one of whose definitions is "noise") one continues southward to the house of Lucca's sculptor, Matteo Civitali, whose praises, sung from the wall, include the statement that he was the first to portray the male nude in the full round after the resurgence of art. This makes sure that detested Florence doesn't claim the honors with Michelangelo, born thirty years after Civitali. The enthusiast apparently forgot about Donatello, born fifty years earlier. Another tower or two, one of them attached to a neatly restored house of the 1200s, brings a confrontation with the church of San Cristoforo, which asks nothing but a long, admiring look, deserved for its good proportions and rose window, the easy flow of the gray and white banding and the carving in the restrained decorations. The effect is more Pugliese than exuberant Lucchese, except for the presence of two metal bars that determined the standard measure for silk in 1296, when San Cristoforo was the church of the silk merchants' guild. Under the modest wooden ceiling, a Madonna remaining of a pillar fresco, a few candles on an unadorned altar, a stone that represents the tomb of Matteo Civitali (although his actual remains are in an unknown place), his artist sons remembered on one of the pilasters, and the names of Lucchese war dead, to whom the church is now dedicated. The rest is nothing but solemn emptiness enclosed in a calm, sure drawing of arches, pillars and ceiling.

Near the house of Catalani, on the via Roma, find the Corte dell'Angelo, which leads into a neighborhood that is so artfully picturesque as to seem to have been arranged for the nineteenth-century sketches that poured out of Italy by the thousands—a collage of mattresses airing and sheets on lines, cats, and pigeons stepping around each other, wooden balconies spilling flowers, a newly painted door, an old door swinging from one hinge and a glass-covered shrine painting. By way of a meager alley one emerges to a piazza shaped by a café, a house that bears the tracery of older shapes and the side of the church of San Giusto, of the twelfth century and lavishly carved at its main portal. At the end of the piazza, the well-designed dark-yellow Renaissance palace, attributed to Civitali, which now houses the Cassa di Risparmio.

The church of San Martino, the Duomo, was designed in the thirteenth century. The tower, rising as increasing numbers and slenderness of openings, crested with battlements, is in the Gallic-Lombard style, as is the façade, much like that of San Michele though it lacks the ambitious height. That which San Martino lacks in height, it makes up in density. (The naïve, show-off joy of both façades brings to mind the story of the juggler whose best form of worship was to juggle the balls for the virgin's amusement.) Lions nip at something or other on the bundles of columns of the lower arcade, and the columns above, again different from each other, sprout fruits, leaves and animal figures that prophesy Le Douanier Rousseau. A few columns make do with diamonds and linear abstractions, and one seems to be a misplaced souvenir of the leaning tower of Pisa. Heads meet at the joining of arches, so do roses and pomegranates, and all connective tissue is engraved, stamped and embroidered in every imaginable way while it maintains the predominating contrast of green and white.

Inside the portico there is more unique matter, less gaudy and more imposing as significant places in art history. Among the brilliantly colored griffins and snakes, there are sculpted panels of the life of Saint Martin and a group of allegories of the months that escape the dry stiffness of the early thirteenth century to become sculpture with a fullness of volume and freedom of movement that indicates high talent and singular advance, particularly marked in the decapitation of Saint Regulus which appears over the portal. Above another door there is a Deposition that at first glance seems to follow the crowded compositions of Roman sarcophagi, but the urgent gestures and emotion that force their way through dust and wear, the sagging deadness of Christ and the fluidity of draperies make important departures from the classical model.

A drop from the near-sublime is to notice that one corner of a wall is protected by spiked arcs of iron, an ornament in corners of many churches. They may have had a particular, other purpose in older times; now they serve to keep the corrosion of urine from seeping through exhausted walls. Turn back to the façade, to Saint Martin dividing his cloak with a beggar, a copy of the original inside the cathedral and, like the portico panels (though not necessarily by the same artist), a breakthrough to Gothic naturalism, the nature of man and horse restudied from life rather than Roman and Byzantine art alone. The tall, serene interior space encloses a light Gothic matron's gallery and a *tempietto* designed by Matteo Civitali to house the famous Volto Santo, rarely brought to public view. There are innumerable picture postcards to show you the large Crucifix of wood in Byzantine style, laden with armorlike chunks of worked gold, the image a Romanesque copy of a ninth-century original. At one side of the large reliquary is a Civitali Saint Sebastian, easy in his arrow-pierced flesh as the Renaissance liked him to be, and elsewhere, several works of the Civitali family—font, pulpit and tombs, one of them accompanied by angels as fresh and free as Bernini's, almost two centuries younger.

The dome is too high and foggy to show anything of its painting except that it swirls cloudily, nor are several paintings by masters easily visible, particularly those buried in thick marble frames. The masterpieces inside the church are two works of Jacopo della Quercia, created within the first ten years of the fifteenth century. One is an austere, spare translation into stone of Saint John the Evangelist and the other a tomb for the young Ilaria, the wife of Paolo Guinigi. As other sculptors have wrested from the marble religious awe and the might of princes, Jacopo has drawn tenderness, which breathes from the folds of Ilaria's gown and the little dog of fidelity at her feet; it perfumes the chaplet on her head, makes silk of her stone cushion and hushes the wings of the cherubim that guard her.

Walking to the right from the apse of the Duomo, past antique shops and clutters of old things, looking back on the campanile and sides of the church, one comes soon to a magnificent yew tree on the via della Rosa and near it, the tiny church of Santa Maria della Rosa in Pisan-Gothic style (look at the detail along the sides), built by the Merchant's Guild at the beginning of the fourteenth century. Continuing on the retiring street, the Pisan-Gothic enthusiast will find, to the north, the church of Santa Maria Forisportam (thus called because it was outside the city walls in the thirteenth century, when it was built), which shields the familiar lion chewing on a lizard and a Virgin and Child of the twelfth century. The avoider of churches, scorning their age and spinsterly charms, can take the via dell'Arcivescovado, a street of antiques and religious articles, of a large shrine with an ugly Crucifixion and several old street lamps. Or, find the gayer street of the Battistero, which leads to a small introductory piazza that announces the amiable Piazza dei Servi and its Santa Maria church. (There is no avoiding ecclesiastical bulk for long.) That piazza narrows, then opens to the battered face of the church of San Bernardini and a long ocher house of steady, remorseless horizontality, the apogee of Renaissance fortress. It is a sulky building, but get close enough to examine the door knockers, a design of cross-barred Saracenic circlet under the head of a Moor in a mantle of leaves.

The via dell'Olivo, off Santa Croce, wanders inviting curves of paths, where one meets the church of San Quirico serving as a movie house, stable doors, horses' heads as rosettes on a band of stone, small cafés, balconies, shrubs, flowers, always laundry, arches with green beards, cats and orange peel and a fountain that forgot its purpose centuries ago. And this can go on all day and into the night and more days and more nights, if extra feet were part of the imperfectly planned equipment of the human body and if time would allow itself to be held. You might start back via the city's later adornments, mainly commercial and busily concerned with cute babies. A *profumeria* on the via Roma has draped ten lively ceramic children along its façade. Near the back of San Michele, a high-class emporium of imported groceries fancies itself in elegant pillars, and over its doorway, babes gamboling among leaves. A shop that sells cloth, an electrical-supplies neighbor and a pharmacy are each host to a pair of ceramic children, all white and plump and nude, under flowers or sitting on wine kegs or involved with grapes; one precocious Lolita wears a small shawl, a hat and an umbrella, nothing more. A shop of the via Veneto scorns vulgar appeal and announces itself as a Negozio d'Ombrelle in aristocratic sweeps of gold lettering. And everywhere there are plaques. Possibly more than any other city, with the exception of London, Lucca praises its famous men, indigenous or merely passing through, with wall ornaments. They stay even when the legends have been erased by years and the elements, as has happened to two handsome, romantically mustachioed and coiffed gentlemen, apparently brothers, who turn their stormy, artistic glares down on the Piazza dei Mercanti where you have returned for a final mound of *granita di café* and another last gaping at the *passeggiata*.

Tobias Smollett

(1 7 2 1 – 1 7 7 1)

Tobias Smollett, Scottish-born writer and surgeon, was well-known for his pica-resque novels like *The Adventures of Roderick Random* and *The Adventures of Peregrine Pickle*. He developed a taste for travel while a surgeon's mate on British sailing ships and for a while lived in Jamaica, where he met and married his wife. After the death of their only child, the couple set out for the Continent. Smollett himself was ill, sick at heart and sick in body, and not well disposed to life abroad.

In Italy Smollett found little that pleased him and seemed to be the victim of a conspiracy. He complained of lame horses, spoiled food, and bad advice. As a surgeon he abhorred disease and squalor, but found it at every turn. He even dis-liked the language: "You have often heard it said that the purity of the Italian is to be found in the *lingua Toscana,* and *bocca Romana*. Certain it is, the pronun-ciation of the Tuscans is disagreeably guttural . . . it sounds as if the speaker had lost his palate."

"Why is he [Smollett] still readable?" asked the twentieth-century travel writer V. S. Pritchett. "It is a pleasure to be the spectator and not the victim of bad temper . . . it recalls the blisters of travel, the times **we** have been cheated, the times **we** threatened to call the police, the times when **we** could not face the food or the bedroom."

Ironically, Tobias Smollett died not in his beloved England, but in Tuscany (Dickens notes the town of Livorno was "made illustrious by Smollett's grave"). This excerpt is from *Travels through France and Italy* (1766), his travel diary.

TRAVELS THROUGH FRANCE AND ITALY

LETTER XXVII.

Nice, January 28, 1765.

Dear Sir,

Pisa is a fine old city that strikes you with the same veneration you would feel at sight of an antient temple which bears the marks of decay, without being absolutely delapidated. The houses are well built, the streets open, straight, and well paved; the shops well furnished; and the markets well supplied: there are some elegant palaces, designed by great masters. The churches are built with taste, and tolerably ornamented. There is a beautiful wharf of free-stone on each side of the river Arno, which runs through the city, and three bridges thrown over it, of which that in the middle is of marble, a pretty piece of architecture: but the number of inhabitants is very inconsiderable; and this very circumstance gives it an air of majestic solitude, which is far from being unpleasant to a man of a contemplative turn of mind. For my part, I cannot bear the tumult of a populous commercial city; and the solitude that reigns in Pisa would with me be a strong motive to choose it as a place of residence. Not that this would be the only inducement for living at Pisa. Here is some good company, and even a few men of taste and learning. The people in general are counted sociable and polite; and there is great plenty of provisions, at a very reasonable rate. At some distance from the more frequented parts of the city, a man may hire a large house for thirty crowns a year; but near the center, you cannot have good lodgings, ready furnished, for less than a *scudo* (about five shillings) a day. The air in summer is reckoned unwholesome by the exhalations arising from stagnant water in the neighbourhood of the city, which stands in the midst of a fertile plain, low and marshy: yet these marshes have been considerably drained; and the air is much meliorated. As for the Arno, it is no longer navigated by vessels of any burthen. The university of Pisa is very much decayed; and except the little business occasioned by the emperor's gallies, which are built in this town, I know of no commerce it carries on: perhaps the inhabitants live on the produce of the country, which consists of corn, wine, and cattle. They are supplied with excellent water for drinking, by an aqueduct consisting of above a thousand arches, begun by Cosmo, and finished by Ferdinand I grand-dukes of Tuscany; it conveys the water from the mountains at the distance of four miles. This noble city, formerly the capital of a flourishing and powerful republic, which contained above one hundred and fifty thousand inhabitants within its walls, is now so desolate that grass grows in the open streets; and the number of its people do not exceed sixteen thousand.

You need not doubt but I visited the Campanile, or hanging-tower, which is a beautiful cylinder of eight stories, each adorned with a round of columns, rising one above another. It stands by the cathedral, and inclines so far on one side from the perpendicular, that in dropping a plummet from the top, which is one hundred and eighty-eight feet high, it falls sixteen feet from the base. For my part, I should never have dreamed that this inclination proceeded from any other cause, than an accidental subsidence of the foundation on this side, if some connoisseurs had not taken great pains to prove it was done on purpose by the architect. Any person who has eyes may see that the pillars on that side are considerably sunk; and this is the case with the very threshold of the door by which you enter. I think it would have been a very preposterous ambition in the architects, to shew how far they could deviate from the perpendicular in this construction; because in that particular any common mason could have rivalled them; and if they really intended it as a specimen of their art, they should have shortened the pilasters on that side, so as to exhibit them intire, without the appearance of sinking. These leaning towers are not unfrequent in Italy; there is one at Bologna, another at Venice, a third betwixt Venice and Ferrara, and a fourth at Ravenna; and the inclination in all of them has been supposed owing to the foundations giving way on one side only.

In the cathedral, which is a large Gothic pile, there is a great number of massy pillars of porphyry, granite, jasper, giullo, and verde antico, together with some good pictures and statues: but the greatest curiosity is that of the brass gates, designed and executed by John of Bologna, representing, embossed in different compartments, the history of the Old and New Testament. I was so charmed with this work, that I could have stood a whole day to examine and admire it. In the Baptisterium, which stands opposite to this front, there are some beautiful marbles, particularly the font, and a pulpit, supported by the statues of different animals.

Between the cathedral and this building, about one hundred paces on one side, is the famous burying-ground, called *Campo Santo*, from its being covered with earth brought from Jerusalem. It is an oblong square, surrounded by a very high wall, and always kept shut. Within-side there is a spacious corridore round the whole space, which is a noble walk for a contemplative philosopher. It is paved chiefly with flat grave-stones: the walls are painted in fresco by Ghiotto, Giottino, Stefano, Bennoti, Buffalmaco, and some others of their contemporaries and disciples, who flourished immediately after the restoration of painting. The subjects are taken from the Bible. Though the manner is dry, the drawing incorrect, the design generally lame, and the colouring unnatural; yet there is merit in the expression: and the whole remains as a curious monument of the efforts made by this noble art immediately after her revival. Here are some deceptions in perspective equally ingenious and pleasing; particularly the figures of certain animals, which exhibit exactly the same appearance, from whatever different points of view they are seen. One division of the burying-ground consists of a particular compost, which in nine days consumes the dead bodies to the bones: in all probability, it is no other than common earth mixed with quick-lime. At one corner of the corridore, there are the pictures of three bodies represented in the three different stages of putrefaction which they undergo when laid in this composition. At the end of the three first days, the body is bloated and swelled, and the features are enlarged and distorted to such a degree, as fills the spectator with horror. At the sixth day, the swelling is subsided, and all the muscular flesh hangs loosened from the bones: at the ninth, nothing but the skeleton remains. There is a small neat chapel at one end of the *Campo Santo*, with some tombs, on one of which is a beautiful bust by Buona Roti. At the other end of the corridore, there is a range of antient sepulchral stones ornamented with basso relievo, brought hither from different parts by the *Pisan* fleets, in the course of their expeditions. I was struck with the figure of a woman lying dead on a tomb-stone, covered with a piece of thin drapery, so delicately cut as to shew all the flexures of the attitude, and even all the swellings and sinuosities of the muscles. Instead of stone, it looks like a sheet of wet linen.

For four zechines I hired a return-coach and four from Pisa to Florence. This road, which lies along the Arno, is very good; and the country is delightful, variegated with hill and vale, wood and water, meadows and corn-fields, planted and inclosed like the counties of Middlesex and Hampshire; with this difference, however, that all the trees in this tract were covered with vines, and the ripe clusters black and white, hung down from every bough in the most luxuriant and romantic abundance. The vines in this country are not planted in rows, and propped with sticks, as in France and the county of Nice, but twine around the hedge-row trees, which they almost quite cover with their foliage and fruit. The branches of the vine are extended from tree to tree, exhibiting beautiful festoons of real leaves, tendrils, and swelling clusters a foot long. By this œconomy the ground of the inclosure is spared for corn, grass, or any other production. The trees commonly planted for the purpose of sustaining the vines, are maple, elm, and aller, with which last the banks of the Arno abound. This river, which is very inconsiderable with respect to the quantity of water, would be a charming pastoral stream, if it was transparent; but it is always muddy and discoloured. About ten or a dozen miles below Florence, there are some marble quarries on the side of it, from whence the blocks are conveyed in boats, when there is water enough in the river to float them, that is, after heavy rains, or the melting of the snow upon the mountains of Umbria, being part of the Appenines, from whence it takes its rise.

Florence is a noble city, that still retains all the marks of a majestic capital, such as piazzas, palaces, fountains, bridges, statues, and arcades. I need not tell you that the churches here are magnificent, and adorned not only with pillars of oriental granite, porphyry, jasper, verde antico, and other precious stones; but also with capital pieces of painting by the most eminent masters. Several of these churches, however, stand without fronts, for want of money to complete the plans. It may also appear superfluous to mention my having viewed the famous gallery of antiquities, the chapel of St. Lorenzo, the palace of Pitti, the cathedral, the Baptisterium, the *Ponte de Trinita*, with its statues, the triumphal arch, and every thing which is commonly visited in this metropolis. But all these objects having been circumstantially described by twenty different authors of travels, I shall not trouble you with a repetition of trite observations.

That part of the city which stands on each side of the river, makes a very elegant appearance, to which the four bridges and the stone-quay between them, contribute in a great measure. I lodged at the widow Vanini's, an English house delightfully situated in this quarter. The landlady, who is herself a native of England, we found very obliging. The lodging-rooms are comfortable; and the entertainment is good and reasonable. There is a considerable number of fashionable people at Florence, and many of them in good circumstances. They affect a gaiety in their dress, equipage, and conversations; but stand very much on their punctilio with strangers; and will not, without great reluctance, admit into their assemblies any lady of another country, whose noblesse is not ascertained by a title. This reserve is in some measure excusable among a people who are extremely ignorant of foreign customs, and who know that in their own country, every person, even the most insignificant, who has any pretensions to family, either inherits, or assumes the title of *principe*, *conte*, or *marchese*.

With all their pride, however, the nobles of Florence are humble enough to enter into partnership with shop-keepers, and even to sell wine by retail. It is an undoubted fact, that in every palace or great house in this city, there is a little window fronting the street, provided with an iron-knocker, and over it hangs an empty flask, by way of sign-post. Thither you send your servant to buy a bottle of wine. He knocks at the little wicket, which is opened immediately by a domestic, who supplies him with what he wants, and receives the money like the waiter of any other cabaret. It is pretty extraordinary, that it should not be deemed a disparagement in a nobleman to sell half a pound of figs, or a palm of ribbon or tape, or to take money for a flask of sour wine; and yet be counted infamous to match his daughter in the family of a person who has distinguished himself in any one of the learned professions.

Though Florence be tolerably populous, there seems to be very little trade of any kind in it: but the inhabitants flatter themselves with the prospect of reaping great advantage from the residence of one of the arch-dukes, for whose reception they are now repairing the palace of Pitti. I know not what the revenues of Tuscany may amount to, since the succession of the princes of Lorraine; but, under the last dukes of the Medici family, they were said to produce two millions of crowns, equal to five hundred thousand pounds sterling. These arose from a very heavy tax upon land and houses, the portions of maidens, and suits at law, besides the duties upon traffick, a severe gabelle upon the necessaries of life, and a toll upon every eatable entered into this capital. If we may believe Leti, the grand-duke was then able to raise and maintain an army of forty thousand infantry, and three thousand horses; with twelve gallies, two galeasses, and twenty ships of war. I question if Tuscany can maintain at present above one half of such an armament. He that now commands the emperor's navy, consisting of a few frigates, is an Englishman, called Acton, who was heretofore captain of a ship in our East India company's service. He has lately embraced the Catholic religion, and been created admiral of Tuscany.

There is a tolerable opera in Florence for the entertainment of the best company, though they do not seem very attentive to the musick. Italy is certainly the native country of this art; and yet, I do not find the people in general either more musically inclined, or better provided with ears than their neighbours. Here is also a wretched troop of comedians for the bourgeois, and lower class of people: but what seems most to suit the taste of all ranks, is the exhibition of church pageantry. I had occasion to see a procession, where all the noblesse of the city attended in their coaches, which filled the whole length of the great street called the *Corso*. It was the anniversary of a charitable institution in favour of poor maidens, a certain number of whom are portioned every year. About two hundred of these virgins walked in procession, two and two together, cloathed in violet-coloured wide gowns, with white veils on their heads, and made a very classical appearance. They were preceded and followed by an irregular mob of penitents in sack-cloth, with lighted tapers, and monks carrying crucifixes, bawling and bellowing the litanies: but the great object was a figure of the Virgin Mary, as big as the life, standing within a gilt frame, dressed in a gold stuff, with a large hoop, a great quantity of false jewels, her face painted and patched, and her hair frizzled and curled in the very extremity of the fashion. Very little regard had been paid to the image of our Saviour on the cross; but when his lady-mother appeared on the shoulders of three or four lusty friars, the whole populace fell upon their knees in the dirt. This extraordinary veneration paid to the Virgin, must have been derived originally from the French, who pique themselves on their gallantry to the fair sex.

Amidst all the scenery of the Roman Catholic religion, I have never yet seen any of the spectators affected at heart, or discover the least signs of fanaticism. The very disciplinants, who scourge themselves in the Holy-week, are generally peasants or parties hired for the purpose. Those of the confrairies, who have an ambition to distinguish themselves on such occasions, take care to secure their backs from the smart, by means of secret armour, either women's boddice, or quilted jackets. The confraries are fraternities of devotees, who inlist themselves under the banners of particular saints. On days of procession they appear in a body dressed as penitents and masked, and distinguished by crosses on their habits. There is scarce an individual, whether noble or plebeian, who does not belong to one of these associations, which may be compared to the Free-Masons, Gregoreans, and Antigallicans of England.

Just without one of the gates of Florence, there is a triumphal arch erected on occasion of the late emperor's making his public entry, when he succeeded to the dukedom of Tuscany: and here in the summer evenings, the quality resort to take the air in their coaches. Every carriage stops, and forms a little separate conversazione. The ladies sit within, and the cicisbei stand on the foot-boards, on each side of the coach, entertaining them with their discourse. It would be no unpleasant inquiry to trace this sort of gallantry to its original, and investigate all its progress. The Italians, having been accused of jealousy, were resolved to wipe off the reproach, and, seeking to avoid it for the future, have run into the other extreme. I know it is generally supposed that the custom of choosing cicisbei, was calculated to prevent the extinction of families, which would otherwise often happen in consequence of marriages founded upon interest, without any mutual affection in the contracting parties. How far this

political consideration may have weighed against the jealous and vin-
dictive temper of the Italians, I will not pretend to judge: but, certain
it is, every married lady in this country has her cicisbeo, or servente,
who attends her every where, and on all occasions; and upon whose
privileges the husband dares not encroach, without incurring the censure and ridicule of the whole community. For my part, I would rather
be condemned for life to the gallies, than exercise the office of a
cicisbeo, exposed to the intolerable caprices and dangerous resent-
ment of an Italian virago. I pretend not to judge of the national character, from my own observation: but, if the portraits drawn by
Goldoni in his Comedies are taken from nature, I would not hesitate
to pronounce the Italian women the most haughty, insolent, capri-
cious, and revengeful females on the face of the earth. Indeed, their
resentments are so cruelly implacable, and contain such a mixture of
perfidy, that, in my opinion, they are very unfit subjects for comedy,
whose province it is, rather to ridicule folly than to stigmatize such
atrocious vice.

You have often heard it said, that the purity of the Italian is to be
found in the *lingua Toscana*, and *bocca Romana*. Certain it is, the pronunciation of the Tuscans is disagreeably guttural: the letters C and G
they pronounce with an aspiration, which hurts the ear of an Englishman; and is, I think, rather rougher than that of the X, in Spanish. It sounds as if the speaker had lost his palate. I really imagined
the first man I heard speak in Pisa, had met with that misfortune in
the course of his amours.

One of the greatest curiosities you meet with in Italy, is the
Improvisatore; such is the name given to certain individuals, who
have the surprising talent of reciting verses extempore, on any subject you propose. Mr. Corvesi, my landlord, has a son, a Franciscan
friar, who is a great genius in this way. When the subject is given, his
brother tunes his violin to accompany him, and he begins to rehearse
in recitative, with wonderful fluency and precision. Thus he will, at a
minute's warning, recite two or three hundred verses, well turned,
and well adapted, and generally mingled with an elegant compliment
to the company. The Italians are so fond of poetry, that many of
them have the best part of Ariosto, Tasso, and Petrarch, by heart;
and these are the great sources from which the Improvisatori draw

their rhimes, cadence, and turns of expression. But, lest you should think there is neither rhime nor reason in protracting this tedious epistle, I shall conclude it with the old burden of my son, that I am always

Your affectionate humble servant.

LETTER XXVIII.

Nice, February 5, 1765.

Dear Sir,

Your entertaining letter of the fifth of last month, was a very charitable and a very agreeable donation: but your suspicion is groundless. I assure you, upon my honour, I have no share whatever in any of the disputes which agitate the public: nor do I know any thing of your political transactions, except what I casually see in one of your newspapers, with the perusal of which I am sometimes favoured by our consul at Villefranche. You insist upon my being more particular in my remarks on what I saw at Florence, and I shall obey the injunction. The famous gallery which contains the antiquities, is the third story of a noble stone-edifice, built in the form of the Greek II, the upper part fronting the river Arno, and one of the legs adjoining to the ducal-palace, where the courts of justice are held. As the house of Medici had for some centuries resided in the palace of Pitti, situated on the other side of the river, a full mile from these tribunals, the architect Vasari, who planned the new edifice, at the same time contrived a corridore, or covered passage, extending from the palace of Pitti along one of the bridges, to the gallery of curiosities, through which the grand-duke passed unseen, when he was disposed either to amuse himself with his antiquities, or to assist at his courts of judicature: but there is nothing very extraordinary either in the contrivance or execution of this corridore.

If I resided in Florence I would give something extraordinary for permission to walk every day in the gallery, which I should much prefer to the Lycæum, the groves of Academus, or any porch or philosophical alley in Athens or in Rome. Here by viewing the statues and busts ranged on each side, I should become acquainted with the faces of all the remarkable personages, male and female, of antiquity, and even be able to trace their different characters from the expression of their features. This collection is a most excellent commentary upon the Roman historians, particularly Suetonius and Dion Cassius. There was one circumstance that struck me in viewing the busts of Caracalla, both here and in the Capitol at Rome; that was a certain ferocity in the eyes, which seemed to contradict the sweetness of the other features, and remarkably justified the epithet *Caracuyl,* by which he was distinguished by the antient inhabitants of North-Britain. In the language of the Highlanders *caracuyl* signifies *cruel eye,* as we are given to understand by the ingenious editor of Fingal, who seems to think that Caracalla is no other than the Celtic word, adapted to the pronunciation of the Romans: but the truth is, Caracalla was the name of a Gaulish vestment, which this prince affected to wear; and hence he derived that surname. The Caracuyl of the Britons, is the same as the *ύπόδρα ἰδῶ ν* of the Greeks, which Homer has so often applied to his Scolding Heroes. I like the Bacchanalian, chiefly for the fine drapery. The wind, occasioned by her motion, seems to have swelled and raised it from the parts of the body which it covers. There is another gay Bacchanalian, in the attitude of dancing, crowned with ivy, holding in her right hand a bunch of grapes, and in her left the thyrsus. The head of the celebrated Flora is very beautiful: the groupe of Cupid and Psyche, however, did not give me all the pleasure I expected from it.

Of all the marbles that appear in the open gallery, the following are those I most admire. Leda with the Swan; as for Jupiter, in this transformation, he has much the appearance of a goose. I have not seen any thing tamer: but the sculptor has admirably shewn his art in representing Leda's hand partly hid among the feathers, which are so lightly touched off, that the very shape of the fingers are seen underneath. The statue of a youth, supposed to be Ganymede, is compared by the connoisseurs to the celebrated Venus, and as far as I can judge, not without reason: it is, however, rather agreeable than striking, and will please a connoisseur much more than a common spectator. I know not whether it is my regard to the faculty that inhances the value of the noted Æsculapius, who appears with a venerable beard of delicate workmanship. He is larger than the life, cloathed in a magnificent pallium, his left arm resting on a knotted staff, round which the snake is twined, according to Ovid:

Hunc modo serpentem baculum qui nexibus ambit
Perspice—

Behold the snake his mystic rod intwine.

He has in his hand the *fascia herbarum*, and the *crepidæ* on his feet. There is a wild-boar represented lying on one side, which I admire as a master-piece. The savageness of his appearance is finely contrasted with the ease and indolence of the attitude. Were I to meet with a living boar lying with the same expression, I should be tempted to stroke his bristles. Here is an elegant bust of Antinous, the favourite of Adrian; and a beautiful head of Alexander the Great, turned on one side, with an expression of languishment and anxiety in his countenance. The virtuosi are not agreed about the circumstance in which he is represented; whether fainting with the loss of blood which he suffered in his adventure at Oxydrace; or languishing with the fever contracted by bathing in the Cydnus; or finally complaining to his father Jove, that there were no other worlds for him to conquer. The kneeling Narcissus is a striking figure, and the expression admirable. The two Bacchi are perfectly well executed; but (to my shame be it spoken) I prefer to the antique that which is the work of Michael Angelo Buonaroti, concerning which the story is told which you well know. The artist having been blamed by some pretended connoisseurs, for not imitating the manner of the ancients, is said to have privately finished this Bacchus, and buried it, after having broke off an arm, which he kept as a voucher. The statue, being dug up by accident, was allowed by the best judges, to be a perfect antique; upon which Buonaroti produced the arm, and claimed his own work. *Bianchi* looks upon this as a fable; but owns that Vasari tells such another of a child cut in marble by the same artist, which being carried to Rome, and kept for some time under ground, was dug up as an antique, and sold for a great deal of money. I was likewise attracted by the Morpheus in touchstone, which is described by Addison, who, by the bye, notwithstanding all his taste, has been convicted by Bianchi of several gross blunders in his account of this gallery.

With respect to the famous Venus Pontia, commonly called *de Medicis*, which was found at Tivoli, and is kept in a separate apartment called the *Tribuna*, I believe I ought to be intirely silent, or at least conceal my real sentiments, which will otherwise appear equally absurd and presumptuous. It must be want of taste that prevents my feeling that enthusiastic admiration with which others are inspired at sight of this statue: a statue which in reputation equals that of Cupid by Praxiteles, which brought such a concourse of strangers of old to the little town of Thespiæ. I cannot help thinking that there is no beauty in the features of Venus; and that the attitude is awkward and out of character. It is a bad plea to urge that the antients and we differ in the ideas of beauty. We know the contrary, from their medals, busts, and historians. Without all doubt, the limbs and proportions of this statue are elegantly formed, and accurately designed, according to the nicest rules of symmetry and proportion; and the back parts especially are executed so happily, as to excite the admiration of the most indifferent spectator. One cannot help thinking it is the very Venus of *Cnidos* by Praxiteles, which Lucian describes. "Hercle quanta dorsi concinnitas! ut exuberantes lumbi amplexantes manus implent! quam scite circumductæ clunium pulpæ in se rotundantur, neque tenues nimis ipsis ossibus adstrictæ, neque in immensam effusæ pinguedinem!" "Heavens! what a beautiful back! the loins, with what exuberance they fill the grasp! how finely are the swelling buttocks rounded, neither too thinly cleaving to the bone, nor effused into a huge mass of flabby consistence!" That the statue thus described was not the *Venus de Medicis*, would appear from the Greek inscription on the base, *ΚΛΕΟΜΕΝΗΣ ΑΠΟΛΛΟΔΟΡΟΥ ΑΘΗ-ΝΑΙΟΣ ΕΠΩΕΣΕΝ. Cleomenes filius Apollodori fecit*; did we not know that this inscription is counted spurious, and that instead of *ΕΠΩΕ-ΣΕΝ*, it should be *ΕΠΟΙΗΣΕ*. This, however, is but a frivolous objection, as we have seen many inscriptions undoubtedly antique, in which the orthography is false, either from the ignorance or carelessness of the sculptor. Others suppose, not without reason, that this statue is a representation of the famous Phryne, the courtesan of

Athens, who at the celebration of the Eleusinian games, exhibited herself coming out of the bath, naked, to the eyes of the whole Athenian people. I was much pleased with the dancing faun; and still better with the Lotti, or wrestlers, the attitudes of which are beautifully contrived to shew the different turns of the limbs, and the swelling of the muscles: but, what pleased me best of all the statues in the Tribuna was the Arrotino, commonly called the Whetter, and generally supposed to represent a slave, who in the act of whetting a knife, overhears the conspiracy of Cataline. You know he is represented on one knee; and certain it is, I never saw such an expression of anxious attention, as appears in his countenance. But it is not mingled with any marks of surprise, such as could not fail to lay hold on a man who overhears by accident a conspiracy against the state. The marquis de Maffei has justly observed that Sallust, in his very circumstantial detail of that conspiracy, makes no mention of any such discovery. Neither does it appear, that the figure is in the act of whetting, the stone which he holds in one hand being rough and unequal, no ways resembling a whetstone. Others alledge it represents Milico, the freedman of Scævinus, who conspired against the life of Nero, and gave his poignard to be whetted to Milico, who presented it to the emperor, with an account of the conspiracy: but the attitude and expression will by no means admit of this interpretation. *Bianchi*, who shews the gallery, thinks the statue represents the augur Attius Navius, who cut a stone with a knife, at the command of Tarquinius Priscus. This conjecture seems to be confirmed by a medallion of Antoninus Pius, inserted by Vaillant among his Numismata Prestantiora, on which is delineated nearly such a figure as this in question, with the following legend, "Attius Navius genuflexus ante Tarquinium Priscum cotem cultro discidit." He owns indeed that in the statue, the augur is not distinguished either by his habit or emblems; and he might have added, neither is the stone a cotes. For my own part, I think neither of these three opinions is satisfactory, though the last is very ingenious. Perhaps the figure alludes to a private incident, which never was recorded in any history. Among the great number of pictures in this Tribuna, I was most charmed with the Venus by Titian, which has a sweetness of expression and tenderness of colouring, not to be described. In this apartment, they reckon three hundred pieces, the greatest part by the best masters, particularly by Raphael, in the three manners by which he distinguished himself at different periods of his life. As for the celebrated statue of the hermaphrodite, which we find in another room, I give the sculptor credit for his ingenuity in mingling the sexes in the composition; but it is, at best, no other than a monster in nature, which I never had any pleasure in viewing: nor, indeed, do I think there was much talent required in representing a figure with the head and breasts of a woman, and all the other parts of the body masculine. There is such a profusion of curiosities in this celebrated musæum; statues, busts, pictures, medals, tables inlaid in the way of marquetry, cabinets adorned with precious stones, jewels of all sorts, mathematical instruments, antient arms, and military machines, that the imagination is bewildered; and a stranger of a visionary turn would be apt to fancy himself in a palace of the fairies, raised and adorned by the power of inchantment.

In one of the detached apartments, I saw the antependium of the altar, designed for the famous chapel of St. Lorenzo. It is a curious piece of architecture, inlaid with coloured marble and precious stones, so as to represent an infinite variety of natural objects. It is adorned with some crystal pillars, with capitals of beaten gold. The second story of the building is occupied by a great number of artists employed in this very curious work of marquetry, representing figures with gems and different kinds of coloured marble, for the use of the emperor. The Italians call it *pietre commesse*, a sort of inlaying with stones, analogous to the fineering of cabinets in wood. It is peculiar to Florence, and seems to be still more curious than the Mosaic work, which the Romans have brought to great perfection.

The cathedral of Florence is a great Gothic building, encrusted on the outside with marble; it is remarkable for nothing but its cupola, which is said to have been copied by the architect of St. Peter's at Rome, and for its size, which is much greater than that of any other church in Christendom. The baptistery, which stands by it, was an antient temple, said to be dedicated to Mars. There are some good statues of marble within; and one or two of bronze on the outside of the doors; but it is chiefly celebrated for the embossed work of its brass gates, by Lorenzo Ghiberti, which Buonaroti used to say, deserved to be made the gates of Paradise. I viewed them with pleasure: but still I retained a greater veneration for those of Pisa, which I had first admired: a preference which either arises from want of taste, or from the charm of novelty, by which the former were recommended to my attention. Those who would have a particular detail of every thing worth seeing at Florence, comprehending churches, libraries, palaces, tombs, statues, pictures, fountains, bridges, &c. may consult Keysler, who is so laboriously circumstantial in his descriptions, that I never could peruse them, without suffering the headache and recollecting the old observation, that the German genius lies more in the back than in the brain.

I was much disappointed in the chapel of St. Lorenzo. Notwithstanding the great profusion of granite, porphyry, jasper, verde antico, lapis-lazuli, and other precious stones, representing figures in the way of marquetry, I think the whole has a gloomy effect. These *pietre commesse* are better calculated for cabinets, than for ornaments to great buildings, which ought to be large masses proportioned to the greatness of the edifice. The compartments are so small, that they produce no effect in giving the first impression when one enters the place; except to give an air of littleness to the whole, just as if a grand saloon was covered with pictures painted in miniature. If they have as little regard to proportion and perspective, when they paint the dome, which is not yet finished, this chapel will, in my opinion, remain a monument of ill taste and extravagance.

The court of the palace of Pitti is formed by three sides of an elegant square, with arcades all round, like the palace of Holyrood house at Edinburgh; and the rustic work, which constitutes the lower part of the building, gives it an air of strength and magnificence. In this court, there is a fine fountain, in which the water trickles down from above; and here is also an admirable antique statue of Hercules, inscribed *ΑΥΣΙΠΠΟΥ ΕΡΓΟΝ*, the work of Lysippus.

The apartments of this palace are generally small, and many of them dark. Among the paintings, the most remarkable is the Madonna de la Seggiola, by Raphael, counted one of the best coloured pieces of that great master. If I was allowed to find fault with the performance, I should pronounce it defective in dignity and sentiment. It is the expression of a peasant rather than of the mother of God. She exhibits the fondness and joy of a young woman towards her first-born son, without that rapture of admiration which we expect to find in the Virgin Mary, while she contemplates, in the fruit of her own womb, the Saviour of mankind. In other respects, it is a fine figure, gay, agreeable, and very expressive of maternal tenderness; and the *bambino* is extremely beautiful. There was an English painter employed in copying this picture, and what he had done was executed with great success. I am one of those who think it very possible to imitate the best pieces in such a manner, that even the connoisseurs shall not be able to distinguish the original from the copy. After all, I do not set up for a judge in these matters, and very likely I may incur the ridicule of the virtuosi for the remarks I have made: but I am used to speak my mind freely on all subjects that fall under the cognizance of my senses; though I must as freely own, there is something more than common sense required to discover and distinguish the more delicate beauties of painting. I can safely say, however, that without any daubing at all, I am, very sincerely,

Your affectionate humble servant.

LETTER XXIX.

Nice, February 20, 1765.

Dear Sir,

Having seen all the curiosities of Florence, and hired a good travelling coach for seven weeks, at the price of seven zechines, something less than three guineas and a half, we set out post for Rome, by the way of Sienna, where we lay the first night. The country through which we passed is mountainous but agreeable. Of Sienna I can say nothing from my own observation, but that we were indifferently lodged in a house that stunk like a privy, and fared wretchedly at supper. The city is large and well built: the inhabitants pique themselves upon their politeness, and the purity of their dialect. Certain it is, some strangers reside in this place on purpose to learn the best pronunciation of the Italian tongue. The Mosaic pavement of their duomo, or cathedral, has been much admired; as well as the history of Æneas Sylvius, afterwards pope Pius II painted on the walls of the library, partly by Pietro Perugino, and partly by his pupil Raphael D'Urbino.

Next day, at Buon Convento, where the emperor Henry VII was poisoned by a friar with the sacramental wafer, I refused to give money to the hostler, who in revenge put two young unbroke stone-horses in the traces next to the coach, which became so unruly, that before we had gone a quarter of a mile, they and the postilion were rolling in the dust. In this situation they made such efforts to disengage themselves, and kicked with such violence, that I imagined the carriage and all our trunks would have been beaten in pieces. We leaped out of the coach, however, without sustaining any personal damage, except the fright; nor was any hurt done to the vehicle. But the horses were terribly bruised, and almost strangled, before they could be disengaged. Exasperated at the villany of the hostler, I resolved to make a complaint to the *uffiziale* or magistrate of the place. I found him wrapped in an old, greasy, ragged, great-coat, sitting in a wretched apartment, without either glass, paper, or boards in the windows; and there was no sort of furniture but a couple of broken chairs and miserable truckle-bed. He looked pale, and meagre, and had more the air of a half-starved prisoner than of a magistrate. Having heard my complaint, he came forth into a kind of outward room or bellfrey, and rung a great bell with his own hand. In consequence of this signal, the post-master came up stairs, and I suppose he was the first man in the place, for the *uffiziale* stood before him cap-in-hand, and with great marks of humble respect repeated the complaint I had made. This man assured me, with an air of conscious importance, that he himself had ordered the hostler to supply me with those very horses, which were the best in his stable; and that the misfortune which happened was owing to the misconduct of the fore-postilion, who did not keep the fore horses to a proper speed proportioned to the mettle of the other two. As he took the affair upon himself, and I perceived had an ascendancy over the magistrate, I contented myself with saying, I was certain the two horses had been put to the coach on purpose, either to hurt or frighten us; and that since I could not have justice here I would make a formal complaint to the British minister at Florence. In passing through the street to the coach, which was by this time furnished with fresh horses, I met the hostler, and would have caned him heartily; but perceiving my intention, he took to his heels and vanished. Of all the people I have ever seen, the hostlers, postilions, and other fellows hanging about the post-houses in Italy, are the most greedy, impertinent, and provoking. Happy are those travellers who have phlegm enough to disregard their insolence and importunity: for this is not so disagreeable as their revenge is dangerous. An English gentleman at Florence told me, that one of those fellows, whom he had struck for his impertinence, flew at him with a long knife, and he could hardly keep him at sword's point. All of them wear such knives, and are very apt to use them on the slightest provocation. But their open attacks are not so formidable as their premeditated schemes of revenge; in the prosecution of which the Italians are equally treacherous and cruel.

This night we passed at a place called Radicofani, a village and fort, situated on the top of a very high mountain. The inn stands still lower than the town. It was built at the expence of the last grand-duke of Tuscany; is very large, very cold, and uncomfortable. One would imagine it was contrived for coolness, though situated so high, that even in the midst of summer, a traveller would be glad to have a fire in his chamber. But few, or none of them have fire-places, and there is not a bed with curtains or tester in the house. All the adjacent country is naked and barren. On the third day we entered the pope's territories, some parts of which are delightful. Having passed Aqua-Pendente, a beggarly town, situated on the top of a rock, from whence there is a romantic cascade of water, which gives it the name, we travelled along the side of the lake Bolsena, a beautiful piece of water about thirty miles in circuit, with two islands in the middle, the banks covered with noble plantations of oak and cypress. The town of Bolsena standing near the ruins of the antient Volsinium, which was the birth-place of Sejanus, is a paultry village; and Montefiascone, famous for its wine, is a poor decayed town in this neighbourhood, situated on the side of a hill, which, according to the author of the Grand Tour, the only directory I had along with me, is supposed to be the Soracte of the ancients. If we may believe Horace, Soracte was visible from Rome: for, in his ninth ode, addressed to Thaliarchus, he says,

Vides, ut alta stet nive candidum
Soracte——

You see how deeply wreath'd with snow,
Soracte lifts his hoary head,

but, in order to see Montefiascone, his eye-sight must have penetrated through the Mons Cyminus, at the foot of which stands the
city of Viterbo. Pliny tells us, that Soracte was not far from Rome,
haud procul ab urbe Roma; but Montefiascone is fifty miles from this
city. And Desprez, in his notes upon Horace, says it is now called
Monte S. Oreste. Addison tells us he passed by it in the Campania. I
could not without indignation reflect upon the bigotry of Mathilda,
who gave this fine country to the see of Rome, under the dominion
of which no country was ever known to prosper.

About half way between Montefiascone and Viterbo, one of our
fore-wheels flew off, together with a large splinter of the axle-tree;
and if one of the postilions had not by great accident been a remarkably ingenious fellow, we should have been put to the greatest inconvenience, as there was no town, or even house, within several miles.
I mention this circumstance by way of warning to other travellers,
that they may provide themselves with a hammer and nails, a spare
iron-pin or two, a large knife, and bladder of grease, to be used occasionally in case of such misfortune.

Matthew Spender

(1945–   )

Sculptor Matthew Spender moved to Tuscany in the late 1960s. The son of poet Stephen Spender, he was born in London and studied at the Slade School of Fine Art. He married Maro Gorky, with whom he has two daughters, moved to Italy to study painting, and stayed. This excerpt from his memoir *Within Tuscany* (1992) describes his daughters' early education in the small schools of the countryside.

Although he is the author of several books (including a biography of his father-in-law, the painter Ashile Gorky), Spender considers himself primarily an artist, a figurative sculptor who works in clay. His art is heavily influenced by his adopted Tuscan home and he wrote that he "appreciated the comment of the Italian artist Arturo Martini, 'The Etruscans made their sculptures like they made their bread.' I find this observation beautiful. Those who make bread are used to a certain manner before they start. Nothing is improvised . . . When working, I often think of the landscape itself, formed by hand over many generations with mattock and pick until the shapes of the hills themselves have assumed the character of sculpture. This feeling is reinforced in that the local clay is dug out from beneath those same shapes which I can see on all sides on the horizon around me."

Spender has had many one-person exhibitions in Europe and his work is widely collected. Ironically, he received his greatest exposure when the director Bernardo Bertolucci used forty-seven of his sculptures in the film *Stealing Beauty*, shot on location in Tuscany in 1995.

from WITHIN TUSCANY

Our elder daughter Saskia was born in Florence, in 1970.

I remember trundling through the night in a very small Fiat, stopping every ten minutes for Maro's labour pains, while the cars piled up behind us tooting in protest.

The obstetrician had an urgent appointment on the ski slopes, and our daughter emerged slightly mauled about the head. She was a nervy infant, flinching if I laughed in the small room, which I did quite often for she was my first child, and I had never imagined the event could be so exciting.

Our second daughter Cosima was born at home, the last child in the *Comune* to be born outside hospital more or less on purpose. Odd things happened to my wife as she was carrying out the tea things to the local midwife and my mother-in-law, one warm afternoon in August. The midwife had got it wrong by a month, and was planning a short trip to Paris. She had just come round to check up and say goodbye.

"And are you going to beat the pavements, when you get there?" asked my mother-in-law politely as they sipped, meaning "Are you going to go window-shopping?"

"*O Signora*," said the dear lady, "I'm much too old to do *that*!"

Maro laughed so much that the tea things came crashing down, and the midwife had no time to go home and get her "nice new little bag" of gloves, rubbing alcohol and string.

At dusk, the electricity failed. I was told to boil water, lots of it, and refused, thinking it a ploy to get rid of useless husbands. We lit candles.

"What nice candles," said the midwife cheerfully, as she smoked a cigarette with her left hand and explored the child, still inside her mother, with her right. "It looks just like a funeral."

Her name was Azzurrini, and indeed for me she had for evermore the pragmatic aura of the Blue Fairy in *Pinocchio*, whenever I read this masterpiece to the children, before bed.

Cosima was born neatly, in subdued light (courtesy wildcat strike at Enel), a mere half-hour after labour began, in a bed carved and joined by my own hand, surrounded by a remarkable number of unmarried aunts, there to see how childbirth went.

When the doctor came he disapproved of everything. Such a risk, these days, having a baby at home. We stood to attention like good soldiers in front of their sergeant. Afterwards, we had a party, mid-wife, baby and all.

Still smoking, the midwife kept flipping over the newborn child. "What shoulders!" she said admiringly, though it was not a part of her that the rest of us found particularly interesting. Signora Azzurrini compared Cosi's anatomy to that of an adult hare.

SCHOOL

Time passed, and the moment when the young needed schooling caught up with us. The garden was still full of legumery and the light of London still seemed unattractive to this "alternative nuclear family," as an Italian would have called us in the early seventies. Once immersed into the educational system it seemed just too hard to return to London and the dull tubercular north.

The village school had one classroom for everyone. There were only seven pupils, all of different sizes. The teacher was a very gifted woman and all the children learned to read and write between September and Christmas.

Our elder daughter's first day of school was unforgettable. She rode her tiny bicycle to the end of the drive, turned, waved and then took off down a short cut through the vines. Blue bike, blue raincoat, wet leaves. She was five.

In winter the whole school, all eight of them if one included the teacher, huddled around a stinking stove with a leaky and illegal outlet right through the window. There was no question of getting this fixed. The stove and the classroom belonged to the industrialist from Brescia, Vittorio's employer, who wanted to evict them so that he could fill their hall of learning with farm equipment. He was perfectly prepared to risk finding all the scholars asphyxiated one day, their grammar books still clutched in their hands, one collective past participle.

The little room had a hat rack by the window, benches and a closed cupboard called *Biblioteca*. I looked inside once, to check their collection of books. It was entirely filled with empty beer cans.

The existence of the school itself was eventually threatened by the central authorities, who decided to close all the outlying village schools and bus the children to larger premises where they could enjoy the benefits of efficient plumbing in a haven of white tiles, under the eye of a watchful beadle during break.

We protested, held stormy meetings, confronted a small sad official sent out from Siena, who suddenly decided to let us run the place ourselves if we could. For three months I taught English at the school in the next village but one, while my wife taught art in ours. Her class was neat and orderly. Mine was hell. At one point, I descended so low as to poke a little boy in the bum with a Biro, to make some point concerning the pronunciation of the definite article. I said to myself, now perhaps this is not the gesture of a true professional, and gave up.

But the school that was taught art by Maro flourished in the creativity which comes from innocence. She claimed that puberty brought with it non-artistic aims, like the Vespa and the disco on Saturdays, the lure to drive to hot spots like Montevarchi and San Giovanni. Pending this moment she taught a quiet, respectful group, male voices teetering on the brink of sudden baritone, female chests still more or less flat. A couple of years later these beautiful children had vanished, leaving behind animated statues worked over by a later hand.

Our children also grew up, and faced the trauma of moving from Gaiole to Siena. For me this was triggered when Cosi came back one day with a report beginning with the words, "*contenutisticamente possibilista, però* . . . ," meaning roughly, "She's got some good ideas, but . . ." How can this poor child, I asked myself, go through life with a language so pompously fluffed out with Ciceronian constructions? Bullied by dog Latin? So we sent them south to a better school in Siena.

I followed, by becoming the parents' rep. There was not a great deal of competition for the job. The teachers were polite, and listened to any kind of didactic argument, but as far as I could tell they never changed their curriculum for anything a parents' representative ever said.

In theory we had some power. We could choose the textbooks and veto the history course if it failed to coincide with our own high standards. We could dictate the flavour of religious studies and re-route the annual school outing. All interesting problems—especially the school outing, that fascinating rite of passage where the kids discover cigarettes and French kissing, and the notion that love can be a public spectacle carried out among an audience of ululating peers. For thousands of Italian schoolchildren the Leaning Tower of Pisa or the Uffizi is a warm primal memory, far from the small historical point the teacher might have wanted to make at the time. Be patient, tourist, as you thread your way among them.

As for the right to veto the school books, we annually attended a meeting where parents, teachers and books were lumped together and stirred.

Italian schools used to arrange their own curricula according to a series of cautious negative parameters laid down by the state, dictating that each theme should have not less than x and not more than y pages devoted to it. As long as these parameters were observed, publishers were free to give the subject what bias they wished. Often it was not clear what line a history textbook might be following; working out the political flavour of a book could involve counting pages rather than analysing content.

We were seldom presented with the mayhem of selection. The teacher would have brought it down to a choice of two, which was kind, but once you had sat down in the middle of the hum and gaggle and put a finger in one ear trying to read, to emerge hot and sweaty and breathing hard three quarters of an hour later, having plumped for one particular pile, as like as not the teacher would smilingly point out the attractions of the books remaining on the table. It was after all a choice of one.

Sometimes a left-wing history book might have more (for instance) on the life of Christ than a Catholic one. The reasons for this were complicated. There was a moment when the Italian Communist Party claimed Christ as a forebear; and meanwhile there was always the problem of the Hour of Religion in class.

I always fought for more study of the Bible in class, unsuccessfully, but as usual I missed the point. The fight was whether or not there should be a Scripture class at all. There were deeply anticlerical socialist teachers who would teach the life of Christ in Marxist terms during the history lesson, but who would refuse to teach anything about him in the *Ora di Religione*. There were Catholics who would teach anything to keep the Hour going—Buddha, Confucius, Zoroaster—avoiding for the moment the problems of discussing Christ.

There is no state religion in Italy, and in theory any child was free to opt out of the Hour of Religion. But it was rare that any child claimed this right. For a while the Liceo Classico of Siena enjoyed the paradox that, while their father fought for better teaching in the Hour of Religion in every parents' meeting, Saskia and Cosima alone in all Siena sat quietly in the corridor for the duration, saying politely they were atheist if ever a passing teacher asked.

They had not always been atheists. The elder went through a passionate Catholic phase at the age of seven, though her theology had been strangely tinged by a recent visit to Iran, where a friend of ours was working. There, left in the cook's apartment while we toured the sites, she had emerged a passionate Shiite.

Back in Italy her view of the Mass involved a fat padded carpet and carefully chosen wardrobe. The plastic babies kept in a row in the bookshelf acquired turbans and incense, though the actual ceremonies took place (as in Tehran) behind carefully shut doors. There was an occasional wail or throb of a drum, heard from the floor below. The empty feel of the desert perceived through a clean tent wall, the beating of a soft childish forehead against the unresilient tiles. A sudden demand for the compass reference for Mecca. Younger sister coopted to a subsidiary role holding Armenian slippers, practically strangled by a loose chador. Garbled bits of what one hoped was classical Arabic followed by references to "*Il Re del Toro*" ("the King of the Bull"), which came from "*il Redentore*," the Redeemer. Her Catholicism was what you might call ecumenical, if ecumenical means shoving in a bit of everything for the greater glory of God.

Every Sunday I would take this eclectic daughter to Mass, on condition that she left her shroud behind.

After a while I decided that I very much liked our parish priest, a man younger than myself, and remarkably straightforward and unsentimental in his sermons. On one particular saint's day he was required to touch the throats of his parishioners with a pair of crossed candles, to save them from sore throats during the ensuing winter. Don

Osvaldo, fired by the revolutionary whiffs of the early seventies, gave his parishioners a speech on the foolishness of superstition. Touching their throats would never protect them against bugs, he said, and if they had flu they should see the doctor. He said it well, and the little flock listened in respectful silence. Then they all queued up to be touched by the candles anyway.

Osvaldo soon became a close friend of the family. We even painted portraits of him, one from each side. Neither Maro's nor mine was successful—he did fidget so, chain-smoking in embarrassment at being looked at for himself alone. If he talked, he could relax, which meant that the sittings usually went on through supper and all night, with many interesting discussions of a cosmological kind.

He was the second parish priest since we had come to live near the village. The first had been there for years, a large and extraordinarily short-sighted man with a soft voice, who would stare up from under at you through glasses like the bottoms of two bottles.

There is an annual ritual just before Easter, in which the parish priest goes round all the houses in the village to bless the walls and beasts therein. A good excuse to evict the spiders and mice accumulated over the winter, beat the carpets, scream at the children for the state of their toy cupboards, etc. When we arrived, strangers in every sense, this worthy gentleman appeared as usual, buoyed by an ample curiosity about our ways and with the perfect excuse to examine them at close quarters.

"My, what a lot of books," he said, after he had admired our comatose angels in their tiny cots and absent-mindedly sprinkled each room with holy water. He took down a book at random. *The Erotic Drawings of Auguste Rodin.* "Ah," he said, "what art!" He took down another. *Frescos from Pompei: The Secret Rooms of the Museo Nazionale in Naples.* Ahem!

"Wasn't it lucky these books weren't in Italian," we said as he rode off—as if there was anything unintelligible about the illustrations.

The following year we had the house nicely scrubbed, walls painted to get rid of the autumnal smoke, and we had meanwhile learned that it was traditional to offer a glass of Vin Santo (from "Zante," apparently—nothing to do with holy wine) and a few dry biscuits. We were all ready and peering out of the window to see his

Vespa trundle through the vines. "There he is!" The robed figure rode with difficulty, a small wind catching the lace of his clean Easter surplice. At the head of the drive he stopped, as if remembering something, and paused to look at us. We waved, but he couldn't see that far. Thoughtfully he turned his bike round and drove off again, leaving our walls unblessed.

He died the following year, in a tragic but spectacular accident. Turning a corner on his Vespa, he rode between two large oxen, not noticing they were carrying the plough slung upside down between them.

Osvaldo was characteristically reluctant to come to the house for a very different reason. I bless people, not walls, he said. What is the point of blessing walls? So he blessed us instead. But it is always awkward to sprinkle water over the doubtful.

When Saskia was in the midst of her Catholic phase, we took her along to Osvaldo to see if he could stretch a point and baptize her. He looked down at the smiling, temporarily toothless nymph in pantaloons and a veil, clutching a black dolly vaguely done up as a Virgin Mary.

"You see, Matteo," he said tactfully, "the thing is that I feel that if you had gone to live in Africa instead of Tuscany, you would have taken her to the witch-doctor with the same serenity with which you now bring her to me."

And he was not far wrong. Elder daughter, now at university studying anthropology, is miffed that she can't participate in certain Yoruba rites, as she hasn't got a religion of her own. Apparently you have to check in one to get another, and if you haven't already got one, you can't start.

When I told Osvaldo all this in the village post office recently, he gave a quiet sigh and said, "Well, I am so glad I get some things right."

Stephen Spender

(1 9 0 9 – 1 9 9 5)

Poet Stephen Spender's friendships read like a pantheon of literary giants: T. S. Eliot, Virginia Woolf, Louis MacNeice, Christopher Isherwood, W. H. Auden, and C. Day-Lewis. His frank autobiography, *World within World* (1951), is often considered one of the best of its genre. One reviewer wrote that the portraits he drew of his friends "have the psychological depth of Rembrandt and the elegance of Velázquez." Despite his trenchant political commentary and keen evocation of pre–World War II Berlin, it was Spender's admission of his lifelong attraction to men, through his long marriage to his wife, Natasha, that drew the most attention.

More than forty years later author David Leavitt borrowed facts from Spender's life for his novel *While England Sleeps*. Spender sued Leavitt and won, but died shortly thereafter. Many thought that the elderly poet did not want his homosexuality rebroadcast after he had become a revered British institution, but Spender maintained that he simply did not want Leavitt profiting from his life and detracting from what he considered his greatest work.

In Stephen Spender's poem "Grandparents" (1971) he relates traveling to Florence to welcome his granddaughter Saskia, child of his son, the sculptor Matthew Spender, and his daughter-in-law Maro Gorky. Like all new parents, Matthew is filled with wonder at this new person, more beautiful than the bambini painted by the masters in the Uffizi.

GRANDPARENTS

We looked at Matthew's child, our granddaughter,
Through the glass screen where eight babies
Blazed like red candles on a table.
Her crumpled face and hands were like
Chrysalis and ferns unrolling.
"Is our baby a genius?" he asked a nun.

We went to the Uffizi and he looked at
Italian primitives, and found
All their *bambini* ugly.
He started drawing Maro and her daughter
Nine hours after Saskia had been born.

(Florence, 1971)

Mark Twain

(1835–1910)

In 1904 Mark Twain and his family were in residence in a Florentine villa, where he was interviewed by a journalist from *The New York Times*. Twain had moved his family from Connecticut to escape crushing debt. The nineteenth-century American master of letters was an abysmal businessman, a genius at losing fortunes. It was not the first time that the Twains had relocated to Europe to regain their wealth.

In his *Times* interview Twain pontificated about Henry James, Charles Dickens, and the art of the novel. (Coincidentally, Twain heard Dickens lecture in New York with his future wife, Livy, on the night they met, Christmas Day, 1867. Livy died in Florence shortly after Twain was interviewed by the *Times*.) "Fact is, nothing is eternal in this world," he said, "and literature is as much subject to the character of the times as any other intellectual manifestation." Then he turned his sights on his inability to master the Italian language. Perhaps, he speculated, it was that his hair was too big. He noticed that the Italians cropped theirs as "smooth as billiard balls." He went straight to the barber and had his white mane shaved close to his head. No effect. Then he tried sleeping with an Italian dictionary under his head. No effect. "I never got hold of an entire sentence. Just a word here and there that comes in handy, but they never stay with me more than a day."

Twain claimed that there was only one person who understood him in Italy— the kitchen maid. "We have quite long talks together and exchange no end of compliments. I talk English; she rattles along in her own lingo; neither of us knows what the other says; we get along perfectly and greatly respect each others' conversation."

This excerpt is from *The Innocents Abroad* (1869), Twain's first book of travel writings. The profits gave him enough financial security to marry Livy Langdon.

from THE INNOCENTS ABROAD

Some of the Quaker City's passengers had arrived in Venice from Switzerland and other lands before we left there, and others were expected every day. We heard of no casualties among them, and no sickness.

We were a little fatigued with sight seeing, so we rattled through a good deal of country by rail without caring to stop. I took few notes. I find no mention of Bologna in my memorandum book, except that we arrived there in good season, but saw none of the sausages for which the place is so justly celebrated.

Pistoia awoke but a passing interest.

Florence pleased us for a while. I think we appreciated the great figure of David in the grand square, and the sculptured group they call the Rape of the Sabines. We wandered through the endless collections of paintings and statues of the Pitti and Uffizi galleries, of course. I make that statement in self-defense; there let it stop. I could not rest under the imputation that I visited Florence and did not traverse its weary miles of picture galleries. We tried indolently to recollect something about the Guelphs and Ghibellines and the other historical cut-throats whose quarrels and assassinations make up so large a share of Florentine history, but the subject was not attractive. We had been robbed of all the fine mountain scenery on our little journey by a system of railroading that had three miles of tunnel to a hundred yards of daylight, and we were not inclined to be sociable with Florence. We had seen the spot, outside the city somewhere, where these people had allowed the bones of Galileo to rest in unconsecrated ground for an age because his great discovery that the world turned around was regarded as a damning heresy by the church; and we know that long after the world had accepted his theory and raised his name high in the list of its great men, they had still let him rot there. That we had lived to see his dust in honored sepulture in the church of Santa Croce we owed to a society of *literati*, and not to Florence or her rulers. We saw Danté's tomb in that church, also, but we were glad to know that his body was not in it; that the ungrateful city that had exiled him and persecuted him would give much to have it there, but need not hope to ever secure that high honor to herself. Medicis are good enough for Florence. Let her plant Medicis and build grand monuments over them to testify how gratefully she was wont to lick the hand that scourged her.

Magnanimous Florence! Her jewelry marts are filled with artists in mosaic. Florentine mosaics are the choicest in all the world. Florence loves to have that said. Florence is proud of it. Florence would foster this specialty of hers. She is grateful to the artists that bring to her this high credit and fill her coffers with foreign money, and so she encourages them with pensions. With pensions! Think of the lavishness of it. She knows that people who piece together the beautiful trifles die early, because the labor is so confining, and so exhausting to hand and brain, and so she has decreed that all these people who reach the age of sixty shall have a pension after that! I have not heard that any of them have called for their dividends yet. One man did fight along till he was sixty, and started after his pension, but it appeared that there had been a mistake of a year in his family record, and so he gave it up and died.

These artists will take particles of stone or glass no larger than a mustard seed, and piece them together on a sleeve button or a shirt stud, so smoothly and with such nice adjustment of the delicate shades of color the pieces bear, as to form a pigmy rose with stem, thorn, leaves, petals complete, and all as softly and as truthfully tinted as though Nature had builded it herself. They will counterfeit a fly, or a high-toned bug, or the ruined Coliseum, within the cramped circle of a breastpin, and do it so deftly and so neatly that any man might think a master painted it.

I saw a little table in the great mosaic school in Florence—a little trifle of a centre table—whose top was made of some sort of precious polished stone, and in the stone was inlaid the figure of a flute, with bell-mouth and a mazy complication of keys. No painting in the world could have been softer or richer; no shading out of one tint into another could have been more perfect, no work of art of any kind could have been more faultless than this flute, and yet to count the multitude of little fragments of stone of which they swore it was formed would bankrupt any man's arithmetic! I do not think one could have seen where two particles joined each other with eyes of ordinary shrewdness. Certainly *we* could detect no such blemish. This table-top cost the labor of one man for ten long years, so they said, and it was for sale for thirty-five thousand dollars.

We went to the church of Santa Croce, from time to time in Florence, to weep over the tombs of Michael Angelo, Raphael and Machiavelli (I suppose they are buried there, but it may be that they reside elsewhere and rent their tombs to other parties—such being the fashion in Italy), and between times we used to go and stand on the bridges and admire the Arno. It is popular to admire the Arno. It is a great historical creek with four feet in the channel and some scows floating around. It would be a very plausible river if they would pump some water into it. They all call it a river, and they honestly think it *is* a river, do these dark and bloody Florentines. They even help out the delusion by building bridges over it. I do not see why they are too good to wade.

How the fatigues and annoyances of travel fill one with bitter prejudices sometimes! I might enter Florence under happier auspices a month hence and find it all beautiful, all attractive. But I do not care to think of it now, at all, nor of its roomy shops filled to the ceiling with snowy marble and alabaster copies of all the celebrated sculptures in Europe—copies so enchanting to the eye that I wonder how they can really be shaped like the dingy petrified nightmares they are the portraits of. I got lost in Florence at nine o'clock, one night, and staid lost in that labyrinth of narrow streets and long rows of vast buildings that look all alike, until toward three o'clock in the morning. It was a pleasant night and at first there were a good many people abroad, and there were cheerful lights about. Later, I grew accustomed to prowling about mysterious drifts and tunnels and astonishing and interesting myself with coming around corners expecting to find the hotel staring me in the face, and not finding it doing any thing of the kind. Later still, I felt tired. I soon felt remarkably tired. But there was no one abroad, now—not even a policeman. I walked till I was out of all patience, and very hot and thirsty. At last, somewhere after one o'clock, I came unexpectedly to one of the city gates. I knew then that I was very far from the hotel. The soldiers thought I wanted to leave the city, and they sprang up and barred the way with their muskets. I said:

"Hotel d'Europe!"

It was all the Italian I knew, and I was not certain whether that was Italian or French. The soldiers looked stupidly at each other and at me, and shook their heads and took me into custody. I said I wanted to go home. They did not understand me. They took me into the guard-house and searched me, but they found no sedition on me. They found a small piece of soap (we carry soap with us, now), and I made them a present of it, seeing that they regarded it as a curiosity. I continued to say Hotel d'Europe, and they continued to shake their heads, until at last a young soldier nodding in the corner roused up and said something. He said he knew where the hotel was, I suppose, for the officer of the guard sent him away with me. We walked a hundred or a hundred and fifty miles, it appeared to me, and then *he* got lost. He turned this way and that, and finally gave it up and signified that he was going to spend the remainder of the morning trying to find the city gate again. At that moment it struck me that there was something familiar about the house over the way. It was the hotel!

It was a happy thing for me that there happened to be a soldier there that knew even as much as he did; for they say that the policy of the government is to change the soldiery from one place to another constantly and from country to city, so that they can not become acquainted with the people and grow lax in their duties and enter into plots and conspiracies with friends. My experiences of Florence were chiefly unpleasant. I will change the subject.

At Pisa we climbed up to the top of the strangest structure the world has any knowledge of—the Leaning Tower. As every one knows, it is in the neighborhood of one hundred and eighty feet high—and I beg to observe that one hundred and eighty feet reach to about the height of four ordinary three-story buildings piled one on top of the other, and is a very considerable altitude for a tower of uniform thickness to aspire to, even when it stands upright—yet this one leans more than thirteen feet out of the perpendicular. It is seven hundred years old, but neither history nor tradition say whether it was built as it is, purposely, or whether one of its sides has settled.

There is no record that it ever stood straight up. It is built of marble. It is an airy and a beautiful structure, and each of its eight stories is encircled by fluted columns, some of marble and some of granite, with Corinthian capitals that were handsome when they were new. It is a bell tower, and in its top hangs a chime of ancient bells. The winding staircase within is dark, but one always knows which side of the tower he is on because of his naturally gravitating from one side to the other of the staircase with the rise or dip of the tower. Some of the stone steps are foot-worn only on one end; others only on the other end; others only in the middle. To look down into the tower from the top is like looking down into a tilted well. A rope that hangs from the centre of the top touches the wall before it reaches the bottom. Standing on the summit, one does not feel altogether comfortable when he looks down from the high side; but to crawl on your breast to the verge on the lower side and try to stretch your neck out far enough to see the base of the tower, makes your flesh creep, and convinces you for a single moment in spite of all your philosophy, that the building is falling. You handle yourself very carefully, all the time, under the silly impression that if it is *not* falling, your trifling weight will start it unless you are particular not to "bear down" on it.

The Duomo, close at hand, is one of the finest cathedrals in Europe. It is eight hundred years old. Its grandeur has outlived the high commercial prosperity and the political importance that made it a necessity, or rather a possibility. Surrounded by poverty, decay and ruin, it conveys to us a more tangible impression of the former greatness of Pisa than books could give us.

The Baptistery, which is a few years older than the Leaning Tower, is a stately rotunda, of huge dimensions, and was a costly structure. In it hangs the lamp whose measured swing suggested to Galileo the pendulum. It looked an insignificant thing to have conferred upon the world of science and mechanics such a mighty extension of their dominions as it has. Pondering, in its suggestive presence, I seemed to see a crazy universe of swinging disks, the toiling children of this sedate parent. He appeared to have an intelligent expression about him of knowing that he was not a lamp at all; that he was a Pendulum; a pendulum disguised, for prodigious and inscrutable purposes of his own deep devising, and not a common pendulum either, but the old original patriarchal Pendulum—the Abraham Pendulum of the world.

The Baptistery is endowed with the most pleasing echo of all the echoes we have read of. The guide sounded two sonorous notes, about half an octave apart; the echo answered with the most enchanting, the most melodious, the richest blending of sweet sounds that one can imagine. It was like a long-drawn chord of a church organ, infinitely softened by distance. I may be extravagant in this matter, but if this be the case my ear is to blame—not my pen. I am describing a memory—and one that will remain long with me.

The peculiar devotional spirit of the olden time, which placed a higher confidence in outward forms of worship than in the watchful guarding of the heart against sinful thoughts and the hands against sinful deeds, and which believed in the protecting virtues of inanimate objects made holy by contact with holy things, is illustrated in a striking manner in one of the cemeteries of Pisa. The tombs are set in soil brought in ships from the Holy Land ages ago. To be buried in such ground was regarded by the ancient Pisans as being more potent for salvation than many masses purchased of the church and the vowing of many candles to the Virgin.

Pisa is believed to be about three thousand years old. It was one of the twelve great cities of ancient Etruria, that commonwealth which has left so many monuments in testimony of its extraordinary advancement, and so little history of itself that is tangible and comprehensible. A Pisan antiquarian gave me an ancient tear-jug which he averred was full four thousand years old. It was found among the ruins of one of the oldest of the Etruscan cities. He said it came from a tomb, and was used by some bereaved family in that remote age when even the Pyramids of Egypt were young, Damascus a village, Abraham a prattling infant and ancient Troy not yet dreampt of, to receive the tears wept for some lost idol of a household. It spoke to us in a language of its own; and with a pathos more tender than any words might bring, its mute eloquence swept down the long roll of the centuries with its tale of a vacant chair, a familiar footstep missed from the threshold, a pleasant voice gone from the chorus, a vanished form!—a tale which is always so new to us, so startling, so terrible, so benumbing to the senses, and behold how threadbare and old it is! No shrewdly-worded history could have brought the myths and shadows of that old dreamy age before us clothed with human flesh and warmed with human sympathies so vividly as did this poor little unsentient vessel of pottery.

Pisa was a republic in the middle ages, with a government of her own, armies and navies of her own and a great commerce. She was a warlike power, and inscribed upon her banners many a brilliant fight with Genoese and Turks. It is said that the city once numbered a population of four hundred thousand; but her sceptre has passed from her grasp, now, her ships and her armies are gone, her commerce is dead. Her battle-flags bear the mold and the dust of centuries, her marts are deserted, she has shrunken far within her crumbling walls, and her great population has diminished to twenty thousand souls. She has but one thing left to boast of, and that is not much, viz: she is the second city of Tuscany.

We reached Leghorn in time to see all we wished to see of it long before the city gates were closed for the evening, and then came on board the ship.

We felt as though we had been away from home an age. We never entirely appreciated, before, what a very pleasant den our state-room is; nor how jolly it is to sit at dinner in one's own seat in one's own cabin, and hold familiar conversation with friends in one's own language. Oh, the rare happiness of comprehending every single word that is said, and knowing that every word one says in return will be understood as well! We would talk ourselves to death, now, only there are only about ten passengers out of the sixty-five to talk to. The others are wandering, we hardly know where. We shall not go ashore in Leghorn. We are surfeited with Italian cities for the present, and much prefer to walk the familiar quarter-deck and view this one from a distance.

The stupid magnates of this Leghorn government can not understand that so large a steamer as ours could cross the broad Atlantic with no other purpose than to indulge a party of ladies and gentlemen in a pleasure excursion. It looks too improbable. It is suspicious, they think. Something more important must be hidden behind it all. They can not understand it, and they scorn the evidence of the ship's papers. They have decided at last that we are a battalion of incendiary, blood-thirsty Garibaldians in disguise! And in all seriousness they have set a gun-boat to watch the vessel night and day, with orders to close down on any revolutionary movement in a twinkling! Police boats are on patrol duty about us all the time, and it is as much as a sailor's liberty is worth to show himself in a red shirt. These policemen follow the executive officer's boat from shore to ship and from ship to shore and watch his dark maneuvres with a vigilant eye. They will arrest him yet unless he assumes an expression of counte-nance that shall have less of carnage, insurrection and sedition in it. A visit paid in a friendly way to General Garibaldi yesterday (by cor-dial invitation), by some of our passengers, has gone far to confirm the dread suspicions the government harbors toward us. It is thought the friendly visit was only the cloak of a bloody conspiracy. These people draw near and watch us when we bathe in the sea from the ship's side. Do they think we are communing with a reserve force of rascals at the bottom?

It is said that we shall probably be quarantined at Naples. Two or three of us prefer not to run this risk. Therefore, when we are rested, we propose to go in a French steamer to Civita Vecchia, and from thence to Rome, and by rail to Naples. They do not quarantine the cars, no matter where they got their passengers from.

Edith Wharton

(1862–1937)

As a young woman, novelist Edith Wharton, accompanied by her family, traveled to Tuscany for the first time. In her autobiography, *Life and I,* she wrote, "I had been saturated in Ruskin, & the result was that, at least, I saw many things which the average Baedeker-led tourist of that city certainly missed . . . To Florence and Venice his little volumes gave a meaning, a sense of organic relation, which no other books attainable by me at that time could possibly have conveyed." Wharton eventually moved to Europe with her husband, Teddy, and wrote articles about architecture and horticulture for *Century Magazine.* They were later collected into two books, *Italian Backgrounds* and *Italian Villas and Their Gardens.*

Early in her career Wharton bristled at the comparison of her books to those of her good friend and frequent traveling companion Henry James. While they both wrote about the European and American upper classes, Undine Spragg of *The Custom of the Country* (1913) is unmistakably a creation of Wharton's imagination. In this excerpt Undine and her new husband, Ralph Marvell, are honeymooning in Tuscany. Ralph is enchanted by Italy, but she finds it hot and unfashionable and begs her husband to take her to Switzerland. Undine is so manipulative, so nakedly ambitious that the critic Harold Bloom wrote that, while he considers it Wharton's best novel, he finds *The Custom of the Country* "rather unpleasant to read." In his only review of Wharton's work, Henry James wrote of the novel (in the London *Times Literary Supplement*) that Wharton illuminated her characters with "almost scientifically satiric . . . light."

from THE CUSTOM OF THE COUNTRY

The July sun enclosed in a ring of fire the ilex grove of a villa in the hills near Siena.

Below, by the roadside, the long yellow house seemed to waver and palpitate in the glare; but steep by steep, behind it, the cool ilex-dusk mounted to the ledge where Ralph Marvell, stretched on his back in the grass, lay gazing up at a black reticulation of branches between which bits of sky gleamed with the hardness and brilliancy of blue enamel.

Up there too the air was thick with heat; but compared with the white fire below it was a dim and tempered warmth, like that of the churches in which he and Undine sometimes took refuge at the height of the torrid days.

Ralph loved the heavy Indian summer, as he had loved the light spring days leading up to it: the long line of dancing days that had drawn them on and on ever since they had left their ship at Naples four months earlier. Four months of beauty, changeful, inexhaustible, weaving itself about him in shapes of softness and strength; and beside him, hand in hand with him, embodying that spirit of shifting magic, the radiant creature through whose eyes he saw it. This was what their hastened marriage had blessed them with, giving them leisure, before summer came, to penetrate to remote folds of the southern mountains, to linger in the shade of Sicilian orange-groves, and finally, travelling by slow stages to the Adriatic, to reach the central hill-country where even in July they might hope for a breathable air.

To Ralph the Sienese air was not only breathable but intoxicating. The sun, treading the earth like a vintager, drew from it heady fragrances, crushed out of it new colours. All the values of the temperate landscape were reversed: the noon high-lights were white, but the shadows had unimagined colour. On the blackness of cork and ilex and cypress lay the green and purple lustres, the coppery iridescences, of old bronze; and night after night the skies were wine-blue and bubbling with stars. Ralph said to himself that no one who had not seen Italy thus prostrate beneath the sun knew what secret treasures she could yield.

As he lay there, fragments of past states of emotion, fugitive felicities of thought and sensation, rose and floated on the surface of his thoughts. It was one of those moments when the accumulated impressions of life converge on heart and brain, elucidating, enlacing each other, in a mysterious confusion of beauty. He had had glimpses of such a state before, of such mergings of the personal with the general life that one felt one's self a mere wave on the wild stream of being, yet thrilled with a sharper sense of individuality than can be known within the mere bounds of the actual. But now he knew the sensation in its fulness, and with it came the releasing power of language. Words were flashing like brilliant birds through the boughs overhead; he had but to wave his magic wand to have them flutter down to him. Only they were so beautiful up there, weaving their fantastic flights against the blue, that it was pleasanter, for the moment, to watch them and let the wand lie.

He stared up at the pattern they made till his eyes ached with excess of light; then he changed his position and looked at his wife.

Undine, near by, leaned against a gnarled tree with the slightly constrained air of a person unused to sylvan abandonments. Her beautiful back could not adapt itself to the irregularities of the tree-trunk, and she moved a little now and then in the effort to find an easier position. But her expression was serene, and Ralph, looking up at her through drowsy lids, thought her face had never been more exquisite.

"You look as cool as a wave," he said, reaching out for the hand on her knee. She let him have it, and he drew it closer, scrutinizing it as if it had been a bit of precious porcelain or ivory. It was small and soft, a mere featherweight, a puff-ball of a hand—not quick and thrilling, not a speaking hand, but one to be fondled and dressed in rings, and to leave a rosy blur in the brain. The fingers were short and tapering, dimpled at the base, with nails as smooth as rose-leaves. Ralph lifted them one by one, like a child playing with piano-keys, but they were inelastic and did not spring back far—only far enough to show the dimples.

He turned the hand over and traced the course of its blue veins from the wrist to the rounding of the palm below the fingers; then he put a kiss in the warm hollow between. The upper world had vanished: his universe had shrunk to the palm of a hand. But there was no sense of diminution. In the mystic depths whence his passion sprang, earthly dimensions were ignored and the curve of beauty was boundless enough to hold whatever the imagination could pour into it. Ralph had never felt more convinced of his power to write a great poem; but now it was Undine's hand which held the magic wand of impression.

She stirred again uneasily, answering his last words with a faint accent of reproach.

"I don't *feel* cool. You said there'd be a breeze up here."

He laughed.

"You poor darling! Wasn't it ever as hot as this in Apex?"

She withdrew her hand with a slight grimace.

"Yes—but I didn't marry you to go back to Apex!"

Ralph laughed again; then he lifted himself on his elbow and regained the hand. "I wonder what you *did* marry me for?"

"Mercy! It's too hot for conundrums." She spoke without impatience, but with a lassitude less joyous than his.

He roused himself. "Do you really mind the heat so much? We'll go, if you do."

She sat up eagerly. "Go to Switzerland, you mean?"

"Well, I hadn't taken quite as long a leap. I only meant we might drive back to Siena."

She relapsed listlessly against her tree-trunk. "Oh, Siena's hotter than this."

"We could go and sit in the cathedral—it's always cool there at sunset."

"We've sat in the cathedral at sunset every day for a week."

"Well, what do you say to stopping at Lecceto on the way? I haven't shown you Lecceto yet; and the drive back by moonlight would be glorious."

This woke her to a slight show of interest. "It might be nice—but where could we get anything to eat?"

Ralph laughed again. "I don't believe we could. You're too practical."

"Well, somebody's got to be. And the food in the hotel is too disgusting if we're not on time."

"I admit that the best of it has usually been appropriated by the extremely good-looking cavalry-officer who's so keen to know you."

Undine's face brightened. "You know he's not a Count; he's a Marquis. His name's Roviano, his palace in Rome is in the guide-books, and he speaks English beautifully. Céleste found out about him from the head-waiter," she said, with the security of one who treats of recognized values.

Marvell, sitting upright, reached lazily across the grass for his hat. "Then there's all the more reason for rushing back to defend our share." He spoke in the bantering tone which had become the habitual expression of his tenderness; but his eyes softened as they absorbed in a last glance the glimmering submarine light of the ancient grove, through which Undine's figure wavered nereid-like above him.

"You never looked your name more than you do now," he said, kneeling at her side and putting his arm about her. She smiled back a little vaguely, as if not seizing his allusion, and being content to let it drop into the store of unexplained references which had once stimulated her curiosity but now merely gave her leisure to think of other things. But her smile was no less lovely for its vagueness, and indeed, to Ralph, the loveliness was enhanced by the latent doubt. He remembered afterward that at that moment the cup of life seemed to brim over.

"Come, dear—here or there—it's all divine!"

In the carriage, however, she remained insensible to the soft spell of the evening, noticing only the heat and dust, and saying, as they passed under the wooded cliff of Lecceto, that they might as well have stopped there after all, since with such a headache as she felt coming on she didn't care if she dined or not.

Ralph looked up yearningly at the long walls overhead; but Undine's mood was hardly favourable to communion with such scenes, and he made no attempt to stop the carriage. Instead he presently said: "If you're tired of Italy, we've got the world to choose from."

She did not speak for a moment; then she said: "It's the heat I'm tired of. Don't people generally come here earlier?"

"Yes. That's why I chose the summer: so that we could have it all to ourselves."

She tried to put a note of reasonableness into her voice. "If you'd told me we were going everywhere at the wrong time, of course I could have arranged about my clothes."

"You poor darling! Let us, by all means, go to the place where the clothes will be right: they're too beautiful to be left out of our scheme of life."

Her lips hardened. "I know you don't care how I look. But you didn't give me time to order anything before we were married, and I've got nothing but my last winter's things to wear."

Ralph smiled. Even his subjugated mind perceived the inconsistency of Undine's taxing him with having hastened their marriage; but her variations on the eternal feminine still enchanted him.

"We'll go wherever you please—you make every place the one place," he said, as if he were humouring an irresistible child.

"To Switzerland, then? Céleste says St. Moritz is too heavenly," exclaimed Undine, who gathered her ideas of Europe chiefly from the conversation of her experienced attendant.

"One can be cool short of the Engadine. Why not go south again—say to Capri?"

"Capri? Is that the island we saw from Naples, where the artists go?" She drew her brows together. "It would be simply awful getting there in this heat."

"Well, then, I know a little place in Switzerland where one can still get away from the crowd, and we can sit and look at a green water-fall while I lie in wait for adjectives."

Mr. Spragg's astonishment on learning that his son-in-law contemplated maintaining a household on the earnings of his Muse was still matter for pleasantry between the pair; and one of the humours of their first weeks together had consisted in picturing themselves as a primeval couple setting forth across a virgin continent and subsisting on the adjectives which Ralph was to trap for his epic. On this occasion, however, his wife did not take up the joke, and he remained silent while their carriage climbed the long dusty hill to the Fontebranda gate. He had seen her face droop as he suggested the possibility of an escape from the crowds in Switzerland, and it came to him, with the sharpness of a knife-thrust, that a crowd was what she wanted—that she was sick to death of being alone with him.

He sat motionless, staring ahead at the red-brown walls and towers on the steep above them. After all there was nothing sudden in his discovery. For weeks it had hung on the edge of consciousness, but he had turned from it with the heart's instinctive clinging to the unrealities by which it lives. Even now a hundred qualifying reasons rushed to his aid. They told him it was not of himself that Undine had wearied, but only of their present way of life. He had said a moment before, without conscious exaggeration, that her presence made any place the one place; yet how willingly would he have consented to share in such a life as she was leading before their marriage? And he had to acknowledge their months of desultory wandering from one remote Italian hill-top to another must have seemed as purposeless to her as balls and dinners would have been to him. An imagination like his, peopled with such varied images and associations, fed by so many currents from the long stream of human experience, could hardly picture the bareness of the small half-lit place in which his wife's spirit fluttered. Her mind was destitute of beauty and mystery as the prairie school-house in which she had been educated; and her ideals seemed to Ralph as pathetic as the ornaments made of corks and cigar-bands with which her infant hands had been taught to adorn it. He was beginning to understand this, and learning to adapt himself to the narrow compass of her experience. The task of opening new windows in her mind was inspiring enough to give him infinite patience; and he would not yet own to himself that her pliancy and variety were imitative rather than spontaneous.

Meanwhile he had no desire to sacrifice her wishes to his, and it distressed him that he dared not confess his real reason for avoiding the Engadine. The truth was that their funds were shrinking faster than he had expected. Mr. Spragg, after bluntly opposing their hastened marriage on the ground that he was not prepared, at such short notice, to make the necessary provision for his daughter, had shortly afterward (probably, as Undine observed to Ralph, in consequence of a lucky "turn" in the Street) met their wishes with all possible liberality, bestowing on them a wedding in conformity with Mrs. Spragg's ideals and up to the highest standard of Mrs. Heeny's clippings, and pledging himself to provide Undine with an income adequate to so brilliant a beginning. It was understood that Ralph, on their return, should renounce the law for some more paying business; but this seemed the smallest of sacrifices to make for the privilege of calling Undine his wife; and besides, he still secretly hoped that, in the interval, his real vocation might declare itself in some work which would justify his adopting the life of letters.

He had assumed that Undine's allowance, with the addition of his own small income, would be enough to satisfy their needs. His own were few, and had always been within his means; but his wife's daily requirements, combined with her intermittent outbreaks of extravagance, had thrown out all his calculations, and they were already seriously exceeding their income.

If any one had prophesied before his marriage that he would find it difficult to tell this to Undine he would have smiled at the suggestion; and during their first days together it had seemed as though pecuniary questions were the last likely to be raised between them. But his marital education had since made strides, and he now knew that a disregard for money might imply not the willingness to get on without it but merely a blind confidence that it will somehow be provided. If Undine, like the lilies of the field, took no care, it was not because her wants were as few but because she assumed that care would be taken for her by those whose privilege it was to enable her to unite floral insouciance with Sheban elegance.

She had met Ralph's first note of warning with the assurance that she "didn't mean to worry"; and her tone implied that it was his business to do so for her. He certainly wanted to guard her from this as from all other cares; he wanted also, and still more passionately after the topic had once or twice recurred between them, to guard himself from the risk of judging where he still adored. These restraints to frankness kept him silent during the remainder of the drive, and when, after dinner, Undine again complained of her headache, he let her go up to her room and wandered out into the dimly lit streets to renewed communion with his problems.

They hung on him insistently as darkness fell, and Siena grew vocal with that shrill diversity of sounds that breaks, on summer nights, from every cleft of the masonry in old Italian towns. Then the moon rose, unfolding depth by depth the lines of the antique land; and Ralph, leaning against an old brick parapet, and watching each silver-blue remoteness disclose itself between the dark masses of the middle distance, felt his spirit enlarged and pacified. For the first time, as his senses thrilled to the deep touch of beauty, he asked himself if out of these floating and fugitive vibrations he might not build something concrete and stable, if even such dull common cares as now oppressed him might not become the motive power of creation. If he could only, on the spot, do something with all the accumulated spoils of the last months—something that should both put money into his pocket and harmony into the rich confusion of his spirit! "I'll write—I'll write: that must be what the whole thing means," he said to himself, with a vague clutch at some solution which should keep him a little longer hanging half-way down the steep of disenchantment.

He would have stayed on, heedless of time, to trace the ramifications of his idea in the complex beauty of the scene, but for the longing to share his mood with Undine. For the last few months every thought and sensation had been instantly transmuted into such emotional impulses and, though the currents of communication between himself and Undine were neither deep nor numerous, each fresh rush of feeling seemed strong enough to clear a way to her heart. He hurried back, almost breathlessly, to the inn; but even as he knocked at her door the subtle emanation of other influences seemed to arrest and chill him.

She had put out the lamp, and sat by the window in the moonlight, her head propped on a listless hand. As Marvell entered she turned; then, without speaking, she looked away again.

He was used to this mute reception, and had learned that it had no personal motive, but was the result of an extremely simplified social code. Mr. and Mrs. Spragg seldom spoke to each other when they met, and words of greeting seemed almost unknown to their domestic vocabulary. Marvell, at first, had fancied that his own warmth would call forth a response from his wife, who had been so quick to learn the forms of worldly intercourse; but he soon saw that she regarded intimacy as a pretext for escaping from such forms into a total absence of expression.

To-night, however, he felt another meaning in her silence, and perceived that she intended him to feel it. He met it by silence, but of a different kind; letting his nearness speak for him as he knelt beside her and laid his cheek against hers. She seemed hardly aware of the gesture; but to that he was also used. She had never shown any repugnance to his tenderness, but such response as it evoked was remote and Ariel-like, suggesting, from the first, not so much of the recoil of ignorance as the coolness of the element from which she took her name.

As he pressed her to him she seemed to grow less impassive and he felt her resign herself like a tired child. He held his breath, not daring to break the spell.

At length he whispered: "I've just seen such a wonderful thing—I wish you'd been with me!"

"What sort of a thing?" She turned her head with a faint show of interest.

"A—I don't know—a vision . . . It came to me out there just now with the moonrise."

"A vision?" Her interest flagged. "I never cared much about spirits. Mother used to try to drag me to séances—but they always made me sleepy."

Ralph laughed. "I don't mean a dead spirit but a living one!" I saw the vision of a book I mean to do. It came to me suddenly, magnificently, swooped down on me as that big white moon swooped down on the black landscape, tore at me like a great white eagle—like the bird of Jove! After all, imagination *was* the eagle that devoured Prometheus!"

She drew away abruptly, and the bright moonlight showed him the apprehension in her face. "You're not going to write a book *here*?"

He stood up and wandered away a step or two; then he turned and came back. "Of course not here. Wherever you want. The main point is that it's come to me—no, that it's come *back* to me! For it's all these months together, it's all our happiness—it's the meaning of life that I've found, and it's you, dearest, you who've given it to me!"

He dropped down beside her again; but she disengaged herself and he heard a little sob in her throat.

"Undine—what's the matter?"

"Nothing . . . I don't know . . . I suppose I'm homesick . . ."

"Homesick? You poor darling! You're tired of travelling? What is it?"

"I don't know . . . I don't like Europe . . . it's not what I expected, and I think it's all too dreadfully dreary!" The words broke from her in a long wail of rebellion.

Marvell gazed at her perplexedly. It seemed strange that such unguessed thoughts should have been stirring in the heart pressed to his. "It's less interesting than you expected—or less amusing? Is that it?"

"It's dirty and ugly—all the towns we've been to are disgustingly dirty. I loathe the smells and the beggars. I'm sick and tired of the stuffy rooms in the hotels. I thought it would all be so splendid—but New York's ever so much nicer!"

"Not New York in July?"

"I don't care—there are the roof-gardens, anyway; and there are always people round. All these places seem as if they were dead. It's all like some awful cemetery."

A sense of compunction checked Marvell's laughter. "Don't cry, dear—don't! I see, I understand. You're lonely and the heat has tired you out. It *is* dull here; awfully dull; I've been stupid not to feel it. But we'll start at once—we'll get out of it."

She brightened instantly. "We'll go up to Switzerland?"

"We'll go up to Switzerland." He had a fleeting glimpse of the quiet place with the green water-fall, where he might have made tryst with his vision; then he turned his mind from it and said, "We'll go just where you want. How soon can you be ready to start?"

"Oh, to-morrow—the first thing to-morrow! I'll make Céleste get out of bed now and pack. Can we go right through to St. Moritz? I'd rather sleep in the train than in another of these awful places."

She was on her feet in a flash, her face alight, her hair waving and floating about her as though it rose on her happy heart-beats.

"Oh, Ralph, it's *sweet* of you, and I love you!" she cried out, letting him take her to his breast.

PERMISSIONS ACKNOWLEDGMENTS

H. V. Morton: Excerpt from *A Traveller in Italy* by H. V. Morton (first published by Methuen Publishing Ltd., London, 1964), copyright © 1964 by the Estate of H. V. Morton. Reprinted by permission of The Spieler Agency.

Eric Newby: Excerpt from *A Small Place in Italy* by Eric Newby, copyright © 1994 by Eric Newby. Reprinted by permission of HarperCollins Publishers Ltd., London.

Iris Origo: Excerpt from *Images and Shadows: Part of a Life* by Iris Origo, copyright © 1970 by Iris Origo. Rights outside the United States administered by John Murray Publishers, London. Reprinted by permission of David R. Godine, Publisher, Inc., and John Murray Publishers.

John Ormond: "Tuscan Cypresses" from *Selected Poems* by John Ormond (Seren, 1987). Reprinted by permission of The Estate of John Ormond.

Elizabeth Romer: Excerpt from *The Tuscan Year* by Elizabeth Romer, copyright © 1984 by Elizabeth Romer. Reprinted by permission of Georges Borchardt, Inc., for the author.

Kate Simon: "Lucca" from *Italy: The Places in Between,* Revised and Expanded Edition, by Kate Simon, copyright © 1970, 1984 by Kate Simon. Reprinted by permission of HarperCollins Publishers Inc.

Matthew Spender: Excerpt from "San Sano" and "School" from *Within Tuscany* by Matthew Spender, copyright © 1991 by Matthew Spender. Rights in Canada administered by Penguin (UK), London (1993). Reprinted by permission of Viking Penguin, a division of Penguin Group (USA) Inc., and Penguin (UK).

Stephen Spender: "Grandparents" from *Collected Poems, 1928–1985* by Stephen Spender, copyright © 1934, renewed 1962 by Stephen Spender. Rights in Canada from *New Collected Poems,* copyright © 2004, administered by the Estate of Sir Stephen Spender. Reprinted by permission of Random House, Inc., and the Estate of Sir Stephen Spender.

Edith Wharton: Excerpt from *The Custom of the Country* by Edith Wharton (first published by Charles Scribner's Sons, New York, 1913). Reprinted by permission of the Estate of Edith Wharton and Watkins/Loomis Agency, New York.